Chronicles of Charanthe #2

REVOLUTION

Rachel Cotterill

Published in the United Kingdom by Rachel Cotterill.

A CIP catalogue record for this book is available from the British Library.

ISBN 978-1-910331-01-9

2 4 6 8 10 9 7 5 3

Cover art by Jessica Soria Gázquez.
Typeset in Gentium.

Also by Rachel Cotterill:

Chronicles of Charanthe

Rebellion

Revolution

Reformation

Novels of the Twelve Baronies

The Golden Elixir

Recipe Books

Design Your Own Cookies

Visit Rachel's website at

http://www.rachelcotterill.com

for future release dates & offers

Chapter 1

Daniel, Eleanor, and the Charanthe trade delegation
disembarked as soon as the ship's first mooring line was tied.
With unfavourable winds, the journey had taken longer than
they'd hoped – they'd been almost two months crossing the
ocean. They hailed a couple of rickshaws by the city gates and
asked to be taken to their embassy, and after a surprisingly
short journey they pulled up outside an imposing building
facing onto the city's main thoroughfare. It was designed in the
local style, with several castellated towers and bulbous cupolas,
and identified only by Charanthe's Imperial crest carved across
the centre of the huge double doors.

At the embassy, once they'd satisfied the guards of their
identities, they were greeted by the young assistant ambassador
– and Eleanor stopped short when she saw who it was. It had
been two years since they'd seen each other, and both girls had
changed in the intervening years, but not beyond recognition.

"Eleanor!" Gisele gasped. "But you–"

Eleanor was startled by how much Faliska's capital
reminded her of Taraska La'on as the city rose out of the sea to
the north. The buildings were in a similar style, with sparkling
domes and arches everywhere, and of course there was the
same hot, dusty climate. Even the city's name echoed that of its
neighbour. Faliska La'un. Yet despite all the similarities, they'd
been told this was a friendly country. Eleanor's fluttering
stomach felt otherwise. It looked too much like the city she'd
fled.

She stopped herself as she caught the look on Eleanor's
face. Driven initially by the need to pass messages unnoticed
beneath the stern watch of their teachers, they'd learnt to
communicate the most important things without words; Eleanor
knew how to scream 'Shut up!' with only the slightest twist of
her smile.

"What a lovely surprise," Gisele continued, recovering

quickly to her usual smooth demeanour. Not for nothing had she progressed so swiftly within the diplomatic corps.

"Delightful," Eleanor said, though she wasn't sure it was. Her cover was blown, and her only chance now was to throw herself on Gisele's mercy and hope their childhood loyalties would be strong enough.

Daniel stepped forwards and extended his hand. "Do you know my wife?"

Eleanor held her face in an impassive smile, but she wondered what in all the Empire had possessed him. His wife? That wasn't part of the story they'd agreed.

"Eleanor and I were at school together," Gisele said. "But I had no idea you were married. And you must be..."

"Daniel, your envoy for weapons."

"Daniel. Excellent."

"We'll have to make time to catch up later," Eleanor said. "We clearly have a lot to talk about."

"Of course. But I'm neglecting your colleagues... let's finish our introductions, and then I can show you to your rooms."

The head of the delegation extended her hand. "Anna, chief trade envoy, with special responsibility for imports, and the export of medicines."

"Philip, representing our cloth trade and wood."

"Oliver, gold and minerals."

After shaking everyone's hands, Gisele led the delegation up two flights of stairs to the embassy's guest bedrooms.

"We'd prepared separate rooms for you," she said to Eleanor and Daniel once the others were settled. "But this one should be big enough for you to share."

"Thanks."

"And it has the best view you'll ever see across the city." She pushed the door open and waved them into a large suite which did, indeed, benefit from a stunning aspect over the rooftops of the Faliska capital. Countless minarets glistened in the sun, but Eleanor and Daniel were too preoccupied to pay much attention to the views.

"Don't ever do that again," Eleanor said as she closed the door to shut out her old school friend. "You can't suddenly invent a marriage."

"It seemed the easiest way."

"You can't change our story without even asking me. How can this possibly help?"

"I had no choice. Why did you not tell me that you know the assistant ambassador? This could ruin everything."

"I didn't know she was working here," Eleanor said. "But I was handling it. We'll just have to explain."

"Oh no." He shook his head. "No, no, no. Why should we trust her?"

"We were at school together."

There was a knock at the door; Eleanor answered it, took their bags from the porter, and turned back to Daniel as soon as they were alone again. "She knows me better than anyone."

"That means nothing."

"So you're prepared to trust some traders we barely know, who are now wondering why we never mentioned being married – but not the assistant ambassador?"

"We were advised to trust this delegation."

"And I'm telling you we can trust Gisele. I grew up with her!"

"You have spent too much time in the company of Venncastle men," Daniel said. "Sharing your school does not make her trustworthy."

"But I know her."

"You have always been too trusting, Eleanor. You insisted on trusting Raf despite everything I told you, and look where that got you."

She took a deep breath, hardly believing what she was about to say. "He never betrayed my trust."

"How can you defend him even now, even after they have tried to kill you?"

"Jorge tried to kill me. Raf didn't know." Their time on the ship had given her plenty of time to reflect, and she was sure of that now. "I know you think they're all the same, but he's not like that."

"He is one of them. I have told you so many times that you cannot trust them... I would have thought after this you would finally believe me."

"You have to let go of your school rivalries some day, you know."

He raised an eyebrow, adopting a half-amused, half-superior expression which made Eleanor want to slap him. "And yet you ask me to trust the success of our mission to the strength of your childhood friendships."

"That's completely different. You're assuming a whole group of people are going to behave badly just because of the school they attended."

"And you are assuming one woman can be trusted because she was at school with you. I see no difference, except that your prejudice is more self-centred."

"Well, we've got no choice. Gisele knows I wasn't assigned to be a trade envoy."

"Which is why we must be married: reassignment is rare, but not unknown," Daniel said.

"I know they do slight reassignments sometimes, like moving someone to a different town. But reassigning a complete drop-out to be an obscure trade envoy? I wouldn't believe it myself."

"We must think very seriously about this. We will talk later, but meanwhile, you will tell her nothing."

He emptied his bag out onto the bed and started to pick out his clothes carefully, folding each item and creating a neat stack in the closet. Eleanor sighed and turned to her own luggage; she was tired from the journey, and all she really wanted was to get washed and have a rest before dinner. Gisele was a complication they couldn't have predicted.

As she started to unpack, her hand scraped against one of the rocks she'd taken from the ballast when they first came aboard. Somehow in the chaos of the journey she'd forgotten to follow through with her plan and she'd still got the rocks – and the briefing notes they were supposed to sink – in her bag.

She pulled out the crumpled papers. "We were supposed to ditch these at sea," she said.

"What?"

"Our instructions. It doesn't matter, I'll burn them now."

She looked around for a grate, but Faliska was a hot country and apparently someone had decided that the room didn't need a fireplace. However there was a sideboard with a large bowl for water and a jug for washing, set on a tiled area at the side of the room, and it looked like the tiles would be enough to contain a small fire.

"I will just check it one more time," Daniel said as she reached for her matches.

"You've read it a hundred times already."

"It is good to be sure." He held his hand out.

"You don't need to." She ripped the sheets in half, set light to one corner, and dropped the burning pages onto the tiles. "It didn't say much, anyway."

She watched as the flames consumed the paper, prodding occasionally with her dagger to keep it burning steadily. Once she'd reduced the notes to a small pile of ash she brushed it into a corner out of the way. The tiles were slightly blackened but she scrubbed at the surface with her sleeve, and soon all signs of the fire were gone.

A bell-cord hung down from the ceiling near the wash-stand; Eleanor gave it an experimental tug, and before she'd even turned away there was a knock at the door, and a young man came in with a pail of steaming-hot water to fill the basin.

"Just ring again if you need more," he said as he left; Eleanor barely had time to call out her thanks before the door closed behind him.

After a hesitant glance at Daniel, who was thankfully still sulking with his back to her, Eleanor stripped off her clothes and set about scrubbing the salt from her skin.

"I'm done," she said as she towelled herself dry. "Do you want me to ring for some clean water for you?"

"Thank you."

She dressed herself in clean clothes before pulling the bell-cord, then stretched out on the bed. She felt she should avert her eyes as Daniel undressed, but she found herself fixated – besides, she reasoned, if they were going to be sharing this room until they completed their mission then they'd have to stop being shy sooner or later. She watched the flexing muscles of his back and his buttocks as he sponged himself clean, peeking from between her eyelashes in case he looked round. Once he reached for his towel she closed her eyes fully and pretended to sleep, only to be disturbed a moment later by something hard landing in her hand.

"Marriage token," Daniel explained when she sat up, fingers tightening around the cold metal chain. "Where is yours?"

"What?"

"As we are to be married, we had better do this properly. You need to give me the wedding half of your name bangle."

She removed her own bracelet, unfastened the clips which held the two halves together, and passed the marriage half to Daniel.

"Doesn't this make us actually married?" she asked as she attached the other half of his bangle onto what remained of her own.

"Technically, perhaps, but we will reverse it as soon as we complete this mission. We do not have to tell the others."

"Just as well!" Eleanor could hardly imagine how their colleagues would react if they arrived back at the Association with wedding signs in place.

"Other wrist," Daniel said as she began to clip the bangle back into its usual position. When she moved it to her right wrist, the metal felt strange and uncomfortable against her skin.

"It feels wrong," she said, twisting the links between her fingers.

"You will get used to it."

Their attention was caught by a gong ringing out in the hallway. "I suppose that's our cue to go down for dinner," Eleanor said. "Come on, it's our first meal as a married couple..."

"Do not even joke about it." Daniel stepped between her and the door. "We must act as though this is completely normal."

"How long have we been married, then?" Eleanor asked. "Where did I meet you? And how did you persuade them to let me be a trade envoy, in this imaginary world?"

"We can decide these details later."

"Gisele will want to know."

"You do not need to tell her anything." He opened the door and they stepped out into the corridor. "We have had a long journey. We have every right to be antisocial."

The others were already seated by the time Eleanor and Daniel reached the dining room, and they slipped into the empty chairs between Philip and Gisele.

"I don't think you've met the ambassador," Gisele said, indicating the middle-aged man to her left. "Eleanor and Daniel, your new envoys for fish and weapons."

"Welcome to Faliska," the ambassador smiled. "I was just saying to your colleagues that, now you've arrived, we'll set up some meetings with your counterparts here. Meanwhile, you should take some time tomorrow to relax and enjoy our city."

"Indeed," Daniel said. "I will enjoy finding out how it differs from the Empire."

"Is this your first time abroad, then?" the ambassador asked.

Daniel nodded. "Yes. I have a lot to learn."

As they were talking, servants filled their plates with steak and vegetables, and poured wine into generous glasses.

"At least the food here looks normal, like home," Eleanor said. "Not like some of the weird things I've eaten."

"Remember you're in an embassy," Gisele said. "We like Charanthe food as much as you do – when supplies allow. And it's always a good day when a boat arrives from home."

"So the local food, out there..."

"You probably wouldn't recognise most of it as food, though it's nice enough when you get used to it."

"How long have you been out here?" Eleanor asked.

"It's been few months, now," Gisele said. "This is my second real posting. But how about you – did you manage to get a reassignment? I'm intrigued by how you've ended up in this job, given your history."

"Well, you know I've sailed a lot, and I learnt a lot about fishing – so here I am, fish envoy."

The ambassador raised an eyebrow. "What interests me is that Faliska don't even buy fish from us."

"Not yet," Eleanor agreed. "It's a developing market. Lots of potential, if we can just identify the kinds of fish that can't live in these hot northern seas."

"How would you even get fish all the way here from Charanthe?"

"Well, if we hung them to dry first, they wouldn't rot on the way over."

"Dried fish?" The ambassador laughed. "It would be a novelty, at least. Still, who am I to know what might appeal to the strange tastes of the Falisanka?"

Eleanor glanced around; it wasn't just the ambassador who looked skeptical. "Okay, listen, just between friends, the fish job is a bit of a sham."

Daniel gripped her thigh under the table, his fingernails digging sharply into her skin.

She ignored the pain, continuing: "It's more of an excuse for me to travel with my husband."

She leaned across to give Daniel an exaggerated kiss on the cheek. His face blushed scarlet, but he relaxed his grip.

"Oh, to be young again." A broad smile spread across the ambassador's face. "Young love, now there's something I understand."

"But of course, I'm still hoping we can make some good deals on the fish," Eleanor added, sipping her wine. "Gisele knows I've always liked a challenge."

For the rest of the meal the conversation hovered around the food, geography, and politics of Faliska. Eleanor listened with interest, constantly making comparisons to Taraska in her head but not wanting to voice her thoughts. There was nothing in any of her cover stories to explain her excursion into what was basically an enemy land, and she didn't want to open herself up to more questions. But she had to convince herself that this place bore no more than a passing resemblance to the city where she and Raf had been tortured.

"We need to introduce ourselves properly," Daniel said as the others started to leave the room. Eleanor nodded, and waited by the door as he took the ambassador to one side and slipped their letter of introduction into his hand. Neither of them had actually read the note, but they expected its Imperial seal to be enough of a reference.

The ambassador split the seal with his fingers, scanned the paper, and nodded. He pocketed the letter without further comment.

"Gisele," he called. She came to the door, looking a little puzzled. "Get some drinks for our guests; we'll retire to the lounge."

"But sir, I thought—"

"My plans have changed. As have yours."

"Of course. Eleanor, Daniel?" Gisele led them to the sitting room of the ambassador's private suite and fetched a large, dark bottle from a cupboard.

"This is the local liquor," she said as she filled four sizeable glasses. "They call it Ngatu'a Karatsa" – she pronounced the strange words without difficulty – "which translates as something like Burning Death. You'll see why."

Eleanor sniffed the contents of her glass, and felt the fumes of the alcohol searing her nose. She was about to take a careful sip of the liquid when Gisele added, "The local custom is to swallow it all as one mouthful. For luck."

Daniel shrugged and threw his head back, tipping the drink down his throat without a second thought. Not willing to be outdone, Eleanor copied him, and a moment later she knew exactly why the Burning Death was so named. By the time they'd both stopped coughing, Gisele had filled their glasses again.

The ambassador took a seat across from them, and raised his glass. "To your health, and to the Empire."

"To the Empire," they echoed.

"Can we take more time over this one?" Eleanor asked, but Gisele shook her head and emptied her glass in one gulp again. Eleanor took a deep breath and followed suit.

Eleanor woke with a pounding headache, wondering for a moment where she was. She pulled the sheets over her head and curled into a tight ball, wishing she could will herself back to sleep, but she'd carefully developed the art of waking quickly: her mind was already racing ahead into plans for their first morning in the city. She stretched out, and started in surprise as her foot brushed against something warm.

Daniel.

She sat up, rubbed her eyes, and looked down at him. He was snoring lightly, lower lip quivering with each exhalation, apparently oblivious to the world. Slowly, fragmented memories of the night before started to come back into Eleanor's mind.

After Gisele had opened the bottle of Burning Death it had all become very fuzzy, very quickly, but somehow they'd found their way to bed. She studied Daniel's features as he slept. His hair fell across the pillow in an untidy mass; it had grown long while they'd been at sea, and the sun had turned it almost white from its usual straw colour.

One of the few vivid recollections she had from the night before was the feeling of that hair between her fingers as she hooked her hands behind his head, his face only an inch or two above hers, the weight of his body pressing down on her... but she couldn't remember how they'd gone from stumbling up the stairs to finding themselves in *that* position.

She shook her head to try and clear her thoughts. How had it happened? She was quite sure that she irritated him just as much as he did her. However drunk they'd been, it was hard to imagine either of them initiating what had been – she recalled this much – a thoroughly exhilarating experience. She ran her fingers across his shoulders, gently kneading his muscles with her fingertips. Yes, he was a pain, but apparently he annoyed her a lot less in bed than he did anywhere else.

"What happened last night?" she asked, pulling her hand away as his eyes flickered open.

"Do you not remember?"

"We drank a lot." She held her throbbing temples in her hands. "I remember that much."

"We should get up. It is late, and we have work to do. I will make something for your headache."

"I remember it was fun," she said, not willing to give up that easily. "We should do it again sometime."

"I think not." He moved to sit on the edge of the bed and started combing the knots out of his hair. "We were drunk. It was a mistake."

"Why not?" She tugged at his arm but he pushed her hand away. "If we're supposed to be acting married, we might as well have the benefits."

"You want to give up?" he asked, getting to his feet. "After all we went through last year, now you want to go home and tell the council that you want to stop work, you want to have babies? We are too young."

She stared at him in shock. "Who mentioned children? I was only talking about having a bit of fun."

He shook his head. "Women bring complications. Vulnerabilities. Why do you think the Association has only ever admitted men before you?"

"How dare you?" She jumped out of bed and followed him across the room. He was splashing himself with cold water from the basin, and she positioned herself between him and the bowl so he couldn't ignore her.

"You do not like me to say women are vulnerable? Look at yourself." He turned her so she was facing her own naked body in the mirror. "We spent one drunken night together and suddenly you want more. Tell me that is not a vulnerability. And women must carry the babies, and you cannot work if your belly is swollen. No, it is not because women cannot fight, but because women cannot be trusted to remain devoted to the task at hand."

She glared at his reflection. "You're just jealous that I'm a better fighter than you, and I don't get seasick, and... And I don't think I want *you* any more, anyway, if you're going to say things like that." She scooped up a jug full of water and began to wash herself vigorously, pounding her skin in an attempt to let out some of her frustrations.

"You think you are a better fighter?" He sounded amused, which infuriated her all the more.

"Yes." She carried on washing, trying to ignore his provocations. Their relative strengths were well established – he was a genius with poisons and potions, but only adequate with a weapon, and she was the opposite. It was what would make them a good team. She told herself she had nothing to prove; it had been proved long ago. Satisfied with her ablutions, she set the jug down and turned to look for a towel.

"Even like this – no weapons, just pure muscle?" As he spoke he caught both her arms and twisted her into a double arm-lock, pinning her wrists into her back.

He had the advantage in height and weight, and she felt cheated into being forced to fight unarmed, but she wasn't going to let him win. His grip on her wrists was solid despite her wet skin, and since she couldn't free her hands she hooked a her foot around the back of his knee and tried to unbalance him that way. They stumbled around the room for some time, he refusing to release her arms, she unrelenting in her attacks on his legs, until a corner of the bed got in the way and they both tumbled onto the sheets.

Eleanor took advantage of Daniel's surprise to snatch her arms away and roll out of his reach. "Call it a draw?" she asked, flexing her wrists. "I don't really want to fight."

"Come on, then, get up." He threw her clothes at her and started to dress himself. "Time for breakfast."

She dressed quickly, clothes clinging uncomfortably to her still-damp skin, and hid a small throwing knife at her hip. It was harder to conceal weapons beneath the light clothes which suited such a hot climate and she felt worryingly under-armed, but at least her hair-pin doubled as a blowpipe, and she had stilettos in her boot-sheaths.

They walked down to the embassy's dining room in awkward silence. A spread of exotic fruit was laid out alongside more familiar breads and cheeses from the Empire, and they found themselves the only people in a room that could easily have seated twenty.

"Looks like we missed the others," Eleanor said as they filled their plates.

"I told you it was late to be getting up."

"Well, it's probably for the best. We would've needed to lose them anyway."

"That is not the point. It would have been useful to have more time."

"We've been at sea for two months – half a day won't make

much difference," Eleanor said. "The only urgency is that we have to do our trade thing tomorrow."

"That does not require much."

"Well, I'd like to wander through the markets and check out the competition."

"But we are not intending to make any deals."

"It's better if they don't realise that. Come on, it's not far, and it won't take long to get a feel for how things work here." She didn't mention her continuing internal fight to convince herself that she wasn't back in Taraska, but she hoped the market would highlight the differences.

"Do you need something for your head first?"

"No, I'll be fine."

They stepped out into the dry heat of the city and walked up the hill to the point where the harbour road intersected with the main east-west route. At the crossroads a paved square made for a convenient marketplace, and Eleanor was pleased to see it was nothing like Taraska's cosmopolitan trade hub. Here, a ramshackle collection of temporary stalls catered mostly to a local crowd; there was no danger of turning a corner and coming upon something as unpleasant as the slave children she'd seen in Taraska.

"We have no competition here," Daniel said, waving dismissively at the little grocery stalls. "This has nothing to do with the Imperial trade routes."

"I need to see what their fishermen have brought in," Eleanor said. "They can't possibly have the variety that we see back home, but it'd be useful to make sure."

Daniel followed a couple of steps behind as she strode towards what appeared to be the fish and meat section of the market. "You are taking this far too seriously."

"And you're not taking it seriously enough. We can't afford to raise any more suspicions."

Most of the fishermen had small carts that were almost empty after the morning's rush, but what remained on display was of a markedly different character to the stock of the fish markets back home: a lot of eels and sea-snakes, and some crates of tiny fish that any self-respecting Charanthe fisherman would have thrown straight back into the sea.

"I need to go down to the harbour first thing tomorrow, when the boats come in," Eleanor said. "But if this is what's normal here, then it's looking good."

"Can we get on with the real work now?"

"Fine." She stepped into the shade of a nearby building. "Where do you want to start?"

"We should find out what the official Taraska presence is. There must be an embassy in the city, at least."

"Yeah, I think they have the building next to ours." Eleanor glanced back along the road they'd walked up. "I saw their crest this morning."

"I cannot imagine who allowed that to happen."

"It works both ways – could be useful if we need to get in there. Anyway, we could walk that way now, and then down to the harbour."

Daniel looked puzzled. "You just said you wanted to go to the harbour tomorrow."

"That's for the fish. We need to find out about boats heading east."

"I had hoped we could find a cart."

Eleanor still found his seasickness amusing – it wasn't what she would have expected of someone who went to school on a ship – but she managed to stop herself commenting on it directly.

"It's a long way," she said. "It'll be more comfortable to sail in this climate, and quicker."

"Perhaps."

"And we should be able to stick to coastal waters, so it won't be too rough. At the very least we should ask around."

Daniel nodded and they started to walk, making slow progress under the glare of the midday sun. They stopped across the street from their embassy and tried to look busy whilst sneaking glances at the grand Tarasanka building next door.

"We will have to go in," Daniel said.

"Do you really think we'll find anything?"

"No."

"Then...?"

"It costs us nothing. It would be foolish to miss this chance to look."

"I suppose. I just don't think they'd be stupid enough to send anything here."

Gisele must have been waiting for them to come in: she appeared the instant they stepped through the embassy doors.

"Eleanor, a word," she said, and though she smiled sweetly her tone left no space for argument.

"I'll catch you up," Eleanor promised Daniel.

He leaned in as if to kiss her goodbye, and whispered into her ear: "Just remember." She didn't need him to elaborate.

Gisele took Eleanor's arm and steered her into a small office, closing the door to separate them from the bustle of the embassy's corridors.

"What is it?" Eleanor asked.

"I was hoping you could tell me. Something very strange is going on here."

"What do you mean?"

"You're no fish envoy, we all know that much."

Eleanor nodded, and wondered how she could possibly avoid the inevitable questions, if Daniel's invention of a marriage hadn't made for a sufficiently convincing story.

"But you turn up here with this new husband and we're under special orders to take care of you both, above and beyond the rest of the delegation, and then the ambassador decides to change his plans to have drinks with you... frankly, it's more than a little confusing."

"I know less than you do," Eleanor said. "Like you said, I'm not really any kind of envoy – I've never done this before."

"Well I can tell you it isn't normal. Are you sure you know everything about this husband of yours?"

Eleanor stared at her, deliberately widening her eyes. "What are you suggesting?"

"There's something not quite right." Gisele cleared stacks of papers from a couple of chairs and sat down, motioning for Eleanor to do likewise. "Are you sure he is who he says he is?"

"He's my husband." Eleanor perched on the edge of the seat, unwilling to allow herself to relax. "I think I know him."

Gisele laughed. "Eleanor, you've always been a little... impulsive. It wouldn't entirely surprise me if you got married without thinking it through."

"I still don't understand what you're suggesting."

"Someone with the power to get you reassigned has friends in high places, for a start. Surely even you can see that."

"I know I'm very lucky."

"After you spat in the face of the assignment system? You needed more than luck. I don't know who Daniel really is, but you'll be careful, won't you?"

"Of course."

"Good."

Eleanor chewed deliberately on her lower lip. "Will you let me know if you find anything out? You've got me worried."

"I'll get to the bottom of it." Gisele got to her feet and opened the door. "Oh, can I take a quick look at your bangle before you go?"

Eleanor bristled at the way Gisele carefully faked a casual tone, but she knew she couldn't refuse such an ordinary request. She held up her wrist and watched as Gisele's eyes locked on Daniel's identification number.

"Thanks. You'll tell me if you notice anything out of the ordinary, Eleanor, won't you?"

"I will."

As she walked back to her room, Eleanor wondered whether the same memory tricks she'd learnt at the academy also formed part of the standard diplomatic training. The brief moment Gisele had spent looking at her wrist was hardly long enough for an untrained eye to pick up a ten character identification number.

Daniel was waiting for her in their bedroom.

"And?" he asked, the moment she stepped through the door.

"She doesn't trust you," Eleanor said, kicking off her boots and sitting cross-legged on the bed. "In fact, she warned me to be careful."

"Good advice. I trust you told her nothing?"

"I just practised looking confused. I'm sure she believes that whatever you're up to, it's nothing to do with me."

"And what does she think I might be up to?"

"She didn't say, but she wanted to see my bangle – she's memorised your number."

"That is no use to her, out here." Daniel turned his own bangle around on his wrist. "She cannot check anything. It would take her too long to send word back to the Empire."

"I still don't understand why you won't let me talk to her. It's not like we have anything to hide, and we could save her a lot of trouble."

"It is not our job to decide for the ambassador whether to trust his staff."

"But now she thinks he's involved in this thing – whatever she thinks it is. I know Gisele. If she's convinced we're doing something wrong, she won't let it go."

"We are doing nothing wrong."

"Let me tell her that."

"No."

"Fine." Eleanor sighed and stretched out on the bed. "Do you think we can get them to bring us some dinner? We've got a busy day tomorrow, and I don't really want another late night."

"We do not have to stay up late."

"I'm just not feeling sociable. Go and tell them you want to spend a quiet evening with your wife, will you? Please?"

"All right."

While he was gone from the room, Eleanor changed into her nightshirt and crawled under the covers. She was dozing by the time he returned with a plate of cold meats, and sat up in bed to make herself a sandwich.

Once they'd eaten Daniel climbed into bed beside her, but instead of reaching out for her he turned away and said, "There is space for you to sleep on the window seat."

"What? Why?"

"You are dangerous to me. Too much temptation, too close."

"Temptation? This morning you said you didn't even want

to do it again." She ran her hand gently along his back, feeling the bumps of his spine beneath her fingers, until he took hold of her hand to stop her.

"I said it would not be wise."

"Then there shouldn't be any temptation."

"Just go over there, please."

"You move, if it bothers you so much."

"Eleanor. You are a head shorter. I would not fit on that seat."

She gave an exaggerated sigh, but arguing was only keeping them both from sleep so she took a spare blanket and settled down on the window seat. As she lay there staring at the ceiling, Gisele's words ran constantly through her head. They were going to need to come up with a good story to put her off the scent, if Daniel kept insisting that they couldn't trust her with the truth.

Eleanor shivered and pulled the blanket closer. It was hard to sleep with so many thoughts nagging at her. Listening carefully to Daniel's breathing, she realised he wasn't sleeping either.

"Why can't I come and lie with you?" she asked at last.

"I told you, you are too dangerous to me."

"I don't know what you mean."

"I could not keep my hands off you if you were right here."

"You haven't convinced me that's a bad thing." Speaking into the darkness felt somehow easier than having the same conversation in daylight. "Last night was fun, and the world hasn't ended."

"You do not wish to throw away your life by getting pregnant, but even aside from that, there are too many risks."

"What risks?"

"People in our situation should not risk falling in love. There is danger in caring too much."

"What makes you think there's any chance of that?"

She waited for an answer, but he said nothing.

"Listen, it's really cold over here. Just let me come back to bed – I'll stay out of your way, I promise."

"Okay. Fine."

Eleanor didn't hesitate: she didn't want to give him chance to change his mind. She climbed back into the bed and, keeping her word, curled up at one side. It was still warmer than the draughty window seat.

She'd drifted halfway into sleep when she was brought back to her senses by Daniel's hand sliding across her skin. She kept her eyes closed and held her breathing steady as he ran his fingers over her hip, along her side, and up to her shoulder. She wondered whether he'd try to wake her if she kept pretending to be asleep, but instead he turned away again and a moment later he was snoring.

Chapter 2

The trade representatives from Faliska were two dark-skinned men with almost-identical features – their sharp noses and narrow chins could have been cut from the same template – but they were distinguished easily by the years which separated them. They both had silky black hair pulled back into long ponytails, but the older man's head was striped with grey.

"My name is Srakanit," the older man said. "And this my son, Sha'on. He is speaking for me in all things, when necessary."

"Anna. I lead the Charanthe delegation." She offered her hand; Srakanit hesitated before stepping forwards to clasp her fingers in both hands.

"Ah, differing customs," he laughed. "I am forgetting my Imperial manners. I am sorry, it has been some years."

"You've been to the Empire?" Eleanor asked.

"Years ago, yes. You have a beautiful country."

"Eleanor is our fish envoy," Anna said. "Her husband, Daniel, represents us on weapons. Oliver is responsible for gold and minerals, I can advise you on medicines, and of course you'll be most interested in Philip's portfolio."

"The most famous Charanthe cloth," Sha'on said.

"Indeed," Philip said. "And I also represent the Empire on wood, which is much less exciting but important nonetheless."

"Srakanit is in control of Faliska's imports," Anna said, stumbling on the pronunciation of his name. "We'll have some proper introductions now, and then tomorrow we can get into more detailed negotiations. Do you want to start us off, Philip?"

"I can do, although the reputation of Charanthe's cloth rather speaks for itself." He stroked the sleeve of his tunic as he spoke. "And of course, the court of Faliska is one of our most valued markets."

They took their seats around the table and Eleanor's attention drifted as Philip began to describe different methods of preparing cottons and linens, tanning leathers and dyeing silks, illustrating his words with samples of fine cloth which he spread across the table. By the time he'd moved on to extolling the benefits of building with planks from Charanthe's tall and straight-growing trees she was thinking instead about the plans she and Daniel had made, in hushed tones over breakfast, for breaking into the Tarasanka embassy that night. So she was caught by surprise when Philip drew to the end of his speech and Anna requested that she introduce her fishing portfolio next.

"Well, as Anna told you, I'm Charanthe's fish envoy," she began, trying to remember why she'd ever thought this was a good idea. "I appreciate this is a new proposal, and maybe you think I'm mad. You have your own fishermen, and maybe you think you have more than enough fish from the seas here."

The two Falisanka representatives observed her in silence, and she found it impossible to read any reaction from their expressions. Daniel, on the other hand, was struggling to suppress his amusement, and she had to look away from him quickly before she lost her composure.

"I think, given the chance, the people of Faliska might enjoy a more varied diet," she continued. "I took a walk down to the harbour before breakfast, and while your fishing boats were bringing in heavy loads, each fish was only a few inches long. Are they fully grown?"

"The little silver ones?" Sha'on asked.

"Yes."

"They come to about this big." He stretched his thumb and forefinger apart to show her.

"At home we'd throw those back as babies. Imagine what Faliska's finest chefs could do with a fish the length of your arm."

Srakanit nodded. "This would be interesting the king. He thinking always to his banquets."

"The waters around the Imperial archipelago are stocked with such a wide variety that you could only dream of," Eleanor said. "And each has a subtly different flavour that I can hardly describe to you, except to assure you that they're all delicious."

"But how you be bringing fishes across the oceans?" Srakanit asked. "In this hot place it will to rotting, no?"

"We preserve fish with salt and smoke for long voyages of our own, so that would be our first suggestion. Dried fish can be packed in crates like any other commodity."

She'd brought samples – what little there was left from the supplies of their own voyage – and handed a plate around for the men to try. Sha'on's lips puckered with the high quantity of salt, and he reached for a mouthful of water, but he was too polite to refuse when the plate came round again.

"There are some other approaches we could try, if my proposition interests you," Eleanor went on. "It seems possible we could fill a hull with water instead of the usual ballast, and create a tank that could sustain live fish for long enough to cross the ocean, or perhaps we could tow a full net behind the ship to keep them alive that way. We won't know until we experiment."

"Let's not get waylaid by too many practicalities today," Anna said. "This is a time for introductions. Eleanor, is there anything else?"

"No, I think that's enough for now," Eleanor said, relieved to have an excuse to stop talking.

She listened with some interest as Oliver presented an overview of Charanthe's current mining endeavours, along with the Empire's hope that further mineral deposits would be found in the southern mountains. Next Anna spoke briefly about the remedies she was offering, sounding like the most boring apothecary lesson as she described the healing properties of the archipelago's native plants, and then it was time for Daniel to take his turn.

He turned to Srakanit. "Do you carry a knife?"

"Naturally."

"Is it a good knife?"

The trader curled his fingers around the rope-wrapped handle at his waist and pulled it from its sheath, laying it flat upon the table: an iron dagger with a slight curve to the blade, and a deep cannelure. "It may looking old, but this was made for my grandfather by the royal armourer, and the edge is sharp."

Daniel reached across and pressed his thumb to the blade. "It may suffice," he said, "but it lacks artistry."

He'd brought a small selection of his own knives, wrapped inside a roll of leather which he now opened out upon the table. Each was a fine example of Harold's craftsmanship, and the inlaid amber and obsidian crystals of Daniel's graduation design sparkled in the sunlight.

"Indeed, I doubt you could find a keener blade than one wrought by a master weaponsmith of the Empire."

Daniel reached across to the fruit bowl and picked out two identical, wax-skinned fruits. Setting one of them beside Srakanit's knife, he threw the other into the air, and as it fell again he sliced it neatly through the middle with one quick swipe of his favourite dagger. Eleanor picked up the half that rolled towards her and sucked on the soft inner flesh; it was sugary but had a bitter aftertaste that she didn't much care for.

"I should like to see your trusty blade in action," Daniel said, pushing both knife and fruit towards Srakanit's hands.

"I am lacking your skill," Srakanit said, hefting the fruit cautiously in his hand. "My son will trying."

Sha'on stood up and took the old knife from his father, but his attempt to recreate Daniel's stunt left the fruit bouncing away with only a chip taken out of the rind.

Daniel wiped the fruit acid from his own blade, slid it back between its leather straps, and rolled the bundle closed again.

"I am not at liberty to discuss the secret methods of our most accomplished craftsmen," he said as he tied the leather thongs to secure the roll. "Yet I am sure you see the value of our offer. No doubt your king will wish to hear more."

"Well, if everyone's happy with these introductions, we'll resume tomorrow," Anna said, getting to her feet. The others followed suit. "I'm sure we've given our hosts plenty to think about."

Sha'on caught Eleanor's arm as she was about to leave the room.

"I would like to talking more with you about the fishes," he said. "If you have time?"

"Oh." She tried to hide her surprise. "Of course."

"I am interesting in your ideas. My father is always speaking well of Charanthe food, and sometimes I am eating here, in the embassy – it is good."

"Thank you."

"Will you walk with me?" he asked. "The market is closed for the afternoon, but my friend brings a cart there. I would like if you come visiting him with me."

"Okay." She glanced across at Daniel but he was engrossed in conversation with Anna.

Sha'on led her into the backstreets behind the embassy, and they walked for about a mile through winding lanes before he stepped into a narrow alleyway and rapped on the door to his left.

An old woman came to the door, and Sha'on said something to her that Eleanor couldn't understand. She disappeared back inside, leaving them on the doorstep, and a short while later a young man came running out and pulled Sha'on into a tight embrace. They exchanged a few words in Falisanka, then Sha'on turned him to face Eleanor.

"This is Bel," he said. "He is working on the market every morning, selling fruits from his parents' land."

"Nice to meet you," Eleanor said, wondering why Sha'on had brought her here, and why she'd agreed to come. This bore little enough relevance to the role she was pretending to – and was of even less interest to her in reality.

"Nice to meet you," Bel echoed. "You are here trading for Charanthe, yes?"

"I'm the fish envoy."

"I am thinking, you should not be limiting yourself to fishes," Sha'on said. "What else good foods could come from Charanthe? You have many plants which will never grow here."

"That's really not my area of expertise."

"Maybe not, but you are interesting in making new areas of trade – like the fishes. You are the right person to think about this."

Eleanor shook her head. "You should talk to Anna."

Sha'on turned and gripped her by both shoulders, and it was

all she could do to suppress her well-trained reflexes and convince herself she didn't need to fight her way free. "My father has meeting with Charanthe trades delegations over many years, and nothing ever changes. You are different."

"Because I'm talking about fish?"

"Because you talking at all." There was an edge of excitement to his voice that caught Eleanor's attention. "And you thinking new thoughts. Usually, the Empire is setting a price, and we buying what we can afford, and that is the end."

"But I don't have the authority to start up discussions in new areas. You really need to speak to Anna."

"You see my shop?" Bel asked. "I will to showing you."

He beckoned her to follow him to the far end of the alley, where it opened up into a small yard. A wooden cart, draped with a heavy canvas cover, was parked against the wall.

"Just listen me," Sha'on said. "If you are agreeing in my ideas, you can talking to Anna."

She couldn't fault his logic. "Okay."

Bel pulled the cover from his cart to show the variety of his produce, which amounted to a dozen different colours and textures of fruit. There were a few sorry examples of the wax-skinned kind that Daniel had used for his demonstration, and none of the other varieties looked much more appealing to Eleanor's eye.

"Here is everything growing in Faliska," he said, waving his hand towards the stall.

"And do you sell a lot?" Eleanor asked, struggling to think of a more intelligent question.

"The king is taking first fruits," he said. "And the rest is mine for selling. People is buying everything we growing. Tomorrow, all will be gone."

"You see?" Sha'on said. "You could bringing fruit from Charanthe, different kinds, and selling here. And vegetables, no? Potatoes. Is much easier transporting than fish, and more rare."

"I'll suggest it to Anna," she said, nodding and wishing she'd thought of being a fruit and vegetable envoy instead. It would, indeed, have been a much easier concept to sell.

28

Bel launched himself at her and for a moment she thought she was under attack, but he simply wrapped his arms around her and hugged her.

"Thank you," he said as he stepped away.

Eleanor turned to Sha'on. "We should get back to the embassy," she said. "They'll be wondering where I am."

Daniel was sitting in the window seat when she came in. "Where in all the Empire have you been?"

"Doing my job."

"Trading? This is not your job."

"Right now, it is."

"Eleanor–"

"It is. I don't want to blow our cover."

Daniel looked unimpressed. "Do you not think your time would be better spent in planning for tonight?"

"I'm sure you carried on without me. You've probably already worked out that the third floor balcony gives the easiest route across."

"I had assumed the roof."

Eleanor smiled. "You never were a climber. The balcony gets us closer, and gives us good anchors for our ropes."

"Then you believe we are ready?"

"It's just an initial exploration. When we get back we'll have enough information to make real plans, but now, all we can do is wait for darkness." She was standing by the fruit bowl and started to pick out different varieties one by one, lining them up along the edge of the sideboard. "Have you found any of these that are edible, yet?"

"Edible, or pleasant to eat?"

"You're a pedant, Daniel, you know. I did assume they wouldn't have given us anything completely indigestible."

"You should say what you mean. But no, I have not found any to my liking."

"Sha'on took me to see his friend who sells local produce on the market here. They don't have a lot of choice. He was suggesting we should import fruit and vegetables."

"Really, Eleanor. You take it too far. You do not even have

the authority to trade."

"What does that even mean? That Anna can overrule me? Of course she could, but she's not stupid."

"Why do you think you know better than her? This is her life."

"And for just a few days it's our life, too. This has to look real until the delegation goes home and we go east." She sat beside him and glanced down into the street, fingers digging into the flesh of the fruit she'd picked up. "And Sha'on had some good ideas."

"About fruit."

"Yes. And this friend sells fruit from his parents' land. Don't you find it interesting? Sha'on shares his father's job, Bel sells his father's fruit. It must be so strange to grow up like that."

"They would find our ways strange."

"Of course."

"They would ask why you would have a child, only to give him up."

"Good question." She tore a mouthful of the fruit, chewed at it, and spat it out. "I certainly don't want to go through that."

"You would not wish to give up your children?"

"I don't want to have any. Pregnancy, birth... it sounds horrible."

"You should not say such things."

"Why not? I don't want to be out of action for a day, let alone months. There are plenty of other women to produce children."

"I am serious – do not say these things when others can hear you. You do not wish to be marked as a rebel."

"We're risking our lives out here in the drylands for the Empire. What more can they possibly want?"

"Others may not see it that way."

They joined the trade delegation in the dining hall, picked a light meal from the available spread, and excused themselves early from the laughing and drinking.

Back in their bedroom, Eleanor strapped throwing knives

into her wrist sheaths and hung a curved dagger at her hip, glad to be able to arm herself properly for the first time since they'd left the Association. An assassin's weapons didn't quite fit the trader's image but sneaking into neighbouring embassies didn't fit with that cover, either, and if they were caught then they'd need every advantage they could carry to defend themselves against Taraska's finest.

She tucked a small blowpipe behind her ear. A cunning device of Ivan's design, this one would take two darts with different drugs, and allowed a simple movement of the tongue to control the air flow and determine which one was released. The darts she carried today were doped with Daniel's choice of poisons: one fast-acting sedative, and another that was slightly less swift but infinitely more lethal.

A heavy belt of throwing stars provided the finishing touch to her outfit. She laced her boots, checked her stilettos were easily accessible, and studied her reflection for a moment in the mirror. She no longer looked anything like a trade envoy.

"Ready?" she asked Daniel, looping a coil of rope over her shoulder. The rough hessian fibres scratched her skin through the thin fabric of her tunic.

"I am."

The stairs leading up to the third floor were at the far end of the corridor and they walked silently, not wanting to disturb their colleagues.

When they reached the balcony Eleanor secured the rope around the balustrade, tied a slip knot in the other end, and threw it so that it looped around a decorative stone curlicue on the Tarasanka building. She hung from the rope, holding on with hands and bare feet, and pulled herself along until she reached the far wall. She slid the window open and slipped inside, glancing around to check the coast was clear before beckoning Daniel to join her.

They left the rope in place and went to explore the embassy. The corridors were dark and deserted, with heavy doors facing off both sides. A floorboard creaked and they both turned to one another, glaring silent accusations though neither of them would risk uttering a word to argue about who had caused the sound.

They peered through a couple of doorways and saw only bedrooms; as in the Charanthe embassy, there were beautiful guest rooms on this floor. Concerned about waking anyone who was sleeping there, they hurried on.

As they made their way down to the next level in search of offices, Eleanor heard another footstep.

Daniel turned on her, and in the relative isolation of the stairwell he dared to voice his frustration: "Hush! You are being careless."

"That wasn't me," she said. It hadn't even fallen in time with her own steps. Daniel didn't look like he believed her, but he said nothing more.

On the next floor they found a corridor that was clearly more administrative, with small engraved plates by each door. From the little she remembered of the Tarasanka script Eleanor tried to pronounce the words in her head, guessing that each one spelt out the name of whichever minor official worked from the room. None of which helped them to work out what they were looking for. She pulled out a piece of paper and began to sketch a map of the building, copying down the letters beside each room on her plan.

Daniel, meanwhile, had opened the first door and was shuffling through piles of papers that he didn't understand. He emerged with a map of Faliska in his hands, annotated in the same foreign script.

"This is only a scouting trip," Eleanor whispered. "We can't start stealing documents or they'll know there's something going on."

"This looks important."

"You can't read it. How can you say if it's important?"

"Look." He pointed to the scribbled notes in the border lands. "This is the area we are to investigate."

She nodded. "Okay. But you still can't take it."

"What if we cannot find it next time?"

"Make a copy, then. We can't take it with us."

Daniel hesitated, shrugged, and sat down at the desk in the office to work, struggling to make out all the detail by the little moonlight which came in at the window. When Eleanor returned from transcribing all the plates along the corridor, he was still squinting at a corner of the paper. Eleanor looked over his shoulder.

"I'm sure that'll do," she said. "Come on, we've got another two floors to look around."

"Go. I will catch you shortly."

"Best not to split up." She leaned across for another pen and dipped it into the ink well. "I'll help."

Once they were sure they'd copied all the notes from the interesting areas in the border lands, they scouted quickly through the remaining rooms on the corridor before descending to the floor below. They were walking along another almost-identical corridor when they heard another creaking floorboard – and with a sudden start, Eleanor realised why they were hearing sounds that neither of them would admit to. She grabbed Daniel's arm and pushed him into the recess of the nearest doorway, tucking herself in after him. In the time it took her to pull the mirror from her pocket to look back along the hallway their pursuer must have ducked out of sight himself; she saw nothing but a slight movement in the shadows. Still, it was enough to convince her that her assessment was right.

She turned to Daniel and mouthed, "We're being followed."

"You are sure?"

She nodded, though she was equally surprised by this turn of events. It was unlike the Tarasanka to be so subtle. She would've expected any guard to raise the alarm and bring a crowd of men running to catch them – or kill them – if they'd been spotted.

"What do you think?" he asked. "Should we fight?"

"If we can get out without a fuss, we should just leave. We'll come back tomorrow or the next night."

He nodded and they moved out into the corridor again, Eleanor walking backwards to keep an eye out for their pursuer. If he looked out and saw her watching, maybe he'd keep himself out of sight and give them time to escape the building.

They got back to the third floor without seeing any further signs that they'd been followed, and scrambled back across to the balcony of the Charanthe embassy. As Eleanor tugged at the end of the rope to release her knot she saw a shadow in the far window, and flattened herself to the floor. She coiled the rope slowly and waited to see if the shadows would move again, but there was nothing more to see, and she shuffled backwards on her belly until she was well inside the embassy.

"What took you so long?" Daniel asked as she straightened and looped the rope over her shoulder.

"He was at the window," she said. "They know we came this way."

"They will increase the guard, then. Just as well to have copied the map."

They made their way back to their room in silence; their own corridors were safer, but they still didn't want to rouse unnecessary suspicions. Eleanor's heart was still pounding as she closed the bedroom door behind them.

"That was close!" She leaned against the wall and let out a happy sigh. "I do love this feeling, don't you?"

Daniel was quiet but she was sure he was experiencing exactly the same thrill. It was, after all, almost the only reason for taking up such a dangerous job. She went to the sideboard and took out a couple of glasses.

"Let's have a quick nightcap," she said, reaching for the bottle of Burning Death. It was horrible, but it was the only drink they'd been supplied with, so it would have to do. She set the bottle along with two glasses on the nightstand.

"We will need to be awake for more meetings tomorrow," Daniel said.

"Who cares? I can't sleep yet."

"But you should try."

She grabbed his hand and held it to her chest. "Can you feel how my heart's thumping? It's going to take me a while to come down."

"Okay."

"So will you sit and have a drink with me?" She sat on the edge of the bed and poured Burning Death into both glasses. He picked one up and sipped it; without Gisele instructing them, there was no need to drink it in the local manner.

"This is not very nice," he said. "I wonder why they drink it."

"Maybe we should think about importing some Charanthe wines."

"You are obsessed with your imports. Honestly, Eleanor, anyone would think it mattered."

"In any case, this mightn't be your favourite drink, but it's what we've got."

She gulped hers down quickly and rang the bell for hot water. Unlike the last time the door didn't open instantly, and Eleanor wondered whether it was too late an hour to try and get a wash. A few moments later, though, the young servant let himself in and filled the basin. She stripped, leaving clothes and weapons in a heap on the floor, and started to sponge herself clean. She posed a little for Daniel but he wasn't paying attention, so she rang for more hot water and enjoyed the youth's blushing attempt to avert his eyes from her blatant nudity.

She towelled herself off and went to sit at Daniel's side. As she poured herself a second drink and leaned across to top up his glass, she allowed her towel to slide down to her waist.

Daniel sipped his drink and Eleanor shuffled a little closer, pressing herself against his side and resting her hand on his thigh.

"We should not do this," he said, moving away. "It is a bad idea."

"You still haven't told me why."

"It is not a good thing for people in our position to fall in love. Love clouds the judgement. It creates only problems when there are decisions to be made."

"We don't have to fall into that." She stroked his arm as she spoke. "I'm not talking about spending our lives together – just making the most of our time here."

She downed her drink, took his glass from his hand, and swung her leg across to straddle him where he sat as her towel fell to the floor by his feet.

"We can have a bit of fun, can't we? Nothing more than that."

"Only while we are here?"

"Exactly." She started to unbutton his shirt, and he made no move to resist this time. "Just while we're already pretending to be married."

Chapter 3

They were woken early the next morning by an apologetic messenger who had been sent to summon them to the ambassador's private office. He could only be persuaded to wait outside with the promise that they'd join him just as soon as they were dressed, and they fell out of bed, heads aching, still feeling fuzzy from the late-night alcohol.

"And this is another reason why you can't try and banish me to the window seat," Eleanor said as she pulled clean clothes from the closet. "We can't have aides coming in and finding us like that, it'd cause all kinds of talk."

"Fine," Daniel said, voice muffled by the tunic he was pulling over his head.

"Seriously. There's no privacy here, and we could do without raising any more suspicions."

"Yes, fine, you win. Is that enough for you?"

"I was just making an observation. If we can't maintain a cover story within our own embassy, we're not much good at this."

The messenger rapped impatiently at the door, and moments later they were following the him along the corridor, their own conversations halted.

"I'm sorry to do this to you," the ambassador said as they were shown in. "I wouldn't normally disturb you, but we find ourselves in a most uncomfortable situation, and I hoped you could lend your expertise."

"Tell us what has happened," Daniel said.

"My deputy wasn't at her usual duties when I got up today." The ambassador pressed his palms together as he spoke, barely maintaining the composure that would normally be expected of an Imperial official. "In the five months she's been here she's always been awake before me, and I got up around my usual time, a little after dawn. Anyway, she wasn't there, so I sent someone to check on her and she was missing from her room."

Eleanor stared at him. "Gisele's missing?"

"Yes. Really, this is most unlike her. I can't imagine a harmless explanation."

"We saw her at dinner," Eleanor said. "What do we know after that?"

"Not much. She retired early, but her bed hasn't been slept in."

"I am not sure how we can help," Daniel said. "She could have gone anywhere in the city."

"Can you show us her room?" Eleanor asked. "That seems like the best place to start."

"There's not much to see, but by all means, follow me."

They went across the hall to Gisele's bedroom, and as the ambassador had noted, there was no indication of anything out of place. Eleanor lifted the pillow to reveal a neatly folded nightdress.

"So she didn't get into her nightclothes," she said. "And as you said, no-one has slept here. Do you have a regular laundry service in the embassy?"

"Of course."

"And your servants would come round every night to collect your dirty clothes?"

"We put them outside the door and then the boy comes for them, yes."

"Could you go and find him, and ask whether Gisele put her laundry out last night?"

The ambassador nodded. "Wait here. I'll send someone to wake him."

"Why does it matter whether she put her laundry out?" Daniel asked as the ambassador left.

"I think I can guess what's happened," Eleanor said. "But I wanted him out of the way for a moment. If I'm right, I'm sure they'll find that she put her clothes out, just like normal. She's smart enough to avoid giving herself away."

"Where do you think she is?"

"I'm not sure where she'll be now. But we know we were followed last night."

Daniel pushed the door closed and lowered his voice. "You

think that was her? Why would she do such a thing?"

"She wanted to know what you were up to. If there's any chance she overheard us mention going out, I wouldn't be surprised if she followed us to see what she could find out."

"Do you have any evidence of this?"

"I know Gisele. I know the kinds of things that'd cause her to go sneaking about in the night."

"We cannot trust something so important to your instincts, Eleanor."

"I warned you she'd do something stupid," Eleanor said. "Besides, she's gone out fully dressed but she's left her boots here. That means she's gone out in her house-shoes."

"That suggests she did not plan to leave the embassy."

"Or that she didn't want us to hear her. She may not have our training, but we spent enough years together creeping down to steal midnight snacks from the kitchens. She wore her slippers so we wouldn't hear her."

"And where is she now, if you are right in your hypothesis?"

"If we're lucky she's still in there, whether hiding or imprisoned."

"And if she is not lucky?"

"On a ship bound for Taraska La'on."

Daniel had his mouth open to speak when the ambassador opened the door, accompanied by a young man who was still in his nightshirt.

"If you could repeat what you just told me," the ambassador said, encouraging the young man ahead of him into the room.

"The ambassador asked me about collecting the assistant ambassador's laundry," the youth said, a slight blush rising in his cheeks. "And I was just saying that everything seemed to be normal last night."

"She was wearing a blue tunic at supper," Eleanor said. "Did she put that out for you?"

"Yes ma'am. Do you need me to fetch it?"

"No, that's fine. Have you worked here for long?"

"About a year."

"And would you say you're quite familiar with the range of the assistant ambassador's wardrobe?"

"I'm not sure what you mean."

"You've collected the assistant ambassador's laundry ever since she arrived here." Eleanor opened Gisele's closet and beckoned him forwards. "Has she been through all of her clothes?"

"At least twice, yes."

"And could you identify what she might be wearing right now?"

He considered it for a moment, shuffling through the stack of clean clothes. "Everything that stands out is here or down in the laundry room. She must be in one of her plain black tunics."

"Thank you. You can go back to bed now."

He nodded, looking immensely puzzled, and left the room without another word.

"Do you have any ideas?" the ambassador asked.

"She put her laundry out and changed into clean clothes that weren't her nightwear," Eleanor said. "And there are no signs of any struggle. She obviously went somewhere of her own accord, but it'll take a while longer to work out where that may be. Can we have full access to her office?"

"Whatever you need. I'm just glad you two happened to be here."

"We'll see what we can do."

"You will make our excuses to the Faliskan traders?" Daniel asked. "They are expecting to see us this afternoon."

"I'll tell them you've taken ill. It's quite normal to lose a day or two when you come to a strange country."

"Thank you."

"I'll unlock Gisele's office for you, and then I'll be in my rooms if you need anything."

"You could have someone send breakfast," Eleanor said. "I can't concentrate on an empty stomach."

"If you are right," Daniel said once they were alone behind the closed door of Gisele's small office, "what do you think we can do about it?"

"If I'm right? Do you have a better explanation?"

"Not yet. So, if you are right, what would you have us do?"

"We have to try and get her back," Eleanor said. "We can't

leave her in the hands of those Tarasanka bastards."

"It is a lot to risk on a hunch, when for all we know she could walk back in at any moment."

"She went out in her slippers! And she's been gone all night. How long would you wait, knowing they'll want to make her talk?"

"Well, we cannot simply walk into the Taraska embassy in broad daylight. We have time to consider other options."

Eleanor picked up a sheaf of papers and flicked through them. "There's nothing here that's going to help us."

"How can you be so sure?"

"Because I'm right. And Gisele's job was boring. Embassy accounts, taking care of visitors, occasional meetings with minor Falisanka officials. Nothing that could possibly be worth disappearing over."

They were disturbed by a servant with a platter of fruit and cheese. Eleanor picked up a slice of something green with watery flesh, and sat down in Gisele's chair to think as Daniel continued to work meticulously through notes and files.

"I wouldn't expect you to know this," she said, reaching for another piece of the same fruit. It wouldn't be her first choice of breakfast, but at least its faint flavour was relatively inoffensive. "But I wonder if there are any plants growing in this part of the world that are illegal in Faliska. Something that they'd refuse to sell to us."

Daniel looked over the top of his papers at her. "Why would you expect me to be ignorant of something so simple?"

"Well, unless you made a detailed study of Falisanka trade laws when I wasn't looking?"

"I would not claim to be a legal expert but ngali'a grows in the sands, and no sane government would permit the sale of such a deadly poison."

Eleanor smiled. "I suppose I underestimated you. That sounds like it'll do nicely for our purposes."

"And what are our purposes?"

"I think I'd like to make a small purchase. We're here with a trade delegation, after all. It'd hardly be out of character for us to visit a neighbouring embassy if we were struggling to fulfil a particularly challenging requirement."

"You cannot possibly be suggesting–"

"I'm going to the Tarasanka embassy." She licked her fingers clean and dried them on her trousers as she got to her feet. "But if Gisele's paperwork is that interesting, you don't have to come."

"Now?"

"Now. Are you coming?"

He made space for his stack of papers on the corner of the desk. "I would not trust you to go alone when you are in this mood."

"What mood?" Eleanor asked. "On second thoughts, don't answer that. Come on, then, if you're coming."

There was a young man guarding the door of Taraska's embassy; though he was heavily armed, he smiled as they approached.

"I can to helping you?"

"I hope so," Eleanor said. "We're here with the trade delegation from Charanthe, and we're having a little difficulty finding something we need. Is there somewhere we can talk in private?"

He waved them into his guard room, where he could keep an eye out for any further visitors as they conversed.

"Have you heard of the plant called ngali'a?" Eleanor asked.

He shook his head. "What it being?"

"It's a plant that grows out in the desert." If he didn't know they were asking about a poison, she didn't need to enlighten him. "Faliska refuse to sell it and it's not practical for us to send an expedition to search the land, but I've heard it's possible to buy anything in Taraska."

"Anything, yes, if you having right money."

"We can pay well."

"Today, five dollars Charanthe," he said. "And the rest when you collecting your parcel."

Eleanor nodded and reached for her coin purse. The guard rummaged on his desk, tore a blank strip from the bottom of a scroll of parchment, and inscribed a few words in the flowing Tarasanka script.

"You writing here what is called," he said, indicating a gap between words. "And here, your names."

Eleanor took the quill, dipped it, and inscribed "ngali'a" with letters of the Charanthe alphabet. And then, because she was afraid her own details might have been noted in some Tarasanka records, she added Daniel's name to the bottom.

"Will they understand Charanthe letters?" she asked.

The guard squinted at her handwriting. "Yes, is fine. I will sending this to ship later, and ship is going for Taraska La'on at daybreak. Your message will arriving in four days. You should expecting your parcel from me when ship returning, ten days from now. Then you paying."

"We'll be going down to the harbour shortly – I can take the message myself, if you let me know the name of your ship."

"Ship is name *Ktasi'on*." He handed her the note. "You should be easy to finding it. You giving this to captain, and he arranging everything for you."

The *Ktasi'on* was easy to spot in Faliska's quiet harbour, its red Tarasanka flag whipping against the mast. Eleanor gripped the note tightly against the winds as she approached the sailor who was guarding the gangplank.

"Is this the ship heading for Taraska at dawn?" she asked.

The sailor nodded. "Taraska, yes." He was a young man, but months of sea air and sun had left heavy lines on his face.

"I have a message for your captain."

"Okay." He held his hand out. "I giving."

"It's an important trade request," Eleanor said as she handed the note across. "Please make sure your captain sees it before you sail."

The sailor tucked the paper inside his waistband without looking at it. "I giving," he repeated.

"Thank you." Eleanor took Daniel's arm and made as if to leave, then hesitated after a couple of steps and turned back to the sailor. "We actually have a number of interests to pursue in Taraska. Is there any space on the boat for passengers?"

He looked blank. "Sorry, not understanding."

"We would like to travel on your boat. As passengers." Eleanor waved her hands to indicate herself and Daniel, and the boat.

The sailor shook his head. "We not taking peoples, no."

"Do you know of any other boats which might be heading that way in the next few days?"

"Sorry?" He looked thoroughly confused.

"Never mind. Thanks anyway – you've been very helpful. Please do make sure our message reaches your captain."

They stopped as soon as they were around the corner and out of sight of the harbour.

"That's the boat," Eleanor said. "I'm sure of it. They won't let us travel with them because Gisele's locked up in the hold."

Daniel shrugged. "Perhaps."

"Do you think I'm wrong?"

"I think he did not understand much of what you were asking. And there are many reasons why a ship may not take passengers."

"Well, obviously, but in the circumstances..."

"In these particular circumstances, we need more information before we act."

"If you can distract that lad's attention, I can sneak on board and check."

"When I said 'before we act,' I meant it. I will not allow you to jeapordise our position."

"Where are we going to get more information without doing something? If you're not going to help, I'll just have to do it alone."

"No." He caught her arm and stopped her as she began to walk.

"Let me go."

"I cannot. Sorry."

"Daniel, don't make me fight you."

He kept a tight grip on her arm. "I should prefer to avoid it."

"Then let me go. I can have her free before lunch and we can get back to business."

"We do not know for sure that Gisele is even there. You cannot destroy our mission on a mere feeling."

"If they hurt Gisele to make her talk she'll blow our cover all by herself. Which way would you prefer it?"

"The boat does not leave yet. We must be patient."

She sighed. "Okay, what do you propose?"

"There are a couple of guesthouses by the harbour. We should take a room with a sea view at one of them, and wait."

"For what?"

"If you are correct, they captured her last night. Would you not prefer to keep your prisoner safely in an embassy cell until the last moment? And would you not wait for darkness to move her to your ship?"

"Okay." Eleanor nodded. "We'll watch to see if they move her in the night, but if we don't see anything then you have to let me go and search the ship."

"If the ship comes to leave, you may do as you wish."

The first guesthouse they tried had a shortage of guests, so it was easy to negotiate a forward-facing room with a view of the harbour. They paid for one night in advance – to knowing looks from the landlord – and went up to make themselves comfortable in their new watchtower.

"We'd better take shifts," Eleanor said, sitting on the pallet which took the place of a bed. "It's going to be a long day."

"Can you sleep now?" Daniel asked.

She stretched out and yawned. "I can sleep any time. Wake me up when you get tired."

He took a seat by the window, and Eleanor watched him from between half-closed eyes until she drifted into sleep. Daniel woke her in the late afternoon, and took his turn on the pallet as she assumed the watch duties.

The harbour was quiet for most of the evening, although a couple of carts stopped near the Tarasanka ship. But the crates they unloaded could never have contained any prisoner who might survive to tell of it, and then darkness fell, and all traffic stopped. She had nothing else to report when she at last woke Daniel to swap roles again.

She slept lightly and dreamed of a man who looked very like Daniel, but in her dreams he was warm and cheery, nothing like his usual reserved and formal manner. She rolled over as she woke and reached out to where she expected to find him, starting in surprise when she found the bed empty. But of course he was still at his seat by the window, watching, waiting. It all came back to her as she sat up and rubbed her eyes, but she couldn't quite shake the alternate reality of the dream world.

"How late is it?" she asked, trying to bring her mind back to the present.

"Not late. You did not sleep for long."

"Have you seen anything?"

He looked round. "I would have woken you."

"I know." She stretched, throwing back the sheets. "Nothing's going to happen, anyway, because she's probably already in there."

"My logic failed to convince you, then." Daniel sounded amused.

"They don't mess about. I don't think they're natural strategists. I think we should just go and raid the ship."

"And warn them of our interest? Better not to give away our suspicions."

"Well if I'm right she's already in the hold, and if you're right then they'll leave it till the last possible moment and bring her just before dawn." She tilted her head and waited for him to respond.

"So?"

"So I don't know why we're bothering with this all-night vigil. We could both get some sleep while we wait." She stretched out on the bed and beckoned him to join her. "We didn't get much rest last night."

"I am fine," he said. "I can stay here. Go back to sleep. It is not your shift yet."

"You're not listening to me. If we both sleep for a while now, we'll be more awake when we need to act." She patted the empty half of the bed. "Come on, we'll both be more effective if we get a good night's sleep."

"Well, she is your friend." He came across to the pallet and removed his trousers before sitting down next to her. "If you are prepared to risk it, I will sleep."

"We'll both wake up as soon as there's any light in the sky, and probably before. It's not much of a risk." She slid her hand

46

beneath his tunic, and rested her head on his chest. "And this is much nicer than sleeping alone."

"Take care," he murmured. "We cannot afford dependencies." But he made no move to dislodge her.

It was still dark when Eleanor woke, only a little moonlight illuminating the room. Her hands wandered beneath Daniel's tunic as he slept beside her; she'd dreamt about him again, and more than anything she wanted her dream-Daniel to be real. He woke suddenly and she pulled away, embarrassed to have been caught out in her daydreams, but he turned and pressed his lips against hers, rolling her onto her back and pushing her down onto the bed as he slid one hand between her legs.

She wrapped her arms around his shoulders and pulled him closer, breathing deeply into his neck, hopeful that her dreams might not have been so far from the truth after all. Reality was more sticky than dreams, and Daniel less expressive, but those were details she was prepared to overlook. At least he'd stopped trying to persuade her that they shouldn't be doing this.

There was no water at the wash stand, and it felt an unreasonable time to disturb their landlord, so they pulled crumpled clothes over sweaty skin. Daniel went to look out of the window as he laced his shirt.

"Look," he said, turning with laces still half-fastened. "The ship is gone."

"No, it can't be." Eleanor yawned and joined him at the window to see for herself. "The guard said they were sailing at dawn. Maybe they moved further along the quay?"

"See?" He waved down at the space which the boat no longer occupied. The rest of the harbour was equally quiet; wherever the ship had gone, it was out of sight, and the sun hadn't yet broken the horizon.

"Bastards!" Eleanor slammed her palm against the wall. "I can't believe it. They must've guessed we were going to try something."

"Impossible."

"They know we were asking questions – and now they've changed their departure. Don't you think it's possible they were suspicious?"

"Any number of things could have altered their plans."

"These things are set by the tides. You don't change your course unless something drastic happens – it must be our fault. We must have made them suspect. Come on, we need to do something."

"Such as?"

"We have to find a fast boat to take us to Taraska La'on," she said. "They'll be half a day ahead of us, at best, and we can't give them time to hide her in the city before we get there."

"We still do not know–"

"They're running," Eleanor said. "That means we know."

Daniel nodded. "Go back to the embassy and fetch an interpreter," he said. "We cannot negotiate this ourselves."

"Where are you going?"

"I need to visit the market. I will meet you back here."

Although it was barely dawn, the ambassador was already in his office when Eleanor arrived. "And?" he asked as soon as he saw her. "What news?"

"A Tarasanka ship left the harbour early this morning," Eleanor said. "We're almost certain that Gisele's on board."

"And you allowed it to leave?" He shook his head. "Sorry, that isn't fair. You don't even have a boat. What are we going to do?"

"We'll follow them. But we need to borrow an interpreter – do you have someone we can trust?"

"Of course. How long will you need her for?"

"We just need someone to come down to the harbour and find us a captain. Can you wake her now?"

"Wait here."

The ambassador returned a short while later, followed by a middle-aged lady with tousled hair and her shirt buttons fastened off-centre.

"Eleanor, this is Lana," he said. "She can speak six local dialects as well as standard Falisanka, and she can get by in Tarasanka and Magrad."

"Pleased to meet you," Eleanor said, extending her hand. "And I'm sorry to get you out of bed."

"It's no problem," Lana said. "Urgent requests don't come

around that often, for translators."

"No, I should think not. But we're in something of a hurry today. If you'll excuse us, ambassador?"

"Of course, of course. I'll be expecting to see you all safely home any day now."

"And you want me to find you a boat?" Lana asked. "Do you have a budget?"

"You'd better ask the ambassador," Eleanor said. "It's his deputy we're trying to rescue. I assume we have whatever resources we need."

"Take whatever you need," the ambassador agreed, and handed across a heavy purse. "Just send Lana back with the rest."

As Eleanor and Lana walked back down to the shore, Eleanor started to give instructions on what she was hoping to achieve.

"Wait here, and I'll see what I can do," Lana said as they came within sight of the harbour.

"It has to be a fast boat," Eleanor added. "We have a lot of time to make up."

She waited by the city gate as Lana walked across and exchanged a few words with a young fisherman who was folding his nets. He shook his head and pointed along the quay towards another boat, and Lana followed his directions to engage an old sailor in conversation. With much muttering and waving of hands they seemed to reach some agreement, and Lana came back to Eleanor.

"I can try some other boats if you like," Lana said. "But that one is about to leave now, heading east, which seems to fit your requirements."

"I'd like to talk to the captain," Eleanor said. "If you don't mind translating."

"That's what I'm here for."

They walked back down to the harbour together, and Eleanor shook the old seaman's hand.

"Is he the captain?" she asked Lana, who nodded. "Can you ask him exactly when he's hoping to leave?"

Lana's voice dropped a few tones when she spoke in

Falisanka, with several sounds which croaked from the back of her throat. Eleanor just looked on with interest. She'd made a short study of the local languages, but not enough to understand a fluent speaker in full flow.

"He was about to leave," Lana said. "He can wait for you, but not for long. He says he must be away before the tide turns."

Eleanor nodded. "That's fine – we don't want to wait as long as that. I just need Daniel to come back from the market. And how long will it take him to reach Taraska?"

"Three days," Lana said after another brief exchange with the captain.

"And his price? I can sail competently, if that helps you negotiate."

Lana turned and said a few more words in Falisanka. The captain shrugged, and held up three fingers.

"Three dollars," Lana said, though the gesture barely needed translating.

"Charanthe?"

"I assume so. They don't really have their own currency here."

"Okay, that's great. Will you ask him to wait? I'll give him a dollar as a deposit, and we won't be long."

Eleanor thanked Lana, sent her back to the embassy with the rest of the ambassador's money, and went up to the guesthouse to wait for Daniel. He came in from the market with a bag full of shopping, and she wondered what he'd thought was so important that it couldn't be bought in Taraska.

"Here." He threw a jar towards her, and she caught it instinctively.

"What's this?" she asked, peering at the thick, dark liquid.

"Indigo paste. To colour your hair – you do not wish to risk triggering any memories in Taraska."

"Now?"

"I think you should."

She held her head over a bowl and slicked the dark gloop through her red hair. "Now what?" she asked. "How long do I have to leave it?"

"Not long. If you wash it now, your hair should be black."

By the time she'd rinsed her hair in three changes of water, she had long black tresses and dull grey fingers. She scrubbed at her hands, but the colour wouldn't shift.

"I look a mess," she said.

"We will be at sea. Who is going to care how you look?"

She pouted. "I thought you might care."

"The colour of your fingertips does not interest me."

"Okay, let's go." She picked up her bag, leaving the half-empty jar of dye on the side.

"Take that with you," Daniel said. "I am not sure how many days before the colour will fade."

"You could've told me that before I used it. The exposure on the boat isn't going to help it last."

"You will be fine. We can probably find more in Taraska, if we must."

"It'd be better to avoid that. If anyone's watching us, we don't want them to suspect a disguise."

"If it is necessary, I will go. There is no chance of my being recognised."

The boat cast off as soon as Eleanor and Daniel were on board, and they'd barely moved out of the harbour when the rain started falling, big droplets splashing on the deck at their feet. Eleanor looked up at the gathering clouds.

"We're going to get a storm," she said to no-one in particular.

The weather turned quickly and before long Eleanor was helping the crew to rig the storm sails, and preparing for a rough day ahead. The boat lurched violently as she climbed back down to the deck, and she glanced across to where Daniel was leaning over the gunwale, regurgitating his breakfast into the sea.

When he turned back to face her, he caught the amused look on her face. "It is not funny."

"But you grew up on a ship," she said, unable to stop herself laughing.

"You know I get seasick."

She nodded; on their journey across the ocean to Faliska,

he'd been green from the moment they moved beyond the sheltered waters of the Imperial archipelago. "It doesn't stop being funny, though. It's just not what I imagined of your school."

Daniel just glared at her and sank to the deck as another huge wave crashed into the boat, clinging to one of the mooring ropes for support. Eleanor made her way across to him, feet slipping on the spray-soaked wood.

"Seriously, are you okay?"

"Could you fetch my bag from the cabin? I need to take some of my peppermint mixture."

"I've got a better idea." She reached out to help him up. "Come with me."

He took her hand and she led him across the deck, supporting him as the boat rolled in the storm, until they reached the hatch into their cabin. She watched him climb down first, then followed to make sure he reached the bunk without further incident.

"Now, lie down, and tell me again what you want from your bag."

"You know, my little bottle for nausea – probably it has fallen to the bottom by now."

She rummaged through the bag until her hand came on something cold and hard, and pulled the bottle out with a flourish. Daniel took it from her, uncorked it, and put it to his lips.

"Lucky you're good at apothecary," she said as he replaced the cork.

"This is only peppermint, with a little adjustment. Even you could make it." He handed her the bottle and she tucked it back inside his bag. "Now, I think I will sleep."

Eleanor glanced around for the nearest bucket and put it on the floor near his head. "Just in case," she said as she turned to scramble back on deck.

When the skies eventually cleared, Eleanor borrowed a telescope and squinted over the bow. She could see a ship ahead of them in the distance, about the size and shape of the *Ktasi'on*, but it was too remote to be sure.

"Can we go any faster?" she asked the one man on the crew who spoke a little Charanthe.

He shook his head.

"But now the storm's died down, surely we can afford to let out the sails?"

She reached for the nearest line, but he put his hand out to stop her from opening the sails.

"Not yet. More winds will to coming."

She kept hold of the rope. "Are you sure?"

"I am knowing this waters – and this winds. We not yet being out of the storm."

"But the wind's blowing eastwards now, and the storm was coming in from the south. We should be clear of it now."

"You must to waiting."

She leaned against the gunwale and watched as the wind whipped up small waves around the boat. "These conditions are fine," she said at last. "We need to go faster."

Before she could insist, though, the wind suddenly turned and picked up again.

"It is how I was telling you," the sailor said, waving at the sails which were now beginning to snap loudly against the mast. Thunder rolled in the distance, and a moment later it was pouring with rain again.

"Okay," Eleanor conceded. "How long until it clears?"

"Maybe tomorrow, maybe not. You should be resting."

There wasn't much else for her to do in the storm and it was getting dark, so after staring forlornly into the distance until the last of the pink light faded, Eleanor took his advice and went down to the cabin. At least the ship on the horizon – if it were the *Ktasi'on* – was also being buffeted and slowed by the storm.

Below decks there was only one small sleeping area for all the crew to share, and Eleanor and Daniel would be squashed together on the narrow bunk he currently occupied. He was curled up on the bed and snoring; she tried to move his feet without waking him, but he stirred.

"Top and tail?" she suggested as she hung her bag from a nail on the bulkhead. "I'm not sure how else we're going to fit in here."

"Fine," he murmured, rubbing his eyes. "Is it late?"

"Just past sunset."

He rolled over and flattened himself against the wall, and Eleanor slid into the narrow space he'd vacated. She gripped his ankles – partly for stability, partly to try and stop him from kicking her in the night – and traced the edge of his foot with her thumb. Unlike her own, callused from so many barefoot runs, his heels were soft.

"You should be training more," she said, prodding gently at the skin. "These are a scholar's feet. No strength."

He ran one hand along her calf and rested it in the crook of her knee. "I am a scholar," he said, his voice low and sleepy.

Moments later, she heard him snoring again. She was awake much longer, finding it hard to sleep in such a precarious position. It wasn't comfortable but she didn't dare move, for fear of losing what little space she had as Daniel thrashed in his sleep.

She replayed the day's events in her head, wondering if there was any way she could have stopped Gisele falling into this mess, or any chance they could have got her out sooner than this, or whether she should have ignored Daniel completely and stopped the *Ktasi'on* before it left the harbour. She chided herself for allowing unproductive thoughts to run away with her; regretting the past would do nothing to get Gisele home safely. Hugging Daniel's soft feet against her cheek, she closed her eyes and waited for sleep to come.

She woke when he tried to climb over her. As she got to her feet she could tell from the boat's movement that the storm had passed and now, finally, they were racing along in the wake of the *Ktasi'on*. She could only hope the Tarasanka ship had also been delayed by the weather.

Chapter 4

They were gaining on the *Ktasi'on* every day but the storm had held them up too much, and the Tarasanka ship had berthed in Taraska's harbour before they even sailed into the bay.

The winds had dropped to almost nothing and all Eleanor's frustration couldn't make the sails fill out any more than they were, so they drifted slowly towards the shore. She watched the *Ktasi'on* through the telescope, hoping for any sign of Gisele, but saw only the loading and unloading of supply crates.

"Maybe we should take the little boat and row?" she suggested to Daniel.

"Have you gone out of your mind? Rowing would gain us very little speed at the expense of a great deal of work."

"But we're losing Gisele. Every moment we're stuck out here is giving them time to hide her further away."

"You said yourself they are not strategic thinkers," Daniel said. "I doubt they are building a maze to conceal her. They will simply deposit her in a dungeon somewhere and assume their defences are sufficient."

"I've broken in to their prison before," Eleanor said. "Although if they've finished building the new citadel, who knows what that'll be like. We should have paid more attention to those plans."

"The trick plans?"

"This might be our chance to find out just how tricky they were. Do you think we can remember the key features?"

"I remember the secret passageway that was so obviously designed to bait us. I doubt we would have any trouble finding its end."

"It's probably got a big sign saying 'Secret passage to the citadel,' with a bright red arrow pointing the way," she said. Even the idea made her laugh. "And it's probably written in Charanthe, just for us. I think I'd rather not take that route, if it's all the same to you."

"Indeed."

They looked up to where the gilded turrets of the new citadel caught the late evening light, shining out even more brightly than the rest of the city's sparkling skyline.

"But seriously, what do you reckon?" Eleanor asked. "The old one that we know, or the new one that they want us to attack?"

"Just because they have built some traps does not mean that the new citadel is just for show. Surely even they would not waste that much money on a mere trap."

"Perhaps not – but the old one seemed fairly well built. I'm not sure why they'd replace it."

"Maybe because you found your way out," he said. "I expect that was not popular. And they are paranoid."

"Well, perhaps we should start by going in the way that I know. If we don't find Gisele in the cells where they held me, we can take a look at the new buildings."

Eventually they reached the quay, and Eleanor and Daniel disembarked with only a hasty goodbye to their shipmates. Eleanor caught sight of her reflection in the water as she scrambled to shore, and was taken by surprise at the dark hair framing her face. She hardly recognised herself, which was reassuring. Even the Tarasanka soldiers who'd guarded her cell would be unlikely to identify her now.

"At least we don't have to wait long for nightfall," Eleanor said. The sun had already dipped below the height of the buildings.

"We will need to eat," Daniel said. "Preferably before we go breaking into citadels."

"There are plenty of food stalls, but you won't like any of them," Eleanor said. "I suggest we go back to the tavern where Raf and I stayed. We can get a meal there and leave some of this baggage."

"I am not sure that is a good idea. What if they recognise you?"

"The landlord probably will, but he's a good bloke. He's helped us before." It was only as she spoke that she remembered how he and his friends had leeched every last coin from Raf – but she didn't have any other ideas, so she kept her reservations to herself. She and Daniel could take care of each other.

"Where is it, then?"

"Follow me."

She led him through the still-familiar streets with an ease that surprised her; it had been a couple of years, but at every turn it felt like only yesterday that she'd last run around these corners. The tavern still had the same tatty bead curtain across the door. Eleanor pushed her way inside and led Daniel through to the landlord's living quarters in the back.

"Is your attic room free?" she asked, gesturing towards the ladder.

The landlord looked at her suspiciously, and she suddenly remembered how different she looked. She held her hands up to cover her hair and recognition flashed into his eyes, followed swiftly by fear.

"You is coming to revenge your friend?" he asked.

"What? Oh, no. No, Raf's fine, he's back home." She studiously ignored Daniel's quizzical expression. "We'd like to stay with you for a few days, if you have space."

He nodded, and waved them up.

"What was he afraid of?" Daniel asked. "What is your history here?"

"It's nothing. Just some business with Raf after I came back to the Empire."

"But you trust this man?"

"I trust him not to turn us in, yes."

"Why?"

"We'll pay him." Eleanor piled their bags under the table, and fished out a couple of coins from her purse. "Come on, let's see what he's got for us to eat."

After a quick supper of fish in a bitter Tarasanka sauce, they ventured out into the night. Eleanor picked out a circuitous route around to the tower she and Raf had escaped from; thankfully, the streets in that part of town were deserted after dark.

"Well, here it is." She waved her hand up towards the tower.

"It's a tough climb. Are you ready?"

"I will follow you," Daniel said, so she started to scout out holds on the wall.

As she reached what she thought was about the half way point she jammed her fingers into a crack that was just wide enough for the job, braced her toes against sheer rock, and turned to look down at Daniel's progress. As she watched him struggle beneath her, she realised she'd overestimated his abilities – and underestimated the smooth black stones. She forced a wedge into the crack, roped herself into a quick harness and dropped a few feet down the wall to face him.

"You should go back," she said, steadying herself against the wall. "I'm sorry, I remembered it being a hard climb but I assumed the academy would have taken us so far on that it'd be easy now."

"It is fine," Daniel said, although the beads of sweat on his forehead told otherwise. "I am fine."

He tried to slide his dagger between two blocks of stone to give himself a hand-hold, but to no avail.

"Are you stable?" she asked.

"Yes."

"Wait there. I'll throw the rope back when I get to the top, and you can climb that way."

"You do not need to worry, I–"

"It's not surprising you can climb ropes better than walls, but it won't help either of us if you end up falling," Eleanor said flatly. "Stay there until I can tie this off at the top."

She pulled herself back up the rope to where she'd lodged the wedge, jammed her fingers again, and loosed her rope. She glanced back to make sure that Daniel was obeying her instruction, and then began to hunt for her next grip. It was slow progress. She was undoubtedly more skilled than the last time she'd made this climb, but that simply meant the wall was merely challenging, rather than near-impossible. No amount of practice would make this into an easy climb, and several times she had to spring from a single hand- or foot-hold to grab at a crevice that was otherwise beyond her reach.

When she finally reached the top she looped one end of her

rope around a stone antefix and threw the end down to where Daniel was still spreadeagled against the stones. He tied a harness and tested it before transferring his weight to the rope; Eleanor braced herself against the wall to support him as he started to climb.

"Wasn't that easier?" she asked as he swung his leg up and rolled onto the ledge.

Daniel nodded, but said nothing.

"Sorry I didn't think of it earlier." She wound the rope around her arm and dropped it onto the ledge. "We can leave that until we get back. Come on."

The tower door was locked, but it was a simple latch and yielded quickly. Eleanor pushed it open slowly, looking for traps or guards, but saw none. She stepped inside, looked around once more, and waved for Daniel to follow her. She led him down towards the cell where she and Raf had been imprisoned: that their captors had chosen to put them in a room together, with all the risks that entailed, probably suggested that they didn't have too many cells to choose from.

Eleanor was sure she knew the way back through the familiar corridors, but something was different. She held her breath as she opened the door to the torture chamber, but found only an empty room. Likewise, the cell where she'd spent so many nights was now unlocked and deserted.

"Looks like I made you struggle with that climb for nothing," she said. "They've cleared up. They must really be using the new citadel."

"Are you sure this is the place?"

She glared at him. "It's not the sort of thing you forget."

"What?"

"Look, this was where they tortured us, okay?" She pushed the door open again with a bang, abandoning any attempt at stealth now she was sure the tower wasn't being used. The sound echoed around the empty chamber. "This room's going to be seared into my memory forever – every flagstone, every brick, every piece of equipment that they've now moved somewhere else. I only have to close my eyes to see it as it was."

Daniel nodded, though she was fairly sure he didn't really understand. There was no way he could imagine it when he'd never experienced anything worse than the academy's interrogation classes.

"Come on, then," she said. "No point in hanging around here when we've got work to do."

"The new citadel," Daniel said. "We must step into the jaws of the trap."

Eleanor held the rope again for Daniel to abseil down the wall, then lowered herself part way before releasing the rope and climbing the remaining distance.

It was easy to find the new citadel, gleaming as it was above the rest of the city, but there was no obvious angle of attack. Armed guards patrolled the walls, and several watch-towers looked out over the streets.

"Looks like you were right," Eleanor said. "They really are paranoid."

"This is a good sign."

"How, exactly?"

"Their defences are all on display. In which case, we need only to devise a plan and follow it."

He said it with such finality as to suggest that was the end of the matter, but Eleanor wasn't reassured. Stating the need for a plan didn't bring them any closer to having one.

"Do you not see?" he asked when she didn't respond. "If they are so unsubtle, they will not be expecting subtlety. We have them at a disadvantage."

"Okay, then, what do you propose?"

He put an arm around her shoulders and pulled her towards him. "Let us walk," he said. "Pretend we are enjoying an evening stroll, and we will see what we can see."

They wandered slowly through the streets which marked the citadel's perimeter. Despite the late hour, this part of town was bustling with activity: hawkers and hookers loitered on the corners, inviting passers-by to sample their wares. Eleanor didn't need encouraging to put a possessive arm around Daniel's waist as they walked.

"This area was all houses last time I was here," she said,

looking up at the sleek grey walls which now towered above them. "And it's only been a couple of years. That's fast work."

"Your escape must have really upset them."

"A couple of kids breaking out of a cell isn't exactly cause for a building like this. Anyway, it looks pretty unassailable, which is all I care about right now – we can't climb up with so many guards looking out."

"I am not looking for a climbing route."

"What, then?"

"Supplies must go in somewhere, as must the staff. If we do this right, they will show us inside."

They eventually found the service entrance at the back of the citadel, a low door set into the inland-facing wall. Even in the dark, a small convoy of carts waited in a line outside the gate.

Daniel fished around under his cloak, pulled out a small bundle, and threw it hard against a nearby wall. It burst into blue flames with a series of popping sounds, sending sparks flying across the street.

"Now!" he said as all eyes turned towards the fire. He gripped her arm and pulled her towards the nearest produce cart. The crates were easily large enough to conceal a person... if only they weren't full of waxy-skinned fruit. Daniel prised up the nearest lid and started to shovel fruits from the crate into the street, kicking them to make them roll down the hill and out of sight. Eleanor scrambled up onto the cart and followed suit with the next crate, scooping out just enough space for her to slide inside. She pulled the lid down and lay still, breathing quietly. She could feel her body beginning to crush the fruit beneath her; juice seeped into her clothes and the acidic smell filled her nostrils. Daniel had also stopped moving around, and for a while she could hear only the popping and crackling of the distraction firecracker, and the alarmed shouting of foreign voices. It wasn't long before that, too, faded into silence, and shortly they felt the cart begin to move beneath them, rattling down towards the citadel.

The crates bumped uncomfortably as they were unloaded and Eleanor braced herself against the wooden walls, trying not to squash any more tell-tale juice from the fruits. Once the room finally fell silent around them, she pushed the lid from her crate and clambered out. Hers was on top of a stack of half a dozen similar boxes, and she dropped to the ground before looking for Daniel. A quiet thudding from inside a nearby stack drew her attention.

"Daniel?" She knocked on the slats of the crate. "Are you in there?"

He grunted his assent.

"Okay, stop struggling, there are a couple of boxes on top of yours. I'll move them."

She heaved the first one down; the corner splintered as it hit the flagstones and powdered spices spilled out across her feet, throwing a fragrant cloud into the air. She pulled the second crate down on top of the first, and reached across to lift the lid from above Daniel's head.

"See?" Daniel said, a smug smile creeping across his features as he swung himself to the ground. "It was simple."

"Now we just need to figure out where they're holding her."

"The plans showed dungeons beneath the east wing."

Eleanor stamped her feet, trying to clear the spices from her shoes, but succeeded only in making another dust cloud. "And you suddenly trust those plans?"

"No – I think that is the last place we should look."

"That doesn't narrow it down much, then. Let's see where we are, and then we can try to be systematic about it."

As it happened, the cells and the food stores were both in an underground segment at the back of the citadel, and it didn't take them long to find where Gisele was being held. There weren't even guards on the corridor; apparently they were putting all their faith in the outer defences. Gisele was manacled to the wall, but the locks on her iron cuffs were crude and Eleanor popped them open with minimal effort.

"Gisele," she said, shaking her by the shoulder. "Gisele, wake up."

She clicked her fingers in front of Gisele's face, slapped her cheeks, and shook her again, harder. Gisele's eyelids fluttered, but she made no real response.

Eleanor draped her friend's arm over her shoulder and hauled her to her feet, but Gisele couldn't support her own weight and there was no chance of holding that position with any stability. Eleanor lowered her to the floor again, hoisted her by the armpits, and edged towards the door where Daniel was waiting. For all that she tried to be gentle, Gisele's body bumped along the floor and she moaned.

"Sorry," Eleanor said. "It's not far."

Daniel came across to see what was happening. "Can I help?" he asked.

"You're supposed to be watching the door. What if someone comes?"

"You sounded like you were struggling."

"Well, if you want to swap you can get Gisele out of here and I'll take over the watch," Eleanor said. "See if you can figure out what they've drugged her with, and whether you've got anything to make an antidote."

Daniel bent over Gisele's limp body and he started to count her pulse as Eleanor went outside to check the corridor.

"Are we carrying any stimulants?" he called.

"I haven't got any drugs," Eleanor said. "Unless you count whatever you've used to dope these darts."

"Assassin's hand and sleepfast," he said. "Well, assassin's hand is a convulsant – that might drag her out of this stupor."

"I thought it was fatal?"

"Oh, it is, when you administer a whole dose into the vein. But if she is heavily sedated already, a drop on her tongue may just work to wake her. Pass me your darts."

"Are you sure? We don't want to risk hurting her."

"Trust me."

Eleanor watched nervously as he held Gisele's mouth open and squeezed a tiny drop of the poison from the tip of one of the darts. Gisele coughed and spluttered, looking for a moment as if she might choke, and then her eyes flew open. It took her a moment to focus, and when she saw where she was she was gripped by pure horror. Eleanor forgot all about the watch duties she'd promised to take on, and hurried across the room to take hold of her friend's hand.

"It's okay," she said. "Gisele. It's me. Don't panic, we're going to get you home."

"Eleanor?" Gisele blinked, confused. "Am I dreaming?"

"You're not dreaming."

"Where are we? And what's happened to your hair?"

"I'll explain later – first, we have to get you out of here. How are you feeling? Do you think you can walk?"

"I'll try."

Gisele struggled to her feet, and with Eleanor and Daniel supporting her on either side she managed to take a few wobbly steps forwards before stumbling. They caught her and kept her upright, but walking out of the citadel was going to be a lengthy process.

"If we meet anyone, we're going to have to put you down quickly," Eleanor said. "And if we do, you just need to keep your head down and stay out of the way. Okay?"

Gisele nodded. They led her forwards a few more steps, through the door and into the corridor, and caught her as her knees gave way.

"You're doing fine," Eleanor said as they propped her up again. "We'll just take it really slowly."

As they turned the corner, though, they came upon a pair of guards – and going slowly ceased to be an option. They ran for the store room, dragging Gisele behind them, and pushed her to the ground behind a pile of crates. Daniel and Eleanor crawled after her and readied their weapons.

"Stay down," Eleanor whispered as the guards came into the room, calling out and challenging in Tarasanka, one banging his staff against the flagstones.

Eleanor stood and loosed stars from both hands, then ducked out of sight again as Daniel stood to take his turn. But although one of the guards fell, the room was too small to keep any kind of distance in the fight. By the time she stood to make her aim again the remaining guard was close beside them, blowing a series of short bursts on a whistle he held clenched between his teeth.

Eleanor leaned on the top of the nearest barrel to topple it, then sent it rolling towards the guard's legs. He jumped from its path straight into range of Daniel's knife, and fell to his knees as Daniel finished him off with a neat cut across the throat.

"Let's get out of here," Eleanor said, wrestling with the first of three thick iron bars which closed the supply gate. Daniel stepped across to help her while Gisele leaned against a stack of crates and watched, still too weak to be of use. They were about to start hefting the second bar when heavy footsteps in the corridor warned them of a dozen guards arriving at a run.

Eleanor slid knives from her wrist-sheaths, but before she could loose a single blade the guards had already grabbed Gisele by the arms. Daniel and Eleanor dashed forwards together, ducking and slashing, but the guards swung their staves like clubs, raining heavy blows and making it impossible to get close without getting hit. A glancing blow to Eleanor's temple was followed by another staff crashing down on the back of her skull; if they struck her again it was after she was already unconscious.

Daniel prodded Eleanor awake; Gisele was already stirring beside them. They were still in the same store room, restrained with iron manacles around their wrists and ankles. A young guard sat on one of the crates, keeping a half-hearted watch.

"What now?" Gisele asked, looking between Eleanor and Daniel. "I take it this wasn't part of your plan?"

"Not exactly."

Gisele leaned forwards to the guard. "What's your name?"

"What are you doing?" Eleanor whispered. "We don't even know if he speaks Charanthe."

"I'm a reasonable woman," Gisele continued. The guard ignored her as steadfastly as she was ignoring Eleanor. "And I'm confident that you're a reasonable man. You're how old, twenty? Twenty-one?"

He shrugged, unable or unwilling to answer.

"I'm sure you think you've done well for yourself. You've made it off the boats, and your master only beats you once or twice a day, I see that. But you know you'll always be a slave."

The boy stared at her now with dark eyes wide, spooked. "How you knowing?"

"I know the ways of Taraska. So what's next? Where do you go from here?"

"What?"

"What's next for you? We've got money. If you help us, you'll never have to go back to your master."

"You having almost nothing," he said, holding up the bag of their possessions. It contained only the few weapons they'd stripped from Eleanor and Daniel.

"Not here," Gisele said. "We're not that stupid. But help us out, come with us, and we'll see you're never a slave again."

He rubbed at his arm, where a black tattoo was just visible through the thin cotton of his sleeve. "Slave always being slave," he said.

"It doesn't mean anything in the Empire, or in Faliska," Gisele said. "Haven't you dreamed of freedom? I can give it to you. You just need to get us out of here."

He thought for a moment, then peered out through the doorway to check they were alone. "I will to helping," he said, loosing their manacles. "But we must going fast."

"You'll have to tell me how you did that," Eleanor said to Gisele as they followed him through the corridors. "How did you know to say those things?"

Gisele smiled. "I'm a diplomat, remember? But it was nothing, just a little local knowledge."

"You knew exactly what to say to make him listen."

"I saw the slave mark on his arm – and I know the shape of their lives."

He led them through quiet passages beneath the citadel, and out of a side gate into the streets.

"Where you wanting?" the youth asked. "We going for ships?"

"Not yet," Gisele said. "We need to go to Hangman's Square."

The youth shook his head. "Not nice," he said. "Better going to ships."

"Hangman's Square," Gisele repeated. "That's where we need to go first."

Eleanor and Daniel exchanged puzzled glances, but if Gisele

had a plan then they weren't about to stop her. The youth reluctantly led the way into an area of tumbledown wooden shacks, in a corner of the city far from anywhere Eleanor had visited before.

Charanthe's embassy in Taraska was small and unofficial – the Tarasanka lords would never knowingly have permitted the Imperial staff to set up offices in their city – but Gisele knew the woman currently serving as the Empire's head of operations in the region. On the first floor of a narrow, half-collapsed building just off Hangman's Square, they found a tiny office with a couple of cluttered desks.

"Is Fan around?" Gisele asked the skinny girl who sat behind one of them.

"She'll be back tomorrow," the girl said. "Can I help you?"

"I'm the assistant ambassador to Faliska," Gisele said. That caught the girl's attention, but Gisele waved her to silence. "Don't ask how I ended up here, but this kid needs sanctuary in the Empire. Can you get him out of the city today?"

The girl nodded. "Do you want me to send him to your embassy in Faliska?"

"Or put him on a ship bound for home, if you can find one. I'll write a letter of introduction."

"Okay, I'll see what there is." The girl rearranged a few things on her desk, and beckoned the lad to follow her downstairs.

"You need to rest," Eleanor said, pushing Gisele into a chair. "Daniel, I think we need your skills – look what those chains have done."

"Yes." He lifted Gisele's arm, examined the wounds, then released her gently. "I will go to the market."

"You might want to pick up some srakol," Eleanor said. "It's a local preparation that seems to help with healing."

"Do you still think I know nothing?" Daniel snapped, then glanced apologetically at Gisele. "Yes, I will get some. I will not be long."

"Are you going to tell me what's going on?" Gisele asked once they were alone.

"You first," Eleanor said. "You're the one who managed to

get yourself kidnapped."

"I assumed you'd worked it out. You managed to follow me, after all – I wasn't expecting that. I thought I'd had it when I came round and realised they'd put me on a ship."

"I guessed a few things," Eleanor said. "Just easy stuff. You got changed into boring clothes and you went wandering in your house-shoes. And I heard someone following us in the night."

"I was careless – I don't have practice at this sort of thing. Whereas you, apparently, do."

"A little, yes."

Gisele narrowed her eyes. "A little?"

"Okay, more than a little."

"What are you, Eleanor? What have you become?"

"Can't you guess? You'll get it wrong, of course, but everyone's always wrong about us."

"You're an assassin."

"That'll do."

"So the legends–"

"They're not legends. All the crazy stuff we thought was fairy stories, well, it's pretty much all true."

"Except the ship-school." Gisele let out a weak laugh. "That one's far too ridiculous."

"As it happens, that one is also true." Daniel said as he pushed through the door.

"Daniel was at Hess," Eleanor said. "Hessekolenisshe. That's the name of the school on the ship."

For a moment Gisele thought they were joking. Then, realising she knew even less than she thought, she shrugged and sank back in the chair. "Have you brought something for these scrapes?"

"I have a number of things," he said, pulling jars and bottles from his pockets. "Here, drink this."

"What is it?"

"It will help you. Drink it."

She prised out the cork and tipped the bottle's contents into her mouth, grimacing as she swallowed. "What was that?"

"I think you would prefer not to know what it contained.

Some things are hard to come by in foreign lands – we must take what we can find. Srakol, on the other hand, is a local speciality."

Eleanor took the wide-mouthed jar and began to smoothe the clear, sticky gel across Gisele's broken skin. "This is good stuff," she said. "The smugglers showed it to me."

"There really were smugglers, then? I wasn't sure if that was all some elaborate story to cover your tracks."

"When I saw you in Almont I didn't have any tracks to cover. I had no idea whether any of this was going to work out."

"And... are you happy?"

Eleanor nodded. "Much happier than I would have been in some stupid police job, certainly. And it's never going to be boring, is it, when we even have to dig our own diplomats out of trouble."

"I'm sorry."

"Don't be. You thought you were doing your job."

"The ambassador knew you were up to something. He started acting strangely from the moment you arrived, but he never told me why. I was worried there might be trouble."

"I know." Eleanor patted her friend on the shoulder in what she hoped was a reassuring manner. "I told Daniel that was the most likely thing – that you were trying to help, and you followed us, and *they* got you."

"Does the ambassador know? Have you sent word that you've rescued me?"

"No, not yet. We'll send you back to Faliska on the next friendly ship, there's no need for you to stay here. You can travel as fast as a letter, and tell him yourself."

"Send me? Aren't you coming?"

"We've got a lot of work to do."

"Here? I thought you were visiting Faliska. Don't you need to come back to the city?"

"There's some stuff in the border lands. We'll have to cross back, but not by far. But we'll make sure we find a friendly boat for you to travel on – we don't want to have to rescue you again."

Chapter 5

"I should come with you."

Daniel and Eleanor looked up from the bowls of rice porridge that Fan had brought them for breakfast.

"What?"

"I should come with you into the border lands."

"Don't you want to get home?" Eleanor asked.

"Believe me, there's nothing I'd like more than to be back in my bed at the embassy," Gisele said. "But you don't know these people like I do. Whatever mystery you're trying to unravel in the borders, it'll be much quicker if you take me with you. Then we can all go home."

"She has a point," Daniel said.

Eleanor barely managed to disguise her astonishment; she'd so expected Daniel to rule it out that she hadn't bothered to consider whether she thought it was a good idea. "We can't guarantee it'll be safe," she said at last.

Gisele nodded. "I know."

"And you're a hopeless fighter, so if we get in any trouble..."

"I'll shut up and do exactly as you tell me. I know."

"Okay, well, if you're sure." She glanced at Daniel, who nodded. "We'll leave as soon as we can find someone to take us in the right direction. Fan can send word to your embassy."

They finished their breakfast in silence, then Gisele went to write a letter to the ambassador in Faliska, leaving Eleanor and Daniel alone.

"Your hair begins to fade," Daniel said, looking critically at her. "We should buy more indigo before we leave."

"Okay."

"Is there anything else we need?"

"I don't think so." She took a deep breath. "But I need to talk to you before the others come back."

"What is it?"

"I was expecting my monthly bleed three days ago. I thought it might just be the disruption of the journey, but I'm afraid, maybe..."

He turned away, cursing.

"Are you angry?"

"I told you we were playing with fire. Do you not see that this could jeopardise the whole mission?"

"I don't see why. We're pretending to be married, and men sometimes do get their wives pregnant... and besides, it'll be ages before it affects what I can do, won't it?"

"So now you want this?"

"No." She shook her head. "No, I don't want it. But if it's happened, it's a bit late for worrying about what I want."

He stood by the window with his back to her, staring out at the opposite rooftops.

"Daniel–" Eleanor began, but he waved her to silence. Knowing a lost cause when she saw one, she sat down again and spread their stolen map on the breakfast table. Whatever he was thinking, it was no excuse for her to stop work.

Eventually he turned back to her. "I think I know how to fix this. Come with me."

He strode from the room without waiting for her to respond, and she had to run to keep up. He led her to the market and stopped at a stall with bunches of dried herbs hanging from its canopy. As she watched, he plucked down a few different branches that she didn't recognise. She had to remind him to pick up a jar of indigo paste while they were there.

Back in the makeshift embassy, Daniel started grinding and blending ingredients while Eleanor knelt over a basin to refresh the colour of her hair.

Daniel decanted his new potion into a small bottle, then poured a few drops into a glass of water and handed it to her. "Drink this."

"What is it?"

"Do you recall saying you would let me be good at apothecary on your behalf?"

She nodded.

"Then let me. Drink it. It is a solution to our little problem."

She did as he said, still not really understanding. The liquid tasted bitter, and she struggled to swallow it all.

"You should probably be prepared for heavy bleeding in the next few days."

It took her a moment to understand what he was saying. "And then... I won't be pregnant any more?"

"That is the plan."

She beamed. "So this," she said, taking the bottle from him, "means we can carry on as before, without worrying. You're a genius."

"With the same caveat."

"Oh, caveats!" She made it sound like a swearword. She was fed up with his silly caveat. It was only a way to pass the time.

"It is important," he said seriously. "Otherwise we cannot."

"Okay, fine, I promise. Again. But I really don't see why this is such a big thing for you. I already care about people, I care about my friends – it doesn't stop me doing my job."

"This is different."

"Do you have any idea how arrogant it makes you sound, assuming that I'm inevitably going to fall madly in love with you? You're worrying over nothing. It's not going to happen."

He hesitated, and she almost thought he might cry, which surprised her – she'd called him arrogant enough times before.

Eventually he said, "I think it is all too late. I thought if I said nothing, and if you did not feel the same, it might not matter. But if I am honest... I already care too deeply for you..." He broke off, choking back a tear.

"Oh no." She knew that wasn't what you were supposed to say the first time someone told you that they loved you, but then, this wasn't how you were supposed to feel. The circumstances could hardly have been further from ideal.

She put her hand on his arm to comfort him, wondering whether his distress was more because he'd failed to meet his own standards or because she'd told him, none too subtly, that his feelings weren't reciprocated.

They were saved from having to talk about it any further by Gisele returning with her letter. "Have either of you got any wax?" she asked. "I need to seal this."

Daniel fished in a pocket of his apothecary case and handed her a stick of black sealing wax. She melted a few drops and pressed it against the paper with the Imperial crest of her ring.

"What's this?" she asked, suddenly noticing the map which covered half the table.

"We're not sure if it'll help," Eleanor said. "But we found it the night you followed us, and it seems to relate to the areas we were told to investigate."

"Can you read it?" Daniel asked.

"It's bad writing," she said. "But this looks like the word for 'good,' and again over here."

Eleanor leaned across to see where she was pointing. "What does it mean?"

"These are settlements, of course, but they're not labelled with their names. Good, trouble, fair, another good... it's like someone's been assessing the villages. But for what, I couldn't say."

"What do you think? Shall we start at one of the 'good' ones?"

"This map covers a huge area," Gisele said. "But this one's only a few miles beyond the border. There should be plenty of carts heading along the westbound road every morning, and we could walk from here" – she pointed at a small junction – "so we'd be there before the sun gets so hot as to burn you."

Eleanor nodded. She and Daniel were too pale for the drylands sun; the Empire had been wise to send a dark-skinned girl like Gisele to represent them here.

"Tomorrow, then."

"Tomorrow." Gisele tapped her letter against the edge of the table. "I'll get Fan to send this as soon as she can. I think we'd better keep out of sight until we're ready to move."

Eleanor removed herself to the floor of their small room that night without needing to be asked. As she lay staring up at the ceiling she wondered if she was the only woman in the world who had to go without sex because the man she'd been sleeping with had decided he loved her. It was all the wrong way round.

And guilt gnawed at her for the way she'd attacked him over the caveats she'd thought so pointless. Guilt, and the nagging feeling that if she hadn't goaded him she might still be sleeping by his side tonight.

She woke the next morning with a crick in her neck and an ache in her back, but she knew better than to mention it. Instead she fell into her regular morning stretches, just a little more carefully than usual.

"Let's go and see about breakfast," she said once Daniel was dressed. "I don't know how much hospitality we'll find in these desert villages."

The skinny girl who'd welcomed them was sitting at the breakfast table with Gisele.

"Cass was just telling me about her success with our slave," Gisele said. "He's on his way back to the Empire in a smuggling ship."

"Smugglers?" Eleanor asked. "Don't they keep well away from people like you?"

"Out here, we're all just Imperial citizens a long way from home," Cass said, smiling slightly. "They'll see him safely across the ocean. They even had a Tarasanka man on their crew."

Eleanor thought back to her days aboard the *Rose*... but the coincidence would be too much to believe. Any number of Charanthe smuggling vessels might have picked up a Tarasanka sailor.

"And with the letter I gave him, someone will find him work when he gets there," Gisele added.

"Are you sure about this?" Eleanor asked Gisele as they finished their porridge and gathered their bags ready for the journey. "Last chance to change your mind and go home."

"I'm sure," Gisele said. "Are you sure you want to go out with that much kit strapped to you? You look like a walking armoury."

Eleanor looked down at herself. It was true, she'd dressed for a fight, while Daniel and Gisele both looked a lot less conspicuous. She laughed a little at her own display of weapons. "Okay, maybe not."

They walked to the northwest gate and passed through the checkpoint without trouble; the guards were focussed entirely on the value of goods coming into the city. The first cart to rattle past them on the westbound road was heavily packed with bleating goats, but the second rode lighter.

"We'll try this one," Gisele said, waving at the driver. "Hey! Ba'utsa! Wait!"

He reined in his horses and turned to look at them across the back of his trailer. "You being Charanthe?"

"Yes." Gisele held her hand up in the traditional Falisanka greeting. "Would you happen to have space for passengers? We can pay our way."

"Where?" he asked. "I not being going to La'un."

"No, that's okay, we don't want to go that far. Just to the second turning north."

"And you not minding sitting with pigs?"

"That's fine."

There were only a couple of piglets in the cart, leaving plenty of space for Daniel, Eleanor and Gisele to scramble in. Gisele adjusted the canopy of the cart to give them a little shade from the morning sun.

The driver seemed to forget about them, and Gisele had to call for his attention so they could get off at their junction.

"What is Charanthe people wanting here?" he asked as they climbed down, but he didn't really seem to expect an answer. Gisele handed him a couple of small coins for his trouble, and he drove off without a backward glance.

It was a pitiful excuse for a settlement, just a couple of houses perched on the corners where the two roads met. One had an optimistic sign offering hospitality to passing travellers, but in reality it was too close to the city for anyone to want to break their journey here.

"The place you're taking us will be bigger than this, won't it?" Eleanor checked as they started to walk north, sun beating down on their faces.

"A little," Gisele said. "But people are spread thinly in this part of the world. Outside of the cities, there's no benefit in living too close to your neighbours."

They walked slowly through the morning heat, along a road that was barely more than two parallel tracks of wheel-compacted sand. Daniel strode ahead of the two girls, but Gisele held Eleanor back when she tried to match his pace.

"Don't tire yourself," she warned. "In a place like this, your priority is to stay comfortable. He'll wait for us."

Eleanor wasn't completely sure that he would, but having convinced Gisele she was happily married she really didn't want to start a new raft of explanations.

"What are we looking for?" Gisele asked as they came in sight of a few low buildings on the horizon.

"We don't know. We've heard odd things – parties of Tarasanka men coming across the border, visiting little villages of no consequence. And then we found that map."

Daniel was waiting for them at the edge of the settlement. "You took your time."

"Desert pace," Gisele said. "We're not even carrying water – it would have been stupid to hurry."

"Well, we need to find somewhere to stay."

Eleanor looked around. Aside from a couple of small boys playing in the shade of a nearby house, there was no-one to be seen. "There's no chance of a guesthouse here, is there?"

Gisele shook her head. "We'll be lucky to find someone with a spare room. More likely we sleep tonight in a shed or on someone's kitchen floor."

They wandered through the streets without any particular purpose, keeping as far as possible out of the gradually-increasing heat of the sun. They found a well at one edge of the village and stopped to refresh themselves. As they were winding the handle to bring the full bucket up, a middle-aged woman came to see what they were doing.

She didn't speak a word of Charanthe, and Gisele's limited Faliska didn't get them far beyond the exchange of names, but it was obvious that they were strangers who didn't belong here. The woman's name was Talika and she turned out to have one of the village's larger houses, overlooking the well. Once they'd drunk their fill she waved them inside. It was much cooler within the house, even with the small cooking fire which glowed in one corner. Talika fussed around her kitchen for a moment and brought out a box of dry biscuits and one large, red-skinned fruit.

"Makta!" she called, and a moment later a skinny teenager appeared from the opposite door. She waved towards the visitors and mumbled something.

The girl Makta nodded, carried the tray of food across to them, and started to cut thin slices from the fruit. When no-one helped themselves, she took out three biscuits, arranged a couple of pieces of fruit on each, and passed them over. Gisele thanked her in Falisanka before eating, while Eleanor and Daniel just smiled their appreciation.

They spent the afternoon with Makta, while her mother came and went on a variety of errands. Though they couldn't hold a meaningful conversation, they passed time pleasantly enough playing simple dice games and sharing food. When darkness fell, no words were needed to indicate that they were welcome to stay.

There were no internal walls in the house, although the two beds were divided from the rest of the room by light, transparent curtains. Makta arranged blankets on the floor for the guests, and they all settled down to sleep. By unspoken agreement Eleanor and Daniel lay close together for the sake of appearances, but the inch between their bodies felt like an unbridgeable gulf.

The next morning they went to look around the rest of the village, trying to get a feel for the place in the early hours of light before it became too hot to accomplish anything.

"We should buy some food if we can," Gisele said as they walked. "It's kind of Talika to feed us, but they can't really afford it."

They eventually found a grocer's shop operating out of one window of a small house. Rows of wilted vegetables were arranged on the windowsill. When Gisele stepped forwards to select some presents for their hosts, a young girl came to the window to take their money. She could hardly have been more than ten years old, and she stared in wide-eyed astonishment at where Eleanor and Daniel waited in the shade.

"What can Taraska possibly want in a place like this?" Eleanor asked as Gisele rejoined them. "It's nonsense. Unless they just want the land to expand the city?"

"That seems the most obvious solution," Daniel said. "But what concern is it to the Empire? Why are we here?"

"Oh, that part's simple," Gisele said. "Faliska's military strength is more of an embarrassing weakness. They don't have anywhere near enough forces to defend their lands."

"And?"

"And with peace in the Empire, our armies are hardly used."

"Would we do that for them?" Eleanor asked.

"Not for them, for us. In the circumstances, Faliska's king won't be able to refuse when we offer our assistance, even if we add crippling conditions."

"What kind of conditions? This isn't exactly a rich country."

"The Empress has been looking for a way to annex Faliska. I think you're here to find her excuse for her."

It took a moment for the idea to sink in. "Why?"

Gisele shrugged. "I can only give you my opinion, but she's getting old. I think she feels her great-grandfather's shadow hanging over her: the whole Empire takes Charan's name. Even if she just gets a strip of villages along the border, it's a foothold in the drylands – and no-one will forget the Empress who first expanded the Empire beyond the great seas."

"She wishes us to find enough proof to terrify the king," Daniel said. Eleanor thought she could hear a hint of disapproval in his voice, but Gisele didn't pick up on it and he said nothing more on the matter.

They headed back to the house and presented Talika with their purchases, to effusive thanks. When Gisele offered to help prepare a salad for the evening meal, Eleanor took Daniel and pulled him outside.

"Something's troubling you."

"No."

"Don't lie to me. You're worried about this job – or what Gisele thinks it is. I could hear it."

"I do not have to answer to you, Eleanor."

"No, but you have to work with me." He turned to go back

inside, but she caught his arm. "Listen to me."

"I have listened."

"I miss you." She blurted the words out, only a half-formed plan in her head. Everything had gone wrong since he'd decided to fall in love with her – and if she couldn't love him back, she nevertheless had to find some way to ease his feelings. The job would suffer if they couldn't find a way forward.

"We are together every day," he said.

"It's different. You're ignoring me, you won't even talk to me about work." She reached for his hand. "Don't shut me out."

"You swore you would never care for me. How am I supposed to take that?"

"I think I was in denial. I think..." She swallowed hard. Unable to conceal her nerves at what she was about to do, she could only hope he'd attribute them to the wrong source. "I think I'm in love with you."

"You do not have good timing, Eleanor. This is not an appropriate time to discuss such matters. We are far too busy to talk of love."

"We don't have to talk about it. I just wanted to let you know."

"Well, now I know. I hope you are happy."

"Don't do this. Listen, I know I've upset you, but this all took me by surprise. I didn't mean to hurt you."

He removed his hand from hers. "You wished to talk about our plans?"

"I want to know what's troubling you."

"If Gisele is right in her assessment, I believe we have much to worry about."

"It all fits, doesn't it? This, and renewed interest in the southern mountains at home, looking to make the Empire bigger in all directions."

He nodded. "I am not sure I like it, that is all. These people have not asked to have our laws imposed upon them."

They sat in silence for a while, until Gisele came out to tell them that dinner was ready, and that night they slept hand-in-hand on the floor.

"We still don't know what these ratings mean," Gisele said.
They sat around Talika's low table with their stolen map spread
out in front of them. "What's good about this village? Is it just a
measure of how easy it'd be to invade?"

They'd spent a few days with Talika and Makta, but nothing
in the village or its surrounding countryside was providing them
with any clues. Short of waiting for visitors from Taraska to
present themselves, they had very little by way of a plan.

"Do you think any of the villages would seriously resist a
Taraskan attack?" Daniel asked.

Gisele shook her head. "Perhaps we should travel out here –
to the one they've marked trouble. At least we might see what
the difference is."

"I think we've been looking at this the wrong way round,"
Eleanor said, picking up a handful of sand-nuts.

"What do you mean?"

"This isn't about the borders. They're not after land – what
use is this land to anyone?" She prised the two halves of the nut
shell apart with her dagger. "It's not like Charan conquering
island after island to feed his growing army. The drylands are
almost completely barren."

"That does not seem to trouble the Taraskans."

"Because they're not trying to take the land. Think about it.
Why would anyone want a few peasant villages and a stretch of
infertile sand? Would you plan an invasion just for a few sand-
nut trees?"

"For building."

Gisele shook her head. "No, she's right. Taraska has always
kept its footprint small. Lots of external trade and visitors, and
not too many permanent citizens to clutter the place up."

"So if they don't want the land," Eleanor said, "what could
they possibly want from here?"

"You've got an idea," Gisele said. "Let's hear it."

"Have you noticed that we've only talked to women? Where
are all the men?"

"I had assumed they were out working," Daniel said.

"Doing what, in these sands? Not farming, that's for certain."

"I am not sure, but we know that some of the foreigners are squeamish about letting women do physical work."

"But there is no work here. There's nothing to do. And manpower is the one thing the Tarasanka lords can't buy – not on any normal market."

"You told me once that you saw children for sale."

"They don't want children, though, if they can help it. You have to look after children. They want at least young teenagers – lads who are strong enough to pull an oar on one of those battleships."

"Slaves," Gisele said, and she looked as if someone had suddenly put a match to a lantern that illuminated the whole of the region's history. "We've always wondered where they find quite so many slaves."

"I do not claim to understand these foreign notions of family," Daniel said, almost too carefully. "But if you have a child, and in a place like this where there are no Imperial schools to bring them up, I cannot understand why you would then sell them."

"They're desperate," Eleanor said. "There's no money here, we know that. Someone's offering them a choice, and they'd rather preserve quality of life for their daughters than keep the whole family together. Think about it. A few dollars is a fortune here, but it's nothing in Taraska."

"And what of the raids?"

"I guess they come back every few months, to get more girls pregnant and take away any lads who are old enough to be useful."

"I wish we'd brought an interpreter," Gisele said. "We could ask Talika about it. But this isn't exactly something we can talk about with hand-waving and smiles."

"If I'm right, what do we do about it?" Eleanor looked to Daniel. "How could we prove this, even if we wanted to?"

"Perhaps we cannot."

"There are two other villages marked between here and the coast," Gisele said, running her finger along the parchment. "If we go this way, we can see if there's a shortage of men everywhere. And if that's the case, we can take a boat back to the city with the news."

Chapter 6

It was dark when the ship finally docked in Almont. After
returning Gisele to her embassy in Faliska La'un, there'd been
nothing to do but head home to report their findings. Gisele had
tried to persuade them to stay for a few days' holiday, but with
a long ocean crossing ahead of them they'd been keen to join
the first available ship.

At the port they rented a small hand-cart for their cases, and
loaded it quickly before picking out an indirect route through
the streets and back to the Association's headquarters. You
could never be too careful.

Mikhail was on watch, and came running down to meet
them at the gate. "Success?" he asked once they were safely
within their own grounds.

"Sort of," Eleanor said, her feet crunching on the frozen
grass of the lawns. The frosts had come early this year. "It's
been quite an eventful trip. We'll tell you all about it tomorrow;
right now, I just need to sleep in a proper bed."

"You'll have to choose your new rooms – I'm opposite
Mack, and there are a couple more spaces along that corridor if
you want to join us."

"I will need to be near the apothecary," Daniel said. "I will
be spending a lot of time there. The last months have been an
interesting diversion, but there are many questions only I can
answer."

"Not that you think much of yourself," Eleanor teased, but
he just looked puzzled.

"Eleanor? They're nice rooms – little suites with your own
sitting room, dining room, whatever."

"Sounds like a plan."

Daniel caught her arm, and spoke quietly so that Mikhail
wouldn't hear over the rattling of the cart wheels. "Do you not
wish to share my room?"

The question surprised her. "I think it might be better for us to have our own space. Don't you think?"

"I have liked spending time with you."

"Yeah. Me too. But sometimes I just want to shut the door and be on my own." After weeks of being forced to share a space all day and night on the ship, she couldn't wait to have a room of her own again, but she thought it might be insensitive to say as much. Besides, it was time to start extricating herself from this accidental relationship.

"Okay." He dropped her arm and picked up his trunk from the cart.

"Really?"

"It is fine. I need to go this way." He waved towards the apothecary.

"Okay." She nodded. "I'll see you tomorrow."

"What was that about?" Mikhail asked as he turned the cart towards the building where his rooms were.

"Oh, it's nothing. You know me and Daniel are always bickering."

"You're like an old married couple," he said, and she laughed. He had no idea that they'd almost forgotten to switch their bangles back to their unmarried state, remembering half a mile from home, just in time to avoid an awkward scene.

Mikhail showed Eleanor where his rooms were, which turned out to be on the same corridor as Ivan. She picked one of the empty suites for herself and deposited her bags there.

"Do you know where they've put the rest of our things?"

Mikhail shrugged. "I'm sure they'll be around somewhere. You've got everything you need for tonight, haven't you?"

"Yeah, I've been living out of this bag for long enough. Another night won't hurt."

They said goodnight with promises to catch up properly the next morning, but instead of going to bed Eleanor marched straight up to Ivan's door. There were things that had been bothering her since before she and Daniel sailed north, and she didn't want to wait longer than she had to for answers.

"Who is it?" he asked when she knocked.

"Eleanor."

A moment later he opened the door, looking sleepy and

ruffled, fastening his shirt as he stood there. "Did you just get back? It's late."

"I know. Can I come in?"

He nodded and stepped back. "Did your trip go well?"

"Can we skip the small talk? I need to know whether you told Jorge to kill me."

He sank onto the sofa, suddenly looking older and more tired than she'd ever seen him. "Would you really expect me to tell you if I did?"

"No, but I'd like to believe I have some skills." She sat beside him and studied his face. "Look me in the eye and tell me that it was nothing to do with you."

"It had nothing to do with me."

"Thank you." She smiled, relaxing back into the cushions. "I didn't really think you'd be so stupid, but I had to check."

"Well, what else would you think? I take it you overheard us in the practice hall. I found your stars... I should've put two and two together when you started acting so strangely."

"I didn't mean to listen, you know. Not that first time."

"There were other times?" He sounded amused, and she blushed.

"I tried quite hard to find out what you were plotting."

"Well you wouldn't have got far, I only gave him the same advice I gave you – become the best that you can be, and the rest will fall into place. I only tried to help him improve. I had no idea he'd decide the best way to win was to eliminate the competition."

"It could've worked, if he'd been a bit more subtle in the attempt. It probably is the most straightforward way to win a contest like that."

Ivan raised an eyebrow. "It's not quite what they had in mind when they came up with the rules."

"No, I'm sure no-one planned for the students to start murdering one another. Anyway, I'm sorry for getting you up. I just had to know."

"I can understand that. Would you like a drink while you're here? I'm sure you haven't stocked your room yet – where are you, by the way?"

"Three doors that way." She pointed at the wall.

"Ah, then you've no excuse not to stay." He threw a fresh log onto the fire and prodded the glowing embers back into life. "Wine or spring nectar?"

"Don't you want to get back to bed?"

"I'd much rather hear about your adventures. The first mission's always the most exciting, especially if you're a long way from home."

"Well, if you're sure – wait just one moment. I've got something in my pack that you might like."

She went back to her room and returned moments later with an almost-black bottle.

"Faliska's famous Burning Death," she announced, presenting the bottle with a dramatic flourish. "Have you got some glasses?"

"Of course. What is that?"

"Something I drank far too much of in Faliska." She cut the heavy wax seal away with her hunting knife, and prised out the cork. "I had to bring some back."

He shuffled his tools to make space for two glasses on the table, and she poured out cautious measures.

"I'm not being stingy, but you might not want much. This stuff makes you do crazy things."

"It sounds like you had fun, then."

"Everything we expected, plus an extra kidnap..." She smiled. "Yeah, we had a lot of fun out there."

"Kidnap?"

"There was a minor official in the Diplomatic Corps who stuck her nose in where she shouldn't have, got on the wrong side of the Tarasanka embassy guards, and got herself swept off to Taraska."

"Are you sure someone like that was worth rescuing?"

"It wasn't her fault, and we couldn't give them chance to interrogate her. She happened to know me from school, so she worked out there was something odd going on, but Daniel wasn't happy to trust her with the truth. We put her in a position where she felt she had to investigate us."

"Well, that's a lesson for you right there – don't let Daniel get in the way of your judgement."

"Yeah, everything would've been that much easier if I'd gone on my own." She thought of the way Daniel's face had fallen when she'd said she didn't want to live with him, and promptly changed the subject. "So what have we missed? We didn't get to hear much news from the Empire."

"Not much of any importance. Rebel attacks are getting a bit more common, but not much more successful. And the Empress is looking at pushing into the southern mountains again."

"We heard a rumour of that last year. Has there been some more movement?"

"She's sending a small advance party – just a few soldiers – to check whether the lower slopes have frozen over yet. Once we get a positive on that, we'll put a group together to go and make contact."

"Everyone acts like the mountain men are immortal or something. No, I don't mean immortal, that's the wrong word." Eleanor took another mouthful of her drink, grimacing as the alcohol bit her throat. "I think I meant invulnerable. Like we can't hurt them. It doesn't make sense."

"I don't think anyone really thinks that, but it's all a bit of a mystery. Attacks have failed in the past, even when we've sent the whole army."

"That's the bit I don't understand. Do we know why?"

"No-one quite knows where they got their skills. They're surprisingly well trained, well armed, and well organised for an uncivilized culture out in the wilds of nowhere – and the Imperial armies aren't exactly on top form these days. Anyway, we're prepared for them to exceed our expectations, so it's nothing to worry about."

The council meeting had already started when Eleanor arrived, but the chamber was surprisingly empty.

"Where is everyone?" she asked as she sat down.

"We've sent a few men out to try and infiltrate rebel groups," Laban said. "Which will be a very slow process, to do it safely, so we'll be quiet for a while."

"Daniel was just telling us about your trip," Ragal said.

"Quite fascinating."

"Looks like those Tarasanka bastards are a bit more subtle than we gave them credit for," Eleanor said. "But I'm certainly no more fond of them."

"You'll need to report back to the palace," Albert said. "I'm sure there'll be questions."

"What else?" Ragal leafed through a pile of papers and handed a few pages across the table. "Daniel, these are the some of the reports you requested before your trip. And a couple of other things have come in that might be of interest."

"Now that Eleanor's back, perhaps we can discuss whether Jorge has served long enough on the punishment watch," Nicholas said. "It's been a few months now."

"Tell him he can come back to normal duties the day he apologises," Eleanor said. "He doesn't have to mean it, but I want to hear the words."

"That sounds fair." Ivan smiled. "I'll tell him. No news yet on the state of the mountains?"

Ragal shook his head. "Nothing yet."

"Well, I think that's everything of immediate importance," Laban said. "Are you two both happy with your new rooms?"

"Does anyone know what happened to the rest of our stuff?" Eleanor asked.

"I think Sebastien offered to keep your trunks in his rooms over at the academy."

Eleanor nodded, and squeezed Daniel's hand under the table, though he was oblivious to her nerves. She'd been avoiding the academy since they got back, but she knew she was delaying the inevitable. Raf must know by now that they were home.

"Shall we go now?" Daniel asked. Unable to think of any good excuse to say no, she agreed.

There was no sign of Sebastien but they retrieved their luggage from the corner of his sitting room.

"I'll catch you up once I've unpacked," Eleanor said as they went their separate ways, but instead of going to her room she she turned into the academy. Better to get this over with sooner rather than later.

She found Raf sparring with Greg in the practice hall, and waited by the door until he had the younger boy pinned firmly beneath the edge of his dagger.

"Good job," she said, and they both turned.

"Can you give us the room?" Raf said, offering his hand to help Greg to his feet.

"Sure." Greg winked at Eleanor, collected his weapons, and jogged outside.

Eleanor and Raf stood in silence, watching one another across the room. Eleanor still didn't know if she wanted to slap him for what he'd said or apologise for her overreaction.

"So..." she said at last.

"Yeah."

"I was an idiot," she said, looking at her feet. "But in my defence, someone had just tried to kill me. And you sort of deserved it."

"I totally deserved it." A smile spread across his face. "I'm sorry."

"So. Friends again?"

He stepped across and swept her into a hug. "I never stopped being your friend, stupid."

"I've missed you," she said as they separated.

"I missed you too." He hooked his arm through hers. "Why don't you stay down here for a bit? We can train together and you can tell me what you've been up to."

"I'd love to, but I need to unpack, and then Daniel and I have to prepare a report for the palace this afternoon. Come round and see me after dinner, I'm only three doors down from Ivan."

"Okay."

"Great. See you later." She kissed him on the cheek and turned to lift her trunk.

"Are you sure you don't want me to give you a hand with that?"

"Let's not have another fight over whether I can take care of myself," she said, laughing. "Not so soon after making up from the last one."

He held his hands up in mock surrender. "Okay. See you

later."

It was late afternoon by the time she made her way down to Daniel's room. He was sitting on the bed, propped up by a dozen pillows and poring over the papers Ragal had given him.

"What are you working on?" she asked, settling beside him and peering over his shoulder.

"Locksure," he said without looking up from the page.

"Do you really think it's important?" She leaned against his shoulder and kissed his neck. "You don't think it could be that I'm just a bit weird?"

"You are not unique." He handed her a page from near the back of the sheaf. "There are a few cases in the archives where locksure failed to work, but it has always been assumed that the preparation was at fault."

"But this time it was the same preparation."

"Precisely. The others were paralysed, you were not. So you see I am on the edge of something important."

"Well, as long as you don't want to try it out on me. It might not have worked properly but it wasn't exactly fun."

"If I develop a new preparation, I may need to test it."

"Oh." She handed the paper back to him, stretched out on the bed beside him and yawned. "Well, just tell me when you want me."

"I always want you." He reached across with his spare hand and loosened the laces of her shirt, slipping his fingers between the strings to stroke her breast. "Just give me time to finish reading these records."

She moved his hand gently away. "As nice as this is, we should really work on our report for the palace."

"What is there to say? We can prove nothing."

"They can send someone else if they want proof. We figured it out – that's all they actually asked for."

They were disturbed by a loud knock at the door. Daniel rolled from the bed and went to see who was there.

"Looking for Eleanor," Raf said, peering past him into the room. "Mikhail said she might be down here?"

"I am." She tightened the laces of her shirt, stepped into her boots, and pushed past Daniel into the corridor. "Come on, let's go back to mine, it's much more comfortable. This place is a lab."

"I went to your room first, but you weren't there."

"You said you'd come round after dinner," she said as they started to walk.

"It is after dinner." He cocked his head to one side and looked at her oddly. "Is there something going on with you and Daniel?"

"Well..." She hesitated. Saying it made it so much more real, and she wasn't sure she was ready for that. "We... I mean... sort of, but not really. Nothing official."

"I thought he annoyed you as much as he does me."

"I've always said he's arrogant, and he is. But I can be like that too. And you. I think maybe it comes with the territory."

"I wouldn't call it arrogance. Except..." – he laughed – "maybe in Daniel's case."

"Will you try and be civil to him, for me?"

"If he'll be civil to me. But honestly, Ellie, why him? Of any man in the Association, why?"

"We got very drunk in Faliska, and somehow... this happened. It's not like it's anything serious – though shhh, don't tell anyone I said that, because I'm a bit afraid Daniel thinks it is."

"Ellie!"

"I know, I know. I'm terrible. I'll tell him eventually."

He shook his head. "I don't know what to say. Really, Ellie, somehow you always manage to surprise me."

"I don't mean to." She paused with her hand on the door to her building. "Do you want to come up, or shall we go out?"

"I was out last night. Let's just have a quiet evening in, and you can tell me all about your adventures."

Eleanor was just setting out for an early morning run when she saw a light already flickering in Daniel's window. She ducked inside the apothecary building and pushed open the door to his room.

"You're up early," she said. Then, noticing that he was

dressed for the cold of a late-autumn morning, "Are you going somewhere?"

"I need to visit the Meadow Isles," he said.

There was a map of the archipelago pinned to his wall, and it took her a moment to find the chain of low, grassy islands in the south. "That's not a short trip."

"No. The supply boat leaves with the tide, I may be gone for a few weeks."

"Were you planning to tell me?"

"You did not feel the need to tell me you were seeing your Venncastle friends again."

"And by 'Venncastle friends' you mean Raf, of course. I wish you two could at least try to get on. You might actually like him."

"I think not."

She wondered vaguely whether another argument about Venncastle would be enough to persuade him to fall out of love again. And it should be easy enough to push him into a fight – they'd certainly argued about it enough in the past. Instead, she changed the subject: "Anyway, what's it about? What suddenly needs your attention down there?"

"The islanders report a new cultivar of yarrow. It may be nothing, but I suspect there is truth in it."

"Yarrow?"

"Woundwort," he translated, and she nodded her understanding.

"So...?"

"They say this is stronger, and if so, there are some things I would like to try. You would not be interested in the details."

"Okay." His natural reticence frustrated her but in this case it was probably true: apothecary had always bored her. "I'm sure you won't be able to resist telling me all about it when you get back."

"If it comes to anything." He picked up his travel bag, the same one he'd been living out of for the past few months. "Anyway. I must go if I am not to miss the tide."

"Have a good trip."

"I will."

She watched him stride away, and wondered what sort of games her mind was playing with her. She didn't even want to be in this relationship, but it irked her that he'd been about to sneak off without even saying goodbye. She slammed his door shut and started running again. There was nothing as good as a furious sprint for clearing the thoughts.

Chapter 7

"Finally, we've got one quick kill in Almont." Ragal looked across the council table. "Eleanor? You haven't been out since you got back, you must have itchy fingers."

"Okay." She held out her hand for the instruction. "Yeah, looks like I could do that in one easy evening. Who's this Princess Sofia, anyway?"

"She's the daughter of the Empress's younger brother," Nathaniel said. "And she's pregnant, which is what the Empress sees as a threat."

"So why do we even need to kill her? If it's the baby that needs removing, Daniel invented a potion that will just make her bleed."

"A dead woman can't get pregnant again next week," Laban said flatly, giving Eleanor a look that suggested she shouldn't argue.

She considered arguing anyway, but it hardly seemed a worthwhile fight to pick. "Fine. Do we have a deadline?"

"Soon," Ragal said. "Before the pregnancy starts to show. But that shouldn't be a problem."

"No, it's a quick job," Eleanor agreed. "I can go tomorrow night."

"The husband is expendable," Ragal added. "It doesn't matter if you have to kill him, but you don't have to go looking for him."

After the meeting split up, Eleanor hurried to catch up with Laban as he walked towards his rooms.

"What was that all about?"

He raised an eyebrow. "What?"

"You're not usually one to advocate unnecessary kills."

"What I said was perfectly true," he said, not slowing his pace as they turned onto the stairs.

"But that's not why you said it."

"So Daniel invented some drug for ending a pregnancy,

94

which I assume is how you two have avoided such inconvenience yourselves."

Eleanor felt a blush rise in her cheeks, wondering how he'd guessed, but he wasn't looking at her. "Yes."

"And why do you think everyone doesn't use it?"

"Daniel invented it. I don't think he's told many people."

"Yes – but that isn't the reason." Laban held open the door to his rooms, and waved her through ahead of him. "Any apothecary could invent such a thing but they don't. Why? Because it's illegal. Every child of the Empire has a duty to produce more children, you remember."

"I remember, but–"

"Preventing children is illegal."

Eleanor flopped onto the sofa and put her feet up on the low table.

"How can something like that be against the law?"

"Why wouldn't it be? The Empire needs children to fill its schools."

"But I've never heard of it. If nobody knows it's the law..."

"There's no reason for them to know. Why would you want anyone to know how many laws they live under? People are happier if they think they're free."

"It's nonsense. You can't have laws that people don't know they have to follow."

"Think about it another way: if you're not assigned to make this substance, why would you try? If it needed doing, someone would be doing it. We're constantly told that we have everything we need, so why would it cross anyone's mind to want something that isn't available?"

"Daniel invents new stuff all the time."

"Of course. Daniel's an inventive young man, and we should all be thankful for that, but his inventions aren't always strictly within the law."

"That's because he mostly invents poisons. And killing people is illegal – isn't it? So we do illegal things all the time."

"Technically, of course. But the Association has a privileged position. Our transgressions are tolerated, within reason. The question is only what the Empress deems reasonable."

"And she'd find this unreasonable. I see." She studied the floor for a moment. "Have I caused trouble for Daniel?"

"Don't worry about it. I'm sure you haven't done any damage this time, but you should be careful."

"Okay." Eleanor got to her feet. "I'll remember that."

"Do you want to stay for tea?"

"No, thanks. This might be a quick job, but I still need to plan it."

She paced around the lawns, her thoughts so preoccupied that she didn't even notice for the first half-circuit that Raf came to walk alongside her.

"You look a bit down," he said at last, and she started.

"How long have you been there?"

"Not that long. What's up?"

"Oh, nothing. I was thinking about a job I've just picked up. Making plans in my head – you know how it is."

He nodded.

"Hey, do you want to come and spot for me? It's just a quickie over at the palace."

"I don't think you're supposed to trust academy kids like me with real work."

"Oh, suit yourself."

"I'm not saying I won't come!"

She grinned at his enthusiasm. "Well, I know you'll do as good a job as anyone, and it'll be more fun this way. Tomorrow night, okay?"

"Sure."

"I'm going to scout it out tonight. Come round straight after dinner tomorrow and I'll talk you through it."

"And you'll definitely be there this time? Not down at Daniel's?"

She blushed. "Daniel's away. Come tomorrow, and dress for the dark."

"You haven't got your graduation set yet, have you?" Eleanor asked as she started to strap her own knives into place.

"No."

"Do you think your practice kit's good enough, or is there

anything you want to borrow?"

From the sheathes at his belt Raf pulled a short curved dagger and a long stiletto. "Harold doesn't make bad knives."

"You're all set, then?"

"I'm only your second. How hard can it be?"

She pulled her hair into a tight bun at the back of her head, and tucked it out of sight beneath a dark cap. "Okay, let's go."

They took their usual route into the city, but instead of walking to a tavern this time they scrambled up a wall at the edge of the Marble Quarter and crept across the rooftops above the gleaming white colonnades.

The palace itself stood apart from its neighbouring buildings, facing proudly over the statues and fountain of the Grand Square. Blue-uniformed guards patrolled the perimeter. The palace guards weren't the Empire's most highly regarded military unit – they had few real threats to defend against – but they'd still be a thorn in Eleanor's side tonight.

"Ready?" she asked. Raf nodded, and they slid down into the street together.

With light cloaks covering their work clothes, and walking with exaggerated instability, they could have passed for any inebriated couple taking a late-night stroll through the quiet streets. Eleanor put her arm through Raf's and leaned close towards him, pretending to whisper into his ear as they came closer to the guard-post near the gate. As the guard stepped out of his office to wave them on their way, she pulled a blowpipe from behind her ear and fired a soporific dart straight at his face.

She and Raf lifted him by one shoulder each, and draped him back into his chair.

"Tut tut, sleeping on duty," Eleanor said as she plucked the dart from his cheek and tucked it safely inside her pocket. "I hope you wake up before the boss finds you."

"They wouldn't get away with such lax security if I was in charge," Raf said as they let themselves in through the service entrance.

"Would you really want to be in charge of the palace guard?"

"Never. Dullest job in the Empire – but after tonight it's going to look a bit more interesting."

Eleanor shook her head. "One of the maids is going to come forwards and confess to an inside job," she said. "It won't trouble the guards."

They had directions to the suite of rooms where Sofia lived with her husband, and they crept along deserted corridors until they reached the right door. They oiled the latch and hinges, then Raf flattened his back to the wall to keep watch while Eleanor went in.

There were two more doors to oil and open before she found the bedroom where the couple slept together. She pulled a bottle of soporific vapours from her belt, opened it, and poured a measure of the volatile liquid onto the pillow by the nose of Sofia's husband. Before Eleanor could even count to five his snores gave way to silent, drug-induced sleep of a deeper kind.

She moved around the bed to Sofia's side and poured another dose of the vapours, before twisting the cork back into the neck of the bottle. As she waited for the vapours to take their effect, she pulled a stiletto from her boot-sheath. She hesitated for only a moment, pondering why this woman and the child she was carrying were such a threat to the Empress... but the Association was being paid to do the job, not to think about it. She drew the knife across the princess's artery and left her bleeding into the pillow.

As she closed the door behind her, she wondered if it had really been a kindness to the husband to leave him with his life. He was certainly going to wake in an unhappier world.

"Done?" Raf asked as she emerged.

She nodded. "Let's go. And we'll take in a tavern or two on the way home – I need a drink."

"What's wrong?" he asked.

"I don't know, everything seems a bit pointless. Trying to annex the drylands and killing some woman because she's pregnant." Eleanor sighed. "I think I'm just tired. Come on, let's get drunk."

"Eleanor!"

She was on her way in from her regular evening run, and she hadn't noticed as she passed that Ivan's door was open. She turned back to see what he wanted.

He got to his feet and walked across to lean on the doorframe. "Just the person I was hoping to see."

"Oh?"

"Have you got a moment?"

"Of course." She pushed open her own door. "Come in."

"Thanks."

"Can I get you a drink? Tea?"

"No, I'm fine." He settled into a chair by her fireplace and stoked the embers. "I was wondering, now you've recovered from your little adventure in the drylands – how d'you fancy teaching for a spell?"

"Teaching what?" she asked, although it was fairly obvious. "Projectiles?"

"You're more than qualified."

"But that's your class. Are you giving up?"

"You might've heard about this mountain expedition? I'd like to go – it's been too long since I got my hands dirty – but I want to make sure my students don't lose out. I can't just abandon them to the vagaries of whoever the council happens to choose."

"Why me?"

"You're the obvious choice. Natural skill at the subject, boundless enthusiasm, and – well, you're not spectacularly impatient, are you? Plus you've just got back from a long trip, so you deserve a rest."

Eleanor hesitated, twisting a loose strand of hair between her fingers.

"It's only one day in eight," Ivan continued. "You'll have plenty of time off, and you can use my armoury if there's anything you need. You know it makes sense."

"I know I could do it," she said slowly. "But I need time to think."

"What's troubling you?"

"I'd be teaching Raf." It sounded silly to say it, and as soon as the words were out she wished she'd kept her reservations to herself.

"You've taught him before."

"And he's taught me plenty of things in return, but this is different. Official."

"He won't mind. He'll see what I see – that you're the best person for the job."

"I know. But if it was me I'd like to be asked, so let me talk to him before I say yes."

Ivan got to his feet. "Come and see me once you're happy, and I'll talk you through where everyone's up to."

Eleanor hadn't even taken off her boots, so she picked up a cloak and followed him to the door. It would be better to get an answer quickly.

"Raf!" He was outside despite the frost, doing backflips on the icy beams of the practice frame. His feet skidded under him as he landed, but he kept his balance.

"Hey Ellie." He dropped to the ground and came across to meet her. "How's things?"

"I think I'm settling, slowly. You?"

"Same as ever." He shrugged. "Getting ready for the contest, I guess."

"I know you'll wipe the floor with them."

"We'll see."

"Listen, Ivan asked me... He wants me to teach his classes for a few months while he goes on this mountain expedition."

"Oh, excellent."

"Really?"

He nodded. "Why not?"

"I'd be teaching you."

"Did you think I'd have a problem with that? You'll be a great teacher."

"But I've only just graduated myself. Won't it be a bit strange?"

"Not for me. Are you carrying any stars?"

"Of course." She pulled a couple from her belt. He took one of them and flicked it hard through the air, until it caught in the wood of the nearest practice beam. The force of the hit made the beam spin on its axis.

"I bet you can hit the same spot with your eyes closed, even while it's spinning," Raf said.

Eleanor watched it for one more rotation until the pattern of movement was locked in her mind, then closed her eyes and counted to three before releasing the second star. She heard the clink of metal on metal and opened her eyes to see the second star lodged neatly alongside the first.

"See?" Raf said, retrieving both stars with a triumphant expression. "You've got nothing to fear from a bunch of academy kids."

"So where's your class up to? I can see you've improved since last time we played with stars together."

"We've been practising, yeah – stars and spikes, against a moving target or from a moving platform. It's still hard."

"It's supposed to be." She took the stars from his hand and tucked them back into their slots. "So you're definitely happy with this?"

"Definitely."

"In which case, I'll see you in class."

She sprinted across the frosty grass and back to Ivan's room. He looked up in surprise when she let herself in and flung herself onto his sofa.

"Did you talk to Raf?"

She nodded, breathless from the run.

"And? What did he say?"

"Just what you predicted. He thinks it's fine."

"So you'll do it?"

"Of course. But you'd better tell me what I need to teach them."

"Let me get you a drink, and we can talk it all through." He already had a half-finished glass of apple wine at his side, and quickly furnished her with a glass of her own.

"Thanks."

"You'll have the second years in the morning, and the first years the same afternoon. They're both good groups, on the whole, but nothing special. Competent but dull."

Eleanor nodded, and tried to suppress a laugh. Trust Ivan to worry about style.

"The first years are just getting started with pipes," he went on. "You'll need to take them through a lot of target practice, different heights and distances and angles. Then take them outside on a windy day, that should sort the men from the boys."

"And the second years?"

"They should be thinking ahead to the spring contest. The projectiles theme won't be much different to last year – there'll be a number of different targets, timing is as important as accuracy, and they'll need to be ready to take a number of shots without pausing for breath. That's if any of them care enough about projectiles to actually choose those tasks."

"They're not keen?"

"They're certainly not at your standard. But then, you're the only student I ever thought might have got through the seventh level."

"You're never going to forgive me for that, are you?"

"You won – I can hardly complain about that. But if you'd had confidence in your strengths, maybe you wouldn't have needed to take such a controversial path to victory."

Eleanor finished her wine in a couple of gulps and set her glass down amongst the clutter on the tabletop. "So how soon do I start?"

"Well, if you're keen you could start tomorrow. I could do with the extra time to pack."

Eleanor paced the hall as she waited for the second years to arrive after breakfast. Greg, Nate, and Raf came in together; Raf winked at her and smiled.

"What's up, Eleanor?" Greg asked. "Come back for some extra training?"

"Not quite. I'm taking over Ivan's classes for a few weeks while he's up in the mountains."

"Really?"

She nodded. "Really."

"But you've only just graduated," Nate said. "How do we know you're that much better than we are?"

"Because Ivan asked her to do this," Raf said, clipping Nate across the head. "And he knows what he's doing."

"Would you rather teach it yourself?" Eleanor asked. "If you think you're almost at my level?"

"No, I didn't say that. It's just a bit unusual. That's all I was saying."

"Well, you can tell me what you think at the end of the lesson. Meanwhile, we've got work to do."

The others had filtered into the room while they were talking, and a quick head count confirmed to Eleanor that she had all the students she was expecting.

"Okay, let's get started." She clapped her hands together to get their attention. "I'm taking over Ivan's classes for a while, but he's caught me up on what you're studying and where you're all up to, so it shouldn't be too disruptive. We're going to start on the balance board – you've done this before, so at least you shouldn't have any trouble hitting the targets. Nate, since you're feeling so confident do you want to come up first?"

The balance board constituted a plank which rested across a thick log, and just standing on it without falling was a trick that required a fair degree of practice. Nate clearly hadn't been practising and he wobbled, struggling to keep his balance while he aimed three knives at the three boards Eleanor had arranged along the wall.

She gave him a score based on his performance across the three targets, and called on a scrawny lad called Stefan to go next. By the time everyone had taken a turn – with only a couple of them falling flat on their backs in the attempt – she felt she had a fair idea of their relative strengths in agility, if nothing else.

She gave them a balance board each, after that, and their own targets to aim at. She watched as they practised a series of shots in quick succession. Much as Ivan had told her, their skill was acceptable but none of them exhibited much polish. After a full morning of balancing and throwing, she sent the exhausted students off to lunch and started to pack everything away.

"Great job," Raf said, coming to help her with the boards.

"I'll get better," she said. "It's hard to take over in the

middle of something like this."

"No, you did fine. Are you coming for lunch?"

"If we're quick – I need to set things up for the first years."

Chapter 8

Daniel returned from his trip to the Meadow Isles just before
the winter solstice.

"Are you coming to watch the contest?" Eleanor asked,
rolling over to face him on the morning of the shortest day.

"I think not."

"It'll be fun. Come on, I know you'd rather watch them
poison each other, but you have to admit that hand-to-hand
makes for a better visual spectacle."

"You go. They are your students."

"Oh, I'm going." She sat on the edge of the bed and started
to pull on her clothes. "I just thought you might want to come
with me."

"No, thank you."

She left him in bed and jogged across to the academy
practice hall, where Karl and Nicholas were setting up ropes to
demarcate the fighting arena. She helped Albert to move a few
benches into position around the ring, then went to see how the
draw had turned out.

Raf's first fight was against Nate. There was never any real
question over the outcome, but Eleanor cheered and applauded
with the rest of the audience at every feint and parry until Raf
had Nate face-down on the ground, stiletto poised at the back of
his neck.

By the time they broke for lunch Raf had annihilated a
second opponent, putting him in a strong position going into the
final round. He stayed in the hall when the others left,
stretching in the middle of the ring.

"Aren't you going to eat?" Eleanor asked.

"Later," he said, dropping into the splits. "Afterwards."

She perched on the end of a nearby bench. "I'm not sure
why anyone else is bothering when you're so clearly going to
win."

"I haven't won yet." He sprung back to his feet and offered

her his stiletto. "Want to help me keep warm?"

She took the knife and dropped into a low stance. "But I'm not wearing my leathers," she said. "So you'll have to play nicely."

"Okay." He reached up to his shoulders and loosed the straps of his own leather breastplate, dropping it to the ground just outside the ring. He threw his greaves and vambraces down after it. "Fair?"

"First to five touches," she said. "I don't want to wear you out."

They fenced carefully at first, in contrast to the vicious attacks of the contest bouts, but neither of them was naturally good at holding back. Eleanor drew blood with her first touch, and didn't quite know whether to laugh or apologise for the scratch.

"I'll get you for that," Raf said, lunging straight back into the fight.

They were still at it – with three points each – when the others started to return from lunch.

"Ellie, get out of the ring," Greg shouted from the sidelines. "You can't win two years running!"

She didn't feel the need to point out that she'd only come second in her own contest, but she turned to Raf: "Want to call it a draw?"

"A draw? No, I want to win. We can finish this later."

They stepped over the rope and Eleanor sat down to watch the next fight while Raf strapped himself back into his leather armour. He should have been tired from the exertion but if anything he seemed to have drawn extra energy from the practice. He faced Greg and Stefan in the final, and both opponents quickly found themselves with blades to their throats.

"Congratulations," Eleanor said, throwing her arms around his neck. "See, I told you you'd win."

"I wonder what this is about," Eleanor murmured to Daniel as they gathered in the council chamber. There had been a lot of unusual meetings since they'd got back from Taraska.

"Ah, Eleanor, glad you're here," Nicholas said as soon as she sat down. "Looks like this one's for you."

"For me?"

She reached out for the paper, but he held it just beyond her reach.

"Let me read, then."

"From the hand of the Empress herself, in the strictest of confidence, et cetera, et cetera," he read aloud. "Understanding that a woman has joined the Association's ranks, we request her attention to the following matter."

"How strange."

"The next bit is the interesting part: young lady to be embedded in the Imperial harem to attend the Crown Prince and administer a potion, to be supplied."

"She wants me to poison the Crown Prince?"

"No, it doesn't say that."

"Let me read it." She took the sheet. "Huh, you're right, it says potion. No details. Very mysterious."

"That is preposterous," Daniel said. "There is no need for Eleanor to enter the Imperial harem when any one of us could find an easier way to answer such a simple request."

"It does sound rather extreme," Nicholas agreed. "What do you reckon, Eleanor?"

"Well, if it's the easiest way to get close to the prince without him suspecting anything, then maybe it makes sense."

"But you shouldn't need to," Laban said. "It's an extremely irregular request. I think we should refuse."

"How long have we got?" Eleanor asked. "Can I have a day or two to think?"

"We'll reconvene tomorrow evening," Ragal said. "You have until then."

"And can we get some more details? I want to know what I'm actually agreeing to."

"Or not agreeing," Daniel added. "As the case may be."

"I'll see what I can find out," Nicholas said. "Though the Empress won't like to be questioned."

Eleanor went down to the academy gardens after the meeting, where she found Raf practising blindfolded throwing techniques. She stood and watched him as he fired blade after blade at the target, then crept up behind him and put her hands on his shoulders just as his last knife sailed towards the board.

He turned in surprise, pulling the blindfold from his eyes. "Ellie! I wasn't expecting you!"

"How are you getting on?" she asked.

He looked over at the target board, where half a dozen knives now protruded from irregular points around the target. "Improving," he said, striding over to retrieve his weapons. "At least they all hit the board this time."

"Well, no-one's going to blindfold you in the real world – or even for the contests. Anyway, I need to ask you something, can we talk?"

"Any time," he said. They wandered over to a nearby grassy bank and he pulled her down to sit beside him on the frozen ground. "What's troubling you?"

"If someone asked you to do a job – when you've graduated, I mean – that meant you had to go and charm secrets out of a girl, would you do it?"

"Of course," he said without hesitation. "Why not?"

Eleanor took a deep breath, unsure whether she should be asking him these questions. She couldn't explain why his answers mattered more than all the views of her fellows on the council. "What if it was sex?"

"If it was necessary." He looked at her troubled face. "But Ellie, if you're not happy you can just refuse – that's why you went to all that effort to get yourself a seat on the council, isn't it?"

"It's not that," she said. "The council aren't trying to make me do anything – quite the opposite. We've had a peculiar request from the Imperial Court, but a lot of people are saying I mustn't. I just don't think there'd be the same fuss if they were asking a man to do it."

"Probably not. But I've told you before, the Association can be old-fashioned sometimes."

"I've noticed." The bitterness crept into her voice despite her best efforts.

He put his arm around her shoulders. "Don't take it

personally, okay? It's not really about you."

"I know." She sighed and sank back to lie on the grass, staring up at the clear winter sky. "I do know that. It's just hard work being the odd one out, and I thought they might've got over it by now."

"Most of them have." He leaned back alongside her. "Most people only care that you're doing a great job. They're just not quite used to you yet."

"How long is it going to take?"

"Well, you were out of the country for months. You haven't been around here for long enough, yet."

"I was two years at the academy!"

"That's two years of people getting used to having a woman anywhere. A woman on the council is going to take a while longer."

"Yeah, I suppose." The cold was starting to bite through her clothes, but she didn't want to go back inside. "Hmm, I've just remembered – we've got a fight to finish..."

"You asked for more details," Nicholas said as they settled in the council chamber. "Reading between the lines, the Empress wasn't happy to be asked, but she's deigned to send half an explanation."

"Oh?"

"She's claims to have concerns about her son's inability to produce an heir. You're to administer a fertility potion to the relevant part of his anatomy."

Eleanor frowned. "I'd have thought that was something he'd be more than happy to do for himself."

"The implication is that he's too proud to talk about such things. You can choose to believe it or not, but I'm afraid that's the best you're going to get. There are some instructions here too, and some rules. You're forbidden to take any weapons into the palace, the message is very clear on that front–"

"What?" Eleanor snatched the paper away from him. "How can they ask me to go anywhere unarmed?"

"That's what it says."

She read and reread the message; there was certainly no

space for interpretation in those words. If she took weapons, she would be summarily executed for treachery.

"That makes it rather a different game," she said. "I don't even sleep without a knife or two."

"You do not have to do this," Daniel said. "Indeed, I believe you should not."

"And I believe you should keep your nose out of it," she said. "I'll still do it, it's fine. I'll just have to be a bit more careful."

The instructions were accompanied by a name bangle by which Eleanor could identify herself as Nina, a young woman registered at the Third City School in Almont, and a copy of Nina's letter of assignment to the Imperial harem. As she clipped the bangle around her wrist Eleanor wondered if she was usurping a real girl, or whether this was a pure fabrication by some forger at the palace. She knew how the Association would arrange things, but evidently the Empress had her own ways of getting things done. There was nothing in the story she'd been given that could explain why a girl would be arriving to her assignment at such a strange time of the year, but although the discrepancy troubled her, Eleanor didn't think there was anything she could do about it.

The Association's tailor had made her a set of clothing in the style of the Almont City 3 uniform. She'd turned her hair blonde with whitening powder, and as she braided two neat plaits, she saw an unfamiliar schoolgirl looking back at her from the mirror.

She walked across the city and introduced herself at the palace gatehouse, presenting the assignment letter as per her instructions. The guard barely glanced at her or her letter, but directed her through a maze of corridors to the apartment complex of the harem.

She was met at the door by a middle-aged manservant who snatched her assignment letter from her hands before grunting his approval.

"I'm his lordship's personal valet," he said, directing her into an empty bedroom. "Any communication from his lordship to you will always come through me. I trust you'll be ready to attend to him this evening."

Eleanor felt nowhere near ready, but there was clearly only one acceptable answer. "Of course," she said.

"Of course, *sir*. You will always address senior staff as sir or madam."

"Sorry, sir."

"Clearly we need to educate you. His lordship has chosen to see you today only because you're new. In future you will be summoned at his pleasure, and you will always be available when he demands it. You will do as he directs you, and call him 'my lord' unless instructed otherwise. Make no presumptions. This will be your room, you'll be brought back here once he's finished with you today. You'll be notified of times when you may visit the city, with a chaperone, of course. You'll have chance to meet the other girls tomorrow. Understand?"

She nodded, although the barrage of rules had little relevance to her temporary position. It gave an interesting glimpse into this strange lifestyle.

"Follow me, then. His lordship will be ready for you shortly, and you're by no means ready for him."

He led her to a large, slate-floored bathroom where a steaming bath was already prepared in the centre of the room, and left her alone there. At least, she thought she was alone, but as soon as she began to undress two young female attendants emerged from a side-chamber. One of them whisked away her discarded clothes while the other helped her into the bath and began, firmly but not unkindly, to plunge her head under the water. They scrubbed her skin, doused her in scented oils, and shaved her in places she'd never thought shaving was possible, before pulling her from the bath and towelling her down. They presented her with a choice of sheer nightgowns, any of which would preserve very little of her modesty, and she opted for a mid-length green slip sewn from lightweight satin. The gown skimmed her hips and fell to just above her knees. She wished she could have worn one of her own dresses, but this skimpy style was clearly what the prince demanded of his women.

Once they'd dressed her, curled her hair, and stained her lips, the attendants directed her to the prince's anteroom where she was to wait until he was ready for her. She perched self-consciously on one of the stuffed chairs and marvelled at the tapestries which covered the walls, embroidered with sparkling gold threads. As she waited for the summons, she tried to imagine the kind of person who would actually get this assignment. There was surely a physical element, but what other characteristics did the Assessors look for? What sort of girl would be delighted to open her letter and find she'd been chosen to be an Imperial concubine?

Someone more placid than herself, Eleanor suspected, trying to think herself into the role. It would certainly have to be someone who didn't mind being told what to do, she could see that much from the way she'd been treated so far. Physically, she guessed any candidate would have to be fit and flexible; maybe someone who would've liked to be an entertainer, but never quite made the grade as a dancer or actor. How they tested for the one essential skill, though, she couldn't begin to fathom: sex certainly hadn't been part of her education at Mersioc.

And what about the prince's wife – was that another job to be filled by assignment, or did he get the same choice in that respect as the rest of the Empire's population? Eleanor wondered how she must feel about the existence of the Imperial harem.

When she was finally called from the anteroom through to the prince's bedchamber, however, any rational thought was dispelled by a flurry of nerves and, she noted with shock, a thrill of excitement that went beyond the rush she normally felt during a dangerous mission.

The prince waited by the window. He was not a tall man but held himself with regal stature, his back straight and his shoulders thrust back. His hair was greying at the temples and a rich diet had given him a rounded silhouette, though she could see from his bare forearms that he kept his muscles well-toned.

"My valet says you're the new assignee," he said by way of an introduction. She nodded, trying to imagine herself seventeen again. "That's all I know about you. Did they tell you much about me?"

"No," she said truthfully, then because she was unsure of the protocols, added a hasty "My lord."

He stepped close to her and rested one arm gently across her shoulders. "Well, you won't have to work too hard," he said, reaching across to brush a few stray curls from her cheek, tucking the hairs behind her ear. "I'm very much in love with my wife. I'll have need of you only occasionally."

"As my lord wishes," she said, impressed by his straight talking. Somehow she hadn't imagined he'd treat his toys with such respect. Unlike the valet with his barked orders, this prince addressed her almost as an equal.

Almost.

"Of course they'll have shown you where you'll be living, and I'm sure someone's outlined the rules. A bit excessive, if you ask me, but the Imperial Household has its odd ways – you'll get used to it." He traced the curve of her breasts through the thin fabric and brought his hands down to rest just above her hips, broad fingers gripping her waist. "Is there anything you don't understand?"

She could feel her heart pounding, and wondered how everything had already strayed so far from the picture of the evening she'd created in her mind. She was supposed to be seducing him, but despite her best efforts to stay professional she was struggling not to respond to his touch. And she still had to contrive a way to retrieve the potion from the spot behind the headboard where she'd been told she could find it.

"No need to be nervous," he said, misinterpreting her silence. "What's your name?"

"Nina."

"Well, Nina, you can call me Leon. Just don't tell the servants – they can get rather hung up on protocol."

"Am I not a servant?" she asked.

"Not quite."

He slipped the straps of her dress down over her shoulders, dropped the fabric to the floor and pulled her now-naked body into a tight embrace. The rosewater scent of his skin filled her nostrils, his fingers were soft against her back, and she could feel his erection pressing through the rough fabric of his trousers. She allowed her body to relax against his; if she was going to do this job, she might as well enjoy it.

Slowly, with a hesitation she felt befitted a young girl facing the heir to the throne only days after leaving school, she began to unfasten his shirt. He stood and watched without moving as she worked her way down from his collar to his waist, finally dropping to her knees to loosen his belt and pull down his trousers.

He slid his hands through her hair and manoeuvred her head gently but firmly until she had no choice but to open her mouth, and suddenly her pretence of virginal innocence no longer felt like such a pretence. This was like nothing she'd done with Daniel, and the pressure against the back of her throat made her gag a little as he pulled her towards him.

"Relax," he instructed, and she forced her muscles to obey. "Use your tongue."

After a few long moments he stepped back and offered a hand to help her to her feet, and led her to the bed before climbing on top of her. His body was heavy and warm, and the hairs on his chest tickled her nipples as he held himself above her, studying her face as his right hand wandered across her skin. He rolled her body between his legs until she was lying on her front, her face pressed into the sheets as he sat astride her buttocks. With one palm resting on the small of her back he ran the other hand along the curve of her spine and up her neck, and leaned in to whisper in her ear: "If you tell me who sent you, I might let you live."

She froze, then let out a slow, deliberate breath and relaxed her muscles, hoping the involuntary stiffening had given nothing away. She could feel the point of a dagger pressing from between his fingers and wondered how she'd allowed herself into this position, furious at herself for letting her guard down.

"What do you mean?" she asked. How had he seen through her so easily? Unless... Her pulse quickened as she ran the options through her mind. Could this whole setup be a trap? Had she been sent here, unarmed, simply so he would kill her? With this new thought pressing on her mind, she wondered whether feigning ignorance would be even more dangerous than just admitting who she was.

"The role you're trying to mimic attracts a certain kind of girl," he said. "You just don't fit."

"Oh?" She had to keep him talking; she needed more time to think.

"You're nowhere near flirty enough, and though you've an alright figure you're a bit too skinny, and these muscles..." He squeezed her thigh as if to emphasize his point. "You've been trained for something quite different. So if you want to live, you'd better explain why you're here."

"I'm not supposed to hurt you," she said, thankful that a truthful answer was relatively harmless. "Your mother sent me to administer a fertility drug, that's all."

"That makes no sense."

"There should be a jar behind your headboard. Go and look."

"Do you really think I can tell a fertility drug from a contact poison? No, I think I'm going to keep you under my knife for now. But whether or not you believed it, my mother has no interest in increasing my fertility."

"Then maybe you're supposed to notice I'm an imposter," she said. "Maybe you're meant to kill me."

He laughed – a loud, hearty laugh completely out of place in the circumstances. "Why would anyone go to this much effort to do away with someone as insignificant as you?" he asked once he'd recovered himself.

"I have no idea. But why else would I be here, naked and unarmed, with a knife to my back?"

He shook his head. "I don't believe this is for your benefit. That's self-centred thinking, and you're not that important."

He was right, she realised, though it pained her to admit it. But his amusement gave her the opportunity she needed and she twisted suddenly, relying on the element of surprise to wrench the knife from his hand before he could use it, and a moment later she held his own blade to his throat, looking up into his face though she was still pinned down by his weight.

"There's an alternative theory," she said, allowing herself a slight smile. "That you're supposed to try to kill me, and in the resulting chaos I'm supposed to kill you. But why would your mother want you dead?"

"Oh, she hates me," he said, his tone strangely casual. "But if that's her plan, you need to think very carefully about whether you want to play into her hands. Do you really want to be the scapegoat for my death?"

She studied his face. Clearly he spoke from a position of desperation, but on the other hand if the Empress truly wanted him dead she must have had some reason not to order it directly. In that context, making a scapegoat of the 'accidental' assassin was a plausible scenario. She wondered whether, if she killed him, she'd even manage to leave the palace before the guards arrived.

"It seems we've both been tricked," she said carefully. "I doubt you like that any more than I do. And since neither of us is going anywhere, we'd better talk this through. Why would the Empress want you dead?"

"I'm not going to talk politics with you."

"I don't care about politics. I care about how I get out of this room, and right now my best chance seems to be to make myself more valuable alive than dead."

"Why should I trust you when you work for my mother?"

"I work for whoever pays me. If you want me to get her out of your way, you only have to find enough dollars to back up your request."

He shook his head. "That's her kind of game, not mine. She's the one who's killing off heirs she doesn't like the look of."

Eleanor thought of Sofia bleeding into her pillow, but she said nothing. Better to let him talk until he said something she could use.

"Mother wants an heir who'll keep pushing the boundaries of the Empire, and she knows I'm not that enthused by conquest. She's already had three of my children murdered – well, the midwives have always claimed they were stillborn, but it's obvious what she's doing. If I don't have an heir by the time mother dies, my little sister can claim the line of

116

succession."

"Is your wife pregnant right now?"

He glared down at her, suspicious. "How did you know that? We've told no-one."

"The Empress seems to have guessed. Okay, I think I have a way out of this mess. What if I can keep your child safe?"

"How?"

"Send your wife away, tonight if you can. She should dress in plain clothes, leave the royal carts behind and travel like a commoner. Tell no-one she's leaving until she's well on her way, then say she's gone to the country for her health. She'll come back a few months from now and report another tragic miscarriage."

"You'll go with her?"

"I'll follow her. With your wife away, you'll need other women more often – no-one will be surprised at that. Send for me on the next full moon," – she picked the easiest day she could think of for them both to remember – "and you can tell me where to find her. I'll make sure the child stays safe."

"How can you promise that?"

"Sneaking around is my job, remember? I can hide your wife until the child is born, and I can hide your child in a suitable school. Now, do we have a deal?"

He nodded and shifted his weight to release her. She passed his knife back to him and was about to roll off the bed when he thrust his fingers suddenly between her legs. The unexpected roughness of the intrusion made her yelp with surprise.

"Can't send you back a virgin," he said as he withdrew his hand. "That would give us both away."

It was too late to be worth telling him she hadn't been so she just picked up the green slip and dressed herself, conscious again of just how little the sheer fabric really covered her. She took the pot of cream from behind the bedstead; without pockets, she had no choice but to keep it clenched in her fist and hope no-one would notice as she returned to her room to change. They hadn't given back her fake school uniform, but there were various everyday clothes in the closet which fitted her adequately.

It was almost dawn by the time she got back to the Association, and she went straight to Daniel's room, but although he woke when she got into his bed he didn't reach out for her.

"Are you still angry at me?" she asked. "I was only doing my job."

"You have the right to turn any mission down," he said. "I cannot understand why you did not do so."

"No-one else could have gone," she said. "It needed a woman, and until we fix our recruitment that means me."

"It did not need doing. We are not here to play power games for the Empress."

She put her arms around his shoulders. "Well, it's over now. I'm back. You can forgive me or not, but I'm not going to stay here if you're just going to sulk."

"I am not sulking," he said, turning to face her. "But this is hard for me. You have been – away. You smell of whatever they have done to you."

"What they did to me?"

"You even look different. Curls in your hair, and your body... you have let them mould you to their own design."

"I let them make me into a member of the Imperial harem, yes. Of course I did. What, did you think I could go in there and then object that they treat me like they treat every other girl who comes in by that route? I wouldn't have even made it to the same room as Leon."

"Fine."

"I know you're not fine." She stroked his cheek. "I know. But how long is it going to take you to get over it? Should I go back to my room?"

"Do not leave," he said. "I cannot get used to your changes if you are out of my sight."

"Okay." She hugged him closer. "Good night, sleep well."

She didn't tell anyone where she was going on the night of the full moon. So far as the council was concerned she'd finished her mission at the palace, and she didn't want to reopen the debate over whether she should have taken the job in the first place.

She let herself into the spare apartment and tried to make sure she looked at home as she waited, hoping Leon would remember to summon her tonight.

It was pitch black outside by the time the valet came to inform her that the prince required her company. She was pushed through the same preparatory regimen as before; knowing she had no need to fool him this time she felt slightly resentful of the time wasted by the endless grooming, but she had to go through this charade for the benefit of all the palace staff. If she acted in any way out of place, suspicions would be raised.

This time she wasn't left to wait in the anteroom, but summoned immediately into the prince's chambers. He sat in a chair by the window, waiting, and waved her to take the seat beside him.

"I trust everything is ready?" he said.

She nodded, feeling strange and self-conscious about conducting business when she was dressed in a flimsy slip of lilac fabric. "Did you do as I suggested?"

"I've told everyone Donna's visiting a spa for her health."

"Excellent."

"In reality, as you suggested, she took a horse and rode out into the country, aiming for Pettiford at the edge of the Silver Forest. She will have found some inn or guesthouse like any common traveller. You'll go and find her, and keep her safe, and take care of the child. And you will do it well, because if any harm comes to either of them then I will come for you with all the might of the Imperial armies."

She looked up and met his gaze steadily. "Remember who you're talking to. I may look like one of your other girls right now, but you don't get to threaten me. We had a deal and I'll keep my side of it, but I can't guarantee your wife hasn't already given herself away."

"She's no fool."

"Maybe not, but she's a princess. She can't have had much practice pretending to be a normal citizen."

"She won't fail. And nor will you."

"And she knows to expect me, and what I'm going to do?"

"She knows you're going to keep her safe."

"And the child?"

"She knows."

"Okay. What name is she travelling under?"

"I don't know."

"What? How am I supposed to go into some unknown inn and ask for a woman whose name I don't know?"

"It's your job to make this work – you'll find a way."

"You're not making it easy for me."

He shrugged. "Don't forget the part where I'm a prince and you're living on my sufferance."

Over breakfast the next morning Daniel kept staring at her across the table, though he looked away whenever she caught his eye.

"You look different," he said once they were alone in her room. "What have you done?"

"Different? How?" She'd carefully stayed blonde since her first visit to the palace; she couldn't believe he'd notice a few extra curls.

"Just different. And you smell of– wait, I do know that smell. You have been back to the palace."

"Yes."

"After everything we discussed, you went back there out of choice? After the mission was over?"

"I agreed to help Leon with his wife – it was the only way I could get out of there alive last time. Listen, he thinks his mother wants him dead, or childless at the very least. And that's not what I signed up for, so I'm helping them."

"You have simply decided the Empress is wrong?"

"She's murdering her son's children, that seems pretty wrong to me. I didn't come here to get involved in the Empress's family feuds."

"You are choosing to involve yourself now."

"I made a deal with Leon to get myself out alive, now I'm just keeping my half of the bargain. Anyway, you're the one who said it: we're not here to play power games for the Empress." She got to her feet. "I'll be away for a few days."

"Where are you going?"

"To finish this. There's a pregnant princess waiting for me; I need to get her out of sight until this baby is born."

"Do you really think, if the Empress wishes to kill the child, simply allowing him to be born will deter her?"

"She'll never know."

"What will you do?"

"I'm not telling you. Don't look at me like that, I'm not telling anyone, not even them. The child will just vanish. It's safest that way. Here, you can help me – figure out what this is for."

She reached across for the pot she'd retrieved from Leon's room. Daniel opened it and sniffed at the contents.

"Careful," Eleanor said. "It might be dangerous."

"I am not stupid." He sniffed once more at the cream, and replaced the stopper. "But I do not know this mixture. I will investigate."

"Thanks." She leaned across for a kiss. "I'll be back before my next class."

It took two days to ride to Pettiford, and when Eleanor arrived she was windswept and chilled by the frosty air. There was only one tavern in town. She arranged a room for herself and settled into a chair by the fire with her cold hands wrapped around a tankard of warm ale. As her fingers began to thaw, she considered how she could ask for news of a woman who could be travelling under any assumed name. At least, she hoped the princess hadn't been so stupid as to give her real name. She watched the flames rising and falling in the grate, looking round every now and then to study the faces of the tavern's other patrons. There were two other women who sat alone in the bar, one tall and severe, the other with a more forgiving expression. Eleanor looked between them while trying not to stare, wondering if either of them could be the princess she was looking for, assessing their waists for any hint of a growing child.

But the woman who swept up to her table and sat beside her without introduction was a homely woman of surprisingly plain appearance. If she was indeed carrying a child, there was no sign that she was anything but naturally full-figured.

"I suppose you must be the girl," she said. "You match Leon's description pretty well."

"Shhhh." Eleanor looked around, but thankfully no-one seemed to have heard. "His is not a common name. You'll be safer if you don't use it."

"I don't understand the need for all this secrecy," the princess said. She followed Eleanor's gaze around the room but she saw only irrelevant commoners, and she dismissed them with a shake of her head. "Nor do I understand why I'm living in a country tavern when I have a perfectly nice home in Almont. But I'm sure you think this is all necessary somehow."

"Your husband believes that you're in danger," Eleanor said. "And I offered to help you and your child."

"He's ridiculous," she said. "He's always bickering with his mother, but then he goes and thinks it's serious. As if she'd really do anything to hurt her own grandchildren."

"Shhhhh. Please." Eleanor leaned forwards and whispered, "Only one family in all the Empire can use words like that and mean something by it. You'll give yourself away if you haven't already."

"If we're not safe all the way out here, then I don't know where you think you're going to find that's safer," Donna said. "We're a long way from home."

"We're only two days' hard ride from Almont," Eleanor countered. "And there's a difference between where it's safe enough to sleep, and where – if anywhere – it's safe enough that we can talk openly. Most people won't recognise your face, but when you talk like that you betray yourself."

"But what does it matter? Why would anyone care who I am?"

"Just the fact that you're here is unusual. People will talk, innocently at first, but gossip spreads and word could easily get back to those who want to hurt you. If you want my help then I won't let you take that risk." Eleanor swallowed the last mouthful of her drink and set the tankard down. "Come on, we can talk more freely outside."

They walked into the trees at the back of the town. Eleanor took a certain pleasure in leading the princess along muddy paths into the forest, enjoying the growing distaste on her face.

"That's better," Eleanor said once they were out of sight of the buildings. "You can use whatever words you like out here."

"It's your turn to talk," Donna said. "What precisely are you expecting me to do?"

Eleanor explained her plan as briefly as she could manage, though Donna interrupted at every opportunity to express her displeasure for various elements. Eleanor simply repeated, until she was sick of repeating it, that she was acting at Leon's request and would be perfectly happy to go home tomorrow if she hadn't promised her assistance.

After the tenth such interruption, however, she'd had enough. "You weren't born into the Imperial family, were you?" she asked.

"No," Donna replied, too surprised by the sudden change of subject to consider not answering.

"And how long have you and Leon been married?"

"Eight years."

"Well, it seems to me that somewhere in the course of the past eight years you've forgotten how to shut up and do as you're told," Eleanor said. "Which might be fine when you've got an indulgent husband and half an army of servants, but when you're in fear of your life and someone's trying to help you, the rules are a bit different."

Chapter 9

Eleanor was slow to respond to the council summons; she'd just got home from Pettiford and wanted to finish her preparations for the next day's classes. By the time she reached the chamber the others were already deep in conversation.

"What was the body count?" Ragal asked as she came in. The target of the question was Ivan; he caught Eleanor's eye and smiled as she slipped into an empty chair.

"Zero," he said.

"Yes, yes." Ragal tapped his fingers impatiently on the table. "I know you all came home alive. I meant the total, including the soldiers who went with you."

"Zero," Ivan repeated. "We didn't have to fight."

"What?" Bill looked astonished. "When has any encounter with the mountain men ended short of massacre?"

"We came to an understanding, of sorts. They use a secret code of hand signals – it seems to be a variant of the Venncastle signs. And as soon as I picked them up on it, they knew they had to listen."

"How can the mountain men know Venncastle secrets?" Nicholas asked.

Ivan shrugged. "It must go back to before the Empire, I suppose. Maybe we're not as unique as we thought. The fact is, they do, and that means we have at least a chance to talk."

"Did you find out what they want?"

"They want what they've always wanted, so far as I can tell. They just want to be left alone."

"That won't satisfy the Empress," Albert said. "She won't rest until every acre of these lands is safely under the rule of Imperial law, and every mountain-born child enrolled in a proper Imperial school."

"Let's wait and see what she says when we turn in our report," Ivan said. "There's no point second-guessing it."

"There's bound to be a second expedition," Nicholas said.

"And we'll have to send Venncastle men, if they really share our hand-language."

"Well, we'd have to wait for the next freeze if we want to send more people," Ivan said.

"Surely summer is the best time to head into the cold regions?"

"You'd think so, wouldn't you? But right now it's pure slush in the mid-ranges, and the thaw rivers are making the lower slopes dangerous. It's only going to get worse as we get into summer."

Eleanor thought back to the view she'd had of the mountain tops from her school. "It never completely thaws up there, does it?"

"Not in the highlands, no. I think that's part of the reason the mountain men don't stray very far down the slopes – their lives are designed around a constant winter, so they stay where the snows are."

"I'm not sure why the Empress thinks it's a good idea to try and start mining up there," Don said. "There must be easier sources of minerals."

"It's not our job to question Imperial policy," Karl said. "We only have to make it work."

"I thought we didn't even have to do that, if we don't want to?" Eleanor asked, her own recent decisions weighing on her mind. "Everyone's always been very definite about the fact that we're outside the Imperial system – surely we can just say no, if we want."

"In theory, yes," Nathaniel said. "But in practice we need the Empress just as much as she needs us. We need her money."

"Do the mountain men have their own mines?" Karl asked Ivan. "Is that why they're so keen to keep us out?"

"No, I don't think they care for that kind of thing," Ivan said. "It's a very simple culture. They make their bows and arrows, their sleds, their cabins, all from the wood of the mountain-top forests. They've a few old knives but nothing special."

"I don't understand it," Bill said. "Haven't we explained

how much more they could have if they adopted the Imperial lifestyle? Hasn't anyone told them how much better it would be for them?"

"I get the impression that's exactly what gets people killed," Ivan said. "They don't like being told what they should want. And who can blame them, honestly?"

"But they're missing out on so much."

"And they think we're missing out on the joys of hunting, and raising our own children, and living in the constant snow. But they don't send military parties to try and persuade us of that."

Daniel had been missing from the meeting, so when everyone else dispersed Eleanor went across to his rooms to see what had kept him. She found him hunched over his desk, making careful cuts into something small and bloody. He discarded most of the flesh into a bucket by his feet, but kept back some parts which he submerged in a clear liquid.

"What're you doing?" she asked, leaning over his shoulder to try and get a better look as he moved another bloody sphere onto his cutting board.

"What does it look like?" He made another incision and pried the flesh apart with his fingers. "I am working."

"You missed a good meeting," she said. "The mountain expedition is back."

"All of them?"

"Yeah, I think everyone was surprised by that."

He nodded, and continued his dissection in silence.

"Sorry for disturbing you," Eleanor said. "Do you want to come round later, when you've finished?"

"This may take a while. It is not a quick preparation."

"What are you making?"

"I read something in the old records that I thought I might improve on: I am attempting to distill the strength of a bull."

"You're what? That sounds like some kind of bizarre magic."

"It is an experiment, if that is what you mean." He threw another lump of flesh into the bucket. "Of course, in the original procedure they took none of this care, but neither did

126

they end up with a perfect tonic."

She was fascinated in spite of herself. "So what was the original procedure?"

"Simply to eat the testes," he replied.

Her eyes fixed on the bowl of meat with sudden understanding. "So that's what those are? Disembodied balls?"

"Yes."

"Where did you get them from?"

"I had a butcher hold some back for me. Most people have no wish to eat them, these days, so he was very happy at my interest."

"Yeah, no wonder."

He continued working through his supply, extracting the slices he was interested in and discarding the rest. Eleanor just watched. Apothecary wasn't usually fun, but this was a step more intriguing than the standard herbal preparations.

"Why do you think no-one's done this before?" she asked at length.

"No-one else is me."

"Yes, but–"

"That is all the difference there is. Who else ever takes the time to create something new? Or to make a recipe better, or a method more precise?"

"What about Albert?"

"He has no imagination. He is methodical enough to make progress, but he has no interest."

Daniel sliced up the final testicle and prodded the lumps he'd submerged in the thick, clear liquid.

"Ah, it will have to sit for a while longer," he said. "I should have known. Then, since you are here, should we order some lunch?"

"Let's go back to my rooms," Eleanor suggested. "I'm not sure I want to eat with the smell of raw testicles up my nose."

In the next morning's projectiles class, Eleanor took the second years out to the practice frame and set an intricate sequence of throws and acrobatics that she knew even her best students would struggle to master: she'd spent a while before breakfast ensuring she could reliably achieve it herself. Once they were each occupied with their own target boards, trying to recreate the individual moves which combined to make the new technique, she wandered casually across to where Raf was warming up.

"You know Ivan's back?" she said, leaning against the frame.

"I didn't." He flicked his stars towards the board, skipping the harder moves to ensure an accurate result, then turned to face her. "Has he asked you to keep on teaching us?"

"He hasn't yet asked me to stop. But they only got in yesterday."

"Any news on how they got on?"

"Not much progress," she said. "But I think we expected that."

"If everyone made it home in one piece that is progress, isn't it? For the mountains."

"Actually, that's probably the main thing we've learnt. We've found a way to talk to them – Ivan said the men in the mountains know some secret sign language that's used at Venncastle."

"Really?"

"Yeah. Do you know it?"

"Of course, everyone does. I mean, everyone at school."

"The mountain men were using it to talk amongst themselves, apparently, and Ivan made it clear that he understood the things they thought they were saying in secret. That made them listen."

"Then that's definitely progress."

"It is." She retrieved his stars from the board and handed them back to him. "Try that again?"

"I can't do this," he said. "You're distracting me with all this talk of the mountains. You're carrying me off into dreams of all the fun stuff I'll get to do once I've graduated... I can't concentrate on making stars go round corners."

"If you want to get that seat on the council, you'd better concentrate on this," she said. "We're only days from the next contest and you never know, you might want to get some points from Projectiles. We'll talk later."

"At lunch?"

"Yeah, come up to mine, I'll order something. Now, show me the best you can do."

At the end of the lesson Eleanor sent him ahead of her up to her rooms while she went to request a light lunch of soup and bread from the kitchens. He was emerging from her washroom when she came in.

"That's better," he said, shaking damp hair out of his eyes. "Human again."

"A bit of sweat doesn't make you any less human," she said, suddenly conscious of her own damp tunic. But she was leading another projectiles class in the afternoon; there was no sense in her getting changed out of her training clothes.

"So, this silent language... you learnt it at school?" she asked as they sat down to eat.

"Yeah."

"And you didn't think to teach me in Taraska?"

"It wouldn't have been much use."

"You don't think it would've helped to have a silent language when we were sneaking around trying not to get killed?" she asked, reaching for a slice of bread but watching his face. "And pretending to be silent monks?"

"It isn't a proper language. It's more a way of modifying what you're saying. So if you do this" – he curled two fingers to his thumb as he spoke – "then you're effectively negating your words. And this" – he flexed his fingers backwards – "signals something to be suspicious of, in the words you're hearing. It's more useful for diplomacy than war."

"I didn't think Venncastle was known for its diplomacy."

He laughed, struggling not to spray his mouthful of soup across the table. "We're known for what we choose to be known for. Much like the Association in that respect."

"You won't be able to keep your secret language to yourselves for long," she said. "Not if the Association needs it to make headway in the mountains."

"Do you think I didn't tell you because I was worried about protecting the school's secrets?" he asked. "Do you really think that would've even crossed my mind out in that dryland prison? I just didn't think it was helpful."

"Okay."

"Honestly."

"I believe you." She copied the gestures he'd shown her; they were certainly of limited use on their own. "You will have to teach us, though."

"Maybe. Or maybe it just makes sense to send Venncastle men into the mountains now. I wouldn't mind going once I've graduated, it sounds like fun."

"You just want to follow in Ivan's footsteps again."

She'd only been making what she thought was a fairly obvious joke, but he set his spoon down and looked seriously at her.

"You shouldn't talk about that," he said. "It's better if we can pretend it isn't... that we don't know."

"Sorry. I didn't think you'd mind, when it's just us."

He shrugged. "I'm being silly, I know, but it's easier to keep the pretence if we pretend all the time. It's something me and Ivan learnt early on."

She was contemplating a stroll down to the kitchens to see what they were making for dinner when there was a knock at the door.

"Daniel asked me to fetch you," Matt said. One of the best students at both poisons and medicines, he'd quickly fallen into acting as Daniel's assistant in his spare time. "He said you should come and eat with us."

"He did, did he? Did he consider that I might already have plans?"

"Have you?"

"No, not really." She picked up her jacket and followed him into the corridor. She was hungry, anyway, but she wondered what Daniel was after. It would hardly be a romantic meal with Matt there, so it couldn't be a social call.

"Today we have chicken," Daniel said when they arrived, indicating the bird which sat, surrounded by a lake of green-flecked sauce, in the middle of the table. "I hope you are hungry."

"I am," Eleanor said. "And I should think Matt will be, after what I put them through this afternoon."

"It was nothing," Matt said, though she knew he was bluffing. He'd succeeded, but only just.

She'd almost finished eating when Daniel handed a small bottle across the table to her. "Here. Five drops on your tongue, morning and evening."

She eyed the it suspiciously. "Is this what I think it is?"

"It is the conclusion of my latest experiment, yes."

"You want me to drink that stuff, knowing what it's made from?"

"I had never thought you squeamish. Besides, you are my only female subject – I need to measure your responses."

"And what responses are you expecting?" she asked, realising that despite her fascination with the method she hadn't bothered to ask what he expected to get out of the end. 'The strength of a bull' was hardly the kind of measurable quantity with which Daniel usually dealt.

"I do not wish to risk influencing your experience," he said. "Once you have taken it for a few days, you can tell me. I will also be taking it."

She pocketed the bottle. "I'll try it this evening, then."

"Why not now?"

"I'm just not sure about testicle juice and chicken."

Matt laughed, but Daniel looked unimpressed.

"You will do what you want," he said. "You always do."

They finished their meal in silence, and Eleanor didn't stay to chat after she'd cleared her plate. Daniel was in one of his obsessive, inventive phases and there was no way she'd get his attention away from Matt and whatever they were working on. Not tonight.

Alone in her room, she pulled out the bottle Daniel had given her. Of all his experiments, this seemed by far the strangest. Just because some people back in history had thought that eating a bull's testicles made them stronger? Most likely they'd just worked harder because they thought it would help.

But of course Daniel was right, she was the only girl he

could test it on. That meant she had to try it. Besides, she wouldn't turn down a little extra strength if there was any truth in it. She pulled out the stopper and dropped some onto her tongue as he'd instructed.

She waited for a moment, but nothing happened. She flexed her muscles, not feeling any stronger, and then laughed at herself for even trying when she hadn't really expected it to work. Unimpressed, she made herself a mug of tea, hoping to wash away the oily residue from her mouth. She sank into a chair and sipped at the drink. Perhaps she was being unfair, perhaps it'd take a few days to kick in. But if that's what Daniel had been expecting, why had he wanted her to try it at dinner?

She was lucky that she'd half-finished her tea before the shaking started, because hot liquid sloshed violently against the sides of the mug. She gripped it more tightly at first, but that only seemed to make the trembling in her fingers worsen.

Setting the mug down by her feet, she stood and took a deep breath, willing her muscles to stop spasming. It didn't work. She could feel her heart pounding in her chest, pulse racing as if she'd just sprinted across the city. She waited, hoping the tremors would subside, but if anything she seemed to be getting worse. Whatever Daniel had inflicted on her, it wasn't strength.

She ran down the stairs and across the grass to the apothecary. It was no great surprise that Daniel and Matt were still working in the lab.

"What have you done to me?" she demanded, sweat beading on her forehead. "Daniel, what is this stuff?"

He looked up. "Do you have something to tell me? Please wait for just a moment."

"I don't have a moment. Can't you see the way I'm shaking? It's killing me."

"Is this the new tonic?" Matt asked. He looked more excited than concerned. "How much did you take?"

Daniel carefully wiped the powders from his hands with a small towel he reserved for the purpose, and reached for his record book. "You are not dying. Now, tell me exactly what has happened."

"I'm shaking like a leaf, my heart is racing at twice the

132

speed it should, and I feel like I'm going to die."

He made a few notes. "You feel unwell? How so?"

"I just told you."

"'Like you will die' is not very precise. What are you feeling?"

She grabbed his hand and held it against her neck. "Can't you feel it?"

He nodded, removed his hand from hers, and scribbled another line in his book. "Is that all? You are fine."

"I don't call this fine."

"It is nothing to worry about. Try just four drops in the morning, and let me know how it goes."

"You're going to have to do a bit better than that if you want me to take any more, at all, ever," she said. Her muscles still trembled, beyond her control. "Don't you have an antidote?"

"You have not been poisoned. If you are so worried, take only three, but you are really fine. Go for a run, use up the energy."

She stared at him. "Are you mad? My heart's already gone crazy, I don't want to explode."

"Try it, or not. Matt will run with you if you need someone to watch you."

"I will?" he asked, but a look from Daniel silenced him.

"Do you really think it'll help?"

"I think it may be the only way for you to get some sleep tonight."

"Okay." Eleanor nodded, and looked at Matt. "But you're definitely coming with me in case I collapse out there."

"Around the lake?" he suggested as they walked outside. "That's not too far."

She glared at him and started to stretch out her muscles. No matter how ill she felt, she didn't like anyone implying she might have difficulty on a simple run. The stretches made her muscles tremble more violently and she wondered if she was making a mistake, but she wasn't about to admit that to him.

They started to run towards the lake, feet bouncing off the compacted mud of the trail. Eleanor could feel her heart racing, but somehow running didn't seem to make it worse. She still felt dizzy, but she could channel the falling sensation into the motion of throwing one foot ahead of the other.

"Wait for me," Matt called, and she realised how far she'd left him behind.

"Am I going too fast for you?"

"A moment ago you were facing death's door. Don't you want to pace yourself?"

"This is my pace." She grinned. "Seems I feel a bit better when I'm running."

Chapter 10

It was five days' ride to Dashfort and the house where Eleanor had hidden Donna away from prying eyes. The man who usually lived there was a half-retired member of the Association who had the unenviable task of resetting the puzzle chamber every time an academy postulant attempted the challenge. He'd been delighted when Eleanor had arrived at his doorstep and told him to take a holiday before the new set of students started to filter through, and he'd hurried off to enjoy springtime on the island where he'd grown up, leaving her with an empty house where she could hide her princess until the summer solstice.

For her part, Donna had protested at almost every aspect of the plan, but she hadn't been able to find an argument strong enough to sway Eleanor's resolve. Although the whole house could easily have fitted into a the throne room of the Imperial palace, it was clean and comfortable, and sat conveniently in the middle of Dashfort. They'd had extensive discussions on that front, too, with Eleanor prepared to allow Donna the freedom to wander the city only if she agreed not to engage in any unnecessary chatter.

So it was that when Eleanor arrived back in Dashfort a few days before the solstice, she found a heavily pregnant and very irritable princess waiting for her.

"So what now?" Donna asked. "Since we need to give this house back, and my baby hasn't yet shown any signs of wanting to come out."

"I might be able to help you with that."

Once it had stopped involving trips to the Imperial harem, Daniel had become a lot more supportive of her plan. So while she'd sneaked away from the Association without telling anyone else where she was going, she'd explained everything to him – including the way that the timings didn't quite work out – and he'd given her an experimental potion that he thought might bring on an early labour. She reached into her bag and brought out the bottle.

"Drink this. You've given birth before, so just tell me when it starts working and we'll get you to a local midwife."

"Can we trust them?"

"You're an anonymous woman about to give birth. If you don't say anything stupid, we'll be fine."

It was almost sunset when Donna's waters broke, and Eleanor helped her to walk through the narrow streets to the house of the nearest midwife. Eleanor had dropped in earlier in the day to warn her that her services would be needed, and had primed her with the idea that the child was bound for Venncastle. She didn't want it to come as a surprise when she took the baby away instead of leaving it to the midwife to find a nursery place.

Eleanor tried to keep out of the way while the midwife and her assistant fussed around with various herbal preparations, and Donna screamed and cursed and cried until the child was finally born.

"You'll be taking him away while the young lady recuperates, will you?" the midwife asked Eleanor once she'd cleaned the child and wrapped him in a clean linen sheet.

Eleanor agreed and took the small wriggling bundle, which promptly started to wail. She held him at arm's length. "This," she said, once she was sure the midwife had moved out of hearing range, "is not a very princely way to behave."

Once Donna was ready to walk again, they went back to the house for one final night. In the morning Eleanor would take the child and Donna would find a cart to carry her back to Almont.

By morning, however, Donna had been holding her baby for a whole nearly-sleepless night.

"I don't think I want to let him go," she said, hugging him close to her chest. "Can we change the plan?"

"No."

"I want to take him home."

"You can't. You know it's not safe."

Eleanor held out her arms for the boy and Donna passed him across, tears forming in the corners of her eyes.

136

"We haven't come this far to have you give in to sentimentality," Eleanor said. "This is only what every other woman in the Empire goes through."

"Where will you take him?"

Eleanor strapped the baby tightly into a sling across her back, and swung herself up onto her horse. "You'll tell me when the time is right for him to come home," she said. "And I'll fetch him. For now, it's safer that you don't know where I'm going."

Donna nodded, swallowing back her tears.

"Go home now," Eleanor said, "and put your grief to good use. Let them see you cry."

"Someone will ask me what's wrong."

"We're counting on it. You'll tell them that you had a baby son, and you lost him to a tragedy of nature. You'll be very clear with everyone – especially your husband, within his mother's hearing – that your heart's broken, and you could never put yourself through that again. He'll be disappointed, but he'll understand."

"And you'll make sure my son is hidden until it's time for him to claim his birthright?"

"Until the Empress is dead and Leon established in her place," Eleanor said. "Or whenever it makes sense that he's safe. We'll see how things go."

The princess nodded, and watched in silence as Eleanor carried her child away. For her part, Eleanor was sure the immediate danger had passed. If anyone saw her now she was just another woman with another child, on her way to lodge him safely in an appropriate school. That she'd picked Venncastle only served to give her a better excuse for making a journey with the child; in that respect, she was lucky the princess had produced a son.

She caught the regular supply boat from Dashfort to Flying Rock Island, crewed mostly by the same sailors as the last time she'd made this trip. She wasn't sure whether they recognised her, but none of them said anything and she was more than happy to remain anonymous. One mother and child was much like the next, to their eyes, and if they noticed she was feeding him from a bottle then they didn't comment on it.

At the gate she was met by curious stares from the guards, but no-one challenged her, and Venncastle's head of admissions came down to talk with her in the gatehouse. She claimed a military background for herself and an invented Association father for the child, and he was accepted easily, with only a few cursory questions. And if she seemed more than a little interested in how he would be named, well, it was only natural that a mother would find parting difficult. A name to hold in her heart was the least they could do in exchange for the right to raise her son.

It was a speedy process, and Eleanor rejoined the supply boat before it went on to complete its circuit of the neighbouring islands, satisfied in the knowledge that the youngest heir to the Imperial throne would grow up to become a Venncastle man by the name of Damien. She didn't even need to send word to Leon. Donna would be home by now, weeping with a genuine sense of bereavement, and the least said beyond that the better.

She got back just in time for the academy's graduation dinner. It had come as no great surprise to anyone that Raf returned victorious from the third contest, in which the task had been to retrieve the key to a cipher one of the rebel factions had adopted. Raf had pick-pocketed a sheet of parchment from one of the rebels as he left his home, while Greg and Stefan had still been contemplating how best to get inside the rebel meeting house.

Eleanor dressed for the evening in her favourite green gown, with only a single stiletto hidden in the strategic boning of the bodice. They weren't expecting any trouble tonight. The artificial blonde had long since grown out of her hair, returning it to its usual deep red shade, and she built an elaborate mound of curls on top of her head.

She walked with Ivan to the banqueting hall, where he took the empty seat next to Raf, and Eleanor found that Daniel had saved a space for her.

"Venncastle continues to take over the council," he muttered as she sat down.

"Can't you leave it for just one night?"

Daniel mumbled to himself as he counted heads around the table. "They are almost half," he said. "It makes fair voting impossible."

"How many times have we needed to vote on anything? I can only think of twice in the whole year."

"But soon we will have to vote on whether we indulge our Empress by sending a second expedition into the mountains."

"I don't think we can stop her."

"Then perhaps we should remove her from the equation. Give your Crown Prince and his heir the chance."

Eleanor was saved from having to think of a suitable response by Ragal standing and striking his glass to get their attention.

"A few words before the feasting begins," he said. "Tonight we celebrate the growth of another cohort of our students from hopeful young men into competent members of our Association. Although it's natural that we give particular attention to Raf's ascension to the council, tonight is for all of you. Make the most of it. Tomorrow, the hard work begins."

Everyone clapped and cheered at that: the graduating students anticipating a fresh challenge, the first years looking a year ahead to their own graduation, and all the older members of the Association who remembered their own first days.

The banquet was as impressive a spread as every year, and the wine flowed freely as everyone heaped second and third helpings onto their plates. Eleanor was relieved that Daniel fell into conversing with Albert about his latest experiments, giving her at least a temporary reprieve from having to work out whether he was seriously threatening to decapitate the Empire.

By the time she was drunk enough and tired enough to want to go to bed, half of the hall had already emptied, but Daniel and Albert were still arguing furiously over some theoretical corner of apothecary. She tried to get Daniel's attention but he waved her away impatiently, more interested in winning his point. She sighed; when he got so absorbed in work, it could be days before he'd want to talk to her.

"I'm going to bed, then," she said. He grunted an acknowledgement, though Albert was still talking and she was sure he was paying more attention to his words than hers. "See you tomorrow."

Eleanor spotted Raf ahead of her on the otherwise empty path, his purple tunic billowing in the warm summer breeze. Creeping along behind him, she slipped a dart into her pipe and aimed it at his ear. He reached up to see what had pricked him, found the tiny needle caught in his skin, and turned in alarm.

"It's okay," she said. "It's only a blank."

He flicked the dart onto the path and ground it with his heel while he waited for her to catch up. "Normal people might've just called out."

"But you prefer me," she said with a smile. "What are you doing alone on your victory night? Don't you have some more celebrating to do?"

"It's exhausting, isn't it? Spending a whole evening being the centre of attention."

"So I shouldn't congratulate you again?"

"You can."

"I'll settle for welcoming you to the real world. Council seat and everything – you've finally caught up with me again."

"Does that mean I can come and spot for you more often?"

"It means I can spot for you for a change. It's about time I got a break."

"Nice to see you're still wearing your necklace." He reached out to lift the pendant from her skin, twisting it to make the emeralds sparkle in the moonlight. "I wouldn't want to think I'd made myself a thief for nothing."

She stared at him. "You just won a thieving competition."

"Yeah, but that's different. That's work, this was... just because I could."

"Well, it's the prettiest thing I own. Which is not to say I don't sometimes think about how to improve it."

"How would you improve it?"

She looped the chain from around her neck and held the pendant where they could both see it. "See the long edge here?"

He nodded.

"I can't help noticing that if it were hollow, it'd be just about long enough to hold a useful dose of something."

He laughed. "You've spent too much time with Ivan."

"No, Ivan would have made it by now. Whereas I'd have to ask Harold to do the real work for me."

"Get him to do it, then. Just the same, but with that bit hollowed out and maybe a spike on the end to administer whatever you keep in there."

"But then this wouldn't be my favourite pendant any more."

"Never mind that, just do it." He took the chain from her hands and put it around her neck again, making tiny adjustments until the pendant lay flat against her skin. "I won't be offended, promise."

"I'll think about it. Now, are you really going straight to bed or shall we get a drink first? It seems a shame to waste such a lovely evening."

"It's nearer dawn than midnight."

"So it's been a long evening. But it is beautiful, isn't it? Come on, it's your last night of freedom – let's sit out on the lawn for a bit."

Chapter 11

Winter was closing in, and the shortening days gave a perfect excuse for quiet evenings in front of the fire. Eleanor had persuaded Daniel that even he needed a break from constant studies, and they were enjoying one such evening playing dice in Daniel's sitting room when Raf came to fetch them to an unexpected council meeting.

"Do you know what it's about?" Eleanor asked him.

He shook his head. "There was an Imperial messenger," he said. "And Ragal wants everyone there, right now, no exceptions. That's all I know."

"Interesting. I wonder what it could be about."

"We will see soon enough," Daniel muttered, striding ahead of them down the hall.

They arrived at the council chamber a little later than most, and found the room so full that they had to squeeze in wherever they could around the sides. Ragal banged his fist on the table to silence the murmurs.

"Good evening," he said. "And my apologies for this interruption of your evening. However, I'm sure you will understand. We've just received a rather significant message, signed by the hand of the Empress herself."

A couple of people exchanged whispered comments; Eleanor caught Raf's eye across the room and raised an inquisitive eyebrow.

"It appears," Ragal continued, "that we are to be outlawed. Or rather, that we have been declared outlaws as of now. There's a lengthy list of unfounded allegations, objections to our status, et cetera. From the night of the solstice there will be a price on each of our heads."

Ragal paused, giving them a moment to absorb this news.

"There will be an amnesty to last until the solstice, which gives us a little over a month to organise ourselves. The Empress offers lenient terms to anyone who hands himself in and agrees to work for the new secret police service which is to be formed, but there are no details of that offer."

"So we prepare to fight?" Don asked.

Laban shook his head. "Not yet. We'll wait out the amnesty here."

"Acting now would give us an element of surprise. We know there's nothing to be gained by handing ourselves over."

"It's true that some of us already know which way we'll jump," Ragal said. "But others may need more time to consider their options. This is not a decision to be taken lightly."

"But the way the Empress has been behaving... how could anyone take her side in this?"

"Everyone must make his own choice," Ragal said firmly. "We can't assume we'll remain united, and we can't make plans until every man has chosen his side."

They were interrupted by a knock at the door, and a young messenger slipped in to deliver a letter to Nicholas before excusing himself as quickly as he'd arrived. Nicholas read quickly, the creases on his forehead deepening.

"A letter from Venncastle," he said, folding the paper and tucking it into his breast pocket. "The Empress has offered them terms, and they've decided to accept. No more Venncastle students will come to the Association."

"What would you expect?" Daniel muttered. Eleanor wished he could set aside his bitterness for long enough to realise the implications of the news they were hearing. Considering that a couple of the academy's intake usually came from Venncastle each year, their supply of good students would be seriously reduced if the school decided to take the side of the Empire.

"A fast decision," Ragal said. "I hope they've thought it through."

Laban shrugged. "As a school, they have little choice. A fugitive school has no future, no students... a refusal would require Flying Rock Island to attempt a secession from Imperial control, and that would be highly impractical."

"But the alumni will follow the school," Don said, looking pointedly at the Venncastle men around the table. His eyes settled on Nicholas. "Well, you will, won't you?"

"I would echo Ragal's sentiments," Nicholas said. "This is a very personal decision. I would not wish to influence any of my colleagues."

"A month isn't long, though," Eleanor said. "We can't wait until the last moment to decide where we go next. And we need to recall everyone who's away on missions."

"We'll send messages tonight," Ragal said. "We must give the Empress's choice to everyone, at home and abroad, but we will make it clear that the Association continues with or without Imperial sanction. Nathaniel, Nicholas, will you help me with the lists? Meanwhile, if anyone wishes to take up the Imperial offer, you need only let me know as you leave."

"Hang on." Eleanor had been reading the list of charges over Ragal's shoulder as he spoke. "There's something wrong with this. There are things on this list that no-one outside of this room should know."

"What sort of things?" Laban asked, peering across the table.

"For a start, Daniel's potion for halting a pregnancy is cited," she said, turning the paper so he could read it more easily. "And we've never even used it. And I don't think we reported back anything about Gisele's little adventure, but here we are, being acccused of recklessly endangering diplomatic staff. Almost everything they're claiming we've done wrong should have been private council business."

"Anyone want to own up?" Don said, one hand sliding towards the hilt of his dagger. "Because I'd certainly like to hear about it."

"We'll respect this period of amnesty on both sides," Ragal said. "If Eleanor is right, I only hope whoever did this has enough sense to get out before the amnesty expires."

"Spies and traitors don't deserve an amnesty," Don said, but he said it quietly, knowing he wasn't going to win this one.

As they left the council chamber, Raf hurried to catch up with Eleanor.

"You're in favour of this split then, Ellie?" he asked, catching her arm to stop her.

"It seems to be happening," she said.

144

"And you're not going to join the new organisation?"

"No," she agreed. "Are you?"

He'd managed to keep very quiet during the meeting, and she suddenly realised that he might be planning to defect. The idea alarmed her – she'd so easily assumed that they'd be in agreement, despite the news from Venncastle.

"I don't like it. But if you're not doing this for the Empire then what are you doing it for?"

"Fun? Seriously, though, that's one of the things we have to work out." The Association would certainly be different without Imperial funding. "But we're not here to do the Empress's dirty work for her. Part of what I wanted was to help the Empire – but that means everyone, and playing in her little power games isn't the point. She's been changing the rules too much lately."

"We can't change anything from outside."

"Well... maybe."

"If we leave, if we go renegade, then that's it." He took hold of her shoulders, forced her to look into his eyes. "Fugitives for life – ours or hers. Where's the chance to change things then?"

"I don't know," she admitted. "But you realise the first job for these new secret police will be to round up the rest of the Association, if they can find us? They won't let us live if they can help it."

"Don't you think the Association will take a similar line?" He looked sadly at her, suddenly seeming much older than his twenty-one years. "Track down the traitors... protect our secrets... it'll be a dirty game all round."

Instinctively, feeling overwhelmed by the enormity of what was facing them, she threw her arms around his neck. She'd only intended to hug him as she usually did but then her lips brushed against his and she found herself kissing him. He wrapped his arms around her waist and brought her towards him, lifting her slightly off her feet as he pulled her further into the kiss, holding her tightly to him as though he never wanted to let her go. As she relaxed against him she realised she'd longed for this since the nights they'd spent hand in hand in that cold Tarasanka cell.

As they eventually pulled apart, she smiled up at him. "Whatever happens, I'll never do anything to hurt you – you know that, don't you?"

"I know," he said, hugging her close again. "I hope we can always say that."

"Always." She rested her head against his shoulder, arms tightly around his waist. "I promise."

He ran one hand through her hair and rested it at the back of her neck. "Whenever I'm with you, whenever there's a problem, I just want to pick you up and tell you everything's going to be okay. But somehow..." he faltered. "This time I just don't know if it will be."

"Just tell me we'll be okay." She looked up at him and he leaned forwards to kiss her again. As their mouths met for the second time, with more purpose this time, she was sure in that moment that if she asked him to stay then he'd do it for her. Tears welled up in her eyes as she felt herself losing the worlds of opportunity she'd only just glimpsed. She hadn't thought he liked her that way... but she couldn't ask him to become a fugitive for her. If there was one thing certain about the coming trials, it was that everyone had to be free to choose which side he wanted to be on. Everyone in the council had instinctively realised that any restriction of that choice would breed weaknesses, or resentment, or treachery. It was too much to risk.

They walked hand in hand down to the lakeside and sat side by side on the shore. For a long time they were silent, watching the ripples in the moonlit water, thinking about everything that was happening.

"You'll definitely go, then?" Eleanor asked, though she knew what the answer would be.

"Sooner rather than later," he said. "Best to get in early, more chance to make a difference that way."

She nodded. "That makes sense."

"Promise me you'll at least think about it over the next week or two. You don't want to throw your life away for sentimentality."

"I have thought about it. I just don't like some of the

146

decisions the Empress has made – and the Association goes back to way before the Empire, we can handle being one step more independent."

"If anyone can survive this, you can," he said. "But be careful who you trust, won't you? It's going to get very dirty before this is over."

"You too." Tears were running down her cheeks and she avoided looking at him, preferring to flick pebbles into the lake and watch the patterns they made in the water. As much as she wanted to persuade herself this wasn't really goodbye, it felt pretty final. Unless the Empress rescinded the edict, she'd never again be able to go and seek him out when she needed a friendly ear. Not for fear of her life.

"I don't want to say goodbye forever," she said. "How long do you think all this is going to last?"

"The worst of it should be over in a year or two. Once everything settles down into whatever the new order is going to look like, and the Association figures out how things will work without Imperial money, then it'll get easier for everyone. Till then, we'll just have to keep our heads down."

Eleanor leaned against him and he wrapped his arm tightly around her shoulders.

"You'll come and find me, won't you?" she asked. "Once it's safe."

"It'll be easier for you to find me – I'm sure the Association won't stay here, and you'd be better not to tell me where you move to. You'll know when it's safe to come out of hiding."

"Okay." She could hardly believe the conversation they were having. How could he calmly tell her that she shouldn't trust him with her secrets? She'd tried not trusting him before, and it had been nothing but horrible. "I'll miss you."

"I'll miss you, too. Please take care of yourself."

She turned to face him and they exchanged one final kiss, lips salty from tears, before walking back to the academy in silence.

As Eleanor got ready for bed, she was sure that by morning he would have left to find his place in the new organisation. She wiped her eyes and tried to think of other things – anything to distract herself – but somehow nothing else seemed to matter. She was almost asleep when Daniel marched into her room, lantern flickering in his hand.

"You kissed him," he said.

"What?" Eleanor sat up, pulling the blankets more tightly around herself.

"You kissed him."

"So you've been spying on me, now?"

"I was looking for you, you were with him. I cannot believe you kissed him."

She watched him, wondering what would come next. Was he looking for a fight? She was too tired and upset to want to argue, but her hand went to the knife beneath her pillow, just in case.

"I let you be his friend, and this is how you thank me?"

"What was that?" Eleanor's voice was low and dangerous, but he'd never been good at detecting the subtleties of her tone.

"Is this how you repay me for letting you stay friends with him?"

"You didn't 'let me' be his friend. You don't get to say who my friends are."

"I do now. You are not to see him again."

She met his gaze steadily. "Or else?"

"Or you are not my girlfriend."

"Then I'm not your girlfriend." Even though it could be years before she'd have chance to see Raf again.

"Just like that?" He looked hurt, and then angry. "When I have tried to forgive you?"

"I'm sick of you trying to control me," she said. "You don't get to forgive me, or to give me permission, or to condemn me for kissing an old friend goodbye. It has nothing to do with you."

"He is leaving, then?"

"He's probably already left." She wished the thought didn't make her feel like crying. She supposed she should feel upset at this break-up with Daniel, but losing Raf hurt her a thousand times more.

"Then he is not your friend, Eleanor. How can you be so

blind? You have always insisted he was not our enemy, but surely now you can see that is exactly what he has made himself."

"He's not my enemy." She blinked back tears that were threatening to spill again; she couldn't afford to let Daniel see her cry. He'd only assume it had something to do with him. "He never will be. Now, if you've quite finished, I was trying to sleep."

"I have not finished." He sat on the bed, and she tucked her feet out of his way just in time. "Are you thinking of going with them?"

"No."

"You have always been closer to Venncastle than is really wise. It would hardly surprise me if you went."

"I said no. I'm not leaving the Association."

"Then you must learn to think of them as the enemy they are. Within a week or two the defectors will have left us, and we will make our plans for the future. It is important we are able to trust you."

"Don't talk to me about trust. I've never given you any reason to mistrust me."

"Today, you did."

"You know what I mean. Whatever might have been between the two of us is irrelevant – professionally, you've had no reason to doubt me."

"It is all the same trust. If you are too close to Venncastle, how can you be trusted in anything?"

"You know, if they didn't have to face people like you who hate them just because of the school they grew up in, maybe more of them would be choosing to stay."

"We would not wish them to. The Association has no need of people whose first loyalty lies elsewhere."

"Are you going to let me sleep, now?" Eleanor asked. "It's quite late."

"Remember what I have said. We will not have chance to make mistakes this time."

"And we won't. But it won't help anyone if we start fighting amongst ourselves – so let's just sleep it off, okay?"

It was ten days before the end of the amnesty when the last of the Venncastle men left the Association. The remaining members of the council gathered in their chamber at daybreak the next morning. It was strange to see the room so empty; Venncastle's contribution to the council had far outweighed its proportion of men in the wider organisation. They hadn't been the only defectors – a handful of others had reluctantly expressed a feeling that their duties to the Empire outweighed any allegiance to the Association itself – but they were by far the largest group to depart.

"Before we begin, I must ask whether anyone is still undecided," Ragal said once they were all seated.

Silence.

"Then, if you are all certain, we must plan our next steps."

"What are we considering?" Bill asked.

"First, we move," Laban said. "We're vulnerable here."

"Where can we go?" Eleanor asked.

"We always knew we might lose favour with the Empire one day – the plans for a new headquarters were made years ago."

"But won't the others have told the Empress's forces where we'll go?"

"We knew there would be traitors, too," Nathaniel said. "None of us knows where we'll be falling back to, but three people hold keys to the vault where that information is stored. I have one and Ragal has one – the third is with Nicholas. We'll have to get that one back from him, but that's all."

"How do you propose we do that?" Ragal asked. "We must assume it's in Imperial hands now, and they won't surrender it willingly."

Nathaniel shook his head. "No. Nicholas will have kept it for Venncastle. If we've learnt one thing, it's that any alliance with that school lasts only as long as it serves them."

"Quite right," Daniel agreed. "Venncastle will not surrender a single ounce of power to the Empire without proper payment, and the Empress would not know to be interested in this."

"Indeed, even most of the Association never knew of these

plans," Laban said. "It's bad for morale to have people thinking you might need an escape route. Aside from the key-holders only a few of us have ever known, even within the council."

"Why bother with the key?" Eleanor asked. "Why can't we just break open the third lock?"

"Remember this was designed by people like us," Nathaniel said. "There are safeguards in place."

"What safeguards?"

"The details are lost to history, but we understand there's some mechanism to destroy everything if anyone tries to break the locks. It would be better not to risk it."

"Do you think Nicholas might bargain for the key?" Bill asked. "Do we have anything left that Venncastle wants?"

"We cannot make any bargain with them," Daniel said. "We cannot trust them."

"But the key can't be any use to them," Eleanor said. "So if they'd trade something for it..."

"We cannot trust them to keep to any agreement." Daniel's voice was firm. "We must not give them chance to create a trap for us."

"We should never have let him leave," Bill said. "We should have taken the key from him while we had the chance."

"He left at the first opportunity," Ragal said. "Before the implications had really sunk in."

"We're still in the amnesty, aren't we?"

"Yes, for a few days."

"Well, couldn't we send someone to meet them under cover of the amnesty? We could scout it out, at the very least, and hopefully work out the best line of attack."

"It's not a bad plan," Ragal said. "Any volunteers? It would have to be one of the younger ones. Someone they might trust to come in peace."

"I think Eleanor is the closest we have to a wild card," Laban said, turning to look at her. "No-one really knew which side you'd choose. If you turn yourself over and claim you've changed your mind, maybe you can get close enough to Nicholas to get the key."

"No," Daniel said. "It is too risky."

"I'll do it," she said. Daniel opened his mouth to protest, but she cut him off, sure he was thinking of Raf. But Laban was right: she was the one who could most easily convince them she'd changed her mind. "I'll go – but it could take a while to work my way close enough to Nicholas. You can't wait here."

"No, we'll move what's left of the Association to a temporary hideout. We have to get out of the city... it's probably best to fall back to the Black Wolf Caves, we can defend ourselves there."

"You'll have to tell me where that is so I can find you again."

"It's easy. Follow the waymarkers over the pass towards Bastion, then head east along the ridge for two days, and down into the Ice River Valley. The caves are in the woods on the north bank, a couple of miles further east beyond the point where the ice cascade joins the river."

"Okay, I'll see you there. I'd better go and pack, we don't have that much time."

Nathaniel followed her from the room. "I'll walk with you," he said. "We should talk about the keys."

"What about them?"

"Each key is a weight around its owner's neck." He twisted his own gold chain around one finger; the key itself dangled far below the collar of his shirt. "And not in the literal sense. The moment you get that third key from Nicholas, your life changes. No more risks. You come straight back to us."

"That's what I was going to do."

"Yes – but you don't quite appreciate how much it matters. You have a reputation for being impulsive, but once you have a key you can't get sidetracked by anything else. You can't run off at a tangent just because the world offers you some opportunity that looks too good to miss."

"Surely there are some things that are even more important than the keys?"

"Not to you. While you're carrying a key, your only purpose is to keep it safe. Others can do the other jobs. This becomes your life."

"That sounds a bit dull," she said. "I'm glad it's not for

long."

"Yes, it'll be different for you, of course. We actually need to use the keys this time. For me and Ragal this has been a duty of years."

"Can I see yours? I need to know what I'm looking for."

He pulled it out from beneath his shirt and held it up for her to examine, though he kept the chain looped around his neck. For something so important, it looked very small. It was like no key Eleanor had seen before, with twelve pins arranged in a complex pattern across the head.

"I can't promise you this will help," he said. "Mine and Ragal's are definitely similar, but I've never actually seen the key that Nicholas holds. However, we assume they were all wrought by one locksmith."

"Thanks."

They reached the door to Eleanor's building and Nathaniel broke off to finish some business of his own. "Good luck, Eleanor. May the strongest winds blow in your favour."

She started packing a small bag with the clothes she wanted to take, making a separate pile of things she didn't expect to need. She was almost satisfied with her selections by the time Daniel arrived from the now-finished council meeting. He barged into her room without knocking, causing the door to slam into the wall.

"What were you thinking?" he demanded. "You cannot do this."

"Why not?"

"It is very dangerous. You cannot go."

She sighed. "I never liked you telling me what to do when we were together – what makes you think I'd like it better now?"

"What if I do not trust you to come back?"

"The rest of the council trusts me." She made up a leather roll with all the weapons she wasn't already wearing, stuffed it into the top of her travel bag, and pulled the drawstrings closed. "If you try to stop me, it'll be quite obvious it's personal. I don't really care if you hate me, but don't try to stop me doing my job."

"I am not happy with this."

She ignored him, and progressed to filling her trunk with the clothes she was leaving behind. "Someone needs to take this to the caves when you go," she said. "Will you see to that for me, or are you feeling too petty to be helpful?"

"I will take it."

"Thanks."

"Remember why you are there," he said as he left. "Do not let them tempt you to betray us."

She wanted to scream after him, but there was no point. Instead, she slammed the lid of the trunk closed, and hefted her travel bag onto her shoulder.

Chapter 12

For all the supposed secrecy of the new organisation, the headquarters of the Shadow Corps was easily found. Greg was manning the ostentatious archway which marked their gate, looking uncharacteristically smart in his new uniform. The deep blue jacket had the Imperial crest embroidered on the breast pocket, and the matching trousers were edged with silver piping. He beckoned Eleanor into the guard room as soon as he recognised her and closed the door, bolting it behind them.

"What are you doing here?" He sounded somewhat alarmed.

"We're still in the amnesty, aren't we? I came to see Raf." It was honest, even if it wasn't the whole truth, and he'd easily believe it.

"You shouldn't have come. I know we've got this amnesty, but we've been given lists. Anyone from the old council is 'kill on sight,' if you didn't come straight across with us."

"Regardless of the amnesty?"

"Something like that. You're marked – you can't be seen. And I don't want to have to kill you."

"Don't worry, I wouldn't let you." She smiled to let him know she was teasing, though she felt nothing but cold inside. Would the others be killed before they managed to escape the city? She wished there was some way to send a message, but she'd blow her cover if she tried it. "Seriously, though, if they're not honouring the amnesty then you have to help me out. I made the wrong decision."

"What?"

"The old Association is crumbling, they're fighting each other, there's no sense of direction... I realised I should've come with you in the first place. I didn't think I'd be too late to change my mind."

"Really? Well, Raf will be thrilled when he gets back – you can't imagine how much he misses you."

"Where is he?"

"Off somewhere... working. We don't get told much, that's the one disadvantage to the Shadow Corps over the old ways. It's all a bit military: too much hierarchy, too much interference from the Empress's favourite generals, and they never tell us anything. Anyway, he should be back in a few weeks. He'll be delighted to see you."

A few weeks? Her heart sank; she hoped it wouldn't take that long to achieve her goals here. Still, she couldn't afford to be distracted by personal concerns. "You'll help me, then? I don't know who I need to see."

"Hide in here – don't let anyone in – and I'll see what I can do."

"Thanks Greg. You've probably saved my life." Her gratitude was entirely genuine: at the very least, he'd saved her a fight she wasn't looking for.

He stepped outside and she bolted the door behind him, then took advantage of the time alone to take a look around the guard room. There wasn't a great deal to see; an inventory of equipment, a rota for gate duties (listing a slew of familiar names, mostly the Association's younger defectors), and a couple of maps of the city were pinned to the whitewashed walls. The blue jacket of someone's Shadow Corps uniform hung on the back of the door, there were two plain wooden chairs, and a couple of crossbows and quivers of arrows had been slung in a corner. Other than that, the space was clear and impersonal. She tucked her own bag under one of the chairs and sat down to wait.

The knock at the door made her jump, and suddenly she realised just how vulnerable she was in this dead-end room. There wasn't even a window to escape through if the wrong person chose to force his way in.

"Open up, El, it's me!"

She unlocked the door with her hand on the hilt of her dagger, just in case, but it was indeed Greg and there was no sign of a trap.

"Eleanor!" Ivan was following just behind, and pulled her into a tight embrace as soon as he stepped inside the guard room. "It's true, then? You've finally seen sense?"

"Something like that. Greg was worried I might be too late, though."

"Nah, we're still in amnesty – though I wouldn't recommend going out on your own before everyone knows you've come back to us, if you know what I mean. I wouldn't want you to end up hurting any of my men."

He winked at her, and she suddenly felt sick at what she was about to do. Was this a worse betrayal than the general slaughter that was about to break out? It felt more personal.

"You'll be okay with me, though," he went on. "And of course you're fine to change your mind, how could we refuse? Come on, let's get you kitted out."

He took her arm and led her round the corner to a small cupboard stacked full of folded uniforms.

"You'll need the smallest size, of course, and even then you might need to make some adjustments..." He fished out a pair of trousers and held the waistline level with her waist; the hems trailed on the floor. "Well, these are the smallest we've got, I'm afraid. Not to worry, you can turn them up until you've got time to sew them."

"No tailor here?" she asked, amused at the idea that the Shadow Corps might be less well resourced than the remnants of the Association.

"I'm sure there will be, eventually, but at the moment we're still setting up." He rifled through the piles of linen and passed her a second pair of trousers, three matching shirts, and a cloak in the same shade of blue. "Now, we're going to have to decide what rank to make you. Where d'you think you'd be up to by now if you'd gone military after school?"

"Oh, I don't know. I've never really thought about it."

"Well, have a couple of stars, that's what we gave Raf." He handed her a jacket with two silver stars riveted above the crest; she noted his own had three. "It's probably about right, though I'm sure it won't take you long to get promoted once you find your feet. I assume you've still got all your weapons?"

"Of course."

"Good girl." He clapped her on the back. "I'm glad to see you here, Eleanor, I really am. I knew you were a pragmatist at heart. The dreamers have always picked out a dangerous path for their ideals, but this time more than usual, if you ask me. Come on, you can get changed in the guard room and then I'll show you round. You'll be safer once you're in uniform."

Greg and Ivan waited outside while she changed. As she straightened her jacket, she thought how useful it would be to take these clothes with her when she went back to the caves. A Shadow Corps uniform was likely to be a safe disguise in much of the Empire, and possibly a terrifying one, if the Shadows lived up to the initial whispers of their reputation.

She pinned the cloak around her shoulders, stuffed her own clothes into her pack along with the uniform spares, and went out to see what was what.

"Looking good, El." Greg smiled at her as she emerged into the gatehouse.

"I definitely need to take up these trousers." She'd folded the hems for now, but that wasn't a solution that would hold if she had to do any running or climbing. She felt vulnerable just wearing such ill-fitting clothes.

"Don't worry," Ivan said. "We won't make you do any real work until you've had chance to settle in and sort yourself out. But let me show you the barracks, you can see your room, and we'll have a walk around the training grounds."

"Thanks."

She followed him into the cobbled courtyard, through another arch at the back, and into the low U-shaped building which surrounded the second quadrangle.

"It's not a patch on our Association quarters, I'm afraid. Everything here's a bit military, it's all bunks and barracks and horrible food, but there are enough good people here. We'll make it our own in time."

He hesitated for a moment, then pushed open one of the many identical doors spaced along the corridor.

"Thought so. This room's free – no point worrying about where you're based, they're all the same. Well, except for the commander and his deputies, but they have suites up at the palace."

It was a plain, whitewashed room with a sleeping pallet and

a small trunk. She put her pack on the floor, thankful that she wouldn't have to live in this characterless box for long. However basic the accommodations in the Black Wolf Caves might be, at least it would feel like a home once the Association moved in.

"Who's in charge round here, then?"

"Nicholas is commander. Then almost everyone who was on the council is three-starred, except you youngsters who've got two. Haven't really worked out who gets a single star yet – at the moment, all the others are just foot-soldiers. But, like I said, we haven't really bedded in yet. I'm sure it'll all make a lot more sense when we've been here a while."

"It's going to take a bit of getting used to, that's for certain." She came back into the corridor and closed the door, wondering what features she could use to remember which room was hers. "I'm not used to anyone telling me what to do."

"I'll make sure you're under me," Ivan said. "And I know I can trust you, so I won't be doing that much ordering. You'll get your third star in no time, but I think it's better to start you off with two, then no-one can question that you've earned it."

They took a short tour of the buildings; aside from seemingly-endless corridors of identical cubicles, there was a large dining hall and a gymnasium. The armoury was tucked away in a corner.

"But they're military weapons," Ivan explained. "Not so beautifully crafted as ours, so you'll want to hang on to yours as long as they last. And maybe one day we'll get our smithy back. Harold's the man I'm most disappointed to lose, out of all this."

They looped around and made their way back to the guard room, where Greg was handing over to a youth that Eleanor didn't recognise.

"Did you get a good tour?" Greg asked.

"Yes, thanks. This is going to be very different, isn't it?"

"It's military," he agreed. That seemed to be everyone's favourite word. "Takes a bit of getting used to, but you'll get the hang of it. Should we put your name down for shifts on the gate?"

"No," Ivan said, before Eleanor had chance to guess at an answer. "She's going to be working for me."

"Oh. Oh, well. That's different." Greg turned back to Eleanor. "In that case, we won't. I'm sure Ivan can keep you very busy without any gate duties."

"Any chance of a drink?" Eleanor asked. "I think I could do with a little something."

"A few of us usually go out about now," Greg said. "You're welcome to come."

"Actually, I think you should come with me," Ivan said. "You'll excuse us, won't you, Gregory? I've got a plan."

Greg nodded. "Catch up soon, El."

"Let's go up to the commander's rooms," Ivan said, resting his arm across Eleanor's shoulders and steering her out into the street. "He's got a much more civilized apartment, and I'm sure he'll have spring nectar or wine if you fancy a drop."

"Won't he mind?" she asked. She felt a few cold spots as flakes of snow landed on her nose, but nothing was sticking on the ground yet. She pulled her cloak more tightly closed anyway.

"Not at all. In fact, I'm sure he'll be delighted to hear your news."

Ivan nodded at the guard on the palace gate, who waved them through without a challenge, and led Eleanor into a nearby tower. Nicholas opened the door almost immediately when they knocked.

"Ivan, what a delight. And you've brought... Eleanor? What are you doing here?"

"The girl's seen sense," Ivan said. "I thought you'd like to know."

"Ahhh, I see. Well, that's very welcome news. Come in, sit down. What can I do for you?"

"I'm sure we'd both like to raise a large glass of nectar to the Empress's health," Ivan said, ushering Eleanor ahead of him into the room and taking her cloak from her.

Nicholas returned a moment later with a bottle and three glasses, and sat down before pouring generous measures for each of them.

"So, I see you've already given young Eleanor some stars," he said as he handed one glass across to her and another to Ivan.

"To the Empire," she said, deliberately amending Ivan's suggested toast.

"The Empire," they echoed.

"Two stars," Nicholas continued. "That might be a bit stingy, for such a feisty girl. It'd look good to have a woman in the higher ranks if we're moving into the general assignment process. We're strongly unbalanced as it stands. Anyway, we can discuss that later, but I take it you're here to ask my opinion on where she should be slotted in."

"Actually, she's going to work for me."

"Really?" He stared at Eleanor for a long moment, and she met his gaze steadily, wondering what he was thinking about. "And has Ivan told you what his little area of responsibility is, Eleanor?"

"Not yet."

"Ahhhh. Well, Ivan, don't you think you should enlighten your newest recruit? You can't expect her to work in the dark."

"It's simple enough," Ivan said, and took a large mouthful of his drink before elucidating. "Eliminating the traitors."

It took a moment for her to work out what that meant. "You mean..."

"He means everyone who's stayed with the Association, yes," Nicholas said. "It's a dirty job, but someone's got to do it."

"Anyway, we know Eleanor and Raf make a great team, so I thought I'd assign them together once he gets back."

"That may not be possible. We may have a more important job for your girl. Is she totally reliable?"

"Of course. She's practically one of us."

Again, Eleanor felt her stomach knot up. It was strange to hear them talking as if she wasn't there, and stranger still to hear Ivan praising her when she was plotting to betray them. But she wasn't here to kill 'traitors' – only to get the key. And there was no going back without that.

"Good." He turned back to her. "Now, Eleanor, the most important question: did you tell anyone you were coming here?"

"What?" She was momentarily blindsided by the question. "No, of course not. They wouldn't have let me leave."

"Excellent. The thing is, I think we'll have to ask you to go back. You're the only one of the Shadows who could possibly slip back into the heart of the Association. Yes, Ivan, she definitely needs to work for your division."

"But how can I go back?" She felt her chance to find the key slipping away. "What can I say to them? They'll kill me."

"I'm sure a girl of your calibre can think of a suitable excuse for a short absence. And you'll have your third star the moment you get back here."

Eleanor nodded. These were people who knew how much she enjoyed a challenge; a refusal would destroy her cover immediately. She took another sip of her drink and forced a smile. "Tell me exactly what you need me to do."

"Ivan can fill you in on his strategy later," Nicholas said. "But at the moment we've been working one stroke of luck at a time. We can't mount a full-out assault in the amnesty period, and of course the Association's leaders are being very careful. But they'll have to move eventually – they can't defend the old headquarters if we send in the full weight of the Specials."

"What do you think they'll do?"

"That's what I want you to find out. You were on the council – hasn't the planning started already?"

"It's chaos," she said. "No-one can agree on the most minor of things, let alone a big question like what to do next."

"Well, they know they've got a deadline," Nicholas said. "They must know we'll attack if they don't move."

"So you want me to find out where they go?"

"That, and then some," Ivan said. "We'll need to know every possible weakness of their new base, wherever that is. When we move the armies in, we need to be absolutely prepared. Yes, Nicholas is quite right – you're the secret weapon we've been waiting for."

Eleanor downed what was left of her nectar in one large gulp, and picked up the bottle to refill all their glasses.

"To success," she said, raising her drink and being careful

not to specify whose success she was toasting.

"Success," Ivan echoed. "Welcome home, Ellie."

They lapsed into general chit-chat for a while before Nicholas steered the conversation back to asking about the disputes at the heart of the Association. Eleanor made up some more stories of fighting and general dissatisfaction, gaining a little silent enjoyment from the opportunity to blame Daniel for a couple of the imaginary problems. She hoped that if the Shadows believed the Association was crumbling, they'd be more likely to make dangerous mistakes later.

"I was thinking about what I can say to the others," she said to Ivan as they walked back to the barracks. "If I tell them I came here to spy on you, is there anything I can give them to make them believe me?"

"What are you thinking?"

"Something like the layout of your buildings. I don't think it'll help them much, but at least it'd sound like I've been doing something useful."

"I don't see any problem with that. We're going to destroy them by spring, anyway."

"Okay, great." That would buy her at least a day of plausibly wandering around the new buildings before she needed to go back to the Association, although she'd have to leave before the end of the amnesty. It remained to be seen whether it would be long enough to get the key.

As she lay on her pallet that night, she grasped her pendant with cold fingers and wondered what Raf would do. But, she soon realised, that was obvious. He was doing it. He wasn't the one playing double-agent games. He'd accepted his place in Ivan's division and was already off on some mission to that end. And if she hadn't happened to come across to the Shadows, maybe she'd be his next target.

She flung the pendant across the room. It made a satisfying clattering sound as it bounced off the far wall and onto the flagstones.

Raf was one of 'them' now. The enemy. However much she wanted to persuade herself otherwise, they'd picked different sides, and that was it. That he was off "eliminating the traitors" only highlighted the gulf between them. It was better that he wasn't expected back for a few weeks. At least then she wouldn't be tempted.

She picked the pendant up the next morning. One of the emeralds had fallen from its setting, and it took her a long time searching the floor before she finally found where it had rolled into one of the cracks.

She tucked both pendant and gemstone safely in a corner of her pack; she'd get Harold to mend it later. It would be a shame to waste a beautiful piece of jewellery just because it reminded her of Raf's decision. If nothing else, she could sell it for a small fortune.

She sat with Greg and Hal at breakfast, then went for another walk around the compound, still feeling uncomfortable in her oversized new uniform. By lunchtime she had a good idea of how all the buildings fitted together, but she was no closer to getting the key from wherever Nicholas might have hidden it.

By the next morning, however, she'd got no further – and Ivan came to encourage her to go back to the Association buildings as soon as she could.

"You can leave most of your things here," he said. "Just take whatever weapons you need, leave the rest in your room. And make sure you change out of that uniform."

"Okay." She tried not to sound disappointed; the uniform would have been the most useful thing she could have packed. But since she was returning without the key, she'd have to plan to come back here. This was looking likely to be a very long game.

As she walked back home, she turned the situation over in her mind. Perhaps this could be twisted into an even greater advantage. If the Association could set up a suitably convincing retreat, into a new headquarters with suitably enticing flaws, then perhaps they could draw out the Shadows in force. Meanwhile, she'd have plenty of time to think about how to get the key from Nicholas when she went back to feed him the details. By the time she reached the Association grounds, she was ready to summon the council and lay out her plan.

But there was no-one there to summon.

She checked the dining hall, the council chamber, and a few bedrooms at random. There was little sign the buildings had ever been inhabited. They'd already moved on to the caves, then. Well, that simplified matters.

She ran all the way back to the Shadow Corps headquarters, and banged at Ivan's door.

"Eleanor? I thought you'd left. What's happened?"

"They've gone!" She was breathless from her sprint, and hoped she managed to sound surprised. "I got there, and it's empty. Deserted."

"Shit." He sat at one end of his pallet. "Come in, and shut the door."

She pulled the door until it clicked closed, and stood with her hands clasped behind her back, waiting. Was she about to find out what the military-style response to failure looked like? Ivan just looked sad, and tired.

"Sit down," he said. "And tell me everything."

"I went back to the old buildings, and there's simply no-one there. They've all gone."

"And you've no idea where they might be?"

"No."

"Nick was convinced that you were going to be the solution to all our problems. But you can't be our insider if you can't find them."

"I can start a search," she said. "Some places are more likely than others. But I thought it was best to come back here first and see if anyone had any ideas. You were on the council before I was, and some of the others long before that – if anyone had made fallback plans, someone here must know."

"Of course, you did the right thing. This isn't your fault. We'll talk to Nick, see if he has any ideas before you start from nothing."

They walked up to the commander's suite in silence.

"Let me do the talking," Ivan said as they waited outside. He looked nervous, and Eleanor felt a creeping anxiety herself.

"Bad news, Nick," Ivan said when Nicholas eventually came to the door. "They've gone."

Anger flashed across his face, but it was gone in a moment. "Of course they have," he said. "Would you stay in a place where your enemies know every inch of the grounds? No, we cannot be surprised. It's just unfortunate that they suddenly managed to get organised so quickly."

"I wondered if you knew where they might fall back to," Eleanor said. "Has anyone ever drawn up emergency plans?"

"A plan was made decades ago," he said. "In the earliest days of the Empire, when the Association's elders suspected they might one day be driven underground. Before my time, of course, and well before you were even born. So yes, there were plans."

"Do you know where they've gone, then?" Ivan asked.

"Even if I did, despatching Eleanor there would only give away our knowledge – it's evident they've given up on her. But no, things are never that simple. Our predecessors were far more subtle than that. There's no way the remnants of the Association can have followed through with that old plan, because I hold one of the keys to it."

He reached under his shirt and brought out an intricate silver key which hung from a chain around his neck. Eleanor had to suppress a smile that would have seemed highly inappropriate. But they'd been right: he hadn't handed it over.

"There's a vault in the old silver mines at Flintmoor, you see, locked with three keys. I hold this one on behalf of Venncastle; Nathaniel and Ragal have the others. So they can't have gone there."

"Might they try to break into the vault?" Eleanor asked.

"I suppose it's possible. That would be a fool's errand, though, and I don't rate them as fools."

"No," Ivan agreed. "It would all be much easier if they were."

"What next, then? If we don't know where they've gone."

"They'll turn up," Nicholas said. "And I'm sure Ivan can find plenty of things to occupy you in the meanwhile."

"I'm sure he can." And she was quite sure she'd be occupying herself, trying to work out how to get that key from around his neck. She wouldn't risk an open attack within the palace, though. Not if there was any possibility of succeeding by a subtler method.

"You should take some time to settle in properly," Ivan said as they walked down to the barracks again. "We won't be busy till the traitors dare to raise their heads again."

"Where do you think they've gone?" she asked.

"I don't know."

"But what's your instinct?"

"If it was me... Well, if it was me, I'd make use of Venncastle, but of course they don't have that option. They'll be looking for somewhere with strong defences, though, as a first priority. They want to be sure of surviving while they work out a new strategy."

"And I guess they'll be trying to get that key from Nicholas, one way or another?" She studied his face closely as she spoke but if he suspected anything, he gave nothing away.

"We'll be ready for them if they try anything. Meanwhile, we'll wait and see."

Eleanor was relieved to have a few days without pressure before she was expected to start hunting her Association colleagues, but she found herself no closer to a plan for stealing the key from Nicholas.

She next saw Ivan at lunch a couple of days later, and took a seat beside him. "I take it there's still no sign of the traitors?"

"They've gone well and truly to ground," he said. "We haven't had a hit for days."

"I'm sure you could use that key as bait to tempt them out. If that's the only way they have to learn their own fallback plans, they'd bargain for it, surely."

A smile spread across his face. "I like your thinking. But how could we get a message to the council?"

"Where's the lock that fits that key?" she asked. "Someone must be working on opening that thing, if it's so important."

"Nick knows the way – he said it was near Flintmoor, didn't he?"

"Well, you might find someone there. But you don't have to pass them a secret note – just make as much noise as possible about the fact that you're open to a deal. Someone will bite."

"Are you happy to set this up yourself?"

"Sure. Let me go and see Nicholas first, and then I'll get things moving."

"Thanks."

"Should I keep you up to date?"

"Come back to me if there's anything you need. And let me know when Nick decides you should have your third star."

Eleanor walked across to Nicholas's rooms at the palace, passing through the gatehouse unchallenged. As the only woman so far to wear a Shadow Corps uniform, she was easily recognized.

Nicholas invited her in and supplied her with tea and cake before asking the reason for her visit.

"I had an idea to lure the Association out of hiding," she said. "But I need your help."

He raised an eyebrow. "Oh?"

"I want you to make it known that you're open for offers to sell that key you wear around your neck."

"I can't possibly–"

"You're not listening. I don't want you to sell it, I just want you to arrange a sale. We can bring the armies with us to take care of the rest."

"You think it's enough to bring them to a meeting."

She sipped at her tea. "Precisely."

"How will we make them believe this is real?" he asked. "I wouldn't expect them to trust me."

"It's of no use to you, is it? They must know that. And you can ask a suitably ridiculous price – they'll pay."

"I'm still not sure they'll believe it."

"It doesn't matter if they suspect a trap. If it's the only hope they have, they'll walk into it with their eyes wide open."

"And if they send more people?"

"Assume that they'll send everyone they can spare. Which means more heads above the parapet for us."

He nodded. "You know, this could just work. Have you run it past Ivan?"

"He said I should just get on with it."

"He's probably right. What do you need me to do?"

"Not much. I'll start putting the word about. Don't deny it too strenuously if anyone approaches you directly, but don't agree anything, either."

"Okay."

"I'll tell you if we get any word back – and I'll probably need you to come along to whatever meeting we agree."

"I'm the bait in the trap?" He laughed and poured more tea. "That's fine, just let me know."

"The key is the bait," Eleanor said. "You're just there to see it safely carried, and to give the attack signal."

Chapter 13

Eleanor walked out into the city without a clear idea of where she was going. She couldn't send a messenger to the Black Wolf Caves without betraying the Association's temporary headquarters – as well as exposing her own precarious position. But somehow she needed to make sure they saw her messages... and unless an idea struck soon, she'd be relying on the exact plan she'd proposed to Ivan and Nicholas. Make enough noise, and someone would crawl out of the woodwork. She only had to hope her colleagues were smart enough not only to see the trap, but to spot her influence in setting it up.

She'd chosen to go out in her ordinary clothes this time, preferring to forgo the fearful respect that the Shadow Corps uniform engendered. It was a strange feeling after the anonymity of the Association's operations, and not entirely pleasant. Besides, today she needed to whisper quietly into the ears of strangers.

She started in the market, but Almont's neat rows of stalls were all carefully staffed by Imperial assignees, and there was no evidence of any additional interests. No-one looked like they'd care about whether the Association could get their third key, even if there was profit in it: smugglers kept their trade well beyond the Imperial capital.

It was early in the day for barflies but she was running short of other ideas, so she made her way to a well-known rebel tavern in the outer streets of the Market Quarter. The proprietor had always been careful to stay on the right side of the law, but everyone knew his sympathies. Her heart thumped as she pushed the door open; even without her uniform she was a distinctive figure, and there was always a chance that someone who'd seen her over the past few days would recognise her as one of the Shadows.

Three men were drinking in a corner, and Eleanor watched them as she waited for the barman to fill her a tankard of frothy beer. They were speaking in hushed tones and she struggled to pick out more than a couple of words. Once she'd paid for her drink she stepped across to join them.

"May I?" she asked, indicating a spare seat at their table.

The nearest man eyed her suspiciously. "Is it wise to be drinking so far from home?"

She recognised the phrase as one of the traditional rebel challenges, and met it with the expected response: "Are we not safe to pass the time wherever we have friends?"

He nodded and pulled the chair out for her. She sat and sipped her beer in silence, wondering if they'd trust her enough to continue their business, but their conversation had turned to banalities.

"I heard a rumour," she said at last. "And I was hoping you could tell me if there's any truth in it."

"What kind of rumour?" asked the skinny, grey-haired man who'd given the test.

"I heard that the assassins have joined the rebel cause now, and that they might be in the market for a certain key."

"What's that to you?" The man who interrupted was the youngest of the three, and he gripped the edge of the table as he spoke.

"Just a passing interest," Eleanor said. "Because I also heard of an old man at the palace who's looking to supplement his Imperial stipend with a sale. I wondered if there was scope for a little profit, if I could arrange a deal."

"There's no deals to be made between honest men and Imperial chattels," the young man said, leaning back in his chair. "So it's probably time you were moving on."

"Calm, Petor." The older man rested his hand lightly on the youth's shoulder. "Let the girl finish her drink."

The third man remained silent, head bent towards the table, his face hidden under the folds of his hood.

Eleanor took another sip of her beer, and watched them.

"Well, if you do happen to hear of any interest, you could always leave me a message at the Old Barrel Yard," she said, naming another tavern with rebel leanings. "I won't trouble you further."

171

She left without another word and turned into the alleys behind the inn. This first attempt hadn't felt like a success, but she knew better than to expect immediate feedback. She'd go and put the word out in a couple more places, but after that, it was a waiting game. The rumour mill was sure to do its work, given enough time.

She stopped to talk to a couple of beggars, passing out coins in exchange for promises of assistance, then went to investigate the early clientele of the Old Barrel Yard.

The tavern was empty, so Eleanor sat at the bar and addressed herself to the landlord. "I'd like a little something to warm me up," she said. "What do you recommend?"

"We've a good spiced ale," he said. "We simmer it with apples and sugar, a few imported spices, and a dash of strong spirits. Does that sound like it might be to your tastes?"

"I'll try it," she said, though she'd never heard of anything quite like that before.

He filled a tankard for her and she wrapped her cold fingers around the sides, inhaling the highly fragranced steam. The spices caught at her throat and made her cough, but the drink was sweet and warm and soothing.

"Good choice," she said. "Thanks."

She settled down to wait, hoping for more patrons to fill the tavern. By the time she swallowed the last gritty dregs from the bottom of her tankard, a few small groups had gathered around the room. She put her tankard back on the bar, picked out one group of young rebels, and addressed them in a deliberately loud whisper as she passed: "I'm looking for a contact from the exiled Association," she said.

"Association?"

"The assassins. I expect there's a lot of money in it if you can help me."

She left them to think about it, and strode back to the Shadows.

"Hold!"

The youth who challenged her at the gatehouse was someone she didn't recognise, though he wore the Shadow Corps uniform. He stepped in front of her with his sword at the ready.

"Who are you?"

"Eleanor." She held out her wrist so he could read her identity from her name bangle. "I work here."

He shook his head. "I don't know you, sorry. And you're not even in uniform."

"I work for Ivan," she said. "And for obvious reasons, I left my uniform in my room. Now, are you going to get out of my way?"

"Sorry," he repeated. "Can't be too careful these days. The rebels are getting restless, as you'd know if you worked for Ivan."

"Well, send for him, he'll vouch for me," she said.

"No, I can't do that. How do I know this isn't a trick to get at him?"

Eleanor was trying to think of a suitable argument when Jorge walked past, caught sight of the guard's unsheathed blade, and came to see what was happening.

"Is there a problem?" he asked.

"Jorge, tell this kid you know me," Eleanor said, relieved to see a familiar face.

"Of course I know her," Jorge said. "She's a filthy traitor – and we're not under amnesty any more."

"Didn't Ivan tell you? I'm in the Shadows now, in his unit."

"Lying isn't going to save you," Jorge said, drawing his own dagger.

"Listen, there are loads of people who'll tell you – Ivan, Greg, even Nicholas. I've just been out setting something up, but I've been living here for weeks."

She slid knives from both wrist sheaths as she spoke, but she knew she was setting herself up for disaster. Even if she could bring both men down without attracting anyone else to join them, she'd have trouble convincing the Shadows afterwards that it had been their mistake and not her treachery at work. And being labelled a traitor would make for a very short life expectancy in this company.

She turned and ran into the street. The young guard couldn't desert his post, and she knew she could outpace Jorge with ease. She sprinted round to the palace gatehouse, hoping against hope that there she might find a guard who knew her.

"I'm here to see Nicholas," she said to the girl behind the desk, who'd seen her a couple of times before. "He won't mind if I go straight up, will he?"

As she jogged to the tower without waiting for an answer, she heard Jorge skidding to a halt in the gatehouse. And by the time Nicholas answered his door, she could hear footsteps pounding on the stairs below.

"It sounds like a herd of cattle down there," Nicholas said as he waved her inside.

"Oh, that's just Jorge," she said. "He didn't want to let me in to the barracks, and when I headed here he followed me."

"Jorge? But why?"

"I have no idea." She sat and poured herself a glass of spring nectar. "Anyway, I've had a good day, I think. Drinking strange beer and leaking rumours all over town."

Before Nicholas could reply, there was a pounding at the door.

"Jorge, what is the matter?" Nicholas demanded as he opened it. "You're making a lot of noise."

"I'm hunting a traitor," he said. "That Eleanor dared to show her face again, and then she had the nerve to..."

"Eleanor works for me," Nicholas said, cutting him off. He threw the door wide open, and Eleanor waved across the room. "She's got a very important post under Ivan, so I'd prefer it if you didn't try to kill her."

Jorge looked flustered, then stormed off without another word, stomping down the stairs again.

"Sorry about that," Eleanor said. "I didn't want to have to fight him to get to my room, so it seemed easiest to just come here."

"It's always good to see you," Nicholas said. "And I really would like to hear about your day. Do you think you've found a buyer for me?"

"Not yet, but have patience. It's started. I expect it to take a few days to reach the right ears."

Eleanor made a habit of passing through the Old Barrel Yard daily after that, gradually getting to know a few friendly faces, and exchanging pleasantries with the landlord, whose name turned out to be Ade. She didn't give her own name, and he was smart enough never to ask. She didn't have to wait very long for her plan to bear fruit: it was only four days later, as she was sitting and shivering over her now-regular tankard of spiced ale, that Ade came over and sat at an empty seat across from her.

"Someone was in here asking about you, miss," he said.

"Oh?"

"Young chap. Dark skinned, lanky, wouldn't give a name. One of those assassin types, if you ask me."

Eleanor made what she hoped was a noncommittal noise in the back of her throat, and took another mouthful of her drink.

"I didn't tell him nothing, mind. You don't run a place like this for long if you're in the habit of snitching on your customers. But he said he'd be back tomorrow, and something about making a deal, if you were interested."

Eleanor nodded her thanks. If she'd learnt one thing about the rebel mentality, it was that she could hide behind silence. Keeping your own counsel was simply good sense where the rebel groups were concerned, and that suited her purposes.

Ade retreated to his chair behind the bar, and Eleanor sat in silence until she finished her drink. The rest of the tavern was still quiet at this hour.

She went to leave, then turned back to the bar as if an idea had struck.

"I'll leave that lad a message," she said. "Just in case he calls again. Tell him that if he puts fifty dollars down with you as a mark of his good faith, then I'll give him a meeting place and time."

"Fifty dollars."

"Ten percent for you," Eleanor said. "What he wants to buy is worth ten times that much, so if he's serious, he won't even hesitate."

"Fifty dollars," Ade repeated, and she could tell he was wondering what sort of business he was involving himself in. "I'll tell him."

175

When she called back the following day, her fifty dollars was waiting.

"Same lad?" she asked as she split off five for Ade. He nodded, and she wondered who it could have been. None of the Association would ever have exposed themselves with such an elementary mistake, so presumably they'd found themselves a runner amongst the younger rebels.

"I told him to come back tomorrow," Ade said. "So you can hold up your end of the bargain."

"Tomorrow?"

"That feels quite long enough to wait for something he's already paid fifty dollars for."

Eleanor sighed. She'd hoped to have longer to consult with Nicholas, Ivan, and the others, but the landlord seemed determined to ensure both sides of the deal were completed as soon as possible. "Okay," she said. "Tell him to come alone to the fountain in the Grand Square, at sunset on the night of the full moon. He'll need to come prepared to negotiate a price, a date, and conditions for the exchange. Do you need me to write any of that down?"

"D'you really think I can't remember a few words?"

She shrugged, and picked up her ale. "That's fine, then. Thanks for all your help."

When she got back to the Shadow headquarters, Eleanor went straight to Ivan's room.

"Shall we talk over dinner?" he said when he saw her. "I'm almost getting used to the food here, but we could go out if you prefer."

"Does Nicholas have a better chef?" she asked. "Because I think he might be interested in the latest developments, and we need to finalise our plan."

Ivan smiled. "I always knew you were a smart girl. Yes, the palace chef is much better – come in for a drink, and I'll send one of the kids round to let him know to expect us."

Once he'd dispatched a young Shadow with a message to Nicholas, he poured two large glasses of wine and sat beside Eleanor on the pallet. "Sounds like it's all going well, then?"

"We're getting close," she said. "I'm meeting their boy – or whoever else they send to negotiate – on the full moon."

"And then?"

"Then we organise the exchange, and make sure we're ready for them."

"Good work. Nicholas will be pleased."

"I hope so." She swallowed the last mouthful of her wine. "Shall we go and find out?"

The palace chef was not only good but speedy, and their first course was already waiting on the table in Nicholas's room when they arrived. They sat down to eat straight away and Eleanor kept quiet throughout the meal, allowing Ivan and Nicholas to fill the conversation with meaningless gossip from Venncastle. It was only as they began their dessert that Nicholas asked the reason for the sudden visit.

"Eleanor pointed out that you had a better chef than down in the barracks," Ivan said.

"Well, of course, and you're very welcome. But I suspect you had another reason."

"We're getting close to our targets," Eleanor said. "I had my first bite yesterday, and I'm meeting with their representative on the night of the full moon."

"Do you need backup for that meeting?" Nicholas asked.

"No, I'll make sure he's alone before I show myself," Eleanor said. "And they wouldn't risk playing games with this – it's only a preliminary meeting, and the prize we're dangling in front of them is worth much more than any satisfaction they might get from trying to slit my throat."

"Well, just shout if you want anyone else to come along."

"I'll be fine, and it'll be a short meeting. My goals are just to check it's really one of their people rather than someone looking to make a few quick dollars, and then to arrange the details of our sale."

"And then you'll need me," Nicholas said. "I see."

"Only if you want to be there. If you'd prefer not to take the risk, I'm sure Ivan or I would take the key and play bait."

Nicholas put down his spoon and leaned across the table towards Eleanor. "You've never had anything like this key to take care of," he said. "So I wouldn't expect you to understand. But I was given this responsibility, and until I'm too old and have to hand it on, it's my duty. This is one job no-one can take on for me."

"Well if that's how it is, then yes, I'll need you. Do you have any preferences for dates?"

"The new moon would give us the best cover of darkness," Ivan said. "That gives us an advantage in ambush, especially if we pick a place we know well."

"With that much notice they'll try and arrange an ambush themselves," Nicholas said. "You can't give them two weeks to think about the location. No, if we're arranging this on the full moon, we can't give them more than a couple of nights to think."

"We don't have to give them a meeting place yet," Eleanor said. "We can give them a date, some rules, and directions for how they can find more information nearer the time. That way we can keep the location up our sleeve until the last moment."

"I'll look into a suitable location," Ivan said. "Since I'll be in charge of the men on the ground."

"Okay," Nicholas agreed. "Eleanor, what else do you need for your meeting?"

"I need to set a price, but that's not really important. I suggest we demand some fairly basic rules for the meeting – their man has to come alone, we'll show him the key, and then he has to count out his money before we hand it over. The sort of things we'd insist on if this were real. In practice, we won't get that far."

"No, quite. So that sounds fine."

"And I need to know where we can send them to get the next message, on the day. I think that's all for now."

"Where do you think you'll set this up?" Nicholas asked Ivan.

"Not in the city," Ivan said. "Maybe out in the pines – there are a couple of possible spots, but I'll need to head out there to check."

"I'll come with you," Eleanor said. "Unless it clashes with my negotiating meeting."

"We can take a trip tomorrow," Ivan said. "Then you'll definitely be back in plenty of time."

"If you're thinking of that side of town, then you can probably set up the preliminary meeting for the old market square," Nicholas said. "Does that sound okay, Eleanor?"

"That works for me. I think I'm ready, then."

The next morning Ivan and Eleanor took a pair of horses and rode north, beyond the city limits and into the old pine forest. Ivan led the way along well-worn tracks until they came to a small clearing.

"This was one of my options," he said as he dismounted and tied his horse to a nearby tree.

Eleanor glanced around, but she couldn't see much through the dense firs. That, she supposed, was the point.

"So... what? They'll come here to make the trade, and we'll lurk between the trees?"

"Come with me," he said, pushing ice-frosted branches aside to clear a path. "And I'll show you."

The young man was already standing at the corner of the fountain, glancing nervously around the square, when Eleanor arrived across the rooftops. She didn't recognise him, but from the descriptions Ade had given, she was fairly sure it was the same youth who'd paid her fifty dollar demand. She watched as he paced and shivered until she satisfied herself that he wasn't making contact with any hidden allies, and then she dropped into a side street and walked slowly across the square.

"Cold night, isn't it?" she said. "I hope you're not kept waiting much longer."

He turned and studied her. "For a moment there, I thought you'd taken the money and run," he said. "It all seemed a bit too good to be true."

"Well, thanks for coming."

"After paying that much for the privilege of meeting you? I think my friends would be very unhappy if I didn't follow this through."

"And who are your friends?" she asked.

"What's it to you?"

"I need to know who I'm dealing with."

"They didn't want to show themselves," he said. "So I don't think they'd like me to give you any more details."

"Tell me who you talked to and where you met them. You're not the customer I expected, so I need you to convince me this is real. Otherwise I'll have to go back and wait for the next buyer to contact me. I'm not interested in dealing with middle-men."

"I spend a lot of time in Almont's rebel taverns, and your story's been going around. One lad was very interested, but he didn't want to risk showing his face to your people."

She thought for a moment, and took a guess. "A young, dark-haired lad, skinny build, and a little taller than me?"

"I don't think I should tell you," the youth said, but his eyes gave him away. And Mikhail had always known Almont well; he was the obvious choice for someone to stay behind in the city.

"Did he give you authority to agree a price?"

"He gave me a limit."

"Which was...?"

The youth shook his head. "I'm not that stupid. I'll tell you if you hit it, not before."

"Okay. First, my seller has a few rules. You'll make your purchase on the night of the new moon. Whoever comes for the key has to come alone. He'll meet me in the old market square and I'll give him the location for the trade. Payment in gemstones, which the seller will check before handing over the key."

"And the seller will also be alone?"

"Of course," she lied.

Again she wished she could send a clearer message to her Association colleagues, but she couldn't risk trusting this unknown. If Mikhail had only come in person, she might have dared to speak a few words... but naturally, Mikhail wasn't stupid enough to expose himself.

She finished the meeting off quickly, and with precious little interest in the numbers that she fired back and forth with the Association's young agent. She'd started stupidly high, but since the number was purely academic, she couldn't force herself to care. It just had to be high enough to make sure they took her seriously.

Chapter 14

She packed her bag two days before the new moon; she couldn't take luggage to the ambush, but she'd hardly be able to come back for her things after everyone had seen where her loyalties really lay. She considered trusting it to the safekeeping of the Old Barrel Yard, but Ade still suspected her of being some kind of Imperial lackey and she didn't want to imagine what he'd make of her array of weaponry and spare Shadow Corps uniforms. In the end, she settled for lashing the bag to a high chimney in the Market Quarter. It wasn't likely that anyone would be bothering to creep over rooftops in this part of town, and anyone who did would probably have other things on their mind.

On the night of the ambush, she sent Greg to the old market square for the first stage of the meeting. Eleanor crouched between the trees with a group of the younger Shadows, watching as snow drifted down into the clearing and hoping it wouldn't cover the ground enough to highlight their tracks. Despite the agreement that the Association's negotiator would come alone, no-one expected that arrangement to be honoured. She doubted that anyone on either side was naïve enough to assume this could pass off without some degree of betrayal and double-dealing, and she could only hope she'd been right in her assessment of their relative strengths. At least the Association knew that Eleanor was working for them within the Shadow Corps.

As for the Shadows, tonight they were backed up by soldiers from the Military Special Corps but they didn't have much experience of directing a military operation, and as a unit they were still very new. Even those who knew each other well from their Association days were having to learn to adapt to their new militaristic structure, and so far they simply didn't have a proper training programme in place for the younger recruits they'd been assigned.

Eleanor studied the faces of the kids who knelt beside her, and she almost felt sorry for what they were about to witness. So far they'd seen only gate duty, and unlike the Association's defectors they had no idea what they were getting into. Their only crime had been to accept their assignments; if she'd been given the Special Corps position she'd dreamed of, she could be on the other side of the fence right now.

She realised with a start that this was it, though it would be a footnote – if it even merited that – in the annals of history. This was the first small battle in the war they all knew was coming. And wars didn't stop to care about whether the soldiers had been fully conscious in choosing their sides.

Nicholas walked out into the clearing, brushed the dead leaves from a tree stump, and sat down to wait. He glanced up towards where Eleanor and the others were hiding and winked. She hoped he was just acting from what he knew of the plans, and where he expected her to be hiding; he shouldn't be able to see them from down there, though they could look down on him from between the branches.

As the sun dipped beneath the horizon, Eleanor wondered whether the Association would have sent their own man to the old market square, or whether the young rebel was still running their errands for them. She hoped they'd understood the importance of sending more than a sacrificial messenger along to this meeting – but she trusted her colleagues to spot the opportunity she'd engineered for them.

It grew gradually colder as they waited, and the flurries of snow became steadily more frequent. Eleanor was still wearing her Shadow Corps uniform but she knew she couldn't fight in a long cloak, so she was having to make do with what little warmth her jacket afforded.

Eventually, Don stepped out from between the trees. As per the instructions, he'd come this far alone, but Eleanor wondered who else was creeping through the woods. There was certainly no way a man of his standing would have come here unprotected: if the Association had been intending a sacrifice, they would have sent someone less important.

Don and Nicholas regarded one another across a distance of

a few yards, not even stepping forwards to shake hands, two men with a long and not entirely happy history.

"I was surprised to get this message," Don said. "We weren't expecting you to be interested in a trade."

"Everyone has his price," Nicholas said. "And by all accounts there's money in this for the Association, so we're only splitting the profits. It'd be a shame for it all to go to waste."

"I thought the Empire would have seen to your needs. You've a good position in the new organisation, haven't you?"

"I have my Imperial stipend, of course, but I miss our old lifestyle. I need a little private money."

"Well, this should certainly make you more than comfortable." Don reached inside his cloak and pulled out a small purse. "Eight hundred dollars in diamonds and firestones, as our representatives agreed."

Nicholas nodded, and Eleanor reacted instantly to the signal. She spun on her heel and slashed with twin daggers, sending the bodies of the two nearest Shadows falling to the ground. She sheathed the knives and flung a pair of stars at the other two as they turned in surprise.

"Sorry," she whispered as they crumpled. "It's nothing personal."

They died silently, and she had a moment to consider her position as she cleaned the blood from her weapons. She crawled to the overhang and looked down to where several of the others were fighting. Dozens of Shadows and Association men had emerged, and it looked like an even match.

She hesitated. If she could keep out of the fight there was a chance of maintaining her position in the Shadows; she'd come to realise that being in the heart of Ivan's operations was a valuable position. This one catastrophe could probably be forgiven so long as the Association left a handful of survivors. It wasn't as if she'd actually colluded with her colleagues; everything she'd arranged had been agreed with Ivan and Nick. She looked back at the bodies – admittedly the sudden death of the four young Shadows hadn't been part of the plan they'd agreed. But given how easily they'd gone down, it didn't look like they would have contributed a great deal to the battle – if she hadn't killed them, it would only have been someone else's job.

As she watched, though, a number of the Special Corps soldiers appeared from between the trees. That changed the balance; suddenly the Association were fighting for their lives, and she knew she had to join them. There wouldn't be much point surviving as a spy for an organisation that was about to be decimated.

She slid down the slope and flung herself into the fray, hoping her Shadow Corps uniform would be enough to protect her from the Imperial forces – for a moment, at least – without confusing her Association allies too much.

As she attacked a pair of Specials she caught sight of Nicholas from the corner of her eye. He was duelling with Mikhail, towering over his shorter opponent and gradually gaining ground as they exchanged blows. Then a knife sailed in from the side, and Nicholas dropped. Mikhail moved towards the body but he was kept occupied first by a girl from the Specials, and then by Jorge who was clearly relishing the opportunity to fight his old rivals for real. Eleanor brought down one of her opponents, blocked another thrust from the other, and wished she could get across to the key. She stepped back and sideways, turning so that Nicholas's body was more clearly in her sights as she fought. At least she'd see if anyone else got to him first.

As her stiletto slashed the throat of her opponent, Eleanor saw Mikhail from the corner of her eye, falling to the ground as Jorge bludgeoned him. She leapt over bodies and pushed her way past a couple of fights to get a clear shot, and pulled four stars from her belt. The first tore into Jorge's throat, leaving the others somewhat redundant, but she was furious enough to just keep throwing. She'd felt a pang of guilt for steering Nicholas into a death trap, but part of her thought that Jorge had had this coming for a long time. She felt no remorse as she turned from his crumpled body.

Once the remaining Shadows and Specials were either routed or killed, she ran to Nicholas's corpse and bent over to snap the chain from around his neck. She pulled the key gently out from beneath his shirt.

"Got it," she said, holding her arm aloft in triumph. The others were busy searching the field, looting whatever cash and weapons they found. One or two even stripped Shadow Corps uniforms from the bodies: each suit was potentially a valuable disguise, if the tears could be sewn up neatly and the blood stains washed out. In any case, they were too preoccupied to notice Eleanor's jubilant announcement.

As she tucked the key safely inside the pouch at her waist, Nathaniel's words echoed in her memory. She was a key-holder now. She had responsibilities – and she wished she hadn't unthinkingly broken the chain when she could have used it herself. She got to her feet, brushing the dirt and leaves and blood from her knees. It hadn't been an easy victory and they had a few Association bodies to gather, but her role was to get home as fast as possible. The others were more than capable of clearing up by themselves.

Safely back at the caves, Eleanor dug out Nicholas's key and placed it on the table next to the other two – then stopped, frozen in surprise and horror. She hadn't really looked at it in the forest, but here it was obvious. It was a completely different design.

"Bastard!" she muttered. "That bastard. He was carrying the wrong key."

At some point when she wasn't looking, Nicholas and Ivan had changed her plan. Ragal picked up his own key and the new one, holding them side by side.

"Are you saying this isn't the third key, after all?"

"Yes. Nicholas showed me his key in his office – it was clearly the same design as these two." She picked up Nathaniel's key from the table. "Just with these pins spaced a bit wider, this one up a bit..."

"Then we have failed." Ragal looked even older than usual. "We won't get a second chance."

Eleanor was still studying Nathaniel's key. She turned it slowly in her hand, squinting at the head, considering every detail.

"Wait," she said. "Let me have that back a moment." She held her hand out to Ragal for the second one.

"What is it?" he asked as he placed it into her palm.

"I have an idea." She held the two keys side by side, looking from one to the other, and smiled. "I think I can do this. Now, I just need Harold."

The others looked confused, but she offered no explanation before pocketing the keys and almost running to the makeshift smithy. Harold had set up his workshop in a high-roofed cave, and was engraving the hilt of a small curved dagger when she came in. He looked up as she approached.

"I love that you still care about the details, even in days like these," she said. "Really. But I think I'm going to need to divert your efforts for a time."

"Oh?" He laid the dagger down on his worktop. "Wait a moment, I've got something for you first."

He reached into one of the pockets of his leather apron and brought out a small silver object.

"Young Raf gave me a sketch and asked me to make this up. Now, what can I do for you?"

Eleanor took the pendant and stared at it, speechless. She wasn't sure she'd be able to tell it apart from the original if she held them side by side, except for the slightly sharpened point that would make the bottom of this one into a lethal weapon just as soon as she filled it with an appropriate poison.

"Thank you," she said at last. "When did he possibly have time..?"

"He came to see me just as he was leaving for the Shadows. Said you'd want me to do this one thing before I gave up my smithy."

"Unbelievable." She tucked it safely inside her coin purse and brought out one of the keys. "Now, back to business. If I asked you to make a copy of this, that'd be so easy as to be boring, wouldn't it?"

"It'd be easy enough to make a moulding, yes."

"Well, I'd hate to bore you." She pulled the second key from her pocket. "What I need is a third key, that happens to be similar to these two."

"Similar?"

"Yeah, I need this middle pin brought into line with this left one," – she held the keys side by side and pointed as she spoke – "and this second pin somewhere to the right, and this..."

Harold interrupted her: "Are these what I think they are?"

"If you think they're the keys to our fallback plans, then yes."

"You've seen the third key."

She nodded.

"And you want me to make a copy, based on your memories of its shape."

"Yes."

"And you know that if we get this wrong..."

"I know. We can't afford a mistake."

"Okay." He reached across and took both the keys from her hands. "Let's get to work."

He pulled a ball of soft clay from his bag and broke it into three chunks. He made one deep impression with each of the keys, then turned back to Eleanor, kneading the third lump of clay in his fingers.

"Now you're going to talk me through this one pin at a time. Are there any that are in exactly the same place as pins from the other two keys?"

"I'm afraid not."

"Start from the top, then."

"Okay. We'll need those two closer together – so that left one lines up here, and the right one just here." She pointed with the tip of her littlest finger, but still couldn't get enough precision. She thought for a moment before pulling a hairpin from her head. "Hang on, let's try that again. This line *here*, and then *here*."

Harold nodded and made two small, careful pin pricks in his clay, then held up both other keys in turn to compare the alignment of the marks to Eleanor's description.

"The next one's more complicated," she said. "It was a pin the size of this one, at the bottom, but up here. No, not quite where that one is, just a fraction further right."

The negotiation of each pin – size, position, angle – was a long and painful process, but eventually Harold had etched a plan of the key into the surface of his clay.

"And what about depth?" he asked. "They're all different depths, look."

She examined the jagged pattern of the other two keys. "Give me a moment to think," she said. "I didn't really have that long to study it."

"Take as long as you need. I'm going to make up wax models of these other two."

He took his two clay imprints, poured molten wax into the holes, and set them aside to harden while he continued his engraving. Eleanor sat with her eyes closed, visualising the moment when Nicholas had shown her the key. Every so often she opened her eyes to check something against one of the two keys on the table in front of her.

When the wax had solidified Harold broke the clay away from the moulds, using first his fingernail and then a slim file to scrape fragments of clay from between the pins of the wax keys.

"One more time," he said. "If you could remind me which of these other pins corresponds to each of these marks I've made. And then, the depths."

Eleanor started to repeat herself, and then stopped short. "Wait. We're doing this all wrong."

"What do you mean?"

"Whoever created these keys wasn't quite as smart as we've been giving him credit for. I don't need to remember the depths and the settings. You don't need to trust my memory, there's a pattern here."

Harold squinted at the two keys. "A pattern? I can see they're the same style, of course, but I don't see any pattern."

"It's complicated. I never could have worked it out if I hadn't seen all three parts." She struggled to believe it herself, it was such a convoluted series of transformations. But as she checked each pin, the mapping held. "Whoever made this, he's... he's like Daniel. Obsessed with symmetry and logic and neatness. He couldn't make three keys and just make them different, even though they needed to be distinct. He had to do something that would make a kind of sense if you looked at all three together."

"Okay, we're going to try this a couple of different ways," Harold said. "We'll do one just as you described it to me, and one by following this pattern. And if we get the same result, we might yet dare to trust it."

"Are you sure it'll work?" Gerald said when she'd presented her results to the council. "If it's even slightly imperfect, we could destroy the vault."

"We won't do better," Eleanor said. "This is Harold's finest work."

"And the days are passing," Ragal said. "If we hesitate too long, they will send someone to destroy it all regardless."

Eleanor pushed the key towards the middle of the table. "So who wants to take it?"

"You got us our third key," Don said. "You should be the one to go."

"What about the original key holders? Ragal and Nathaniel have been guarding this secret for years."

Ragal shook his head. "I'm getting a little too old for this kind of nonsense. I'll be quite happy if you just come home with news of a new headquarters."

"Nathaniel?"

"He's right. This is a job for younger men – and women. If you'd like to go, you've earned the right."

"I'll need to take someone with me," she said. "Or preferably two. I'd put money on the Shadows having some presence at the vaults."

"Who do you want?"

"I'll take Sebastien." She thought for a moment. "Who else isn't too busy right now?"

"Mack's already there to keep an eye on the vault. You could pick him up when you arrive."

"Good thinking," Eleanor nodded. "We know they work well together. I'll tell Sebastien to be ready to leave in the morning."

They got up before daybreak and rode west towards the Flintmoor mines, stopping only for a quick lunch and to give their horses chance to drink from a nearby stream. By nightfall they estimated they'd made almost half of the distance. They pitched their tents away from the road and lit a small fire to roast a couple of rabbits for dinner.

The next evening, having ridden their horses to the point of exhaustion, they came within walking distance of the mines.

"Let's tie up here," Eleanor said, picking a spot from which the horses could reach both grass and water. "We have to assume we've got enemies here, and we'll draw less attention if we go by foot."

They walked a little further before making camp for the night, and Mack found them while they were cooking breakfast the next morning.

"We were about to come looking for you," Eleanor said. "We've got a job to do."

"Did you get the third key?"

She hesitated, wondering how much she should tell them. "Sort of."

"What's that supposed to mean?" Sebastien asked. "I thought we'd come out here to open the vault?"

"And that's exactly what we're going to do. It'll be fine, Harold's good at what he does."

"What?"

"We've got a very careful replica of the third key. It'll be fine."

Mack and Sebastien exchanged glances, but they knew better than to question her.

At the vault, she gave them each one of the real keys while she slid Harold's reconstruction into the third keyhole. For the thousandth time she questioned whether her descriptions had been accurate enough, whether the pattern was more than a figment of her imagination, and whether Harold's reconstruction held to the necessary level of perfection in its detail... but it was too late for second thoughts.

"On the count of three," she said, turning the key just enough to check she'd lined it up in the lock.

"One."

Sebastien's fingers tensed.

"Two."

Mack shuffled a little closer to the door, positioning himself ready.

"Three."

As she said the final word they each turned their keys, watching one another's hands to ensure that their movements were synchronised. After a prolonged and steady turn, they felt the locks click under their fingers.

Eleanor realised she'd been holding her breath, and exhaled slowly. The world hadn't ended. Nothing had exploded or vanished or broken. She pulled the door towards them, and it creaked on rusty hinges that hadn't been opened in generations. Even with a squirt of oil, the movement was still stiff.

The inside of the vault was lined in thick metal sheeting, but otherwise unimpressive. For a moment as they looked through the door, Eleanor wondered if they'd come too late. Had someone already removed the critical plans? And what of all the money they were expecting to inherit? The vault would have been big enough for all three of them to stand comfortably inside, yet it was empty aside from one small, flat box on the floor.

She picked up the box and tried to lift the lid, but it wouldn't budge.

"Puzzle box," she said, slipping it into her bag. "Come on, let's get back to camp, we can open it more safely there."

"Do you really think anyone's going to bother attacking us here?" Mack asked.

"You've been watching this spot since we realised it mattered – don't you give the Shadows credit to have done likewise?"

"I haven't seen anyone."

"I'd like to believe they wouldn't have seen you."

He nodded. "Okay, let's go back to the camp."

They closed the vault carefully and scuffed the ground to disguise the marks they'd made in opening it. If they hadn't been seen already, they didn't want to give themselves away by leaving careless tracks.

Eleanor left the others building the evening's fire and sat alone in her tent with the box. She slid the pieces of the puzzle gradually back and forth until at last the box popped open. The parchment inside was old and brittle, but the ink was still bright and clear. She turned it around until the map made sense to her; it showed a few streets in a suburb of Almont, not a part of the city she knew well. One house was highlighted.

She stuck her head out of the tent and called the others across from the fire pit.

"This is really strange," she said, smoothing it out on the ground. "It's back in town."

"That's just a house," Mack said.

"Maybe there's a tunnel or something?" Sebastien suggested. "Like the route from the fountain into the old headquarters."

"We'll start back tomorrow and have a look," Eleanor said. "For now, let's think about food and sleep."

There was no question that this was the place the plans described, but they'd all expected to find something more impressive at the end of the trail. Something more in keeping with their established traditions and accumulated wealth. For all that the Empire had been funding the Association over the past three generations, they knew that they'd had no shortage of money in earlier days. This cottage, squished between its neighbours, didn't look like a secret headquarters to be proud of.

"It's a bit small," Mack said. "Are you sure this is it?"

Eleanor pushed the door open and peered into what looked for all the world like a small cottage. It wasn't even uninhabited. The furniture was well worn and the plates had scraps of last night's dinner. And as if any more proof were needed, the last embers of a fire glowed in the grate.

"I thought I was sure," she said. "But someone lives here."

"Keep going," Sebastien said, stepping past her. "It must be a marker along the way – there must be something here that'll point us in the right direction for the real headquarters."

"Wait," Mack said, pulling them both back outside. "We'd better check there's no-one home before we go hunting around their house, don't you think?"

"There's no-one here," Eleanor said. "If there was anyone at home, they would've come by now to see what the noise was."

They fanned out into the cramped living space and began examining chairs and walls and curtains, looking for any kind of clue. But everything was merely domestic. A small kitchen area, a low sofa, an old trunk that was doubling as a table by the fire. Eleanor lifted plates, cups and trinkets from the top of the trunk and opened it hopefully, but it contained only a couple of dead spiders.

Mack climbed the ladder into the attic bedroom, but stuck his head down a moment later to report that there, too, was apparently nothing beyond homely furnishings and bric-a-brac.

Sebastien rolled back the hearth rug and checked the flagstone floor for any stones that might be loose or marked. When nothing made itself apparent he sank back into the sofa to think, while Eleanor left the house by the back door to look around the yard.

They reconvened a short while later, feeling somewhat dispirited. The directions had seemed clear enough, but this was just somebody's house.

"Do you think we're too late?" Eleanor asked. "Do you think it used to be here, but now...?"

"They were smarter than that," Sebastien said. "We'd be disappointed if they'd left something obvious to a cursory search like this. There's something we're missing."

Eleanor paced the room, studying the furniture and fittings for a second time, wondering what hidden meaning they could possibly read into these nicknacks. It was hardly the Code Tower.

"Let me have another look at the map," Eleanor said, holding her hand out until Sebastien passed it across. If the map had brought them to the wrong place, maybe they'd misread the map. She laid it on the table and followed the outline of streets with her fingertip until...

"I've got it!"

"What?"

Sebastien and Mack both stared at the page again, but they still saw a pattern of Almont streets.

"It's not really a map of the city," she said, smiling at the cleverness of whoever had designed it.

"But it's obviously–" Mack started to protest, but stopped himself.

"Everything has to be deniable," Eleanor said. "Nothing is as it appears."

"Even after all the safeguards they built around the vault?" Sebastien asked.

"It's like you said: they were smarter than we're giving them credit for. If we can't follow our own predecessors' trail, that's our failure. Think of it like the tests we had to pass to get into the academy."

"So what do you think it is?"

"Look where they've stopped the edges of the streets." She traced the ragged line again as she spoke. "Doesn't that shape remind you of anything?"

"It's... it's the coast of the mainland."

"Exactly. And if that's a map of the coast, and we need to find the region enclosed by this house, then at a rough guess we're looking for an island about five miles out."

Mack and Sebastien exchanged stunned glances but she knew she was right, and she was sure they saw it too.

Chapter 15

"We need to unite our allies," Don said, speaking at the first meeting in their new council chamber. "That much is obvious."

They'd found the new headquarters without difficulty on their second interpretation of the map. An extensive series of underground rooms had been carved out of the heart of a rocky islet that was generally considered uninhabitable. The whole place had been perfectly set up, even down to the concealed harbour where they could moor a couple of small boats out of sight of both the surrounding islands and the nearest mainland town of Woolport. It hadn't taken long after that for the Association to move their centre of operations. While Daniel and Albert had gone off on a short trading expedition to bring their stocks of medicinal herbs up to siege quantities, the rest of the council were preoccupied with the question of what they should do next.

"What do you mean?" Ragal asked.

"We have natural allies in our exile. The Empress has inadvertently given us access to the whole body of rebels. There's enough will out there to completely overthrow the Imperial family, but the little knots of rebels don't stand a chance of organising a proper revolution. We can be the force that brings them together."

"Since when do we want to overthrow the Empire?" Gerald asked.

"She cast the first stone."

"Yes, we all know the Empire's being stupid, but I thought we were just going to wait for this to blow over."

"There's going to be a war," Don said, leaning back in his chair. "Whether or not we take a part in it. If we stay out of it, the Empress might win, and she won't be forgiving in victory. This way we get to be in control, and we make sure ours is the winning side. If we play this out cleverly enough, we can name our own Emperor."

"Or Empress," Eleanor added.

"Whatever. You see my point."

"So what exactly are you suggesting?" Laban asked.

"We need to change what we mean by recruitment. We'll keep up with our plans to gather up our normal cohort of new students, of course, but we need to start getting the word out to the rebels that we've got a flag they can march under. Eleanor, you've got good contacts in some of the rebel taverns in Almont, haven't you?"

"There are a few who know me, yes."

"Great. You're going to the city to visit the Assessors anyway – you need to take a detour across town. We need to know rebel numbers, strategic points... anything that might come in useful. And start, gently, to give them a few lessons."

"Okay."

"Just enough to let them understand how much we can help them... not enough to let them run a revolution on their own."

"What does it matter if they manage it on their own?" Bill asked.

"You haven't been listening. We need to be central to their success – how else can we make sure of our place in the new regime?"

"But..."

Don didn't let him finish his objection. "There are three possibilities, and only one appeals to me. Either the Empress continues to quash little pockets of rebellion" – he made squashing motions with his thumb against the table – "and grows more confident, and decides to lock us out for longer. Or some form of revolution succeeds. If it succeeds without us then we have to go on scavenging for jobs where we can find them. Whereas if we can make sure we're instrumental, we can dictate our own terms to the new government."

After a long and tiring ride from Woolport across to Almont, Eleanor tied her horse in a quiet alleyway and ducked inside an open doorway to change into an outfit of cleaner and smarter clothes. She entered the Assessors' College by a top-floor window, and casually asked the first passer-by where she could find Lucille's office. He pointed her downstairs, and a moment later Eleanor was knocking at a half-open door.

"Eleanor?" Lucille could hardly believe her eyes when she looked up. "What in all the Empire brings you in here?"

"I needed to talk to an Assessor," Eleanor said. "So you seemed like the obvious choice. May I?"

"Of course, by all means. Can I get you a drink?"

"No, I won't be long." Eleanor sat in the empty chair, facing her friend across a cluttered desk. "I just came to ask you a favour."

Lucille stacked the papers she'd been working on and looked up. "What is it?"

"I need some assignments changing in time for this summer. I know it's short notice, but there are certain students – Level One students – who need to be given Level Three assignments."

"What? Why?"

"Do you remember a very long time ago, when we were just girls, and Gisele told us a story about assassins and some very strange recruitment processes?"

"Those old myths? Sure, I remember."

"It's not a myth, Luce. I was one of those students."

"An assassin?" Lucille's eyes widened.

"After a fashion."

Lucille shook her head. "Of course I can see you'd have the skills, but honestly, that's not a real job. I would have heard about it."

"Well, it's not really got much to do with assassination – that's just the bit that makes good stories to scare schoolgirls. There's a lot more to it than that."

"But the whole thing's a myth. It's just a childhood story. Even Gisele never believed it when she told it to us."

"Of course she didn't believe it, but it's not a myth." Eleanor pulled a knife from her wrist-sheath and handed it across the desk. "Even you can see that's no military design. The Empire would never spend this much on making their weapons beautiful."

Lucille held the knife cautiously in both hands, using thumbs and forefingers to grip both the handle and the flat of the blade. "It's very pretty," she said, tilting it to make the gems sparkle in the lamplight. "But I'm not sure what that's supposed to prove."

"I can't prove anything to you. But I also can't think of any good reason why I'd lie about this."

"So assuming you really are an assassin – or whatever you'd prefer me to call it. Why are you here?"

"Well, the thing is, there are some students that will have been picked out already, and someone needs to downgrade their assignments to make sure they get something thoroughly unsuitable. I was hoping you could make that happen."

"What?"

"I need you to find out who my students are, and change their assignments."

"From One to Three?"

"Precisely."

"Are you really asking me to go against the system? Against my own job?"

"This was part of the system, till this year," Eleanor said. "Until the Empress decided... well, let's not go into the politics. The thing is it's always been this way, we've just lost our official route. But I'm sure the list is still somewhere in this building."

"You're asking me to choose sides in a tussle with the Empress." It wasn't exactly a question, but there was incredulity in her voice.

"You can't avoid making a choice. Sitting there and doing your job, keeping things as they are, is a choice you make every day."

"But that's a harmless choice. You're asking me to go against everything."

"No decision is harmless. You might not have seen the signs yet, in here, but there's war on the horizon. A real civil war that's going to come to everyone, whether you like it or not. No-one gets out of making that decision."

"I can't," Lucille said. "My job is to place people where they'll be happiest and most productive. I can't do something so wrong."

"You wouldn't be giving people assignments they'd be completely unhappy in. Just something below their level – so that they'd know, if they thought about it in the right way, that there might be a better option."

"And this is what happened to you, to make you turn down your assignment?"

"Yes."

"What were you offered?"

"Something in the local police in Port Just."

"And you're trying to tell me that that wouldn't have made you completely unhappy? It would have driven you insane."

"Yeah, it would," Eleanor admitted. "I would've gone slowly mad. But that's why I turned it down, you see? It's sort of a test."

"Eleanor, people don't throw away their lives because something seems a bit beneath them. To make someone do that the alternative has to be hateful, and I can't do that. I'm sorry."

"You have time to think," Eleanor said, getting to her feet. "I won't hurry you."

"I'm not sure there's a lot to think about. It's just wrong."

"This the only way to make sure we get the best people where they belong. Write to Gisele – she should be back from Faliska by now. I know you've always trusted her judgement more than mine, but I saved her life last year. Maybe she'll have something to say."

"And she knows about this strange job you claim to have?"

"She does now, yes. Write to her, or drop in for tea. I'll come back in a couple of weeks."

"But if I did agree to help you – just imagining I did – wouldn't I lose my job?"

"No-one needs to find out, and they certainly wouldn't know it was you. This has been part of the assignment system since the first days of the Empire, so someone will already have identified the right students. You only have to make a couple of switches."

"I'll write to Gisele," she conceded. "But I can't promise anything."

"Just promise me you'll think about it."

Lucille nodded. "Okay."

Eleanor left the College by a more conventional route and walked her horse across the city until she reached the Old Barrel Yard. She went in via the stables and sat down; Ade recognised her and put a tankard down at her table before she even had chance to take a seat. She waved him into an empty chair beside her and he sat, puzzled. Though she'd briefly been a regular patron of the tavern, she'd never been one for initiating conversations.

"I think we've known each other long enough to speak openly," she said. "At least while we're alone."

"What d'you wish to speak of?" he asked.

She glanced around to check no-one else had come in behind her, then leaned towards him and whispered one word: "Revolution."

"I'm not sure I've much to say on that subject."

"You must've noticed there's a war brewing. The rebels are getting restless."

"True enough."

"But without proper organisation, they're just making noise. The Empire continues to crush every uprising."

He nodded, though his expression was still cautious.

"My people want to make sure this goes the right way."

"Who are your people?"

"I don't think you need to know that yet."

He opened his mouth to object, closed it without speaking, and thought for a moment. Then: "What are you offering?"

"A plan."

"And your price?"

"This isn't about money." She slid one perfect throwing knife from its home at her wrist, spun the blade quickly in her fingers, and sheathed it again in one smooth motion. The whole display took only a couple of heartbeats, but she watched as the flash of the knife caught his attention. "But I need people who'll follow me – any strategy will only work if we get the majority of rebel factions on board."

"Tell me what you need from me."

"You understand the different factions in a way that I don't

– I'll need your knowledge in time. But right now, I just need to get the word out. There's no shortage of rebels in the city here, and plenty of others in hiding across the archipelago, but this will only stick if everyone's working to the same plan. I need people to commit to joining the revolution, and I'll need to know how many soldiers I can count on."

"You can't ask me to make a list of people the Empire would like to see dead."

"No, not a list of names. I trust you'd never be so stupid. But I need an idea of numbers, and we'll create a set of secret challenge phrases to identify the new order." She pulled out a sheet of parchment on which she'd already inscribed a dozen question and answer pairs. "Oh, and we need to put a stop to all the little acts of vandalism until we've agreed our common goals."

"You're asking a lot if you want rebels to stop rebelling."

"Setting fires and smashing windows isn't a meaningful rebellion – it's just spite. I want to see that energy put to good use."

"And you really have a plan?"

"Yes. Will you help me to spread the word?"

He nodded.

"Find the leaders if you can," Eleanor said. "We'll have a meeting here on the night of the full moon, when we'll lay out a little more detail, but we want to keep it small for now. We don't want to attract attention from the Imperial forces just yet."

"The full moon? I'll see what I can do."

"Thank you. Meanwhile, my horse is in your stable, and I'd very much like to take a small room for a few nights."

The night of the full moon was foggy and damp, making the streets dark and cold. As she hurried along to the meeting at the Old Barrel Yard, Eleanor wished she'd thought to bring her winter cloak. She'd presumed too much from the early spring sunshine.

When she arrived the bar was already crowded and she was amused – and somewhat impressed – to find a young lad at the door who was using her own pass phrases to control who he allowed to enter. After she'd satisfied him of her identity, she pushed through to the bar.

"Good turnout," she said to Ade. "Thanks."

"It's your idea that's brought them," he said. "I can't claim any credit for that. Are you having your usual?"

She nodded, and he filled a tankard for her. The spiced ale warmed her fingers and her insides, and by the time she reached the bottom she was more than ready to call her meeting to order. She drummed her fists on the bar until the room fell silent, and stood on a chair to address the crowd.

"Men and women of Almont," she began. "Welcome to the revolution."

They clapped and cheered and stamped their feet, and she had to wave to quieten them down before she could go on.

"The Empire has gone too far! The Imperial family flouts their own laws! We must act!"

Again there were cheers, and again she waited for the excitement to subside before continuing with a more serious tone.

"The Empress is looking to expand into the southern mountains, against the will of those who live there. She's trying to extend her influence into the drylands across the ocean, by sending our soldiers to die in the sands. She's ordering the assassination of those who dare to disagree, even her own flesh and blood."

She looked around the room, and her eyes met those of the astonished audience who were soaking up every word. They might be longstanding rebels, but she guessed most of them had never before come close to knowing what went on within the palace walls.

"This can't continue. To succeed, the revolution needs every one of us. It requires every woman and man and child we can call on. It requires us to give up our petty acts of personal rebellion and join together to follow a new path. A path more challenging, but more rewarding. A path to overthrow the Empress and her poisoned family. This is the only way to stop them crushing us with laws they don't even follow." She could feel tension mounting in the room as she spoke. "So who's with me?"

The crowd erupted with cries of "Yeah!" and "Forwards!" and "Revolution!"

"Because anyone who's not with me can leave, right now." She pointed towards the door, but nobody moved. "There's no space left for playing at rebellion. There's no more time for vandals and petty thieves. For our revolution to succeed we have to be much more than this. We're at war now. This is a battle. You are an army!"

Again she waited for the clapping and cheering to subside. There was something strangely addictive about this leadership game. The crowd fell into silence again and watched her expectantly.

"Like any army, we need to have discipline," she said. "You need training and weapons and strategy – I can give you those things. In exchange, you have to give me your word. If you're prepared to trust me, we can do this together."

"I'm in," cried a young man at the back of the room, punching his fist into the air. A smattering of others echoed his sentiments, while others just watched.

"Now, I need you to go out and tell your people. Tell your neighbours and friends that this is the shape of the new order. The revolution is starting tonight."

She barely slept that night. The excitement of what she'd started filled her veins; there was something exhilarating about the crowd's responses. Suddenly Don's idea seemed to have a real prospect of success.

The next morning, feeling a little more optimistic about everything, she made her way back to Lucille's office.

"I won't do it," Lucille said. "I can't."

"Okay," Eleanor nodded. She was disappointed but she'd promised herself she wouldn't exert any more pressure – she still felt some loyalty to the girls she had grown up with. Besides, she was sure she could find someone else at the College who would be just as easy to break.

"But I've got you a list," Lucille added, pulling a couple of sheets of paper from her pocket. "I thought, maybe, if you had the names... well, you could talk to the schools, couldn't you?"

Eleanor had to fight to stop the triumphant expression that was trying to shape her features; Lucille might reconsider if she understood just what she was offering. Talk to the schools? Not likely. But talking to the possible candidates, now there was a plan that might work.

"Perhaps," Eleanor said casually. "I'll have a go."

"Here."

"Thanks, Luce. You've saved me no end of trouble." She read the names and noted the schools. There were a couple from Venncastle; that was no surprise. The others were spread across the Empire. "Could I come back later in the week and take a look through their records?"

"I have them here," Lucille said, offering up a stack of folders. "I can't let you take them out of the building, but you can read for as long as you like."

Eleanor sat there for almost half a day, flicking through the files while Lucille continued to work. Once she was convinced she'd committed every important detail to memory, she put the pile of papers back on the desk and got to her feet.

"Thanks for that."

"Is there anything else?"

"I'd appreciate it if you could pass one message to whoever makes these lists," Eleanor said. "Just tell him to include the female students from next year."

"What?"

"Didn't you notice? There aren't any girls on this list. It's time that changed."

"I thought you said this was the way you found your job."

"Well, yes. I was a special case. They haven't traditionally taken any women."

"Okay, I'll do that. And come back if you need anything else, won't you?"

"I won't need to," Eleanor said, tucking the list of names safely under her belt. "But I'll be back around this time next year, and I'll be very happy if there are some girls' names on the list."

She was almost at the door when Lucille spoke up again.

"Do you really think there's going to be a war?"

"It's looking more and more that way."

Lucille wasn't the kind of person who liked things she couldn't measure, and she looked troubled at the very idea. "What's going to happen to us?"

"I don't know. It probably depends which side you choose."

"What do you mean?"

"The Empress has already set about killing any rebels that her people can track down. Even children. It won't be long before the revolution has to become equally violent to stand a chance of success."

"But you think the rebels are going to win? You must, or you wouldn't be supporting them."

"I can't promise you anything like that. I don't know who's going to win. I just know what's right, and the Empress has been wrong a lot lately."

"Do you think I should...?"

"I think you should stay out of it for as long as you can."

"But last time you were here, you said everyone would have to choose."

"That day will come – and I think it'll be soon – but it's not here yet. For as long as you're able to keep doing your job without danger, that's what you should do," Eleanor said. "When that becomes impossible, only you can decide which way to jump."

Lucille stared at her, tears welling in her eyes. "I don't want this."

"I know. Neither would I, if there were any alternative."

"But what should I do?"

"I think you should pick the winning side," Eleanor said. "It might well be obvious by the time you're forced to choose. But listen, if you do join the rebels, just make sure you mention my name. You'll find friends quickly that way."

Lucille nodded. "I'll remember."

"You've done me a huge favour today," Eleanor went on. "And you know I'll always help you if I can."

"Would I have to fight? You know I was always hopeless at that kind of thing."

"No, my friends will hide you until I can find you. You're

not cut out for fighting – no-one's going to try and put you on the front line."

Chapter 16

Eleanor spread Lucille's paper on the table in front of the council. "The Assessors won't change the letters for us, but I've got names," she said. "There are eleven."

"Good work," Don said, leaning across to study the list. "What now?"

"I suppose the next step is to go and make ourselves known to these students. Make sure they have our invitation in their minds when they get their letters of assignment."

"Well, you can't go to Venncastle, that's obvious."

She rolled her eyes. "If you don't think I can survive visiting a school, we've got bigger problems than recruitment!"

"I don't think they'd kill you," he said. "But if you go there, two things will happen. First, they'll ignore you anyway. And then, once you've gone, they'll report your visit and the Empire will know what we're planning."

"You don't think they already know what we'll do? The Shadows know us. They know we're not stupid."

"I agree with Don. You cannot go to Venncastle," Daniel said.

"Fine. Where does that leave us?" She consulted her list. "Bastion, Hess, Almont 5, Almont 9, Dashfort 2..."

"You should not go to Hessekolenisshe," Daniel interrupted.

"Why not? Are they going to turn me in to the Empire, too?" Eleanor could feel the frustration creeping into her voice. Why couldn't she just take the list and work through it? It didn't matter if the Empress got word that they were recruiting; it would be more surprising if they weren't.

"No. I should go."

"Why?"

"They know me. Besides, I am not sure a woman should take any part of this job. It is important to get it right, this first approach."

"Are you honestly saying I'm going to get it wrong because

I'm a woman?" She glared at him, daring him to answer. "Because if you're going to say things like that where I can hear you, you might want to make sure you've drawn your knife first."

"Eleanor." That was Laban. "Please calm down. Everyone's on edge at the moment, but you know Daniel doesn't think badly of you."

"I am serious," Daniel said. "No student will expect a woman to be recruiting for the Association. They may not believe you are who you say you are."

"If I turned up in your bedroom in the middle of the night, crept up to your bed without even waking you, and I had your entire school record in my memory, don't you think you'd take me seriously? I didn't even believe in your school when I was a girl, we thought it was just a myth, but I think I've done a pretty good job of pretending to take you seriously."

"Fine. Go. But if it does not work, remember that I have said this."

"And what news of the rebels?" Nathaniel asked.

"The word is spreading," she said. "I told them to stop the mindless vandalism, and there's certainly been less disruption in Almont over the last few days. We need a few messengers to carry this to the islands. We'll leave things quiet for a couple of months – that should be long enough to give the Empire a false sense of security – and then we'll start to consolidate."

"Consolidate? What do you mean?"

"There are a few rebel areas in the city already, but that's more of a convention. We need to put some force behind it and teach them how to defend their ground. They need guards and pass phrases and weapons – so if anyone has old blades that you don't really use any more, we'll get Harold to smooth off your identifying marks, and we can send them across to the city."

"And when we've consolidated the ground? What then?"

"We'll take a step back and see what we've got. We can start expanding street by street, and when the time is right, we can run assaults against some of the Imperial infrastructure. For now, though, let's focus on securing what we've got."

She'd hoped to get away without having to talk to Daniel. Aside from bickering across the council table she hadn't spoken to him since he'd tried to dissuade her from going to the Shadows, and she would have been perfectly happy to continue with that state of affairs indefinitely. Unfortunately he seemed to have other ideas, and came after her as she left the council chamber.

"Eleanor."

She wondered whether she could get away with pretending she hadn't heard him, but he'd only follow her to her room.

"Eleanor," he repeated, quietly.

She turned, mentally preparing herself for an argument. "Yes?"

"If you are intent on going to Hess," he said, "you should at least let me draw a map for you."

She was about to snap something about being perfectly able to navigate a school when she realised that, actually, he was right. "Okay, thanks. That'd be helpful."

"Yes."

He looked like he was expecting her to say something else, but she couldn't imagine what. "Well? I said yes, I even said thank you. What are you waiting for?"

"I am only wondering when you might realise that you are not some hero of legend and you do not have to solve everything all by yourself."

"Probably about the same time you realise we're not at school any more, and this isn't a game, and we don't have time to *take turns*. We just have to get things done."

He stepped forwards and planted his lips on hers, gripping the back of her head so fiercely that she had to struggle to pull away. She slapped him sharply across the cheek.

"Do that again and I won't fight the urge to pull a knife on you," she said. "Just because you broke us up doesn't mean you can unilaterally put us back together again. We're broken. It'll take more than that to fix it."

"Then... I apologise." He looked stunned. "I only..."

"Don't." She put her finger across his lips to shush him. "You have a map to draw, and I have to pack. We can talk

210

about this another day."

She started in Almont, with the Fifth City School. The low grey building was sandwiched in the middle of the Artisan Quarter, with easy access over the rooftops, and the windows weren't even latched. The boy was called Richard and, it turned out, he shared a dormitory with seven others. She found his room without difficulty, but the challenge would be to extract him from his bed without waking the others.

She peered into the room, watching for any sign of movement – or too-careful stillness – that might indicate a boy was awake. Satisfied that they were all really sleeping, she tiptoed across to her target and clapped her hand across his mouth before he could make a sound. She rolled his body across her shoulders and carried him from the room, only lowering him to the ground once they were back in the corridor outside. He tried to speak through her fingers.

"If you promise to keep your voice down, I'll let you talk," she said. "Is there somewhere we could go for privacy?"

He nodded.

"Which way?"

He indicated left with a jerk of his head and she helped him to his feet, still keeping one hand firmly across his mouth. She couldn't afford to risk a disturbance.

"Who are you?" he asked as soon as she allowed him to speak. "What d'you want with me?"

"I've come to recruit you." She gave him a moment to think about it, watching the questions flicker across his face, but he didn't voice them. "You don't need me to tell you that you're an exceptional student. You're top of your class for hand-to-hand, and one of the best in the Empire at apothecary. You're quiet when you need to be quiet, but people will listen when you speak. You have all the skills we need."

"We?"

"Have you heard of the Association?"

He looked blank. "What's that?"

"Okay, let's start with something you've definitely heard of. There are plenty of legends telling of a secret society of assassins, though they're seldom much good on the details."

"Um, yeah... but you're not telling me you're an assassin, are you?"

"Well, that's not all that I am." She smiled, amused by his reaction to the idea of having been hauled from his bed by an assassin. There was a time when she would have felt the same. "But of course those are the stories that tend to get told, since assassination is infinitely more exciting to talk about than, say, politics."

"Politics?"

She'd guessed from his records that that might pique his interest, and the timbre of his voice now told her she'd judged correctly.

"What you need to understand is that the Association does a little bit of everything. If it needs doing, and if other people might be reluctant to do it or lack the necessary skills, that's where we step in. We know how to move silently through the shadows, how to arrange a situation to turn the way we need, how to steer people subtly in the right direction... as well as how to slip a knife between the ribs or a poison in the drink."

"But you work for the rebels?"

"Not exactly. We used to do a lot of work directly for the Empire, but sadly that's no longer an option – which is why, instead of a Level Three assignment to make you think, you'll almost certainly get the Level One you deserve. But even if you get your dream job, we can offer you something beyond any of that."

"And if I'm interested... what do I do? How do I contact you for more information?"

"What more information do you want? You can ask me now."

"I'm not sure, I just thought I might have questions."

"Well, generations have managed without anyone to guide them," she said, though she thought of Venncastle's approach and wondered whether the Association would have done better to swallow its pride a long time ago. "If you want to join us, you just need to come to the Black Wolf Caves at the full moon after you get your assignment."

She had one more boy to visit in Almont that night, and then she returned to her room at the Old Barrel Yard, though she waited until it was morning and the tavern was empty before she asked Ade how her plans had been progressing in her absence.

"People are impatient," he said. "You're asking them to pull back but they don't see any alternative. There's a lot of doubt."

"So they'd prefer to go on setting fires that last just as long as it takes for the fire wardens to arrive, rather than planning to actually achieve something?" she asked, trying not to sound too disappointed.

"You make it sound as though a sacrificial fire has no effect."

Eleanor just stared at him, unable to even form an intelligent question around what she thought she'd heard. Eventually she managed, "Sacrificial... what?"

Ade sighed and sat down. "What do you know about the cults?"

"Aside from being illegal?"

"They must have taught you more than that. What about your histories?"

"Charan identified religion as a serious threat to the peace," she said, almost reciting from her schoolbooks. "It undermines the foundations of the Empire to give power to any beings which aren't bound by our laws."

"And what d'you believe?"

"Me?"

"Do you really think the gods can't see you just because you haven't done any sacrifices lately?"

Eleanor twisted a corner of her tunic between her fingers. "I hadn't really thought about it."

"Well, there's a thing to think about. For now it'll do you to know that the cults aren't nearly so dead as they'd have you believe, and if you're going to throw your lot in with rebels then you'd best find out who you're dealing with."

"Cults." Eleanor nodded, trying to assimilate all this new information whilst maintaining a coherent plan. "And does that account for all of them?"

"Maybe one in ten's like you and just doesn't enjoy being bossed around by some woman whose only claim to anything is the name of her father's grandfather. The rest are devotees of one god or another."

"And this is why they like to set things on fire?"

"There's nigh on a thousand gods mentioned in the old lore, but the Lady of Fire sits over them all, and her followers are the largest faction. You do want her on your side."

"Okay. Do you have a map of the city?"

He shuffled beneath the bar and pulled out an old, slightly faded plan of the central districts. "It's a little out of date," he said. "Why?"

"I'll be away for a while, and I want to give people something to do while they wait for me to get back. Now, as I understand it there are rebel streets where we are, and nearby here and here," – she traced the roads with her fingertip – "and then in the Exchange Quarter around this square, and then down here in the south... is that about right?"

"Those are the main areas, yes. There are a few houses just over here, and a couple more here along the old mining road."

"Okay, this is what we'll do. Everyone who lives between two rebel houses in these areas needs to be persuaded to leave if they can't be persuaded to join us. That way we can strengthen up the areas where we're already strong. Anyone who wants to start a fire should be encouraged to take out houses along here or here to strengthen our perimeter."

"Our perimeter? How can we ever defend ourselves when the Imperial forces come? Most of our volunteers haven't lifted a weapon since school combat classes."

"Don't worry about that for now. Find out who wants to be a soldier in the rebel guard, and suggest they work on their fitness. When I get back I'll start some combat training."

After that she moved as quickly as she could from one school to the next, hitching lifts on carts between cities, and giving each boy the same basic message: you have a choice, and we're it. She tried not to think too hard about the strange things Ade had said. The rebels were only one part of the plan, and if some of them followed arcane cults that was simply

214

another lever to use in moving them.

Finally, Hessekolenisshe was the only school left on her list. As she followed Daniel's instructions to where the ship lay permanently at anchor, she finally admitted to herself that this was going to be much harder to sneak into than any normal, land-based school.

The ship wasn't far from the shore, sheltered between a pair of thin islands. Eleanor borrowed a small skiff and sailed out into the channel on a cloudy, moonless night, but she still didn't dare approach the ship too closely. Just because she couldn't see anyone on watch didn't mean that there was no-one looking out to see her.

She lowered her anchor, folded the sails, and dived over the side. She left the skiff bobbing in the waves and struck out towards the school ship, swimming mostly beneath the surface and lifting her face for air as infrequently as her lungs allowed.

She paused under the shadow of the bow and contemplated her options. The ship's hull was built from large, thick planks that would provide surprisingly good holds for climbing. She tested her weight on one of the lowest boards above the water line, lifting herself half out of the water. She thought she felt the ship move, but it was almost imperceptible, and she wasn't sure if she'd imagined it. It certainly wasn't enough to wake anyone.

She pulled herself slowly up the hull, flattening her body against the planks as she climbed, and reached the deck after slipping only a couple of times on the slimy boards.

She'd brought dry clothes wrapped tightly inside her sealskin bag, and she ducked into an empty classroom to change. For all that she wanted to surprise the boy, she didn't quite want to look like she'd just crawled out of the sea. Her hair, however, was irredeemably drenched; water and seaweed dribbled down her back as she went to look for the boy called Lukal.

With Daniel's sketch of the ship in her mind, she knew she didn't have to go far to find the bunks of the students in their final year. Lukal was asleep just where she expected him to be, and she put her hand firmly across his mouth before waking him.

He opened his eyes, stared at her in horror, and tried to scream; Eleanor put her finger to her lips while keeping her other hand clamped on his face, but it was no use; he tried to wrestle himself free, and though he wouldn't succeed she knew he was going to be trouble. She flicked a dart from her sleeve straight into his arm, and waited for him to slump back into his bunk. It was the second time she'd had to sedate a panicked youth, but the last one had been small and easy to carry. Lukal was twice Eleanor's size, and she struggled to move him without waking his friends.

The boy in the next bunk started to sit up and, frustrated, Eleanor shot a dart towards him before he had chance to work out why he'd woken. She plucked the dart from his skin and pocketed it; he wouldn't remember a thing when he woke, and though he'd have a slight headache it shouldn't be enough to rouse his suspicions.

She turned her attention back to Lukal and eventually managed to manoeuvre him out of the room. Once she was sure she'd taken him a safe enough distance from his colleagues, she gave him a small dose of stimulant to wake him again, silently thanking Daniel for equipping her with such carefully paired potions.

"Do you know what just happened?" she asked as he came round.

He peered at her from beneath heavy eyelids. "Who are you?"

"I'm representing the a body known as the Association," she said. "That's all you need to know."

"But... this isn't how it's supposed to happen. Only Venncastle breaks the rules like this."

"It may not be what's supposed to happen, but since the Empress decided to take away the old routes, I'm afraid it's what we're stuck with. If we can't change your assignment, we have to get the message through some other way."

He blinked slowly, three times, and shook his head. "You've drugged me. I don't feel right."

"You panicked. We'll have to train that out of you, if you're going to be any use at all. But you'll be fine, trust me. I wouldn't go to all this trouble just to poison you."

"What's this about, then?"

"I'm just here to tell you that you're on our list. You've got the option to come and join us – and if that's your choice, make your way to the Black Wolf Caves on the night of the full moon following your Day of Assignment."

He looked unconvinced but he didn't ask any more questions, so she left him thinking about her proposal and changed back into her wet clothes to swim back to her boat. She dried herself off again before settling down for the night, curled up beneath the folded sails, and slept until the dawn light woke her with its warmth. She was about to return the skiff to its owner and look for a cart back to Almont when a new thought stopped her in her tracks. She'd finished her rounds more quickly than she'd expected... and it wasn't far to Venncastle. No-one would have to know if she failed, but to get even one of the students to shelve their legendary loyalty for long enough to consider the alternative she was offering, now that would be an achievement. And there were two names left on the list Lucille had provided.

Her mind made up, she turned the boat and sailed along the coast in the direction of Flying Rock Island. It would take a day or two at most; there was nothing to lose.

She thought they might have improved their security since the last time she'd managed to climb in via the sea-walls, but she saw no flicker of lights in the old guard towers as she approached. It looked like the school's guards were still focused exclusively on their duties at the front gate. She dropped her sails and rowed into a small cave beneath the cliffs to wait for darkness to fall more completely. As she waited, she lay back in the boat and tried to recall the detail of the Venncastle students' records; unlike the others, she hadn't been constantly rehearsing this meeting in her head.

The clearest sign of her unpreparedness, though, was that she didn't really know where in the castle to look for the two boys who'd been on Lucille's list. As she scrambled up the cliff face she remembered James, the lad who'd caught her last time she'd tried this. It was a shame he would have graduated and moved out into the adult world by now – otherwise she could have asked him for directions. As it was, she'd just have to work it out some other way.

She made her way to the tower which housed the Provost's chamber, and found a small administrative office on the ground floor. There was a plan of the castle pinned to the wall, with names pinned into the rooms, and it didn't take her long to spot the two she was looking for.

She checked and double-checked her position on the map, then marched straight into the nearer of the two rooms.

"Tal."

The youth sat up in bed, and jumped to his feet almost immediately. He was tall, with stringy muscles that flexed as he moved to position himself between her and the door.

"Who are you?" he demanded, reaching for a sword from the wall rack.

"I wouldn't bother with that," she said. "If I was here to hurt you, you wouldn't even have woken. And you certainly don't stand a chance if you try to attack me."

"Who are you?" Still he held the sword in front of him. "Why are you here?"

"I'm from the Association," she said. Addressing Venncastle's students certainly demanded a different approach. "You've heard of us, of course. In fact, until about a year ago, I expect you imagined you'd be joining us."

"Didn't know the Association had girls in it," he muttered. "Anyway, that's by the by. The Association's dead. It's Shadow Corps, now."

"The Association is far from dead, believe me. You might get assigned to the Shadow Corps, you might not – that's in the Assessors' hands. It's not your choice."

"You still haven't said why you're here."

"I wouldn't want you to be misinformed when you come to make the most important decision of your life. The Association is still an option that's open to you. It's important that you're aware of it."

"Venncastle doesn't support the outlaws."

"You support only yourselves."

He shook his head. "We back the Empire, but you're no part of that now. And there's war on the horizon."

It amused her to hear this child tell her there was war brewing, as if he had any concept of what that might mean.

"No," she said firmly. "Venncastle only truly supports Venncastle – however much you might wish the Empress to believe otherwise. We know. But the split already happened, which means things are different now."

"How is it any different?

"Your choice is personal, but if there's to be a war, the school would be wise to have people on both sides."

He turned his sword slowly, watching her reflection in the blade. "Why shouldn't I just kill you now? I'm sure I'd be well rewarded for it."

"If you think you stand a chance, you're more than welcome to try. After all, I'm not even holding a weapon." She held up her empty hands to illustrate her point. "But if I disarm you as easily as I think I will, promise me you'll think seriously about what I've said."

"Why should I promise you anything?"

"You owe it to yourself."

He lunged as she started the sentence, and before the final word left her lips she had his sword in her hand and he was lying on the floor, trapped beneath her. To his credit, he didn't tremble.

"So, do you promise?" she asked, stepping towards the door and tossing the hilt of his sword back towards him. "We'll be waiting for your decision."

"How would I contact you? I mean, if I even wanted to."

"There's a full moon three days after you get your assignment. If you think you might prefer my alternative, you just have to come to the mouth of the Black Wolf Caves that night. We'll take it from there. Now, if you'll excuse me, I have to pay a visit to one of your colleagues."

"Gaven."

"Well, I'm sure you'll talk to him about all this tomorrow. Just remember your decision is your own." She turned and left before he had chance to respond.

She jogged lightly through the corridors until she reached the tower where she expected to find Gaven, squirted oil into the hinges of his door, and pushed her way into his room without a sound.

"Gaven."

He barely seemed to stir beneath the sheets but she knew he was looking at her, and probably with a weapon now aimed in her direction.

"I've come to talk to you about the Association."

He still didn't move. "Go ahead."

She smiled into the darkness. He was a deep one, this one.

"I'm just here to make sure you have all the facts you need to make your decision. You'll be given your assignment in just a few weeks, and until recently you were expecting something meaningless. Just a formality, something to refuse without even reading it." He made no acknowledgement of her words, so she pressed on. "Things have changed – you're probably expecting the Shadow Corps now and you'll probably get it. But the alternative hasn't disappeared. You still have the choice to refuse their offer and join us."

He remained impassive; immobile. She wondered if she'd get any reaction at all.

"Well, if you think you might be interested, I had a little chat with Tal earlier. He knows how to find me. There's always a welcome in the Association for good people who choose to seek us out."

She backed out of the room, not trusting to turn her back on this quietly dangerous youth. He seemed the sort who'd put a dart in her neck and claim his reward without bothering to ask her for any reason why he shouldn't.

As she made her way back to the Association headquarters, she couldn't get him out of her mind. It would be an unlikely victory, but she wanted his quiet confidence on her side.

By the time she reached the council chamber, news of her arrival had spread and most of her colleagues had already assembled.

"Well?" Laban asked.

"I think we'll get a good showing," she said. "I was very persuasive."

"Can you estimate a number?"

"I'd say somewhere between eight and ten out of eleven."

"There were not eleven names on the list we agreed." Of course, it had to be Daniel to throw the first stone.

"We need all the good people we can get," Eleanor said. "Venncastle have always supplied talented students."

"How could you? Do you not see what you have done?"

"And it went well, actually – thanks for asking."

"It did not go well. We must assume they have reported your plan."

"Well, of course we have to prepare for an ambush. We've always had to assume an ambush, that's why we picked the caves in the first place."

"But now you have guaranteed it."

"It's too late for regrets now," Ragal said. "All that remains is to make the best of it. If we're lucky, we may gain one more recruit from this."

"I'll make sure of it," Eleanor said. "An ambush is the best gift they could ever give us – by the end of that, we'll have our own brand of loyalty nailed in place."

"If we could compete with Venncastle loyalty, why have we lost every last one of them?" Don asked. "They care only for their own."

"We can play them at their own game," Eleanor said. "We just need to invent some rules that suit us. And I think I'm starting to get the hang of this."

Daniel shook his head. "You cannot win."

"Watch me." She turned and strode from the room, feeling a little taller with every step. The more she thought about it, the happier she was with her decision to change the plan. An ambush was almost certain. Now she just had to make it work in her favour.

But they were still weeks from the solstice, and before any of that she had a revolutionary force to train in Almont. She went back to her room to start preparing everything she expected to need.

The door opened without a knock and she knew who it was before he opened his mouth.

"I don't want to hear it," she said. "You don't even think I have a chance."

"No."

"So what are you doing here?" She counted out practice daggers as she spoke, stacking them alongside her travel bag.

"I came to help you."

She turned then. "What?"

"You will not succeed with Venncastle, but that cannot mean you fail in the end. What do you need from me?"

"Well, if you're offering..." She could think of plenty of ways his apothecary's skill could be useful. "There are bound to be injuries, so I'll need painkillers and compresses. And if you've got some of that bull extract, I'm sure I could make use of it."

"When will you leave?"

"Tomorrow, but I'm going to Almont first. Mack's coming to meet me at the caves, so you can make up a case with whatever you think we'll need, and send it with him."

Chapter 17

Eleanor took her usual room at the Old Barrel Yard and asked Ade to start spreading the word to gather everyone who'd volunteered to join her special branch of the revolutionary guards. She had to get them started with a proper training programme before she disappeared to collect the Association's new students.

It was a diverse collection of men and women who turned up to meet her a few nights later, ranging from a handful of youngsters who were barely out of school, to older couples who huddled nervously together and looked as though they hadn't done a day's exercise since their schooldays, to a group of scrawny, weather-beaten sailors with shell talismans strung about their necks. Ade had told her that most seafaring folk wore something similar, in deference to the Lady of the Waves, though in normal company cult symbols were kept safely out of sight. One girl of about Eleanor's age carried a curly-haired toddler at her hip.

Eleanor looked them over. This was certainly going to be more interesting than refining the skills of the Association's usual recruits.

"Welcome to the First Revolutionary Guard Corps," she said. "As you know, we're looking at strengthening the borders of our rebel districts, and undermining the Empire. For that we need people like you. Or rather, people like you will be when I've finished with you. I hope no-one said this was going to be easy."

They watched her with cautious smiles. A plump, middle-aged man put a protective arm around his wife's shoulders, but no-one said anything.

Eleanor pulled a pair of throwing knives from her belt and sent them spinning in opposite directions to lodge in opposite beams of the tavern walls. Her audience gasped.

"I'm here to teach you a few of my skills," she said. "And it won't be long before you can do that, but we've got to start with the basics."

She set them off by outlining a simple jogging route, just a couple of miles out from the tavern and back again.

"Leave him here," she suggested to the young mother, whose name turned out to be Rosemary, as the others headed for the door. "Ade can keep an eye on him for you."

"Ollie's the reason I'm in the revolution. I couldn't give him away. I mean, look at him." She tousled his blonde curls and he smiled up at her. "I was hoping he could come with me on guard duty. I can't make his daddy see sense, so I need to keep him close."

"We'll see about that later," Eleanor said, wondering whether she shouldn't send the girl straight back to regular duties. But she looked fitter than most, and perhaps she could be gradually separated from the child. "You're not doing any guard duties tonight, anyway, just a bit of training – and he'll slow you down. He'll be safe here with Ade and Nasha."

They had to run hard to catch up with the others, who were somehow managing to stay together and sustaining a surprisingly good pace.

"Great work," Eleanor called out as she jogged alongside them. At the front, setting the pace, was a bald, broad-shouldered man in his late twenties who could have picked Eleanor up without breaking a sweat. She fell into step beside him. "What's your name?"

"Dash."

"What do you think, shall we go a bit faster?"

He looked back over his shoulder. "We don't want to lose them."

"You're a natural leader, that's good – we'll need you – but for now let me worry about what they can manage. Show me what you can do."

He sped up quickly, making Eleanor work twice as hard to match his speed with her shorter legs. By the time he'd settled again into his natural pace, only a couple of the youngsters were still keeping up. Eleanor left them to lead the way and fell back to encourage the others.

"Eric, isn't it? How are you feeling?" she asked the plump man; he was wheezing a little, and still gripped his wife's hand as they stumbled along.

"Fine," he gasped. "Just fine."

Eleanor turned to his wife, who looked a little more comfortable, but not much. "And you?"

"This is fun," she said, tugging at her husband's hand to encourage him to speed up. "We're going to enjoy this, you know. It's nice to have a way we can contribute to the revolution."

Eric nodded, but couldn't find the breath to speak.

"Great," Eleanor said. "And what's your name?"

"Lise."

"Okay, keep it up, we're nearly half way." The small leading group was already coming back towards them.

"When are we going to learn to fight?" asked one of the youngest, a skinny girl who looked hardly old enough to have left school. "I thought we'd need to do that first."

"You will," Eleanor said. "But I need you all to have a good level of fitness. There's no point giving you a knife if you don't have the stamina to stand up and use it."

"I'm already fit," the girl said.

"Oh, good. Then you can catch up with Dash, and tell him that when he gets back to the tavern, he needs to form everyone into two teams as they arrive."

The girl nodded and broke into a sprint, but she was panting before she reached the turning point, and had almost collapsed by the time she passed Eleanor again in the other direction. She avoided Eleanor's gaze and kept running, but it was clear she was struggling.

"If you keep going at that speed you won't make it back," Eleanor said, turning to run alongside her. "Let alone catch up with Dash."

"You knew I couldn't do it," the girl said. "That's why you asked me. Isn't it?"

"You told me you didn't need to train. Come on, slow down to a pace you can manage – we'll run together for a bit and you can tell me about what brought you into the revolution."

"Me? I just... we just graduated. It seemed like the right time to come and make a difference."

"Were you all at the same school?"

"Molly and me were..." She paused to catch her breath, breathing heavily as her feet pounded against the road. "Jace was at the boys' school nearby, and he knew some of the others. We all came across together."

"What was your assignment? What were you supposed to be?"

"Teacher," she said. "Little ones."

"This is going to be a bit different, then." Eleanor smiled. "Thanks for putting your name down."

"Like I said. We want to make a difference, and this is it, isn't it? This is going to be the war."

Eleanor nodded. No-one could deny that war was on the horizon, even if they didn't quite know when it would break out and envelop them.

By the time they got back to the tavern, those who'd got there before were half way through fresh tankards of beer.

"Did you think that was it?" Eleanor asked, standing with her arms crossed beside their table. "Or is this what you think counts as good training?"

"I thought we'd done," Dash said, getting to his feet and draining his mug. "But I see I was wrong. What next, boss?"

"Nicole's in charge," Eleanor indicated the skinny girl. "She's going to get you into two teams – as even as you can make it, Nic. And then we're going to have a little competition."

As the stragglers arrived in ones and twos, Nicole divided them into two groups at opposite ends of the bar. She split couples into separate teams, but if she noticed the discomfort some of them felt at being separated, she took no account of it.

"Okay?" she asked Eleanor once they'd all arrived and been sorted. Eleanor nodded. "What now?"

"Healthy competition can be a good motivator," Eleanor said. "So we're going to have a little race. You all know where we are, and I'm sure you all know the way to the cattle market. The first team to get from here to there will win, but after you leave this street your feet mustn't touch the ground."

"What?"

"You heard me. There are plenty of easy routes over the rooftops – if you can get on top of the tavern here, you shouldn't find it hard to get your bearings. But remember, you need to make sure your whole team gets there safely."

"Okay, team, who already knows how to climb?" Dash asked. Nicole nodded yes, and a couple of the other youngsters had already disappeared outside to see what was what. Eric shook his head, looking sick at the idea, and Rosemary looked equally nonplussed. "Okay, come on, let's go out and see what we've got to work with."

"Who died and made you Emperor?" Nicole asked, but she still followed him into the street.

The second team had formed a tight huddle by the bar, talking in hushed voices. Eleanor left them to their discussions and followed the others outside; the interesting stuff would happen in the street. The route she'd given them was short and simple. If they could get everyone onto the rooftops, it was almost a gentle stroll across to the edge of the cattle market. She climbed up the wooden frame of the tavern and sat on the roof – near the skylight of her own bedroom – to watch.

"It looks easy," one young lad called down. He and his friend were already on neighbouring rooftops, and from there they could even see the market square.

"I'm not sure how I'll get up there," Eric said. "It might be easy for you young things, but some of us are past that stage of life."

"Maybe you shouldn't be trying to do this, then," the lad retorted. "Leave it to those of us who can."

"That's enough of that," Dash said. "No more of that, or I'll come up there and you can answer to me. We're a team. Let's act like it."

Eleanor smiled to herself; she'd guessed he was going to be good, and he was proving her right.

"You got a plan?" Nicole asked. "Or are we just going to wait for them" – she motioned towards the door – "to come and catch us up?"

Dash ignored her and addressed himself to Eric and Rosemary, the most nervous members of his team. "Are you both okay with ladders?"

They nodded, still looking troubled.

"Okay, come over here." He put one hand on the timber-framed wall of the tavern, and his other hand on the corner of the window frame. "Watch, and try to remember where I put my feet."

They both obediently watched as he stepped up the wall; the timber framing provided reasonably straightforward holds, and by the time he reached the roof, Rosemary was almost ready to try for herself. Dash perched on the edge of the roof and grasped her hand as soon as she came close enough to reach, helping her to scramble up the last few feet. She made the mistake of looking down, and had to sit for a moment to recover her balance before walking across to where the two young men were waiting, but she had a quietly triumphant expression when she got to her feet again.

"Start walking," Dash suggested. "Everyone who can climb by themselves might as well get up here while I help Eric."

The second team came out into the street just then, and as Nicole swung herself up the wall they moved across to the next building which had a slightly lower roof, where a couple of the younger members formed a bridge with their hands for the others to step up. But Eleanor's attention was divided between the two youngsters who were helping Rosemary to keep her balance as she walked across the tiles, and Dash who was encouraging Eric in every step he took up the wall of the tavern. If they could keep up this level of co-operation, then her revolutionary guards were eventually going to make a formidable force.

Eleanor jogged across to the edge of the market and waited to see how they'd handle the next big challenge: getting down again. She wasn't surprised that Eric turned white when he looked down into the street, but the effort the others made to calm him and help him was both more surprising and more pleasing.

Once everyone had reached street level at the corner of the

cattle market, they all walked back together.

"You can have a drink now," Eleanor said as they came up to the door of the Old Barrel Yard. "You've certainly earned it."

"When are we meeting again?" Rosemary asked.

"Tomorrow, if you like," Eleanor said. "I take it none of you are still working on your Imperial assignments?"

"I am," Eric said. "I don't know how I'd survive without my stipend."

"The revolution will take care of its own. You can't be a rebel guard while you're beholden to the Empire."

He nodded his acceptance; his little bakery would be one man short tomorrow.

"So, you can all come back here tomorrow morning. We'll do a bit more running, and if you impress me, maybe we'll even take a look at what you remember from your school combat classes."

The next morning, after another brief circuit through the streets, she handed out wooden practice knives for them to fight with and waved them into pairs. She was careful to split up the couples again, sure that they weren't going to defend themselves as though it mattered when they were only under attack from their own spouse.

Dash ended up paired with Nicole, who examined her wooden knife with a distainful expression that Eleanor recognised all too well.

"I know," Eleanor said. "You've used metal blades at school. Fine, I get that, and I felt the same when I first started training for the Association. But the point of this exercise is for you all to show me what you can do, and I don't want to have to worry about injuries."

"Okay." She dropped into a mediocre imitation of a textbook stance, feet placed a little too close together to be stable, shoulders sloping a little more than they should.

Dash faced her squarely: feet apart, knees bent, confident in his own bulk. He held the knife as though it was just an extra obstacle to work around, and when Nicole darted forwards to aim a slashing cut at his chest, he deflected the blow with the flat of his hand.

"I know we're using wooden knives," Eleanor said. "I know it's not very realistic, but please, would you pretend it's a real blade coming towards you?"

"I am," he said.

"What I mean is, you might want to try using your knife to block with. You wouldn't want to cut your hand off."

"Begging your pardon, boss," he said. "But I've been in a few fights, over the years, and I've always managed to block the hand that holds the knife."

Eleanor looked at Nicole. "May I borrow your partner for a moment?"

She nodded, looking a little perturbed as Eleanor pulled out a short, very sharp dagger.

"I want you to do what you just did," she said. "Don't worry, I'm not trying to hurt you, I won't do anything fancy."

He nodded, tucked the wooden dagger into his belt as he waited for her to step forwards. As she extended her knife arm, intending only to strike him with the flat of the blade, his hand came out of nowhere and knocked her wrist sideways, taking the knife safely away from his body.

"See?" he said. "Nothing to worry about."

"Where did you learn to do that?" she asked. "I thought you were a carpenter."

"Like I said, boss. Just a few bar fights I've seen. If you don't want to end up getting hurt by some upstart kid with a knife, you have to know how to defend yourself."

"Well, it's a great skill to have, but you still might want to learn how to use that knife – we're not in a bar scrap now. We're at war."

"You said you weren't going to try anything fancy," he said. "But what would you have done if you were being fancy?"

"You don't want me to show you."

"You should. We're going to be up against Shadows, like as not, and I've heard things. At least you could give us a clue what we're expecting."

"Well, if you're sure."

"Don't hurt him," Nicole said, twisting the wooden knife

between her fingers. "He don't know what he's asking."

"Give me that, then." Eleanor sheathed her dagger and held out her hand for the practice knife. "If I get past your guard, you're going to know about it anyway."

She dodged and feinted a couple of times, switching the knife from one hand to the other, watching as his eyes followed the blade. For someone with no formal training, he was very good at this. Nevertheless, she knew she only had to wait. Eventually his eyes would flicker the wrong way, or he'd suffer a moment's lapse in concentration, or he'd simply leave a gap he couldn't cover. She would wait for that moment.

In the periphery of her vision she could see Nicole shuffling anxiously from one foot to the other. She was waiting, too, probably impatient to get some more practice herself.

Eleanor moved forwards, and sideways, and threw her dagger from one hand to the other... but she hadn't waited long enough, and Dash's hand caught the knife before she could strike, snatching it away and turning the blade on her. She ducked, blocked, and flung her leg out in a trip that sent him sprawling to the ground – and immediately felt guilty for using her instinctive reflexes to humiliate him when, in reality, he'd won. He still held the knife, whereas she was now unarmed, and in a real fight that would probably have been the end of her. In a real fight, though, she wouldn't have been arrogant enough to rush into the first half-plausible gap. At least, she hoped she wouldn't.

She extended a hand to help him to his feet.

"You're a natural," she said. "I think you and I need to talk some more, but for now, be nice to Nicole. I want her alive at the end of this."

"Will do, boss."

Eleanor left them to it and went to check how the others were getting on. They were having varying degrees of success – or suffering varying degrees of failure – but everyone still looked happy. More than one had developed purple bruises from cracks against the wooden blades.

"Every bruise would be a cut in battle," Eleanor said. "Don't forget that, when you're at home with your arnica lotion and wishing the bruises away. Every mistake you make now is one you shouldn't make when it matters."

By the time she left them three weeks later to go and collect her new recruits from the Black Wolf Caves, she thought she would have happily put about half of them on a shift of basic guard duties. Of the others, she was less convinced. But she left them with an extensive programme of running and circuit training and sparring, and promised she'd be back within a couple of months. That, she hoped, would be long enough to take the new students and make them presentable.

"Meanwhile, Dash, how do you fancy your first short mission?"

"Of course, boss."

"Great." She steered him out of earshot of the others. "I want you to take a horse and ride to Woolport, and then find yourself a little boat. Wait for darkness and sail out to the rocky outcrop they call the Faery Stacks, and you'll be met by someone from the Association. Tell them that Eleanor sent you, and that we'd like Bill or maybe Andreas to get down here and do some hand-to-hand training."

"Will they believe me?"

She shrugged. "Probably not. You'd better go unarmed, and if they challenge you then let them capture you. Learn to go placidly – they won't kill you out of hand if you don't fight. Ask to see Sebastien, and tell him Eleanor's told you about that time she almost killed Mikhail for calling her Ellie."

He stared at her. "You did that?"

"Why do you sound so surprised? You know I'm a professional killer."

"Sure, but that's professional. You don't have a temper."

She almost laughed, but stopped herself. Maybe he'd just been lucky, or perhaps he was right – perhaps she'd mellowed.

"It was a while ago," she admitted. "I was young, and I was having a really bad day. Anyway, tell him that, and he'll know it was really me."

Chapter 18

Eleanor found a position amongst the rocks where she was thoroughly concealed, but with a good view across to the mouth of the caves. The students wouldn't be arriving until the next night so she had plenty of time to settle herself and ensure she was familiar with every stone of her surroundings. Then, assuming they were right to expect an ambush, the fun would start. She wasn't quite sure how she'd force her plans to fruition if the ambush didn't materialise, but she didn't really doubt that it would. Everyone was just so predictable.

She'd just decided she was satisfied with her vantage point when Mack and Stefan arrived, their horses heavily laden with packs that she assumed contained the weapons, food, and medicines she'd asked for. She ran down the slope to meet them, taking a rocky path between the trees so as to minimise the tracks she left.

"Thanks for this," she said, moving to help them to unburden the horses. "Let's make sure no sneaky Shadows have come early, and then we can move everything inside the caves."

They stepped warily into the cave mouth, looking around for any signs of disturbance. But the subtle markers they'd left when the Association moved out were all still in place; clearly no-one had been here since they'd left. Nevertheless, they kept their knives out until they'd gone over the main cavern from top to bottom.

Then they hefted the packs inside, and Mack started to cut the bindings while Stefan led the horses through to the area they'd previously used for stabling.

"Here, this is the kit Daniel sent," Mack said, passing across a small but surprisingly heavy case. "It's strange to be back in these caves again, isn't it?"

"I didn't spend that much time here."

"No, I suppose you didn't. Too busy pretending to be a Shadow."

Eleanor opened the case and inspected the contents. Daniel had tied neatly-written labels around the neck of every bottle and jar, so she wouldn't have to think too hard. He'd sent a box of prepared woundwort poultices, a wide-necked jar of topical ointment for lesser scratches, six bottles of poppy tea, a jar of arnica lotion, more woundwort leaves, honey, and alcohol for cleaning out wounds. And then there was a large bottle labelled 'Strengthening Tonic,' which she guessed was his polite way of saying 'Bull Testicle Extract.'

"Any bandages?" she asked Mack, who himself was busily sorting food and weaponry into neat piles on the ground.

"Somewhere," he said. "I haven't got to them yet."

"As long as they're somewhere." She arranged the jars again and shut the case. "I'm taking this up to the watchtower, do you want to bring the food? You and Stefan can wait up there while the kids defend themselves, I don't want them to know we're here."

Mack straightened, balancing a stack of food parcels in his arms. "You're sure of this ambush, then?" he asked as he followed her to the back of the cave.

"They won't miss this opportunity," Eleanor said. She turned into a narrow passageway and started up the steep staircase that was carved into the rock. It was tight enough that her elbows brushed the walls, the rough surface catching at her sleeves as she climbed. "I want you two up here to keep an eye on things. If the kids get themselves in trouble and don't realise they can fall back inside the caves, you can start shooting. You've brought the crossbows, haven't you?"

"Just as you said," Mack agreed.

"Right. But you only get involved if they're really in danger. I want it to feel real."

"Sure, I get it."

The long chamber they called the watchtower was above the mouth of the cave, and featured half a dozen arrow-slits that had been chipped out of the face of the cliff. From the outside, they could have been natural cracks, and were in any case mostly concealed by the thick creepers which grew across the rock. But from within, they gave a perfect aspect across the clearing.

Eleanor set the medicine case down against the back wall, and Mack deposited his parcels alongside.

"We brought more than this," he said, considering the small pile. "It must be in the other packs, but it's all more of the same. Biscuits and saltfish and dried fruit."

Eleanor shrugged. "I wasn't expecting gourmet dinners."

After supplying the horses with hay and water, Stefan had continued working through the packs, and they came down the stairs to find him unpacking daggers and throwing knives from their leather rolls. Along with three crossbows, six full quivers, and a few short swords, there was now quite an array of weaponry on the cavern floor.

Mack bent to pick up a large, light bundle and tossed it to Eleanor. "Bandages," he explained as she caught it.

"Thanks."

Once they'd moved all the food and blankets up to the watchtower, and hidden most of the weapons in a dark corner of the cavern, they retired to the watchtower with their crossbows. Stefan took the first watch, while Mack and Eleanor tried to get comfortable on the uneven rocky floor.

Mack shook Eleanor awake at sunrise, and after a quick breakfast she returned outside to her viewpoint in the forest. She spent the daylight studying every detail her eyes could pick out in the clearing below. She was constantly alert for any signs of movement, but she saw nothing except the occasional bird fluttering between the trees. Then again, she wouldn't have expected to see the Shadows.

She took out a sheet of parchment and crafted a short message in the basic Venncastle code she'd taught herself from Raf's school notes:

Change of plans. Don't let our lads fall out to join attack. More value if they stay with new recruits.

She signed it with a brief and unreadable scrawl; she wanted to give the impression of a message written and sent in haste, and she was relying on the supposed secrecy of the code to vouch for the origin of the message. The reader should, she hoped, be able to think of some appropriate sender whose name fit with the approximate shapes of the squiggle. Satisfied with her work, she tucked the note safely into her pocket for later use.

Then, as the sun began to dip below the horizon, she carved words into the hilts of two wooden daggers, and waited.

The first to arrive, before the moon had even risen, was a tall, thick-set youth with wiry black hair. She recognized him as Simeon, from Dashfort 2.

She aimed the dagger carefully. As he stood there waiting, watching the forest, the wooden blade hit the ground only inches from his feet. He pulled it out of the grass, and she watched the way his eyes flickered as he read the message.

SHOW THIS TO THE OTHERS.
EXPECT AN AMBUSH.
PREPARE TO DEFEND CAVES.

He looked around to see where it had come from, but Eleanor was crouching well out of sight. He moved around until his back was against the rocks, scanning the edge of the forest, now more purposeful in his waiting.

The movement, when it came, was Lukal.

The two young men acknowledged one another with appropriate caution, and though she couldn't hear what they said she assumed that the greetings they exchanged were the challenges and responses she'd given them.

Simeon beckoned Lukal to come closer and handed him the wooden dagger to read. As they pored over it together, Eleanor fired her second message-dagger into the ground between their feet, making them jump apart and tense until they realised it was another message rather than the start of an attack.

This time the inscription gave more practical help, directing them towards the box of spare throwing knives she'd stashed on a ledge inside the mouth of the cave. Simeon scrambled up to find them, and although he passed a couple of blades down to Lukal, he kept the elevated position and most of the stock for himself.

Richard was the next to arrive, closely followed by Kit, and as each in turn read the message from the first dagger they began to form a human shield around the mouth of the cave.

Eleanor simply waited and watched. So far, it was all going to plan.

Tal and Gaven came into the clearing together, as she'd suspected they would. Everything she'd stressed about individual decisions had only pushed them closer together. Well, that was where she wanted them. They were one Venncastle-conditioned unit, so far as she was concerned, and she'd break them together.

She watched them with interest as the dagger was passed across and they read the message together. Tal took a central position in the formation, sword at the ready, while Gaven hovered at the edge. Ready to duck out and join the ambush party, then. That simple positioning gave away more than he could have imagined.

Dan and Aaron arrived a little after sunset, and seemed relieved to find they hadn't missed their chance. The three who hadn't appeared, Eleanor assumed, had chosen to take the Imperial route instead. Assuming they'd all gone into the Shadows or the military, they'd be crossing swords soon enough.

As the moon rose high overhead, she wondered when the ambush would strike. Were they expecting her to make the first move? Did they really think she'd march straight into the teeth of an attack? Well, she could wait all night if she had to.

She pulled her old Shadow Corps jacket over her clothes and took out the message she'd written earlier. She could hardly read the Venncastle code herself without her crib sheet – she hoped, despite his years out of the school, that her target wouldn't have that limitation.

She crept down into the forest, and it didn't take long for her to spot the grey jackets of the Military Special Corps soldiers crouching in the undergrowth, along with one or two blue-suited Shadows. They were so sure of themselves that they hadn't even bothered with camouflage. She picked out a young lad in Special Corps uniform, marched up to him, and slid the note into his hand.

"I need you to take this to Ivan," she said. He nodded and listened, seeing only the uniform, not asking for any proof of her status. "Venncastle have sent word. He'll understand."

"Yes, ma'am." He didn't even unfold the paper. She could hardly believe it. If so simple a disguise were so effective it'd be all too easy for her to slit their throats one at a time... but she wouldn't cheat. She needed this too much.

The youth ran off through the trees, and Eleanor climbed back to a decent vantage point. She'd been gambling that Ivan would be here to command the attack personally, but this was such an opportunity – she'd be amazed if he'd left it to anyone else's charge. That the soldier hadn't been fazed by her request suggested she'd been right in her assessment.

The students took turns to sleep in shifts at the mouth of the cave, but they slept with their school knives grasped in their hands. Eleanor didn't dare to close her eyes for even one brief moment. She wanted them to manage this on their own, but she wouldn't let them be massacred if they made mistakes. And either Mack or Stefan would be keeping a similar watch from behind the creepers.

The ambush party finally moved as dawn was breaking, and Eleanor shimmied up a nearby tree to get a better view of them. Thirty Specials and half a dozen Shadows suddenly materialized from between the trees, closing in on the boys who still waited at the mouth of the cave. Tal kicked Lukal and Kit awake, and they scrambled hurriedly into position.

As she watched the Imperial forces approach she wondered whether she'd made a mistake. What chance did eight sleep-deprived schoolboys have against an elite military unit? But she'd given them a defensible location, the attackers didn't have the element of surprise they'd hoped for, and they'd been arrogant enough to send a fairly small force. Besides, she was relying on it being a close fight. If she'd wanted to stack the odds, she could have brought more backup of her own.

The students exchanged puzzled glances, wondering now if this was a test or whether they should strike to kill. She knew just how they were feeling; she'd asked the same questions of Raf in Taraska.

"It's both this time," she murmured to herself. "Just because I'm testing you doesn't mean it isn't real."

She could only hope they'd work that out for themselves before it was too late.

They banded more tightly together as the Specials drew in around them; the Shadows hovered near the edge of the clearing, waiting. Eleanor saw Kit's eyes track around as he counted them out, noting their positions, and she was glad at least one of them had noticed.

The Specials approached in two rows, moving in perfectly synchronised formation. The back row advanced as the front row stood still to let them pass, then they paused and waited as the roles were reversed. Step, step, pause. Step, step, pause. However much the Shadows had been militarized by the Empress, she could never imagine them adopting this stilted, choreographed motion. Step, step, pause. What could it possibly gain the Specials to walk with such a pattern?

Simeon was still sitting on the ledge, feet dangling over the edge. It put him in the best position, a couple of feet above the heads of the others. As the Specials came closer he took careful aim and flung one of his knives towards the nearest soldier.

That was the moment that Eleanor understood the bizarre formation. On an individual level, the Specials were a long way from the proficiency and expertise of the Shadows, but as a unit they were more than the sum of their skills. The target of the knife didn't even flinch in an attempt to get out of its path, but the man on his left stepped neatly past him and cut the blade out of the air. Eleanor cursed quietly. She had some ideas of how to get past their careful guard, but the boys were fresh from school. She couldn't expect them to see it. Simeon had frozen; his next knife was poised but he didn't release it, not wanting to lose another blade into the dirt for nothing.

They hesitated just long enough for the first line of Specials to reach them – and then hesitation stopped being an option. As the attackers engaged, Gaven turned and was about to plunge his dagger into Richard's side, but from the corner of his eye he saw a flash of iron as one of the Specials came up beside him. He spun round to defend himself, blocking with the dagger he'd been about to use. Though he tried to negotiate his way into the attacking line, the soldiers wouldn't stop pressing him and he was forced to fight back. Richard, exchanging blows with his own Special Corps opponent, was too preoccupied to even notice how close he'd come to being betrayed.

The students were putting up a good fight, but they were both outnumbered and outclassed. Injuries and tiredness combined to slow their movements, and they started to make more and more mistakes. By contrast, on the Imperial side there were soldiers – not to mention the Shadows – who had yet to engage in the fight. Eleanor was considering whether she needed to go down and help them out, when Simeon's voice disturbed her thoughts: "Retreat! Fall back!"

She hadn't even noticed him leave his post until he came running from deep within the cave.

"Are you mad?" Tal asked, shouting over his shoulder as he fenced with one of the Specials. He feinted left and then lunged, taking the girl down with a cruel stab to the stomach. She writhed on the ground, screaming in pain until one of her colleagues knelt beside her and slit her throat.

"Fall back!" Simeon waved his hands as he cried for their attention. "Fall back! There's natural walls inside the cave. We can defend it, come on, quick!"

Eleanor knew the rock formation he was talking about, and was glad he'd found it. If they swallowed their pride and took his suggestion, they could hold off the Imperial attack indefinitely. And – though the students didn't yet know it – they even had plenty of supplies in the caves to withstand a short siege. The Imperial forces would give up after a day or two, not wanting to waste much time starving out mere boys, and particularly not with the occasional crossbow bolt if they got too close.

Dan and Lukal started to pull back straight away, and gradually the others went along with them, edging backwards towards the natural fortifications Simeon had found. Tal and Gaven resisted the longest, until they were almost separated from the line. Tal stepped back in a hurry, not wanting to be isolated and surrounded by the enemy. Gaven made another attempt to change sides, but as three Specials continued to attack him he had no choice but to fight back, and then he too

240

was forced to join the others retreating into the relative safety of the cave.

The twelve remaining Specials formed a barricade across the cave's entrance, but didn't follow the boys inside. Eleanor breathed a little easier. The caves were unassailable. Now it was just a waiting game, and they'd get bored soon enough.

But the Imperial forces didn't look like they were about to give up and go home, or even to settle down and wait. A couple of the Shadows – Ivan, and a towering lad that Eleanor didn't recognise from Association days – stepped out of the shade of the trees to confer with the young lieutenant of the Specials. Of course she couldn't hear them, but their animated gestures toward the caves suggested they were planning an assault. Well, let them try.

The lieutenant barked orders at his men, and the group split in two. Half of them disappeared between the trees while the remainder, joined by the Shadows, formed a knot by the mouth of the cave. In tight formation, they moved inside.

Eleanor slipped down from her treetop perch and crept down towards the clearing. It should all be fine so long as the boys kept their nerve, but she wasn't quite confident in them. Besides, she could take out a few of the forest lurkers while they weren't expecting anything. Every dead Special was one fewer enemy in the battles to come.

She loaded her blowpipe. The dart she selected carried a poison of Daniel's invention, one which would paralyse the victim before slowly killing him. In these circumstances it would be better to avoid the writhing agony which tended to accompany the fast-acting poisons.

She spied her first target crouching between two trunks. Perfect. He wouldn't even have far to fall. She came within a few feet of him before firing the dart straight into his neck, and he seemed not to even notice. He was trying to hold his muscles still anyway; he'd be dead before he realised he was frozen to the spot.

She crept around the clearing and quickly despatched two more, before noises emanating from the caves disturbed her. But the sounds weren't what she expected to hear: instead of the clash of weaponry, there came coughing and shouted curses.

Eleanor broke cover and sprinted across the clearing, trusting the element of surprise to confuse the remaining lurkers between the trees – after all, she was coming from the wrong direction, and she was still wearing her uniform jacket. She felt a knife fly past her ear as she ran, but there was no cover nearer than the cave itself, and no time to stop and worry about other blades that might follow. Inside the mouth of the cave, though, she found chaos. The air was thick with an acrid black smoke. Almost nothing was visible, but most of the coughing came from the back of the cave where she expected to see the students.

She dropped to her knees, lowered her head to where the air was clearer, and spotted the feet of the knot of Imperial troops. After taking a deep breath of clean air, she launched herself into the middle of them. She held a knife in each hand and slashed wildly as she spun, taking down five soldiers and a couple of Shadows before she even paused to draw breath. She dived to the ground, trusting the smoke to cover her as she rolled out of reach, and stopped to consider her next move. Crouched against the wall of the cave, she could see only the backs of their heels as the surviving men ran from the sudden massacre.

She got to her feet and turned back to where the students were watching her through the gradually-dissipating smoke, eyes wide. Only Gaven managed not to look surprised, but she was confident even he wouldn't have seen anything quite like this before.

"Don't know what you're staring at," she said. "Any one of you could've done that."

Then she leap-frogged over the wall and knocked Gaven and Tal to the ground, pinning them down with one bloody knife against each throat while her new colleagues fanned out to defend against anyone who might decide to come back for more.

"Which of you set this up?" she demanded, looking from one young face to the other.

"Why d'you think that?" Tal asked.

"Just answer the question. Did you arrange this?"

He shook his head, and since she'd already decided he was innocent, she released him to concentrate her efforts on Gaven.

"Gaven?"

He looked straight into her eyes, and she wondered what he was planning. He wasn't the sort to rest under her blade without considering his options.

"Don't move," she said. "I'd be sorry to lose you now, but I'll kill you if I have to."

"Do you expect me to defect?"

"You already have."

"No."

"You understand I can't let you go. It's up to you whether I send our thanks to the school – or the regrettable news of your death. So let's talk."

"There's nothing to talk about."

"Where do you think your first loyalty lies – with the Empire? With Venncastle?"

He nodded as though there were no need to choose between the two.

"You're wrong. It's here." She plunged her dagger towards his throat, pulling back only as the point dimpled his flesh. "Whatever they tell you, when it matters, your first priority is to live. Why didn't you fall out to join the ambush party? That's what you'd planned."

He kept his silence, still watching her.

"If you won't answer, I'll tell you. They didn't give you the chance, and in the heat of a battle like that you fight back or you get killed. I'm glad you made the right decision."

"You sound like you planned it."

"I did."

"But we–" he started, then stopped himself just short of a confession. "How could you plan for the Imperial forces to ambush you?"

"I'm sorry, did you think you were being clever when you went to tell the Provost about our little chat?"

She left a moment for him to answer, but he remained characteristically silent.

"Well, it's not your fault you're predictable, though we'll

try to train you out of it."

"I mentioned your offer," he said. "They said we could use the opportunity to take down all the Association recruits. They don't want you trying to steal Venncastle men."

"Theft? How quaint. And what did they promise you for your part in this? A star within weeks of stepping into uniform?"

His face tightened with anger. "I can't be bought."

"No, of course not. Just another of the ways you think you're special."

"What are you doing?" Tal asked. He was still sitting more or less where she'd left him, watching.

"I'm just talking a little sense into your friend," she said. "I know you've already made your mind up, but this one's still half tempted by the idea of a glorious martyrdom."

"Hey! I don't plan on dying."

"Then you'd better get up and make yourself useful."

She shifted her weight to let him move, and watched as his eyes flicked from her face to her weapons. Then his resolve wilted, and he got calmly to his feet.

"I suppose that's how it is, then."

"Good." She glanced across at the others, counted them once, and then again to check. "Where's Richard?"

None of them spoke, but Simeon cast his eyes down and inclined his head almost imperceptibly towards the ground. Peering past him, she could make out a dark lump in the shadows.

"Dead?" she asked, and he nodded.

"Well, this isn't quite how I wanted you to start your careers, but none of us asked for this war." She stepped across and threw her cloak across the body. "Come on, let's get started. We'll move him later."

She led the students up to the watchtower where Mack and Stefan were both still poised at their arrow-slits.

"Any signs of life out there?" she asked.

"Not since you sent them running," Mack said without looking away from the window.

Eleanor turned back to the students, who had filtered in

behind her and arranged themselves in a line along the back wall.

"Welcome to the Association," she said, taking off her Shadow Corps jacket and draping it over the back of a chair. "I haven't introduced myself properly. My name's Eleanor, and these are my colleagues, Mack and Stefan."

She watched the students' reactions as she spoke. None of them spoke, but she could see them studying her with a mixture of fascination and envy, just as she'd once studied the Association's more experienced members.

"We ran the Association from these caves until we got access to our new headquarters," she continued. "And you're going to stay here until I can trust you to travel without getting us killed."

"So this is the academy now?" Tal asked.

"The academy is history, for a while at least. I wish we had the luxury of running a full two-year training programme, but we're in difficult times. We should have a few days before they can bring backup, so we need to be ready to move soon. I'm going to do my best to keep you alive, but anything more fancy than that will have to wait."

As she spoke she was conscious that she'd already failed them. Richard's body lay testament to that.

"You've had a long night and it's time for you to get some sleep," she went on. "But first, I suspect you might be hungry."

A couple of the lads nodded, and she handed two large flasks to Lukal.

"If you go back the way we came, and follow the tunnel down from the back of the cavern, there's a freshwater spring. Fill these and come straight back up here."

While he was gone, she opened the medical case Daniel had prepared for her, and proceeded to dispense woundwort poultices and cotton bandages to patch up the worst of their injuries.

Lukal returned with the water and after the boys had drunk their fill, Eleanor took a swig from one of the flasks. It was a fast-flowing stream that ran in the depths of the caves, and they were close to the source, so the water was always fresh and clear and cold. Just what she needed.

The food parcels contained stocks of biscuits and dried fish and fruit – more akin to emergency stores than the gourmet banquet with which she'd been welcomed to the academy, but she made no apology for it as she handed out rations. Things were very different now. She had no patience for anyone who might worry about home comforts in times of war, but fortunately the students were all quick to suppress their disappointment.

Once they'd seen to the essentials of food, water, and first aid, Eleanor gave out blankets and encouraged the students to sleep. She took one of the crossbows, and brought Lukal with her to guard the entrance while the others rested.

"Will you help me move these bodies?" she asked.

Richard's body lay near their feet, and several Specials and Shadows beyond. They dragged the strangers outside first, stripping weapons and money from the corpses before dropping them in a heap inside the forest. Then they went back for Richard.

"He'd want us to use his weapons," Lukal said, hesitating over the body. "Wouldn't he?"

"I've never understood why people get more squeamish around bodies which used to be on their side," Eleanor said. "It's just another dead weight now. If you want his knives, take them – he won't be using them again."

"I suppose so." Lukal took the daggers from Richard's belt and added them to the pile of recovered weapons, then cut his purse and threw it across to Eleanor.

They sat on the rocks behind the barricade and Eleanor offered him a couple of biscuits.

"I don't really think they'll bother to attack us again," she said. "Certainly not until they can fetch reinforcements from the city. But it's always best to be careful."

He glanced back into the caves. "Am I on duty all night?"

"Give the others a little time – you're the only one who wasn't really hurt in the fight. But you can doze here if you want, I'll wake you if there's trouble."

He arranged himself with his back against the wall, and a

moment later he was snoring. Eleanor didn't expect any disturbances and none came; after a long and boring watch, she woke Lukal and sent him to fetch Tal and Simeon to take over. Only once they were settled in their positions did Eleanor curl up on a nearby ledge and risk allowing herself to sleep, the crossbow still ready in her hand.

Once everyone had rested, Eleanor roused them and brought out more biscuits for a meal she called breakfast, though it was late afternoon. She gave the students each a dose of Daniel's strengthening tonic, as well, though she wouldn't tell them what it was. They'd grow tired enough through training that the extra stamina would barely begin to compensate, but she didn't want to have to explain the tincture's unconventional origins.

She led them down to a cavern that the Association had used as its practice hall when they'd been based here, and unpacked some blunted knives.

"Right," she said. "Let's see what you can do. I've read your assessment files, of course, but I need to get my own idea of what you're each capable of."

She formed them into a circle and directed Kit and Aaron to take the first turn at sparring. After they each had a chance to challenge in a winner-stays-on competition, she wasn't terribly surprised to see Gaven emerge victorious. Pulling her own dagger from its hilt she stepped into the circle herself.

He was as impassive as ever as he watched her approach, barely keeping his guard up. She took a few small steps around the circle and then lunged towards him, flicking her knife into her left hand and bringing the blade up against his throat while with her right hand she took care of his dagger, blocking his thrust and sending his weapon spinning across the floor.

"Sorry," she said as she stepped back. "But you were being careless."

"Let's try that again," he said, retrieving his knife and dropping into a more obvious guard this time.

"Later. I want time for that lesson to sink in, first. Arrogance is a typical Venncastle trait and it's important we get past that sooner rather than later."

"Why did you go to all this trouble to recruit us if you're

just going to slander our school?" Tal asked.

"Some of us would have preferred to manage without you," Lukal muttered.

"Don't misunderstand me," Eleanor said. "I have a lot of respect for Venncastle and its methods."

She punctuated her words with the confirmation hand gesture, a subtle interleaving of fingers, and smiled when even the imperturbable Gaven couldn't quite suppress his shock. Tal didn't even try.

"The Association has always pandered to Venncastle," Lukal said. "Why did I make the mistake of thinking things would be different since the edict?"

Eleanor ignored him and continued to address herself to Gaven and Tal: "There's a fine line between pride and arrogance. However justified your self-confidence, overconfidence is a weakness that needs fixing. As for you," – she turned to Lukal – "We'll have no more of your sectarian whining. We're all in this together. Does anyone have a problem with that?"

The students were silent.

"Okay. Now let's see how well you climb."

As she watched them picking out their routes up the craggy walls of the cavern, she caught herself reminiscing fondly over her own carefree days at the academy, when climbing better and faster than her peers had been one of the few things that mattered. Simeon twisted himself under a particularly challenging overhang, fingers jammed into a barely-stable crack as his toes scrabbled for purchase. When he reached the top, Eleanor called out to him.

"Simeon!"

"Yeah?"

"Come here."

She waited as he scrambled down the rock surface again. He dropped the last few feet and rolled, then got to his feet and faced her, smiling.

"That's the last time you take the hard route just to be fancy," she said. "Understood?"

He looked into her eyes for a moment, caught the

248

seriousness of her expression, and his pride turned to embarassment. He nodded.

"Good. We don't have time to impress anyone – the easy way is the safe way."

"Safe?" Tal asked. "Isn't death an occupational hazard in a job like this?"

"There's a guy called Bill who taught me combat at the academy," Eleanor said. "And in my first class he made us sit down and listen while he told us we weren't in the military. We thought he was a bit crazy, but he was right and it's still true. You're not here to be footsoldiers of the revolution."

"But..."

"No buts. If we need people to die for this, we have hundreds of rebels for that. The Association was here before the Empire and it'll be here after this war. I'm not saying you won't get hurt, but I don't want you throwing your lives away."

She set out targets to check their accuracy with throwing knives and stars, instructed them briefly in the art of aiming a blowpipe, and tested their balance and agility. Only after she was sure she'd got a measure of them all did Eleanor allow them a meal break.

Chapter 19

It was three days after the ambush that Eleanor decided to make a move. It was hard to judge whether the students would be more help or hindrance on the journey, but she wanted to get well clear of the caves before anyone decided to come back and try to wipe them out. They loaded the horses with what remained of their provisions, and started the days-long walk back to Woolport.

They rowed out to the island under cover of darkness. Sebastien was on the night watch and Mack called out greetings before he had chance to challenge them.

"You've brought us fresh blood, then." He glanced across at the students. "Just seven?"

"Three didn't show up, and one was killed in the ambush," she said flatly. "The Empire lost more."

She waved the students forward from the boat, and pointed them towards the rocky tunnel which formed the entrance to their new home.

"Do you want me to wake the council?" Sebastien asked.

"No, it'll wait till morning," she said. "The kids can sleep in the practice hall."

She settled them with blankets and plenty of snacks, and woke a couple of her colleagues to keep watch at the door. In her own mind she was sure she could trust them now, even Gaven, but she'd never hear the last of it if she gave them the run of headquarters and anything did go wrong.

The next morning she summoned the council to convene over breakfast.

"That was fast," Laban said. "I don't think anyone was expecting you home so soon after the solstice."

"They're a good group," Eleanor said. "They need a lot more training, of course, but I brought them back as soon as it was safe to travel."

"Where are they?"

"In the practice hall. I set guards at the door – I know some of you are nervous of our new Venncastle colleagues."

She looked pointedly at Daniel. He raised an eyebrow in surprise, but said nothing.

"I'll need some help with their training," she added. "Someone to take them on with hand-to-hand, definitely, and some sessions of athletics, sailing, climbing, and general sneaking around."

She'd already cut poisons from the schedule entirely, much to Daniel's displeasure, arguing that it was more efficient for everyone if skilled apothecaries like himself made up enough preparations for everyone. It was, she'd insisted, only the equivalent of Harold's mastery in the smithy: no-one argued that every man should have to forge his own blades. Eventually she'd managed to shut him up only with the promise that he could take as much time as he wanted to instruct the new students once everything had stabilized. He knew better than to reopen the issue in front of the council.

"I'll keep up with projectiles for a month or two," she continued, "but then I need to head back to Almont and pick up the revolutionary guards again."

"We had a report while you were gone," Don said. "From one of our people embedded in a rebel group in Dashfort. They've heard about what you're doing in Almont, and three groups there have started to talk about working together."

"Great. Have you sent some words of encouragement?"

"I wrote straight back. It's the perfect opportunity for him to step up and take the lead there."

Daniel caught up with her after the meeting disbanded, leaning against the wall to block her passage.

"I did not think you could succeed," he said. "Not with Venncastle."

"I know."

"I was wrong." She watched as he struggled for words. "About many things."

"Well, you won't make that mistake again."

She smiled to try and signal that she was prepared to forgive him, but he was staring morosely at his feet.

"You said... You said we were broken," he said. "What does that mean? What do you need me to do?"

"It's okay," she said, reaching up to touch his cheek. "Let's just forget it."

He avoided her eyes. "How can I forget you?"

"I mean, let's forget we ever fell out. Okay? Let's start again." A smile spread across her face. "Just like we started the first time – with half a bottle of Burning Death. I've still got some."

"It is early for that."

"Well, we can skip the drink." She wrapped her arms around his waist and tucked her fingers into his waistband. "But I wouldn't mind going back to bed."

She took his hand and led him to his room; it was closer than hers, and for once she didn't mind that it was a laboratory full of strange-smelling potions. She hardly even noticed. She forgot all about the students, too, and Daniel had to remind her to go down to the practice hall after they'd finished making up. She splashed water over her skin, but she was still flushed when she arrived.

"Been busy?" Tal asked. She wasn't sure if she imagined the smirk... but the boy always smirked.

She ignored his question and directed their attention towards the waiting target boards and their varying degrees of competence with the battle stars. As she demonstrated a couple of easy techniques she knew she was flinging the stars with a little more than the necessary force, annoyed at herself for relenting so easily.

Her monthly bleed was five days overdue before she remembered what they'd both forgotten. She barged into Daniel's laboratory, gave Matt a look which told him he could leave quickly or be painfully evicted, and collapsed into a chair.

"I haven't bled," she said the moment they were alone. "We forgot. I need you to make up some more of this." She rolled the empty bottle across the bench towards him.

"Okay." Daniel nodded. "Relax, there is no hurry."

"That's easy for you to say – you're not the one with a tiny person suddenly growing inside you."

He picked up the bottle and turned it between his fingers, his expression suddenly thoughtful. "Do you not think this is ridiculous?"

"What?"

"You travelled across the Empire to find new students, yet we go to these efforts to avoid producing our own children." He came to stand beside her, put one arm around her shoulders and ran the fingers of his other hand across her belly. "You have the power to give us someone untouched by the Imperial schools. No conditioning to break or recruitment to negotiate."

She frowned. "It takes a long time to turn a baby into a useful adult."

"This will not be a short war – and there comes an age where even a child can be useful. I could fight long before I was seventeen."

"Are you serious?"

"I have never been more so."

"Let me think about it." Images swirled in her head, and she suddenly felt sick and dizzy. "If there's really no rush with the potion, then I can have some time to think."

She'd hoped that 'time to think' would mean time to herself, but over the next few days Daniel sought her out more and more often to ask whether she'd reached a decision.

"You have been thinking enough," he said, coming unannounced into her bedroom one morning. "What have you thought?"

"Okay. Fine." As hard as she tried, she couldn't find a good excuse to say no.

"Good." He nodded, looked a little befuddled, and turned away. "Yes, that is good. Well done."

"It wasn't just me." She wrapped her arms around his waist and rested her cheek against his back. "It's a joint effort, this one."

"You have the harder part," he said. "Though you will have around six months before you have to stop working."

"How do you know more about this than I do?"

"I have been studying you for years."

She laughed, remembering some of his more unusual experiments. "Yeah, you have. Anyway, if I've only got six months I'd better head back to Almont sooner rather than later. We've got a revolution to organise. Do you want to come?"

"I have work to do here."

"Of course you have."

"Must you go? I thought Andreas was there."

"Yeah, but he's no strategist. Someone has to steer this."

"Take care of our child." He put his hand on her stomach. "No strong spirits, and no more tonic."

"Why not?"

"Remember when you first tried it, and you thought I had poisoned you?"

She nodded.

"That is why."

The First Revolutionary Guards had been developing their skills under Andreas' guidance, and Eleanor barely recognised the group she'd left just a couple of months earlier. Eric had lost his baker's belly, Rosemary had taught her little son to hold a knife safely by the handle, and they were all developing visible muscles.

"Have you taken them out yet?" Eleanor asked Andreas.

He shook his head. "Not yet."

"Well, I think we should go and get our hands dirty."

"I was planning to go home, now you're back."

"Of course. Go. I can handle it." She turned back to where her new guards were entertaining themselves with casual sparring. "Right, who wants to put their new skills into practice?"

They agreed with enthusiasm, and Eleanor lined them up to check their weapons. Once she was sure they were all properly equipped she led them out into the street.

"Welcome back, boss," Dash said, falling into step beside her. "We've missed you."

"It looks like you've all been making good progress without me."

He shrugged. "It wasn't the same."

As they reached the edge of the rebel district, she left him in charge of the group and jogged ahead to scout out the streets. A large group with obvious weaponry would stand out from the usual Almont crowds, and she wanted to make sure they got a chance to try their blades on an easy target before the Imperial armies were summoned back to defend the city.

Around the next corner there were three men chatting in a quiet street, all dressed in the uniform of the palace guards. Well, that should be a manageable number for a first kill. She was about to call a charge when the man with his back to her laughed, tilting his head just enough to show his profile.

Eleanor ducked back around the corner and held her hand up to tell the others to stop. Why was Raf disguising himself as a palace guard? And what about the other two? She flattened herself against the wall and peered around the corner to double-check – not that there was really a doubt in her mind.

The revolutionary guards stood patiently a few feet behind her, watching for her signal. She kept her right hand raised – they might interpret anything else as their cue to move – and with her left, pulled the blowpipe from behind her ear. She leaned around the corner, tongue playing across the twin openings of the pipe. Sedate or kill? She had no idea whether he'd keep his side of the bargain, even if she gave him chance, but she certainly wouldn't let her fledgling soldiers use his body to blood their swords. It was a simple matter of respect: he deserved better.

He moved as if he were about to turn, leaving her no more time to consider her options. She couldn't let him see her: he'd recognise her in a heartbeat, just as easily as she'd recognised him. With her next breath she puffed a dart straight towards him. He scratched at the back of his neck, but before he could pull out the dart his knees gave way and he collapsed to the ground.

Eleanor waved her trainees forwards, and as they stepped around the corner the two palace guards broke into a panicked sprint. They definitely weren't undercover Shadows, then. She wondered whether they'd even known Raf's true identity. Perhaps his disguise was for their benefit. Most of the revolutionary guards ran after them, but Dash caught Eleanor's arm, keeping her back.

"What about him, boss?" he asked, voice barely a whisper, motioning towards Raf's body.

"Shadow," she said. "Too dangerous for you. Come on, let's go and see if we can catch up with the others."

Dash continued to stare at Raf on the ground. "I don't think he's dead yet."

"It's a slow poison," Eleanor lied. "Now come on or we'll miss all the fun."

By the time they caught up with the others they were already a little too late. The two palace guards lay bleeding into the ground while the revolutionaries stood over them with blood-soaked weapons, looking in equal parts elated and confused. Molly was shaking, sobbing into Nicole's shoulder.

Eleanor surveyed the bodies. It had been a clumsy job – she'd have to work on their style it they were going to be efficient at this – but they'd succeeded, even without her to supervise them. And without Dash, who'd always been the strongest of the new recruits.

"Good job," she said. "There's a fire post just around the corner, go and wash your weapons and your hands in the buckets. Dash, go with them and keep a look-out. Molly, can I have a word?"

Nicole gave Molly one final hug before leaving her to go with the others.

"You okay?" Eleanor asked.

Molly glanced towards the bodies, then turned and vomited against the wall. "Not really," she said. "Sorry, I'm letting you all down."

"The shock catches everyone differently," Eleanor said. "It'll catch up with the others later."

"I don't think I'm cut out for this."

"Here." Eleanor fished a small flask of dark spirits from her pocket and removed the cork. "Drink this, it'll make you feel better."

"I'm not sure I should..."

"Just drink it. Trust me, okay?"

She nodded and put the bottle to her lips, taking a small sip at first, then quickly tipping the flask for a longer draught.

"You're just in shock," Eleanor said as she put the bottle away again. "Go home, get some sleep, take tomorrow for yourself, then come back and tell me what you want to do. There are plenty of other roles for a bright girl like you, if you decide you can't stomach this."

Molly nodded, and bent to pick up her knife from the street.

"Let me clean that for you," Eleanor said, though the knife – like Molly herself – was barely flecked with blood. She'd clearly had no active part in the attack.

"Are you sure?"

"It's one less thing for you to worry about – and I need to catch up with the others at the fire post, anyway."

"Thanks."

"It's fine. I'll see you tomorrow night."

Molly walked away from the bodies; it wasn't her most direct route home, but Eleanor understood. It was more of a surprise that only one of them was having second thoughts.

"Where's Molly?" Nicole demanded as soon as Eleanor rejoined the others. "You can't make her leave just because she cried, it's not fair."

"It's okay." Eleanor laid a hand on Nicole's shoulder. "I didn't make her do anything, I just suggested she should get some rest. Meanwhile, we've got cause to celebrate – let me buy you all a drink or two."

It was hardly a meaningful offer since Eleanor's money – the Association's money, in fact – was the only thing keeping the revolutionary force fed and watered, but no-one objected to the gesture. The Old Barrel Yard was already buzzing with life, but the other patrons recognised the new guards and their bloodstained shirts, and quickly cleared space for them to sit down and celebrate. They settled into a corner with flagons of spiced ale and plates full of hot sausages.

"To my First Revolutionary Guards," Eleanor said, raising her tankard. "May you always be a thorn in the Empress's side."

"To us," Dash echoed.

"And to Eleanor," Lise added. "Without whom we'd still be a ragtag bunch of nobodies."

"The Empress will curse our names tonight," Eleanor said. "But I don't want her to forget about us tomorrow, or next week, or any time before she draws her last breath."

There was a murmur of agreement.

"From tomorrow we'll aim for a kill every night. Just palace guards and police, nothing hard. Those of you whose gods would appreciate the sacrifice, you're welcome to dedicate your actions however you choose. And we'll need to redouble our defences – they'll come for us, and hard."

The next morning she laid out a rota of duties, splitting rebel gangs into morning, afternoon, and night shifts to maintain a constant guard around the perimeter of the main rebel district. The bloody display of the previous night had brought in dozens more volunteers in need of training, and she assigned them to shifts along with more experienced guards. There should be plenty of quiet times when they could practise, and even untrained hands might be useful when the worst came.

That was the defence. For the offensive part of her plan, Eleanor would take one or two of her First Corps guards out every night to spill Imperial blood – at least until she was sure they could manage without her. She pulled Dash to one side and told him that he'd be first.

"You missed the action last night," she said. "And I guarantee I'm not the only one who noticed."

"No-one's going to hold that against me," he said.

"They might in a week or two, when I tell them you're going to be leading this unit on my behalf. Better if we make sure you've got an impeccable record first."

He nodded his understanding. If he was at all surprised by what she said, he didn't show it. For her part, Eleanor was just pleased that he didn't seem to object to the idea of extra responsibility.

"So, you'll come with me tonight and make your own mark on this city. Bring one of the others for backup."

They met again at nightfall, by the door of the Old Barrel Yard. Dash had invited one of the sailors to join them. A middle-aged woman with wiry muscles kept taut by the rigours of a life at sea, Violet had always been one of the group's best all-rounders.

"Are you ready to make trouble?" Eleanor asked.

Violet cracked her knuckles. "Ready as the wind, cap."

Dash simply inclined his head, and stepped out into the damp streets. It had been a grey day and rain still dripped steadily from the rooftops.

"They'll be on their guard after yesterday," Eleanor said. "So we'll go up. No-one ever looks up, even though any fool knows that no-one ever looks up."

They scrambled over wet tiles until they reached an alley just outside the Marble Quarter.

"Close enough that we should get some targets," Eleanor said, "but far enough from reinforcements that we stand a chance of getting away with it. These are the kinds of things I need you all thinking about if we're going to give the Empress nightmares."

"Thanks boss," Dash said, and she was sure he was absorbing every lesson exactly as she intended, his mind focused on his future role as much as on their present outing.

"So what are we waiting for?" Violet asked, peering down into the street where a couple of young women walked arm in arm.

"Uniforms," Eleanor said.

"Stupid Imperial lackeys deserve whatever they get. Anyone who's not one of us..."

Eleanor looked at Dash. "Do you want to explain?"

"It's a message," he said. "Killing people at random doesn't say anything except we're good at killing people. Attacking the uniforms tells the Empress it's personal."

Eleanor smiled. She couldn't have put it better herself.

They didn't have to wait too long for a uniform; the alley was a natural cut-through for palace guards on their way home after the day shift. Eleanor had to hold Violet back from a suicidal attack as a dozen loud, laughing youngsters passed beneath them, but the next guard was alone and lost in thought. Eleanor gave the signal, Dash and Violet dropped into the street, and the young man had barely looked to see what the noise was all about before Violet had him in a double arm-lock and Dash sliced cleanly across his throat.

"Nicely done," Eleanor said, scrambling down to join them.

"If we're in the business of leaving messages, I don't suppose you're going to let me take him to the ocean for my Lady," Violet said, a wistful note in her voice.

"Cut a finger or two to throw into the ocean," Dash suggested as he wiped his dagger clean on the dead man's tunic. "And you could carve your sigil into his chest – that wouldn't be a problem, would it, boss?"

"No problem," Eleanor said, feeling suddenly out of her depth. It was one thing to know that some of the rebels followed the cults, but quite another to hear this talk of carved sigils and sacrifices.

Violet drew her knife to start work while Eleanor and Dash took up look-out positions on either side of her. Once she'd hacked through one finger she set off to take her offering down to the harbour.

"You didn't want to dedicate this one yourself?" Eleanor asked Dash as they turned to walk back to the Old Barrel Yard.

"I'm not pledged to anyone," he said. "And you saw how much it matters to her. No-one keeps the old ways like sailors."

"Oh?"

"Hadn't you noticed? It's hardly surprising – the Sea can pull her victims into the depths without a warning, so it's best to stay on her good side."

"I suppose so."

"I thought you'd been to sea. I'm surprised you didn't see it."

Eleanor shrugged. "I didn't know what I was looking for. Until last spring I thought religion was just a footnote in the history books."

"They might've killed the hearth gods, but you'll never stop a sailor begging mercy from the Lady of the Waters."

"They got your assignment wrong, didn't they?"

He looked at her, surprised by the sudden change of subject. "What makes you say that?"

"You're good at fighting and you know a lot about people. You should've been someone important in the army, but the bastards always seem to get it wrong."

He shook his head. "My assignment was perfect. This is necessary, but it isn't fun. I'm happiest when I'm using my hands."

"You know, once everything's calmed down a bit there's someone I'd like you to meet back at the Association."

She told him about Harold's artistic bent as well as his technical proficiency, and showed him her own graduation knives by way of example. She thought of Ivan's little inventions, too, but there was no sense mentioning him when – she hoped – she'd never see him again. If their paths were to cross, she'd have to try and kill him. So she stuck to describing weaponry, and somehow the discussion occupied them until they reached the Old Barrel Yard. Eleanor turned towards the stairs.

"Aren't you staying up for a drink, boss?" Dash asked, holding open the door to the bar.

"I need to sleep. This child's draining me."

He stared at her waist, though there was nothing yet to see. "You're pregnant?"

"Yep."

"You shouldn't come out with us if it's tiring you."

"I'll be the judge of that."

He held up his hands. "No offence meant. You just take care of yourself, that's all."

Chapter 20

By midwinter Eleanor's belly had swollen so far as to make even walking uncomfortable. Every day as she performed her morning stretches she found herself needing to further adjust her posture to account for the steadily increasing weight she carried at her waist, and it was becoming more and more of a challenge for her to keep up with the others when she took the guards out on exercises.

"I think I'm going to head home in the next few days," she said. She was sitting at her usual table in the Old Barrel Yard with a few of her First Revolutionary Guard Corps. The voluntary force had continued to grow as the movement expanded, with more and more little rebel gangs putting themselves forwards for guard duties, but Eleanor usually socialised with a subset of her own trainees.

"Don't go," Rosemary said.

"You don't really need me any more, and if I leave it much longer it's only going to get harder to make the journey."

"Don't go at all." Rosemary rested one hand on her arm. "It's all men back there, isn't it? What use will they be when the baby comes?"

"Precisely none, I expect."

"Then stay," Molly chimed in. "Rosie can teach you all sorts of things about babies."

Eleanor glanced down to where Ollie sat between their feet. He was playing with a blunted dagger, seemingly oblivious to the adults surrounding him.

"And you don't even like him," Nicole said.

"Who?" Eleanor asked, still thinking of Ollie and wondering how anyone could think she didn't like such an adorable boy.

"Your boyfriend."

Eleanor stared at her. "Whatever gave you that impression?"

"You never talk about him except to complain."

"That's just the way things are with me and Daniel. It

doesn't mean I don't like him. Anyway, I'll only be out of action for a few months and Dash can look after things here. Speaking of which" – she turned to Dash – "we need to talk strategy before I go. Can you spare me some time tomorrow?"

"Let's talk about it now."

Eleanor looked around the table. It wasn't that she didn't trust the others, but Dash was the only one she'd ever really thought of as a potentially serious player.

Dash must have seen her eyes move. "We're all friends here," he said.

"And we're all risking our lives in this war," Nicole said. "You can't just cut us out of the important stuff."

"I just thought it might be boring," Eleanor said. "But if you're sure you don't mind, we can do it now."

"We don't mind, do we?"

Rosemary, Jace, and Molly all agreed that they were positively longing to hear it, and Eleanor realised she was fighting a losing battle.

"I'll probably be gone for about five months," she said. "I need to come back in time to visit the schools so I'll come and see you then, but in the meantime you need to start thinking about long-term security."

Dash nodded.

"Keep Second Corps here to run the regular guard, and maybe bring Sixth across from the eastern district just to make sure. You've been doing a great job with the nightly raids, but now I want you to take First Corps out and get me a gate."

"A gate?"

Eleanor reached for the map that Ade kept behind the bar, and laid it out on the table. The four rebel districts had been shaded in as they developed and grew, and now accounted for almost a fifth of the ground within the city walls.

"If we can secure all three gates – or even stop the supply carts further out – we can effectively beseige the city. But that's just a nice daydream for now. The critical point is that if we don't take one gate quickly, they'll do the same to us."

"Yes boss."

"There's plenty of farmers out there who'd like to keep the

revolution fed and watered, but it won't do us any good if we're trapped within our own walls."

Dash glanced down at Ollie. "I'm not sure all of First should come out on a job like this."

"That's up to you. They're your unit."

"What d'you think, Rosie?"

Rosemary studied her fingertips for a long moment. "Ade and Nasha could look after him," she said at last. "It'd only be a few days at a time, wouldn't it? He's got to learn to live without me some day."

"Anything else you want us to take care of?" Dash asked.

Eleanor shook her head. "Just get me that gate before our stores run low."

She considered going straight to Daniel's room when she reached the island headquarters but it was the middle of the night and she wanted to sleep, not talk. It was only after lunch the next day that he heard she'd arrived and came to wake her.

"Morning," she said, propping herself up against the pillows and rubbing sleep from her eyes.

"It is past noon."

"It was a long trip," she said. "And this kid likes me to sleep, when it's not kicking me awake. Can you see? There."

She pointed towards where the foot – at least, she guessed it was a foot – had been a moment before, but the child was apparently shy. While Daniel was watching there was no movement.

He sat on the edge of the bed and cupped his hands around her waist before leaning across to kiss her. "Welcome home."

"I suppose you want me to get up now."

He frowned. "At some time you should call the council. We need to hear of your progress."

"Well." She yawned and stretched, arching her back to try and stretch the pains from her spine. "You could call them, and I'll be there once I'm washed and dressed."

By the time she reached the council chamber the others were already seated, and the room fell into silence the moment she opened the door. She lowered herself awkwardly into the nearest chair.

"Welcome back, Eleanor." Laban smiled across the table. "What news from the city?"

"We've consolidated four rebel districts in Almont," she said, "defended by fifteen units of Revolutionary Guards, each about a hundred strong. They're not the Specials, by any means, but they're basically okay and we've had a few successful raids on the city's armouries and grain stores. Of course, First Corps are my personal project. They've been continuing a wave of attacks against the palace guards, but I've diverted them now into getting one of the city gates under our control. Further out, we're in touch with similar districts forming in Dashfort and Bastion, all with Association men at the helm. Mistleton was the first town to fall completely to the rebels, and we think Lashquay won't be far behind."

There were murmurs of approval from around the table.

"We haven't really crossed swords with the main Imperial forces yet, though we've had to execute a couple of spies. I think the Empress is waiting to see what we do next."

"And what are we going to do next?" Gerald asked.

"For as long as she's waiting for us to make a move, we'll take it slowly," Eleanor said. "Strengthen our defences and make sure our supply routes are solid. I'd rather take longer and make sure we get it absolutely right."

"You're turning into a proper field commander," Don said. "When I suggested you go and stir up some rebels I never imagined you'd take to it so naturally."

"It's all pretty obvious when you just look at it. Well, this part is. I'm not quite sure how we go from a few towns and districts to control of the whole Empire."

"Slowly," Don said. "Just like you said."

"Well, I won't be doing anything for the next couple of months," Eleanor said. "Although if anyone wants to go out and take my place, I can give you the codes you need to get past our guards."

"Best if you keep control," Don said before anyone could volunteer. "At the moment it's completely clear who's running the show, and we don't want anyone getting confused over that."

"Just tell us when you need backup," Gerald said.

"And when you are ready for us to remove the Empress," Daniel added.

"I'll need all the help I can get when that time comes," Eleanor said. "My guard units aren't cut out for that kind of mission. But before we knock the Empire spiralling into chaos we need to make sure the dice are going to fall the right way."

She went down to the practice hall after the meeting, and was just warming up with some gentle exercises when Gaven found her.

"How's it going?" he asked.

She looked round in surprise; he was the last person she would have expected to engage in small talk. "Tiring," she said, wiping sweat from her forehead. "I'll be glad when this nonsense is over."

He nodded, trying as hard as an eighteen-year-old boy could to look as if he understood the trials of pregnancy. "Have you thought about schools?"

"We're going to keep it here with us," Eleanor said. "I'm not going through all this just to give another child to the Empire."

"Have you considered Venncastle?"

She hesitated for a moment, caught off-guard by the earnest expression on his face. It was almost as though he expected her to not only consider such an absurd suggestion, but to jump on it with relief. "Venncastle sided with them," she said. "We had to prise you away from your assignment, remember."

"But you managed it," he said. "So you could do it again. Think about it, at least. You know he'd be well trained with us."

"No point worrying about that until we find out whether it's a boy or a girl, anyway."

"You mean you don't know?"

She shook her head. "How could I? I can't see through my own skin."

"Venncastle fathers have been testing this for decades." He started towards her and then hesitated, realising she'd be a dangerous woman to touch without invitation. "May I?"

"Okay."

She watched, fascinated, as he pressed his fingers gently to her sides and felt around the bump.

"Have you done this before?" she asked.

"No."

"So how confident are you?"

He placed his hands flat against her skin and held still until the baby kicked him, once and then again.

"All the signs suggest a boy," he said, straightening and stepping away from her. "I could be wrong, of course, but if I'm not..."

He left the sentence hanging, unfinished.

"Thanks."

"So you'll think about Venncastle?"

"I'll think about it," she said. It would be hard not to think about it, though she knew that she couldn't even raise the idea with Daniel without a fight.

"Good." He nodded and made a hasty retreat from the hall.

She tried to get back into her exercises but she struggled to maintain the necessary levels of concentration. The more she thought about it, the more sure she felt that Gaven's diagnosis was correct. They were having a little boy. It made the whole thing feel suddenly more real, as if the blob that was growing inside her had suddenly coalesced into a real person. She walked across to Daniel's lab in a daze.

"We need to think of a name for our little boy," she said as she pulled out a chair.

"A boy?" Daniel asked. "How do you know?"

She wasn't sure what compelled her to lie, but mentioning her conversation with Gaven felt like a bad idea. "I found out in Almont," she said. "One of my volunteers used to be a midwife."

"We have many practicalities to discuss," Daniel said. "Quite aside from his name. Where will he live once he is born?"

"He's going to live here, of course. What do you mean?"

"What had you imagined? Will I keep him in my rooms? Or

yours?"

"Mine. You live in a lab." She waved her arms towards the shelves full of specimens, ingredients, and potions. Even the desk between them was cluttered with neat rows of bottles and equipment.

"But you could both live here, with me. Everything would be easier if we shared rooms."

"You can come round any time you like. I'm not moving into the apothecary, and I know you don't want to leave your work."

"And as we are to be parents, do you not think we should be married?" he continued, ignoring her comments.

"Why?"

"Under the old family ways, marriage was not optional."

"I thought we were trying to breed our own little warrior of the revolution. I'm not sure that's quite what it was all about in the old days."

"But we should do this properly." He unclipped the name bangle from around his wrist and started to separate the two halves. "Here."

She took the half he was offering and removed her own bangle slowly, wondering why it felt so strange. They were bringing their own little boy into the world. Compared to that, the exchange of wedding tokens could make no practical difference to their relationship, and yet it felt inexplicably significant. The feeling made her nervous.

She passed him half of her bangle, connected the remaining half to the piece he'd given her, and snapped the whole thing closed around her right wrist.

"If you will not live here, I will move to your rooms," he said as he fastened his own bangle in place. "I do not need to work all night."

"That's that, then," she said, although it didn't quite seem real. "Married. How long do you think it'll take the others to notice?"

"Everyone here is trained in observation," he said. "I would be disappointed if it was long."

Eleanor nodded. She was afraid he was right. "I'd better get on," she said, getting to her feet. "I promised Don I'd go into a bit more depth on my plans for the next stage of the revolution."

"When will you be ready?"

"Ready for what?"

"To take this revolt seriously. It is all just a game until we take the throne from the Empress."

She sank back into the chair. "It's all about timing. She's useful to us – she's an enemy everyone can hate. We're uniting people against her as much as anything. If you kill her today, someone like Leon inherits, and suddenly the Empire doesn't look so bad."

A smile touched the corner of Daniel's lips. "I think I see. We need to remove the line of succession first."

"That's not what I meant. We just need to have an obvious successor to step into the void, and it takes time to position someone like that."

"Who?" he asked. "You?"

She shrugged. "I don't know." It hadn't crossed her mind, but once he said it she saw that she might be an obvious choice. She'd certainly fallen into a leadership role; in the eyes of most revolutionaries, she was the one holding the reins.

"We should start work on the heirs at once," he said. "It will be easier with the family out of the way."

She thought back to Leon and Donna, and the effort she'd put into hiding their son. "They haven't done anything to deserve it. We could just let them slide into the history books."

"This is a war, Eleanor. It matters little what they have or have not done, if they stand in the way of progress."

She'd been back almost a month when Laban summoned her to his suite. She held her belly as she walked up the stairs, hoping to feel the child kicking again, always heartened that the baby could be active even while she was bored and housebound. She knocked lightly at the door and then let herself in without waiting for a reply.

His rooms here were smaller than the suite he'd had in Almont, but he'd laid out the same furniture in a similar arrangement. His practice dummy leaned in the corner behind the sofa, though the room was too cramped for him to make use of it. She walked in to find him sitting with his feet resting on the table, and he motioned for her to join him.

"Tea?" he asked, and she nodded. "Come, sit. How's the baby?"

"Still kicking, so I think he's okay." She kept her hand on her belly. "He'll be glad to be out of here."

"And you?"

She rolled her eyes. "Me too. I'm getting fed up with this."

"When do you expect the birth?"

"Around three months, by Daniel's calculations. I keep wishing it to come sooner."

He nodded, and they sipped their tea in silence.

"Why did you want to see me?" she asked at last.

"I understand," he said softly, "that you're thinking of keeping your child out of school."

Eleanor nodded.

"Are you sure that's a good idea?"

"He can live here. The Empire won't find him – or if they do find us, we've got bigger problems than hiding one child."

"But what kind of life can you offer him? What if this isn't where his talents lie? I know the system isn't perfect–"

"Perfect?" she interrupted. "It's hopeless."

"I know it's not perfect," he said. "Why do you think the council have always had our own measures in place? But the reasoning at the beginning was sound. No parents can guarantee a life which suits their child, or even know where their strengths lie. Only assessment do that, and the Assessors are good at their testing."

"Don't go saying things like that in the rebel districts."

"You can't threaten me," he said, his face hardening. "I know you had a bad experience, but your assignment was designed to bring you here."

"I'm not just talking about assignments, school was awful the whole time. You know I hated it."

"You were very unlucky."

"It doesn't give me much faith in the system. What was my

assignment before you got them to change it, anyway?"

"I didn't ask."

She looked at him, searching his face for any hint that he might be lying.

"Really," he said. "I didn't ask, it wasn't important."

"Well, I'm not sure it would have been what I deserved, even without your intervention. The Assessors never understood me."

There was a moment's silence, then he said, "That was your mother's doing."

"My mother?" Eleanor didn't even know who had given birth to her. How could the unknown woman have wrecked her childhood?

"Didn't you wonder why your teachers never steered you towards the areas you were best at? They weren't incompetent. Everyone saw where your skills pointed, but she wanted to protect you."

Eleanor took several deep, troubled breaths. Was her own mother really the reason she'd had such a difficult time? Had the woman somehow managed to infiltrate the staff and affect the whole path of her schooling? How had she even known which child was hers?

"Then who is my mother?" Eleanor asked.

His reply was so quiet that she couldn't make it out.

"What?"

"Isabelle," he repeated, louder this time.

She looked hard at him, suddenly skeptical. Surely it was against the rules for a headmistress to enrol her own daughter in her own school. And besides, the whole school knew that Isabelle had never had children; it was an open secret that she was barren. "How can that be? How could you know?"

"Because I'm your father."

The silence which followed felt like an eternity. Eleanor studied Laban's features with renewed vigour, assessing the plausibility of his declaration, trying in her mind to cause some combination of his face with that of her former headmistress to result in a likeness of herself. She'd never really paid much attention to his appearance before. He had black hair and his skin was a few shades darker than her own, but then she definitely shared Isabelle's colourings and complexion. He was short, as she was, though that meant little. But his ears were small like hers, and his nose turned slightly upwards the way her own had done before it had been broken for her. Deciding that she probably believed him, she wondered how she was supposed to feel.

The Empire had outlawed family units three generations earlier, and no records of paternity were even kept, so she'd never given much thought to the mystery people responsible for her existence. Yet now she was surprised to realise that she felt abandoned. If her parents had always known who she was then they should have told her – even if that meant breaking the law.

"Tell me everything," she said, trying not to betray her feelings with her voice.

He nodded, and began to recount how he'd met Isabelle when they were both teenagers just out of school, and how he'd offered to give up on his dream of finding the academy in order to stay with her. But she had told him that he had to go, so he'd gone, and only later found out that he had a daughter. Isabelle had enrolled the girl like any other anonymous child in her school, and had refused to introduce her to Laban however many times he'd asked.

So Eleanor had grown up under her mother's watchful eye, and had been discouraged from anything that might set her to follow in her father's footsteps – particularly after another girl from Mersioc had failed in such spectacularly gruesome fashion in an attempt to find the academy.

"So you thought you'd come and train me yourself?"

"My contacts at the Assessors' College indicated that your skills were in the right areas – you were taking after me whether you liked it or not. I thought you might benefit from a little encouragement."

She shook her head, trying to take it all in. "Why are you telling me this now?" It was too much, too sudden, at a time when her body and her emotions were already in turmoil.

"I should have thought that would be obvious." His gaze strayed to her belly.

"So you can claim your new grandson?"

"Claim?" He laughed. "I'm not laying any sort of claim, to you or to him. I'm just hoping you'll listen to what I have to say."

"Say it, then." Better to get it out of the way quickly, if there was to be more. If this great revelation had just been a prelude, she knew she couldn't leave before he'd finished saying his piece.

"I don't know how to explain what it's like, having a child. But the one thing I have a duty to tell you is that loving someone the way only a parent can love their child – that opens you up to a world of pain beyond your imagination. Every wound you've suffered so far would seem a pin-prick in comparison."

She didn't know what to say. It sounded so much like what Daniel had said about their relationship, back at the beginning. And of course what he'd said had been right, so far as it went: there had been times when worry had weakened her, and times when he'd hurt her more than she should have allowed. But that was only half the story. Eventually she looked up.

"Isn't it worth it, though?" she asked.

A smile twisted the corner of his lips. "Oh, it's worth every second," he said. "But now you can't say I didn't warn you."

Chapter 21

The message from Lucille came earlier than Eleanor had
expected; she'd hoped to put off thinking about the next round
of school visits until after her son was born. But Lucille didn't
even know that she was pregnant, and had already pulled
together the folders. Daniel tried to persuade her to send
someone else, but she wanted to do this one herself. Anyone
else might still be stupid enough to ignore the Venncastle
names on principle. Besides, it would only be a short trip, and
she was seriously bored of being confined to headquarters.

She arrived in Almont late at night and took her usual room
under the eaves of the Old Barrel Yard, adjusting the skylight to
stop the rain dripping onto the floorboards. Ade looked at her
with evident curiosity, but he knew better than to ask what she
was doing back in town.

The next morning she took an indirect route out of the rebel
district, made a few stops to ensure she hadn't been followed,
and walked to the Marble Quarter. It had all been so much
easier when she could just enter Lucille's office by the window,
but she couldn't climb in her current condition. Pretending she
had a normal kind of appointment, she introduced herself to the
receptionist.

"Lucille isn't available today," the young man said, barely
looking up. He tapped his pencil in an irregular rhythm against
the edge of the table, watching each bounce.

"She's expecting me."

Tap. Tap-tap. Tap.

"Sorry. She's indisposed to visitors, with or without an
appointment."

"Do you know when she'll be back?"

He stopped tapping and considered her for a moment, then
leaned forwards and lowered his voice. "Between you and me,
I'd find another Assessor to help you with your business.
Lucille's got herself in trouble with the Empress's special

forces. We're not sure if she'll ever come back to work."

"Okay," Eleanor was careful to hide her emotions. "Thank you for your time."

She turned to walk slowly from the lobby, feeling sick to her stomach and determined not to show it. The irregular tapping resumed behind her. Special forces? She wondered what that meant. Had her little recruitment exercise drawn the attention of the Shadows?

She walked around the block and stopped out of the way in a quiet alley. Apparently she was going to have to go climbing after all. She looked around for an easy route, settling for a gap between two buildings where she could angle her bump into the corner and find holds on the two facing walls. Since returning to the Association she hadn't even climbed for practice, and she struggled with the simplest of movements. It was as if all the strength had gone out of her shoulders, and her muscles felt like jelly. When she eventually hauled herself onto the icy tiles she rested on her side to catch her breath. The baby kicked, and she stroked her belly around where she thought his head might be.

"Sorry Martin," she whispered. "But this is one job that can't wait."

She returned to the Assessors' College over the rooftops, lowering herself awkwardly in through a top floor window and walking down two flights of stairs to Lucille's corridor. And then, because there were two smartly uniformed city guards standing outside Lucille's office door, she strode past without casting even a glance in their direction, walked around the building, and scrambled out again through another window. She cursed under her breath. She'd come too late. If the list had been in Lucille's office then it had fallen into the wrong hands now.

She climbed slowly to the ground and walked to the edge of the Market Quarter where she stopped to exchange pass phrases with a man from Second Corps who was guarding the street. She strode into the Old Barrel Yard, leaned against the bar, and waved at Ade for a glass of water which she finished in three gulps. She couldn't shake the feeling that whatever had happened to Lucille, it was all her fault. It was too close to be a coincidence.

She ascertained from Ade that First Corps were out doing exactly as she'd asked, waging war on the city's northeast gate. She didn't know the other units' strengths so well, but a few carefully chosen questions led her to a tall, muscular woman called Sally who was widely known to be the best climber in Sixth Corps, and possibly in the whole Revolutionary Guard. Eleanor introduced herself, though it was obvious Sally already knew who she was, and briefly explained her predicament.

"And that's where you come in," she finished. "I need to go back tonight, and I really need someone to rope me, because climbing with this figure is a nightmare."

Sally agreed at once and Eleanor sent her to get some rest while they waited for nightfall. She tried to sleep herself, but her old shoulder injury twinged and she found herself staring at the ceiling instead.

Sally returned wearing cropped trousers and a tailored black top which fitted her closely and showed off her curves, with her silver-blonde hair pulled back into a tight bun. They set out in the early hours of the night, long after Eleanor was sure even the most dedicated Assessor would have gone home. She knotted a harness around her torso – the kind of comprehensive support she hadn't relied on since she was a child – and made sure it was well hidden beneath her cloak before leading Sally towards the Assessors' College. The climb was much easier with a rope, and Eleanor left Sally on the roof while she went in to investigate Lucille's office.

Thankfully the guards had gone home for the night, so it looked like they'd been tasked to guard against inquisitive colleagues rather than anything more serious. Eleanor still moved on tiptoes and hesitated before trying the door, mindful of a possible trap. As it happened the door swung open easily and without any surprises. The office was in complete disarray: the incoherent scramble of a half-finished search rather than the messy-but-organised piles that characterised Lucille's normal mode. Eleanor picked her way across to the desk, taking care not to step on any of the scattered paperwork, though the marks of earlier footsteps showed that previous visitors had been less mindful.

She didn't dare to light even a single candle against the dark; a light in the College at this time of night would bring city guards running at the best of times. And if Lucille was in really deep trouble, it could even be soldiers or Shadows.

She found nothing that looked like her list. A couple of complex charts plotted students against test scores, with potential assignment notes jotted in the margins, but they were assignments to areas like trade and manufacturing. Nothing even military; that wasn't Lucille's field. Somewhere, in some other office, would be charts that plotted the strength and agility and speed of the Empire's physical elite, against their skills with weapons and hand-to-hand, against their temperament and other personal qualities. In theory if she had all that information she could reconstruct the list for herself, but she didn't know anything about the methodology. If she had to attempt it, her results would be little better than guesswork.

Eleanor looked around again. Student folders were scattered across the room. If Lucille had already had all the folders waiting for her, was it possible that the relevant files could still be here despite the search?

She picked up the nearest example and flicked through it. A carpenter, the cover sheet proposed, although it hadn't yet been signed off and confirmed. Boring. Eleanor threw it back onto the pile, trying to maintain the haphazard appearance.

The next two were equally dull, but the third had 'Shdw?' scribbled in a curly hand that contrasted with Lucille's neat print. The report gave details of a youth called Daryl, at Venncastle. Eleanor turned the pages quickly: impressive physical scores, high intelligence, good apothecary, exceptional integrity. She was almost certain she'd found one of the records she was looking for. He'd do, in any case.

She worked her way around the room, and found four more folders that seemed to match her mental image of a good Association recruit. If Lucille had kept them in one pile in her office, the search had muddled everything together. At least it seemed to mean that whoever was searching hadn't known what to look for.

Eleanor gathered up the files she was interested in and considered taking them with her, but documents missing from the archives would look very suspicious. Instead she let herself into a few of the corridor's other offices and, whenever she found one that looked busy enough that an extra file wouldn't be noticed, slipped one or other of the folders into high piles of works-in-progress. She hoped it would be too late for anyone to connect the dots – or too late for it to matter – by the time the files turned up again.

And then, with her head full of names and numbers, she went to collect Sally from the roof and headed back to the tavern to think. Once she had a drink in her hand she turned to address herself to the tavern's assorted patrons, daring to speak with relative freedom now that access to the whole district was so carefully controlled.

"Okay, everyone." She clapped her hands to silence the room. "I need to find a new contact in the College of Assessors. Does anyone have any friends who work there? Preferably someone who might be sympathetic to our cause?"

"No honest worker could ever support such an artefact of the Imperial tyranny," said a young woman with an infant strapped to her back. "You'll never find a sympathetic Assessor."

Eleanor slammed her hand into the bar and the woman jumped, startled.

"That's short term thinking," Eleanor said. "And the process of revolution is a long one. If we don't have a tame Assessor right now, we should be working on turning one or two to our side."

"But assessment is the poison at the heart of the Empire," the woman said once she'd recovered from the initial shock. "It's the very symbol of everything we want to destroy."

"I won't argue with that," Eleanor said. "But that's precisely why we need to be able to attack from within."

"I had a friend in the College," said a man from the other side of the room. "I even thought I might marry her, before all this, but she was afraid of what the revolution might mean for her job."

"There are plenty of promises we can make," Eleanor said, though she was painfully conscious of the way she'd failed to protect Lucille when the wrath of the Empire came. "If she's only worried about her role under the new order, we can negotiate something suitable."

"I'll try to get back in touch," the man said. "But I don't know how she'll take it."

"Thanks, I'd appreciate it. Anyone else?"

"There's one old friend I could try," Ade said. "Just let me know exactly what you need."

"Which of the Empire's other organs should we be looking to subvert?" another man called across the room.

"Good question. The palace guards are an obvious target, as is anyone who works in the Imperial household. The police and the city guard. Maybe even the prisons."

"And the Shadow Corps." The young woman who spoke was petite with delicate features, and despite the heat of the fire she was wrapped top to toe in a heavy woollen cloak with a cowl that covered her head and threw shadows across her face. A few wisps of black hair had escaped to stray across her eyes.

Something in her voice suggested she'd had personal dealings with the Shadows, and Eleanor wondered what story lay behind her venom, but it seemed an unwise time to ask. Instead, she said, "We've tried infiltrating the Shadows. Though with all the new recruits it could soon be time to try again. We'll keep an eye on it."

The young woman nodded. "You should."

The crowd gradually thinned, and Eleanor was about to go up to her room for the night when the cowled woman approached her. "You're Eleanor, aren't you? Can you spare me a moment?"

Eleanor nodded. "Shall we have another drink?"

"I'd prefer privacy." She glanced towards the tavern's few remaining patrons, and then at Ade who was cleaning up behind the bar. "Could we step outside?"

"It's cold out there. Come up to my room, we won't be disturbed."

The girl followed her up the stairs, the soft fall of leather soles echoing behind the thud of Eleanor's riveted boots.

"What's your name?" Eleanor asked as she put a match to lanterns around the room. The air was damp, and every wick took long moments to dry out and sizzle into life.

"Lauren."

"Sit down." The attic room had a warm bed but no chairs; hospitality was supposed to happen in the bar downstairs. Eleanor sat cross-legged beneath the skylight, and waved for the girl to sit on the floor in front of her.

As she bent to her knees the light fell across her face and Eleanor could see her features clearly for the first time: olive skin, dark eyes, full lips, and a jagged, deep scar along her jaw. She noticed the focus of Eleanor's eyes and dropped the cloak from her head as she sat. She pushed her hair back, clearing her face. In so doing she revealed more scars: across her left temple, along her hairline, and at the side of her neck. A small chunk was missing from the top of her right ear.

"Mine aren't the first battle scars you've seen," she said when she caught Eleanor examining her face. "They won't be the last."

"What brought you into the revolution?" Eleanor asked. She thought of Lauren's earlier words, and the hatred behind them. "Did the Shadows do this to you?"

"No." She hesitated; looked sideways at the lantern, then down to the floor. "I'm in the Shadow Corps."

Eleanor caught her breath sharply, sliding her knife from its wrist sheath as she exhaled. How had one of the Shadows infiltrated their innermost sanctuary? These days the Old Barrel Yard had passwords on the door, as well as those protecting the whole district, and if one Shadow had tricked her way inside then there was no reason to believe there wouldn't be more.

"Let me speak before you kill me," Lauren said. There was no fear in her voice, but also no threat.

"I think you'd better tell me your story," Eleanor agreed. She folded her hands on her lap but kept the knife in one hand, ready. "And quickly."

"I was in the Specials, to begin with. And very, very good at my job. I was one of the first military reassignments into the new unit when the Shadows were formed."

"When did that happen?" There'd been no military transfers when Eleanor had seen the inside of the Shadows.

"Half a year ago."

"And then what?"

"I'm just like every other revolutionary. An idealist, if you favour that term. I didn't like the way it was going, I hate the things the Empress asks of us... just like you, if you're Association. I've heard enough about the rift to know what I missed."

"But you're still in the Shadows."

"That's what I wanted to talk about. I could leave, of course. I'm often tempted. But I thought... you're the one with the plan, the vision, you see. So when I heard you were back in town..."

Eleanor watched her without comment, letting her falter, waiting for her to fill her own uncomfortable silences.

"I thought it might be more useful if I stayed where I am," Lauren said, composing herself again. "With your permission. If I could be part of your plan."

She searched Eleanor's face for any clue to her thoughts while Eleanor continued to study her in return, giving her another long moment of silence to be sure she'd really finished. Then: "How long have you been playing this game?" Eleanor asked, her attention suddenly focused on practicalities.

"What game?"

"How long have you been sneaking out at night to drink in rebel bars?"

"Just a few weeks. Only a couple of times really. I wanted to see what was what. And then I heard you were here. I knew I needed to see you."

"Well, you were right about that. And you're certain you've never been followed?"

Lauren's expression hardened. "I may be ex-military, but I'm not an amateur."

"Okay, okay." Eleanor held up her hands in a small conciliatory gesture – though she still held her knife against her palm. "Relax. My friends will tell you I'm a perfectionist, but I'm only doing my job. We can't afford a single mistake."

Lauren nodded her understanding.

"It's for your own safety, anyhow. They already know where to find the rest of us."

"Yes, I see that."

"Do you? Well, we could do worse than talk about safety. If you want to do this properly, there won't always be a safe way out. I'll understand if you change your mind, but you'd better change it quickly."

"I won't change my mind."

"I hope you've had enough experience to say that and mean it. I know what you're taking on – I've been there. I know how hard it can get."

"Maybe you could... I mean, maybe if you had any tips. Was there anything you learnt the hard way?"

"You just promised me you weren't an amateur."

"I'm not." She straightened a little; chin up, shoulders back, pouting with offended pride. "I'm professional enough to recognise the value of experience."

"That's more like it." Eleanor allowed herself a genuine smile for the first time since the shock of learning she had a Shadow in her room. "None of this stammering and pleading. Act as if you deserve my respect and you'll get it. Ask me straight for my advice, and I'll happily give it."

"I'd appreciate that."

"Good. And we have more logistics to discuss, but it's getting late. Can you meet me at sunset tomorrow?"

"Of course. Here?"

"No. After you leave the rebel district tonight, you won't be coming back."

"But–"

"You're a Shadow and you need to act like one. The pass phrases will be changed just in case you're ever tempted – you can't compromise your position just because you feel like an evening with friends."

"You still don't trust me."

"You've asked me for a difficult assignment. I'm just doing what I'd do for anyone in that position: protecting you, and protecting the rest of us. It wouldn't do for anyone to notice one of the Shadows coming and going between rebel districts."

"It's okay, I understand. I wouldn't trust me, either."

"I trust you as much as I trust anyone on the day I meet them." She turned her wrist outwards to make a point as she slid her blade back into its sheath, though in reality unsheathing her knife would add only a couple of heartbeats to her reaction time. "And probably a little more: it takes guts to say the things you've said. So, you'll meet me tomorrow on the roof of the tannery, where the cattle road crosses the river, and we can talk."

"I'll be there."

Eleanor had deliberately chosen a low roof that was easy to climb onto, and Lauren was already perched on the tiles, face hidden again by the cowl of her cloak, when she arrived. They settled down in a gutter between two peaked rooftops; from the ground they were invisible, and the workshops were empty by this time of day so no-one would hear them.

"Is this a place you often use for meetings?" Lauren asked. "It seems... unusual."

"I'm not sure I've ever been here before," Eleanor said. "A regular spot would be a bad idea, for reasons that should be obvious."

"I thought the revolution had moved out of hiding. Everyone knows the approximate borders of the rebel districts, these days."

"That's a bit different. Most things aren't this sensitive. For most things a friendly tavern is fine, but we can't even trust our friends with this."

Lauren had been absent-mindedly rocking a loose tile to her left, but she stopped to look straight into Eleanor's eyes. "None of them?"

"None."

"Let me get this straight. Yesterday you told me I couldn't go back into the rebel districts. Now you're telling me you're going to let them think, if they pass me in my uniform, that I'm just another Imperial slave."

"You know the Shadows, so you understand as well as

anyone what you're getting in to. Every gap between you and us makes you safer. We can never guarantee there won't be a leak – that there isn't someone we think is one of us, who's actually spying for the Empire. So until you've finished you can't tell anyone who you are."

"So if I end up in a fight... then what? If they don't know me?"

"It depends. Try to choose your missions so you don't cross the path of the revolution, if you have a choice. What rank are you? Whose unit do you work in?"

"One star – same rank I had in the Specials, which doesn't translate to much choice over anything. But I'm under Karl and looking towards the mountains, so unless you're planning on moving in the south it should be okay."

"That should keep you well clear of difficult situations, then. As for wandering around the city in your uniform – the only ones who'd dare take on the Shadows are Association, and I'm the only one who's been spending much time in Almont lately."

"Okay."

"It's not too late to change your mind."

She shook her head. "It's fine, I just didn't realise I'd be so cut off."

"You'll be horribly isolated, so you need to be extra careful. Don't be tempted by the friendship of your enemies."

"I would never!"

It was another moment of fierce determination, and it caught Eleanor by surprise. There were times when Lauren seemed nervous and unsure of herself, and then she had these flashes of absolute certainty. As if it was physically impossible to have a friend with opposing views. Eleanor thought of Raf, and wished that were true.

"Everything's black and white in your eyes, isn't it? Good and bad. But there are some good guys in the Shadows. Capable, bright, sweet."

"They're still the enemy."

"And you know that, but they can sound very reasonable when they try. They'll be nice to you. They'll give you every opportunity to believe what they say."

"I'll be careful."

"Good." It was easy to picture Lauren spending time with her old friends – chatting and drinking with the Venncastle crowd, or playing dice in the barracks – and it felt very, very important that nothing developed further. There was too much danger there. "A few other things. Don't try to communicate with us, even – especially – when you really want to."

"Especially?"

"The times you most want to get a message through are probably the times that there's most at stake, but you can't risk it. We'll have to agree on somewhere that you can leave your updates."

"Here?" She fingered the loose tile again. "I could tuck a note under the corner."

"Do you have a waterproof pouch – sealskin, or something – to protect it if it rains?"

Lauren fished around under her shirt and pulled out a small wallet of tarred skins. "Will this do?" She tested it under the loose tile, where it slid almost completely out of sight.

"Perfect. The first thing I need you to do is find out what happened to my tame Assessor. She's called Lucille, she was picked up a couple of days ago."

"Lucille the assessor? I don't suppose you know her ID number?"

"M-R-eight-one-J-two-three-L-D-M."

"Okay. Anything else you can tell me?"

"She was working at the College in Almont, she had a list of students ready for me, and then someone came for her. I don't know exactly who, but someone official – they put the fear of death into the staff. I need to know what's happened to her. Plus anything else you can tell me about the Shadows' plans, of course. Leave a note here every new moon, and I'll come by to collect it and leave more instructions."

"When do I see you again?"

"You won't, as long as it's going well. We can't risk it."

"And if it goes badly?"

"I'll give you an emergency code word in case of trouble."

"How does that work?"

"It's your one way ticket back into the revolution. If you need to skip out of the Empire's sights in a hurry – if your life's in immediate danger – this will get you past any checkpoint."

"Sounds like a good system to have."

"Thankfully, we don't need it often. You can have code word river. Don't write it down, don't even say it until the day you need it. It'll only work once, and it'll tell everyone that you're in trouble. And then they'll tell me."

She nodded, mouthing the word in silence.

"All set?"

"And if I need to – what? I just say it instead of the regular response to a challenge at the border?"

"Just say 'code word river' to any rebel guard. Frankly, even someone who's not in the guard should know what their role is... I'm surprised you hadn't heard of it yourself. It's easy for civilians: don't panic, and find a guard who'll know what to do."

"Okay."

"Okay." Eleanor smiled. "Good luck, Lauren. You're doing an important job for us."

They went in opposite directions across the rooftops, Lauren north into the Marble Quarter to resume her place in the Shadow Corps, and Eleanor west towards the markets, the rebel district, and her bed in the Old Barrel Yard.

As she tried to sleep that night she wondered what she'd agreed to. She remembered her own days in the Shadows, how hard it had been to live that double life, and she wondered whether Lauren really knew what she was getting into. Well, it was too late for second thoughts. She'd succeed or – the alternative didn't bear thinking about, so Eleanor curled on her side, pulled the blankets tightly around her shoulders, and tried not to think too hard.

Chapter 22

It was only five days until the next new moon, and it was with some difficulty that Eleanor climbed onto the tannery roof to check for messages from Lauren. As she'd expected, there was a slim package tucked beneath the tiles.

She slipped the pouch into her pocket and set off home. Only when she got back to her room in the Old Barrel Yard did she carefully unwrap it to pull out the note and see what Lauren had to say.

L. in gaol. Under special guard, treason charges, investigation ongoing. Not looking good.

Eleanor lay on her back and stared up through the skylight, searching for inspiration in the gathering clouds. If Lucille was being tried as a revolutionary then she had to do something. Treason against the Empire carried a non-negotiable death penalty.

She could just imagine trying to get this one past the council. Springing conspirators from the Imperial cells would set a dangerous precedent; it would never be practical if everyone came to expect a rescue. But this was different. Lucille hadn't signed up for this. She gave a mental shrug and told herself there wasn't time to go back and discuss it with the council anyhow. It didn't really matter what they would've said, because they weren't going to have chance to say it. Just like she wouldn't have chance to find someone less pregnant to run the rescue mission.

"Are you ready for this, Martin?" she asked the bump. He kicked her hard, which she decided to take as a sign of his agreement.

"Just as well," she said, rolling onto her side. "It's not like we have much choice."

On the back of Lauren's note she sketched out a quick map of Almont's main Imperial prison, or what little she knew of it. She didn't know where they'd put a rogue assessor... would

Lucille really be treated as a dangerous rebel just because she'd been willing to pass along a list of names? The fact that Lauren had been able to find something out so easily suggested the Shadows might have been involved already, which wasn't a good sign. And even with that information there was little chance of tracing a single prisoner before being spotted; the gaol was huge and well guarded. She tore the paper in half and set the corner alight with the flame of her lamp.

On a fresh sheet she scribbled a reply to Lauren, asking for details of where precisely Lucille was being held and when the trial was expected to conclude. It would be useful to know what deadline she was working to.

She went to tuck her reply safely inside the pouch, when her fingers brushed against another scrap of paper. Wondering how she'd missed it before, she unfolded it and read the four short, unfortunate words: *Too late. Don't come.* It was Lauren's writing but in contrast to the neat and measured lines of the longer note, this message was scrawled untidily across the page.

Eleanor cursed and ripped apart the message she'd just written. This changed everything. Lucille was dead, and it was all her fault.

The only thing keeping Eleanor in Almont had been her plan to rescue Lucille, so there was suddenly no reason to stay. Once she'd provided Lauren with new instructions, she made her way slowly back to Woolport on a succession of borrowed horses. There were fewer carts running between towns these days, with every journey at risk of being waylaid by rebel supporters or opportunist highwaymen, so her only choice was to ride. Even sitting sidesaddle and maintaining a very gentle pace, it was an uncomfortable journey.

She wanted nothing more than to go to sleep as soon as she arrived back at the Association, but Daniel had moved into her room, and with him had moved heaps of debris that now cluttered the room.

"Are you going to tidy up in here?" she asked as she undressed ready for bed.

He rolled towards her, yawned, and brushed the hair from

his face. "Hnmmh?"

"You've turned my room into an outpost of your lab," she said, waving towards a precarious stack of books and bottles. "It's clutter and it's dangerous. When are you going to clear up?"

"Welcome back." He reached out and took her hand to pull her into bed. "I missed you, too."

"I'm serious, it's a real mess in here."

"When did you start worrying about a few stray papers?"

She frowned. "We're having a baby. This is his home too, you know."

"I will clear it all before the baby arrives."

"Tomorrow," she said. "Promise me you'll do it tomorrow."

"Okay."

She smiled and allowed herself to relax back into his arms, and then she was asleep before he'd even finished rearranging the blankets around her shoulders.

She got up the next morning with every intention of calling a council meeting straight after breakfast, but she'd barely started her morning stretches whe the stomach cramps began in earnest. She climbed back into bed, sent Daniel to fetch her some breakfast from the dining hall, and curled up under the covers to wait for him to return.

As well as bread and meat, he brought her a hot compress and a mug of herbal tea that wouldn't have been her first choice for flavour but which – he promised – would help to ease the pain.

"I think I'm going to have the baby today," she said as she propped herself up on pillows and sipped at the drink. "This is his way of telling me he wants to come out."

"What?"

"I can feel it. He's ready."

"By my calculation–" Daniel began, but she cut him off.

"Your calculations were wrong! He's ready to come out now."

"How do you know?"

"He moved while I was riding home. It's like he was working his way down inside me, getting ready to escape. I just know."

He shook his head, readjusting the compress he'd positioned around her waist. "We are not ready for this. Not yet. It is too soon."

"It's not like I can stop it, Daniel, do you think I have a choice? It's his decision."

"But we are not ready."

"Just find me a woman who's done this before, please. I don't know how this is supposed to work."

"As soon as night falls," he promised.

"He might be born by nightfall."

"Then all will be well. You know we cannot sail to the mainland in daylight. Now, what news can I take to the council?"

She gave him a very quick recap of events with Lucille, though she missed out Lauren's part of the story. The girl would be safer if no-one knew what she was doing.

Daniel left her alone and Eleanor tried to force herself back to sleep, but the cramping pains were too much. In an attempt to distract herself she shuffled Daniel's materials outside into the corridor, swept the floor, and changed the sheets on her bed. By the time he came back to bring her lunch and check on her progress, she was ready to demand a sleeping potion.

"Not a good idea," he said. "I think it would make you both sleep."

"Would that be so bad? He's not moving much at the moment."

"Better not to risk it."

"But I'm so tired, and I just can't get comfortable." She shuffled in the bed as if to prove her point, turning onto her side and then onto her back again.

"Try walking a little," he said. "I shall go to Woolport soon."

"She is there." Daniel pointed across to where Eleanor was crouching with her arms wrapped around her body, rocking back on her heels.

Eleanor looked round. "Who've you found?"

"This is Melissa," Daniel said. "She has come to help you."

"You?" Eleanor stared hard at her, then turned back to Daniel. "Is this the only woman you could find? Seriously? I asked you to find me someone who knows what's what, and she's about twelve!"

"I'm eighteen," Melissa said, stiffening. "And I've done this before, so I know exactly how you're feeling right now."

"Oh, you do, do you?"

"It's okay. It's normal to be nervous, and of course it's harder for you, without the Imperial midwives to show you what to do."

"You made use of their services, did you?"

"Well, yes, I..."

"And gave your child to their schools?"

"I'm not proud of my mistakes."

"I should think not." Eleanor bit her lip to keep from screaming, then turned her attention back to the girl who was, evidently, no kind of revolutionary. "What kind of Imperial slave are you?"

"I didn't come here to be insulted." Melissa turned towards the door, but Daniel stopped her.

"She is not normally like this. Please, stay."

"Okay." She nodded. "Okay, but Eleanor, you need to calm down. Do you have a herbalist here, or something?"

"I am quite accomplished in apothecary," Daniel said with uncharacteristic modesty. "What do you need?"

"I need to get some drugs in this woman so she'll shut up and listen. Pain relief, if nothing else."

"Come with me."

"Don't you dare leave me," Eleanor said, grabbing Daniel's wrist. "Don't you dare. You did this to me, and you'll see it through."

He turned back to Melissa. "Down the stairs, and on your left. There is a small store room, everything is labelled. I would suggest maybe poppy for the pain."

The moment they were alone in the room, Eleanor gripped Daniel's arm even more tightly and pulled him close. "Daniel, I'm serious. She gave her child to the schools. Isn't she even with the rebels? Where did you find her?"

"She is in the revolution, yes. But she is quite new."

"She's a child herself."

"You wanted someone who has done this, and she has, not long since. She is the best you could hope to find at short notice."

"Maybe I'll wait. When were you expecting him to arrive? Maybe I can just... you know... hold him in."

Daniel put his arm around her. "I know today has been hard," he said. "But it will be over soon."

Melissa returned with her arms full of jars and bottles, and arrayed them on the floor at the side of the room.

"Poppy extract," she said, picking one up and offering it to Daniel. "And I brought a few others."

"Poppy will do for now." Daniel took the jar, opened Eleanor's mouth, and placed a small, sticky brown ball onto her tongue. She spluttered at the bitter taste and struggled to force herself to swallow it without vomiting.

"Fetch some water," Daniel said. "And prepare a tea with ginger root and camomile flowers."

"Maybe you could do that while I find out what's going on here," Melissa said.

"We're having a baby," Eleanor said. "What in all the Empire do you *think* is going on?"

"How bad are the pains?"

"Nothing compared to some I've experienced, but bad enough that I want this to be over, preferably yesterday."

"Has it been getting worse over the day?"

"It comes and goes."

"Come and lie down for a moment, and let me have a look."

Eleanor took off her trousers, lay back on the bed, and watched with strangely detached curiosity as Melissa poked about between her legs.

"I think you've got a while yet," she said, wiping her hands clean. "Perhaps even a couple of days."

"How can that be? I was so sure he was ready to come out this morning."

"He may be ready, but you're not. You're still too tight."

While Eleanor was still struggling to accept that she might have been wrong, Daniel returned with the ginger tea. After she'd swallowed a couple of mouthfuls she turned to him.

"What was that stuff you made for Donna?"

"Donna?"

"The princess. You made up something for her to drink, to make her baby come sooner."

"I remember."

"Can you make some for me?"

"We are not in any rush."

"She says my body isn't ready, but I don't know how long I can just wait around. Please?"

"Wait until tomorrow. If you still want to hurry yourself, we can discuss it then."

"You should try to get some sleep," Melissa said. "You'll need all your energy to push him out."

"And you still won't let me have a sleeping draught?" she asked Daniel.

"You definitely need to rest." He looked to Melissa. "You believe it will be tomorrow before the birth begins?"

"Tomorrow afternoon at the earliest."

"Then I see no harm in a light sedative." He untied the pouch he always kept at his waist, fished around inside it for a moment, and brought out a bottle of small tablets. "Here, this should do."

"Just one?" Eleanor asked as he went to put the bottle away.

"One should be enough."

"Okay, but if I'm not asleep by the time I count to ten, you're giving me a second one." Eleanor stuck the tablet under her tongue and started to count; she was asleep before her lips managed to form themselves around the five.

By the time she came round it was late the next morning, and she woke to find the cramps in her abdomen were even worse than before. Every couple of breaths she found herself struggling against a new pain that was stronger and more intense than the last.

"Where's that girl?" she asked Daniel. "And why are you working in my room?"

He looked up from his pestle and mortar. "I thought you would want me to be here," he said.

"Yes, but not with all your potions and poisons, not when we're about to have a baby. Can't you leave it just for a couple of days?"

"I was only preparing more tea for you." He tilted the bowl so she could see inside, though she couldn't have identified the half-crushed seeds. "It is nothing dangerous."

"If that's for the pain, I could really do with it sooner rather than later."

"Here, eat this."

He brought her another sticky ball of poppy extract, and insisted again that she follow it up with an infusion of ginger and camomile.

"So the poppy does not make you sick," he explained as she sniffed uncertainly at the fragrant steam.

"Where's Melissa?"

"I told her she could rest," he said. "We will need her soon enough."

Another wave of pain hit her, knocking the breath from her lungs, and she gripped the mug so tightly she feared the pot might crack.

"Fetch her," she said. "It's getting worse."

"This is faster than I thought," Melissa said as Daniel ushered her into the room. She parted Eleanor's legs, made a brief examination, and nodded. "You're almost ready to push him out now. Come on, get up."

"What?"

"Get up and walk around. It'll help."

It was the last thing she felt like doing but she wasn't going to argue with anything that might get the whole experience over more quickly. She paced around the room, pausing at every contraction, almost enjoying the worsening pains. At least this meant something was happening.

She wasn't sure how, but some ancient part of her seemed to know exactly what was supposed to happen next. She pulled a blanket from the bed to kneel on, and pushed with muscles she hadn't known she possessed. Melissa crouched beside her and held out her hands to touch the crown of the child's head.

"Great job," she said. "Keep going like that, and he'll be out in no time."

Despite Melissa's encouraging words, progress was slow and painful. In the moments between pushes, whenever she relaxed her efforts to try and catch her breath, Eleanor could feel only an overwhelming burning pain where the baby's head was stretching her body in ways it had never been stretched before. She gripped Daniel's hand and tried to blink back tears.

"I need more poppy," she said. "It's wearing off."

Melissa reached for the jar, then hesitated and looked to Daniel for advice. "Can she have more? Is it wise?"

"I'm not a child, you don't need to baby me – just give me that."

"Two drops of poppy tea, in water," Daniel said. Melissa set down the jar and picked up a small bottle instead. She dripped a little into a glass of water, and Eleanor gulped it down as though it was her first drink after weeks in some dryland desert.

She had a brief respite once the baby's head was out, and then another spell of pushing and wanting to scream until his shoulders came through. After that it was all over quickly, and he fell into the sheet Melissa was holding ready.

The child's head lolled as Melissa wrapped him up, and for a moment Eleanor was afraid he wasn't breathing. Melissa handed her the bundle and she held it close, feeling the tiny body of her baby under the layers of thin fabric. She stroked his face but his eyes stayed closed.

"Is he okay?" she asked Daniel.

Daniel reached across and pressed one finger against the baby's neck, feeling for a pulse. "He lives, do not fear. Shall I wake him?"

She nodded and he left, returning moments later with a bottle of clear liquid. He dipped his little finger into the bottle neck and placed it against the baby's lips.

A moment later, the child opened his eyes and started to wail.

"Why is he crying?" Eleanor asked, suddenly feeling frantic. "What's wrong?"

"Crying is normal," Melissa said. "I'm sure you cried when you saw the enormity of the world. Remember he's only known the inside of your belly until now."

The cries intensified.

"But how will I know if he wants something?"

"Just hold him. If he needs more than that, you'll know."

They helped her back into bed and she wrapped herself and the child beneath layers of blankets, shivering from the stretch of time she'd spent half-naked in the chilly room. She wrapped herself protectively around the child and stroked his hair until he stopped crying. She'd almost dozed off when she was brought abruptly back to her senses by a pair of tiny lips clamping onto her left nipple.

"Melissa?" she asked, not wanting to disturb him by turning to see whether the girl was still there.

"What is it?"

"Look – I think he's hungry. What am I supposed to do now?"

Melissa pulled back the blankets and peered over her shoulder. "I'm not sure," she said, blushing. "They took my son away to the nursery before I got this far."

"I think he's trying to suck," Eleanor said. "Maybe he'll just get on with it."

She shuffled into a sitting position, supporting his head, and watched as his mouth worked. One small hand clutched at the blanket near his head.

"You can go home if you want," Eleanor said.

Melissa nodded. "I think you know as much as I do, now."

"Thanks for coming. And I'm sorry if I was short with you earlier, I was struggling."

"It's okay, I understand."

Daniel escorted her out, leaving Eleanor alone with a hungry child at her breast. She stroked his head and tried to talk to him, but it was hard to know what to say to someone who so plainly didn't understand a word of it. When he eventually released her nipple, she held him up to get a better look at his face. He stared back at her with bright blue eyes that matched Daniel's.

Daniel returned and settled himself in a corner with a pile of papers, and Eleanor thought she might finally get some sleep when she felt dampness seeping through the bundle of sheets. She laid the child on his back and started to unwrap him, but stopped short before she finished cleaning up the mess.

"Daniel?"

"What is it?"

"Our son... he's a girl."

He came across to see for himself, but there was no denying it. The baby boy they'd been expecting had, in fact, turned out to be entirely female. He reached out to take her tiny hand, and she started to cry again.

"Well, she cannot be named Martin," he said. "That much is obvious. Do you have another idea?"

"Maybe we could call her Isabelle," Eleanor said. "It turns out that's my mother's name."

"You knew your mother?"

"I didn't know she was my mother at the time, but she was the headmistress at my school."

"How is that possible? It sounds like Venncastle sedition."

"It really wasn't anything like that. She never even told me."

"Then how did you find out?"

"Can we please leave this for now? It's a long story, and I need to sleep. We can talk about it tomorrow."

"Okay."

"But what do you think of the name?"

"Isabelle. Yes, it is a pretty name."

"That's settled then." Eleanor wrapped the baby in a clean sheet and held her tightly. "Hello, Isabelle."

Isabelle just looked up with wide blue eyes and gurgled.

Chapter 23

"Isabelle needs you," Daniel said.

Eleanor shook her head, looking down at the tiny girl bundled in the sling across her chest. "What you mean is, Isabelle needs milk."

"You are her mother as well as her food. She needs you to be here for her."

"I'm sure you can find another woman with milk in her breasts. Whereas this job needs me."

"I could go."

"You, go to Venncastle? And what? Tell them how much you hate their school? I don't think so."

"Or we could–"

"No, I'm going. I've been out of action for much too long." Eleanor had already packed a small bag and she had every intention of leaving that night to start her journey while the moon was dark. "Go out to the rebel district in Woolport and find any woman with a baby – her milk will be just as good as mine."

"Isabelle needs her mother."

"And the Association needs new students – I'll still be Isabelle's mother when I get back." She leaned across and kissed him on the cheek. "I won't be gone for long."

She took Isabelle out of the sling and put her into Daniel's arms. He still held her awkwardly, afraid he might drop her, though she looked happy enough to rest in the crook of his arm. Eleanor hoped he'd learn to relax with her if he had some time to care for her alone.

She went to Almont first; there was one school to visit there, and she had numerous other loose ends to tie up. She rode around the outside of the city walls, passing along the edge of a dozen green fields before she came in sight of the northeast gate. She slowed the horse to a walk as she approached. If her plans had succeeded and this gate was now guarded by her own people, she wanted to give them chance to see her coming.

Rosemary was the first to recognise her and she left her guard post to run outside, shouting greetings. Ollie ran behind her, although he stumbled after a few steps and fell, arms sprawling across the road. He let out a piercing cry but Rosemary turned and wagged her finger at him, and he picked himself up without further complaint.

"You've got him well trained," Eleanor said. She lowered herself to the ground and embraced her friend. "You'll have to teach me how you do that."

"He's old enough to know that crying at the wrong time could get us all killed," Rosemary said as they started walking back towards the gate. "Where is yours, anyway?"

"She's at home. I'm here to work."

"Are you staying long?"

They reached the spot where Ollie had fallen, and he held his hands up to show off the fresh grazes on his palms. Rosemary ran a hand through his curls and praised him for his bravery.

"Just a couple of days in the city, I hope," Eleanor said. "I've got a few places to visit before I can go back home to Bella."

They reached the gate, but it was only raised by a couple of feet. Rosemary pushed Ollie under first, then dropped to her knees and crawled through the gap.

"Hang on," she said. Then Eleanor heard the creaking of chains and gears from inside, and gradually the gate inched upwards.

"Security," Rosemary explained. "We keep it closed so we only have to guard one direction, and we've brought the border of the eastern district up to the wall."

"Good thinking."

"It was all Dash's idea. He's on night shift, but you'll see him later."

Once the gate was raised enough for the horse, Eleanor led him through. Rosemary reached up to adjust the chains, and the gate fell back into place with a thud which shook the ground. The horse reared up, startled, and Eleanor had to calm him before she could tie him up for the night.

The stairs inside the gate tower were barely wider than a man's shoulders, and rose steeply into the wall. In the guard room above the gate Violet stood with a crossbow in her hands, looking out across the city rooftops, but she turned to see who was responsible for the extra set of footsteps on the stairs.

"Well, if it isn't the captain her very self," Violet said, a smile spreading across her face. "Back in action, are you, lass?"

"I'm getting there," Eleanor said. "I've been training every day since Bella was born, but there's nothing like the real thing."

There were stacks of crates against one wall. Violet rested her crossbow on top of the pile and rummaged through one box, then another, finally coming up with a dark bottle.

"To celebrate," she said. They didn't have glasses, so she poured large measures into three cracked mugs.

"Should we really do this while we're on duty?" Rosemary asked as she sipped at the drink.

Violet snorted. "You think I can't shoot straight after an inch or two of spirits?"

"I'm not sure I could."

"Never mind, so long as one of us can." Violet knocked her mug against Rosemary's. "To Eleanor's return."

"To me," Eleanor said, lifting her mug to join the toast. "And to the defence of the northeast gate."

"We should rouse some of the others," Violet said. "They'll all want to know you're back."

"Let them rest," Eleanor said. "I'm in town for a couple of days, there'll be plenty of time to catch up."

But the noise had already woken Molly, who came climbing down the ladder from the sleeping loft, eyes bleary and hair in disarray.

"What's going on?" she asked, clinging sleepily to one of the stiles of the ladder. And then she looked around and answered her own question: "Eleanor! When did you get back?"

"Just now."

"How's the baby? Can I see?"

"She's not here, Daniel's looking after her."

"Oh, that's a shame. But she's okay? What did you call her?"

"Isabelle. After my mother."

"Your... wait, don't tell me, I'm just going to get the others. Everyone's going to have the same questions."

She scrambled back up the ladder before Eleanor could object, again, to the idea of people being woken up just to see her. Before long her friends started to appear: Jace in his nightshirt; Nicole with a tunic pulled hastily over her slip; Dash who had slept fully dressed and in his leathers since the day Eleanor put him in charge. Rosemary sent Ollie up to bed and the adults arranged themselves in a circle, sitting on the floor. Violet poured more spirits, and everyone started firing questions at Eleanor.

"Boy or girl?"

"When was she born?"

"What's her name?"

And then, in shocked and somewhat envious tones, "How in all the Empire did you come to know your mother?"

Eleanor threw back one drink after another as she answered, abandoning any hope of working that night. She'd go and check on Lauren's messages first thing in the morning.

They were disturbed by a rattle on the door at the bottom of the stairs. Violet slung the crossbow over her shoulder before going to see who it was, and returned with a tall, blonde-haired woman who held her hand and sat beside her, leaning into her shoulder. Eleanor knew she'd seen the woman before but it took her a moment to place her: Sally, the climber from Sixth Corps.

"So what's been happening here?" Eleanor asked. "Aside from this solid achievement?" She slapped the floorboards with the palm of her hand as she spoke.

"You asked us to get you a gate, boss." Dash smiled at her, a little pride creeping into his expression.

"And a very nice gate it is, too. Has our Empress tried to take it back yet?"

"She's sent soldiers a couple of times, but it does its job. We could hole up in here for a while, we've even got a good stock of supplies." He waved towards the crates where Violet had found the bottle of spirits. "And crossbows. We're getting quite good with the crossbows."

Violet raised her bow in one hand and her drink in the other. "Forty six," she said, her words slurring a little. "Forty six little bastards came and stuck their dirty bodies on my arrows."

"That's forty six we never have to deal with again," Sally said, resting her head back on Violet's shoulder and shuffling closer.

Violet looked down at her and smiled, kissing her forehead and stroking her hair. "You're always one for seeing the good," she said. "That's why I like you."

"Someone has to," Sally said. "It's an unhappy enough business."

"We're winning though," Jace said, leaning back on his elbows. "That's what matters."

"We're not losing," Nicole said. "But we're not winning very fast, neither."

"We always knew it'd take a while," Eleanor said. "Tomorrow you can show me the latest boundaries and we'll talk about what to do next."

"Are you staying here?"

"I'd thought of heading for the tavern, but if you've space then I'll stay."

"We've got plenty of mats, haven't we?" Nicole asked Dash, and he nodded. "And blankets. That's settled then, you can stay here."

The whole floor shook as a scrawny, black-haired youth dropped through the ceiling hatch without troubling to use the ladder.

"Fire!" he shouted. "Look south, there's a big fire gone up."

The gate had been built to defend against threats from beyond the city so the outer wall had only arrow-slits, but on the city-side were two large windows. The youth pushed open the shutters and Eleanor's legs wobbled as she got to her feet and joined the others crowding to look out over the city. The flames glowed red against the evening sky, a pillar of thick smoke billowing upwards.

"We weren't supposed to be setting any fires out that way," Dash said, frowning. "That's not part of the strategy."

Nicole had been at the front of the group, leaning right outside. She turned, her face grey. "It's too close," she said. "I think it's one of our buildings."

Dash cursed. "Okay, who's still sober? Nic, wake everyone else. Violet, are you still competent to wield that bow?"

"I've not had much."

"I haven't had any," Sally said.

"The two of you can stay here in case this is a diversion," Dash said. "I'm taking everyone else who's able to run. Anyone who's too drunk, get some sleep and be ready to take the next shift."

Only Rosemary cried off; she'd drunk less than half of what Violet had given her, but she didn't usually drink at all. Eleanor knew that running would feel more like falling, but she also knew she'd be as much use drunk as most of them would be when sober.

Nicole came back down the ladder with a dozen sleepy, half-dressed guards, and Dash led the way into the streets. It wasn't hard to find the fire: the tower of smoke and sparks loomed above the rooftops. They ran towards it until they came upon the knot of people who'd run out into the street to escape the blaze.

Dash sent most of the guards to fetch buckets from the fire post, and asked Eleanor to help him find out what was going on. She held his arm for stability as they ran towards the crowd, her other hand on the hilt of her dagger.

"What started this?" Dash asked, but no-one seemed to know.

"Well don't just stand there gaping like idiots," Eleanor snapped. "Bring water. We need to contain it."

"I can handle things here," Dash said. "You find out what happened."

Eleanor walked around the corner to get a better view. There were three houses burning, and the fire was starting to lick at the edges of the neighbouring rooves, blackening the tiles.

"Where did it start?" she asked. A young woman indicated the left of the three houses, while an older man pointed across her to the right. Eleanor glared at them. "Okay, what exactly did you see?"

"I heard a crash," the man said. "And then there was smoke."

"Lots of smoke," the woman agreed, then burst into a fit of coughing as if to emphasise her point.

"Did anyone actually see anything?" Eleanor asked, but to no avail.

Bystanders and revolutionary guards alike were starting to arrive with buckets from the fire point, as well as various boxes and even canvas bags that they'd filled themselves from the nearest springs. Dash was directing them to start at the edges, but Eleanor grabbed one bucket and carried it with her as she approached the middle of the blaze. She looked up and down, scanning for traces, but the soot and ash and water were being trampled into black mud by the enthusiastic rescue force. If someone had set the fire deliberately, their tracks were now long gone.

She heaved the bucket of water towards the nearest window, turned to hand the bucket to the nearest volunteer, and then spun back to face the buildings again. The windows. She cursed herself for not seeing it sooner. The windows had all been blown out by the fire but there was nowhere near enough glass in the street.

Ignoring numerous cries of protest, she ran inside the nearest house. The ceiling above her head creaked ominously and a shower of sparks fell down into the room, but she ignored the disturbance. What she needed to check wouldn't take long. She edged across to the window and there, as she'd predicted, the missing glass littered the floor. A rock the size of her fist lay on blackened floorboards, giving extra weight to her theory: someone had smashed the windows from outside.

She turned back towards the door. A burning beam crashed down across her path and she ran, leaping over the timber and throwing herself into the street just as the rest of the ceiling collapsed behind her. She hit the ground and rolled, and someone threw a bucket of water over her.

"Learnt anything?" Dash asked, offering his hand to help her to her feet.

She shook herself, sending droplets of water flying, and shivered. "Not an accident," she said. "You need to change the pass phrases. And make sure you're protecting the gate with an extra challenge only First Corps know."

"Only First? Don't you trust the others?"

"I trust you more."

"Can you find out who it was?"

Eleanor looked again at the chaotic mess of footprints tracked across the cobbles. "Not likely," she said. "Not now. But we know it was *them*, inside our very heart, and that's all that matters."

"They'll pay for it," Dash said.

A man from a nearby house came out with a towel for Eleanor, and she dried her hair as the human chain continued to pass buckets of water towards the flames. Eventually they managed to contain and finally quench the fire, and the First Corps regrouped around Dash and Eleanor.

"We learnt one important lesson tonight," Dash said as they started to walk home. "We need to recruit more fire wardens into the revolution."

"We did alright," Nicole said, glancing back at the blackened shells that had been houses. "We stopped it quick as the fire wardens ever stopped our fires."

"We haven't had a good fire for months," Jace said. "But they're asking for it, if they come in here and burn our homes."

"You'll have your revenge," Dash said. "But we'll work out the very best way to do it."

Eleanor woke the next morning feeling better than she would have expected given the excitement of the night before, and the extra bottle of spirits they'd shared on their return. She left the others snoring in the sleeping loft, greeted Rosemary and Jace who'd kept watch on the night shift, and went out into the city.

Two notes from Lauren waited beneath the tannery's loose tile. Eleanor skimmed them while she crouched on the roof but there was nothing that required her immediate attention, only vague indications that the Empress would be pulling her forces back from the mountains to focus on squashing the pockets of revolt in her cities. It was news, but it was no surprise.

She left brief instructions asking Lauren to look into how many new recruits the Shadows were expecting, asking her if possible to provide names and schools before the assignment letters went out at the solstice. If she could fill the gaps on her list when she next passed through the city then she'd have time to go and approach a few more schools.

She dropped in at the Old Barrel Yard to exchange snippets of news with Ade, and found the tavern full of patrons eager to hear more about the previous night's fire. She told them what little she'd discovered, and encouraged everyone to be vigilant with their challenges if they saw anyone they didn't recognise in the rebel districts. Especially if that someone was carrying a torch.

After a light lunch she made her way back to the northeast gate, where she knew she could pass the time until evening with dice games and friendly conversation. Sally was picking out lively tunes on slim silver pipe when she arrived. Violet sang along, while Molly and Nicole kept watch and hummed occasional harmonies.

"Would you like to play?" Sally asked, offering the pipe to Eleanor. "We've only got the one."

Eleanor laughed. "I wouldn't inflict that on you."

"Go on," Molly said. "I bet you're better than you think."

"No, really. I'd much rather just listen."

"Shall we do 'Safe In The Storm' again?" Molly said. "Violet's been teaching us some of the prayer-songs that they sing on the boats."

"D'you remember the words?" Violet asked.

"I think so."

It was an energetic round with two parts; Violet conducted the others as she sang, until they'd gone through the words three times and she waved her hands to silence them.

"Have you spoke to Dash yet?" Nicole asked Eleanor once the song was finished. "He's got big ideas for tonight."

"What sort of thing?"

"He's calling it the night of a thousand flames."

"We're going to set the city alight," Violet chipped in. "By way of paying them back for the fire last night."

"Tonight? Is that long enough to organize everything?"

"How much organization do we need?" Molly said. "Grab a few torches and away we go."

"Ah, you're probably right. Well, I've got other things to see to, but I'm sure I'll have time to start a fire or two on the way." She'd been hoping to get her first school visit out of the way that night.

"Talking about me?" Dash asked, coming through from the stairs.

"I'm just catching up on the plans for tonight," Eleanor said.

"You'll come, won't you? I think we can get a hundred guards out with torches and still have enough people on watch across the city."

"I need to get up to the Second City School tonight," she said. "But I can drop a torch or two on my way there, if that helps?"

There was a map pinned to the wall, and he studied it until he found the school. "You could take one of the silk factories, you'll be that end of town."

Eleanor nodded.

"What are you doing at a school, anyway?" Molly asked.

"Association stuff."

"You recruiting someone?" Violet asked. "We should do that. All the kids, not just the one or two your people care about."

"They've had seventeen years of Imperial brainwashing," Eleanor said. "And the revolution's still pretty new. It's a hard sell."

"We came," Jace said, indicating Molly and Nicole. "We knew what mattered, even as kids."

Eleanor smiled at that. It was only a year since they'd graduated themselves, but they'd seen a lot in that year.

"Tonight should help," Dash said. "It's a rallying cry as much as it's revenge. We always get more volunteers when we do something flashy."

"Just be careful who you trust," Eleanor said. "They're not above sending someone to try and make friends with you."

"We've restricted the gate to First Corps, like you said," Dash said.

"First and Sally," Violet corrected.

"Of course." Eleanor smiled to hear the protective note in Violet's voice; it was nice to see them so happy. "Why don't we just bring Sally into First, Dash? She might as well be."

"She's leading Sixth Corps's planning for tonight," Dash said. "But she's bound to come here after. I can talk to her then."

"Maybe you should leave her there," Violet said. "They need her more than I do."

"She can choose for herself," Dash said. "Meanwhile, we need to decide on our targets."

They huddled round the map to discuss their plans. Eleanor suggested the armoury buildings, which no-one seemed to have thought about, and Dash firmly quashed Molly's suggestion that they could save everyone a lot of time in future by just torching the schools.

Eventually night fell and they equipped themselves with matches, torches, and oil-soaked rags. Eleanor set out alone and made her way to the factory district where a number of Charanthe's most famous cloths were manufactured. It was deserted at night, the looms silent and the dye baths still. She laid oily rags along the window sills and lit her torch, using it to set light to one window after another. Then she swung herself onto a nearby rooftop and ran, the fires steadily growing behind her.

At Almont 2, she found her target in a dorm room full of sleeping boys. She was about to pour sleeping vapours onto his pillow, but even beneath the sheets she could see the bulk of his body: she'd never be able to lift him. With a quiet sigh, she started to work her way around the room, dropping vapours on the other boys' pillows instead. Once all but Bren were knocked out she shook him awake.

"Who are you?" he asked. "What are you doing here?"

"I came to offer you a choice," she said. "I'm from the Association. I want you to know that our path hasn't closed to you just because the Empress decided she doesn't like us."

"You're working with the rebels, aren't you?" he checked, looking a little confused.

"We're using the rebels. See that?" She pointed him towards the window. He got up to look, and she gestured expansively across the city, where flickers of red and orange now peppered the skyline.

"Fires?" he said. "Rebel fires, I guess. So what?"

"Someone set a fire in the eastern rebel district last night – this is retaliation. Proof to the Empress that anything she does to us, we can repay tenfold or a hundredfold. The rebels give us the numbers we need to make big moves like this, but we tell them when and where to move."

As she spoke, she realised that wasn't quite true any more. Dash was becoming the leader she'd asked him to be. If she'd asked him not to set the city on fire, she knew she would have had to give him a very good reason. But there was no sense in confusing the boy with all that. For now, it was enough that she had a light-show to impress him with.

She went to Venncastle last. Though she'd travelled back through Almont to check, there were no extra names from Lauren. In the pouch on the rooftop she'd found only an apologetic note explaining that the Shadows wouldn't find out exactly who they'd be getting until after the solstice, and some wittering about a new poison-flower that she'd have to pass on to Daniel. So Daryl was the final name on her list.

His bedroom was in one of the towers of the old castle, with a view out across the sea to the north of the island. As soon as she opened the door he rolled from the bed, knife in hand, and considered her from between half-closed eyelids.

"I've been warned about you," he said. "The Provost said you might come."

Eleanor smiled. "I'm sure he did."

"And?"

"Did he also warn you not to be so foolish as to think you're being original if you try and trap me into an ambush?"

"Something like that."

"Well, he's saved me a lot of time in explaining things to you. I trust I don't need to tell you about the Association, either."

"Slaves of the revolution." He said it with a venom that surprised her.

"The Association doesn't work for anyone."

"Then why are you working against the Empire?"

"The Empress made us outlaws, remember? If they've told you to avoid us, they must have told you that."

"You could've gone into the Shadows, but you've joined the revolution instead."

"Joined it? Don't you see? It's our revolution. Didn't you notice when the rebels suddenly started to get organised? They never would have got this far on their own."

"I could just kill you," he said, toying with his knife. "They'd make it worth my while."

"The people who might be able to kill me aren't the sort of people who'd talk about it first," she said. "So I'm going to pretend you didn't say that. Anyway, I just wanted to make sure you're aware of all your options. If you want to see me, you don't have to wait for your assignment – just come to any of the rebel districts in Almont."

"And now you're going to talk to Billy?" he asked as she turned back to the door. "Or have you just come from there?"

Billy was a new name to her. If someone of that name had come to Lucille's attention at all, then his was one of the folders which had already been taken or lost before Eleanor searched her office. That Daryl named him was a gift, she could look up his room now and...

She hesitated, an idea forming at the back of her mind. There were risks, but it was certainly a more interesting path to take.

"Just you," she said. If it didn't work, she'd lost nothing she'd been expecting to achieve.

"But I thought–"

"We're being a lot more selective this year. And it's only

fair to let the Shadows get one or two of their assignees, don't you think?"

She turned and left him gaping at her as she strode from the room, and was certain that Billy would hear all about this at breakfast if not before. The only question then was, would she hear from him?

Eleanor returned from the schools in high spirits. She was sure she'd made a good impression on the boys, and she was glad to be coaxing her body back into the peak of fitness. She almost felt human again.

Daniel and Matt were working in his lab when she got home, while Isabelle slept in a trunk that he'd propped open in one corner.

"I'm back," she said, somewhat unnecessarily.

"Isabelle missed you," Daniel said. "She cried for days."

"She can't possibly know who I am," Eleanor said, picking up the baby and cradling her. The girl had grown noticeably bigger, and had developed a shock of messy, white-blonde hair on her head. "She's a helpless, mindless baby – babies can't recognise people."

"She knows you. You should not have left her alone."

"And I had a good trip, thanks for asking."

"Good. But you must catch up with our daughter's progress. Whenever I give her something to play with she puts it in her mouth."

"I can see that," Eleanor said, looking down to where Isabelle had woken and was chewing on her sleeve.

"And she is hungry often. I think she will be ready for real food soon."

"Speaking of food, have you eaten yet?"

"We are busy," Daniel said, waving towards a beaker resting above a small burner.

"You two go and get some dinner," Matt said. "I can finish up here."

"Are you sure?" Daniel checked, but Matt waved them away.

They went down to the dining room, and Eleanor balanced

Isabelle on her knee while they ate. She dipped her finger into her soup to offer a taste to the girl, who was so enthusiastic that she nipped Eleanor's finger with a tooth that hadn't been there before.

"You're right," she said to Daniel. "We should try giving her more normal foods. I think she likes the soup."

Daniel dipped a piece of bread in his soup, left it until it was soggy, and pushed it between Isabelle's lips. She smiled and gurgled and dripped soup all down the front of her blanket, but she still seemed happy about it.

"Oh, and I've got something you might be interested in," Eleanor said, fishing around in her pocket for the note from Lauren. "Details of a couple of new poisons, developed from mistflowers that Ivan brought back from the mountains."

"Let me see," Daniel said, taking the paper and scanning across it. "Mistflowers. I have not heard of these. Where did you get this?"

"Contacts in the Shadows," she said. "It's complicated. But I thought you'd like to know."

Lauren had included one example stalk of tiny lilac-and-white flowers, pressed and dried, which Daniel examined reverently.

"We have missed them," he said, scanning the notes again. "A very short flowering period, this says, in the early spring."

"Maybe next year."

"Next year, yes." He got to his feet. "If the effects are as described, then we must study this."

"Right now?"

He held up the dried-out sprig of flowers, stalk pinched tightly between thumb and forefinger. "I have to store this safely. Poison flowers are not meant for the dinner table."

"You haven't even finished..." she started to protest, but he was gone. She wiped a drip of soup from Isabelle's chin. "Looks like it's just the two of us, then, Bella."

While Eleanor was wiping her face, Isabelle reached up and wrapped her fingers around the edge of Daniel's bowl. Then she pulled, hard, and sent the whole thing crashing onto the floor. Eleanor cursed as soup splashed around her feet, but

Isabelle just giggled.

With one arm firmly wrapped around the baby to prevent any further mishaps, Eleanor finished her own soup, and then bent to clear up the spillage. Isabelle reached out to put her fingers into the puddle of soup and smeared red lines across Eleanor's face, beaming as she did so.

"Okay, fine," Eleanor said, glad there was no-one else in the dining hall to see the mess. "You've covered mamma's face in soup, was that fun? Now let's go and get clean."

She left the crockery fragments on the table with her dirty bowl, carried Isabelle back through to Daniel's lab, and left her there while she went to bathe. Her ablutions were disturbed, however, when Isabelle started screaming.

"She is hungry," Daniel said, carrying the child awkwardly into the bathroom and holding her out towards Eleanor. "You should feed her."

"Hang on, let me finish." Eleanor scrubbed quickly at her skin, clambered from the bath, and picked up her towel while Isabelle continued to bawl at her. Once she was dry she took Isabelle from Daniel's arms and held the little mouth up to her breast, just as she'd done so many times before she left, though the new tooth made her nervous.

Isabelle stopped crying, sucked, and... nothing happened. The expected flow of milk didn't come. Eleanor squeezed her breast, wondering if something was blocked, but to no avail. She tried her other breast, but the same thing happened.

"It's not working," Eleanor said, looking to Daniel for an explanation. "There's just nothing happening."

Daniel studied her for a moment. "Your breasts have shrunk while you were away," he said. "Perhaps the milk is gone."

"Do you have something I could take for that?"

"I will think on it."

"Well, who did you find to feed her while I was gone? We'd better keep her here a bit longer."

Chapter 24

Simeon came into the room, leaned over her shoulder, and whispered into her ear: "We have code word river."

Eleanor nodded and continued with her work, putting together tiny darts and dipping their tips in poison, as if there was no urgency to the situation. She hadn't told anyone here about Lauren, and until she found out what had happened she didn't want to have to answer questions. The guards and messengers didn't know what any of the code words stood for, only what they needed to do. When she'd used it, someone would have swept Lauren away – ostensibly for her own safety – while others passed the message along to the Association's council. Or in this case, directly to Eleanor.

After a suitable pause, she put away her kit and carried Isabelle through to where Daniel was working.

"I need to go to Almont," she said. "Something's happened."

"What?"

"A code word just came in, an emergency shout from one of my network. You don't need to know the details, but I have to deal with it."

"You should call the council first."

"It's not necessary. This is an easy one, I'll be back in few days. No-one else needs to worry about it."

"Eleanor—"

"No arguments. I need you to look after Bella."

Lauren had been given a small room with no windows, a makeshift cell converted from an old coal cellar in the eastern rebel district. She lay on the sleeping pallet with her eyes closed until she heard the door.

"I thought that code word was supposed to help me, not get me arrested," she said, sitting up when she saw who it was.

"It kept you alive, which was the primary goal," Eleanor

314

said. "But you're not a prisoner – shall we take a walk?"

"Okay." Lauren stood and stretched. "It'll be nice to get some exercise."

"We just have to get you out of that uniform first. It'll only cause problems."

She'd brought a spare outfit of her own old clothes and turned away while Lauren changed. The trousers were a little short on her but she looked passable and, importantly, no longer stood out as a Shadow would. In the heart of a rebel district like this, the Shadow Corps uniform would guarantee trouble.

Two of the Second Revolutionary Guard Corps flanked the door; when Eleanor and Lauren walked out they nodded an acknowledgement to Eleanor and let them go without question, not needing to understand why their captive was suddenly walking out from under their noses.

"You say I'm not a prisoner," Lauren said. "That's not how it's felt."

"They don't know what the code words mean." Eleanor motioned over her shoulder, waving dismissively back towards the guards. "They don't need to. They just know what to do."

"Which in this case involved locking me up."

"Don't take it so personally. They have a list of code words, and when they hear one they take certain steps. The first thing is to be suspicious: the codes are given to spies, we expect that some might leak or be guessed. The guards take custody, and they're under instructions to be very careful. Then they send word back to the Association, guard their guest, and wait."

"Guest. Right." Lauren almost laughed. "Am I free now?"

"Absolutely. They were just waiting for me to verify that you were who we expected, so now I'm here, you're fine. You don't even have to stay with me if you don't want."

"Thanks."

The last of the evening sunlight filtered through the turning leaves, warming their faces as they walked.

"So do you want to tell me what happened?" Eleanor asked.

"You mean they didn't even pass the story along to you? I assumed they would."

"When you invoke a code word, everything else is irrelevant

detail. The code word comes to me; you're taken somewhere safe. That's all that matters, and it's safer to keep the process simple."

"I was just walking home. I'd been – well, it doesn't even matter. I was out in uniform, I was walking near the edge of this district, and I walked into a gang who thought they'd get points for a Shadow scalp."

"How many? I would have thought you could handle a few stray ruffians."

"Oh, I was winning. Easily. That wasn't the problem. I didn't have much choice left: end it with the code word, or... do what a real Shadow would have done."

"It's a pity. You were useful in there. I was hoping we'd be able to keep you in place for a year or two."

"You wouldn't have preferred me to..." Eleanor watched as fascination and horror played across her face. "No, that's unconscionable. Impossible."

"You made a decision. And given how little time you must have had to make it, I could have understood either argument."

"Are you seriously suggesting... what I think you're suggesting?"

"I'm not suggesting anything. Things work differently in war. You could certainly have argued that your value – right then, with where you were embedded – was more than theirs."

"Anyway, it's happened now." She shook her head as if to clear out the images she didn't like. "So here I am."

"It was a fight that did for me, as well, with my brief stint in the Shadows. But I was in Ivan's unit, when his job was to hunt and kill whatever remained of the Association, so I could hardly avoid a battle."

"I can imagine."

"Anyway, we'll have to replace you. Was there one of your colleagues who you think we could turn?"

She shook her head. "We didn't really talk about it. It's not safe to talk about things like that when you're in the Empire's sights. Even within the Shadows, no-one says what they really think."

"Okay. We'll get on to it soon."

"Besides, you said I shouldn't try to get to know them on a personal level."

"That's probably for the best. Are you ready to come back to the Association with me tomorrow?"

"You need me to come back with you?"

"Well, only if you want to. What were you thinking of doing next?"

"I don't know, but... Association? I assumed I'd find somewhere to lodge in one of the districts, and then..." She hesitated. "I hadn't really thought beyond that. Revolutionary guard, or something."

"You're virtually one of us – you'd be wasted on guard duty."

"True."

"So you'll come?"

"Oh, I'll come, if you're sure they'll have me."

"I can't give you a seat on the council, but you'll have a lot more freedom than you ever did in the military. And I could really use your insight when we get down to planning the next steps of our attack."

Lauren nodded. "Where's the Association based these days?"

"It's not far from Woolport, we'll set out in the morning. Do you have any business you need to tie up first?"

"I disappeared from the Shadows without a word. I doubt there's much of my old life left to attend to, and I can hardly go back for my things."

"No, you can't go back. Do you want to buy anything before we leave the city? We've our own tailor, but it'll take a few days for him to kit you out."

"I could do with a change of clothes – these are a little small."

Daniel was sitting cross-legged on the floor, sharpening his knives while Isabelle played by his side. He'd given her a whetstone so she could pretend to sharpen her own wooden blade, but instead she chewed on the handle.

Eleanor scooped the girl up and kissed her. "Mamma's

home," she said. "How are you getting on? No, no. You're still holding it wrong – here, you need to do it more like so. Daniel, haven't you been correcting her?"

"She is very young. Let her play, there will be time for correction later."

"She's falling into bad habits already. See, Bella, like this." She picked up one of Daniel's knives to demonstrate, holding it slanted against the whetstone, her thumb on the blade. Isabelle ignored the instruction and bashed her knife against the stone.

"Did you succeed?" Daniel asked.

"Yeah, I told you it wasn't much. I've brought Lauren back with me, I suppose I'd better introduce her to the council later."

"You have done what?"

"I've brought Lauren–"

He cut her off. "Who is Lauren?"

"She was my mole in the Shadows."

Isabelle tugged at Eleanor's hair then, when she didn't get the quick response she was expecting, started to hit her on the head with the wooden knife.

"That's not what knives are for, sweetie," Eleanor said, catching the child's hand and holding it. Then, to Daniel: "The one whose code word I was responding to, you know?"

"I do not know, because you would not tell me where you were going."

"She was reassigned from the Specials to the Shadows last year, fell in with the revolutionaries, and I picked her up before she quit her job. She's been passing information back – very useful stuff."

"I struggle to believe it." He shook his head. "However well I know you, I struggle to believe it every time you do something this stupid."

"You didn't say it was stupid when I brought you mistflowers."

"You have invited the enemy into our midst."

"We're recruiting everywhere we can. How could I possibly turn down such a perfect candidate?"

"When will you learn that you cannot do these things without permission? Recruit her to the revolution, by all means.

318

But to bring her here?"

"She stayed in the Shadows for us. With them. We owe her for that, we can't just leave her to die of boredom guarding a rebel district somewhere."

"Better she dies of boredom than we all die of treachery."

"You are in a happy mood, aren't you? Come on, Bella, let's go and make a new friend."

Isabelle gurgled happily as Eleanor carried her into the hall, still clutching the wooden knife.

"Oh, and you finally got me pregnant again," Eleanor called over her shoulder, but she didn't wait to see what he'd have to say about that. Not while he was in such a bad mood.

"This is Isabelle," Eleanor told Lauren. "You last saw her when she was just a lump in my belly."

"You're keeping her here? I had no idea."

"Well I could hardly surrender her to the Imperial schools, could I? Not while we're plotting to overthrow them."

Isabelle sucked on her knife blade.

"Oh, absolutely. All the rebel families are doing it – holding on to their kids, I mean. I was just surprised to see her here. Rather than out in the districts. I didn't imagine kids in the Association."

"Just the one, so far, but I've another on the way." She patted her stomach though there was nothing to see yet, even if you knew to be looking.

"Hi Isabelle." Lauren waved but Isabelle had buried her head in her mother's shoulder, looking out only from the corner of one eye.

"Say hello to Lauren, sweetie."

Isabelle looked up briefly, then resumed chewing on her knife handle.

"Nice to see she's already got her own knife," Lauren said, smiling. "It must be good to start early."

"We thought that, but she's hopeless. She just hits things with it."

"Well, you've only given her a wooden blade. It's not much use for anything else."

"I can't give her a real knife until she stops eating

everything in sight."

"It's a bit circular, isn't it? Until you give her something she can use, she won't learn to do anything with it beyond hitting things and eating it." Lauren crouched and pulled a dagger from her boot sheath. "Isabelle? Try this."

Isabelle reached for the sharp edge of the blade, and Lauren had to pull it quickly beyond her reach.

"Okay, maybe that wasn't such a good idea."

Eleanor looked at Lauren's plain, military-issue knife. "Do you want to come and meet our weaponsmith?" she asked. "You'll need to come up with your own design before he can make you anything special, but I can introduce you, anyway."

Eleanor led the way through the corridors to the smithy.

"Harold? I've brought someone to see you."

"Oh?" He hammered a few more times at the blade he was working, and plunged it into the cold bath. Plumes of steam rose around him, condensing in beads on his forehead. "Come in, then, don't be shy."

"This is our newest recruit," Eleanor said. "Harold, meet Lauren. Lauren, this is Harold, the best weaponsmith in all the Empire."

"I wouldn't say that." He laughed and held out his hand. Lauren grasped it firmly.

"Pleased to meet you."

"Lauren's going to need some nice knives," Eleanor said. "She's got military junk at the moment."

"Well, we can soon fix that. Let me take your measurements, and then you can start thinking about a design."

It was a couple of weeks later that Sebastien, who'd been living on the mainland for a few weeks, returned with a very unusual message. He went to Eleanor first, and found her and Lauren sparring in one of the practice rooms.

"What are you doing back so soon?" Eleanor asked, sheathing her knives.

He looked across at Lauren, who had sat down to wipe the sweat from her face and hands. "Who's this? Can I talk?"

"It's fine. What's up?"

"You're not going to like this," he said. "I got a message – a proposal. The Taraskan lords want to involve themselves in the war."

Eleanor frowned. "Here?"

"Yeah."

"How, exactly?" Lauren asked.

"Their letter suggests that they're sympathetic to our cause, and they offer to bring their ships to oppose the Imperial navy. At a cost, of course."

"We'll never deal with those bastards," Eleanor said. "Surely they know that."

"I told you you wouldn't like it."

"Next time, don't even bother to bring their stupid messages here. You're not their messenger."

"You know I have to take this to the council."

"No, it's fine, just burn the letter and forget about it. No need to waste everyone's time."

"I have to," he said. "Something big like this, there has to be a vote."

Eleanor sighed. "Fine, give it to me, I'll deal with it."

Sebastien shuffled uncomfortably. "Are you sure I shouldn't take it myself?"

"Look, I'm going to call the council, okay? Don't you even trust me any more?"

"Sorry." He handed the paper across. "It's not that I don't trust you, I just know how much you hate them. It's totally understandable."

Eleanor pocketed the letter and toyed briefly with the idea of burning it anyway, but it wouldn't gain her anything. Sebastien would just tell the others.

"Can you go and check on Bella?" she said to Lauren. "I'd better deal with this."

Once the council were assembled Ragal called the meeting to order, rapping sharply on the table.

"We really only have one thing to discuss today," he said. "An offer of assistance from a rather unexpected quarter – the lords of Taraska. Eleanor, can you outline the terms of the arrangement they're offering?"

"I don't care what the terms are," Eleanor said. "Why waste time even considering their terms? We know we can't trust them."

"The revolution is losing ground," Don said. "We're clinging on to the rebel districts, but we're certainly not growing the way that we were. It's time for drastic action."

"We need something to tip the balance in our favour," Bill agreed. "And this might just be it."

"You're not doing yourself any favours by refusing to even listen," Laban said quietly. "Hear them out, and then make your argument."

Eleanor nodded, though she knew there could be nothing in the letter that would change her mind.

"This came via Sebastien, through some convoluted line of messengers from the King of Taraska," she said, holding the paper aloft. "It reads: To the honourable men of the southern lands, it being understood that we stand in common cause against the tyranny of the Empire, Taraska having long opposed the imposition that the Imperial regime has made on its citizens..."

"Get on with it," Gerald said shortly. "We don't really need to hear all this nonsense."

"It really is nonsense," Eleanor said. "Opposing tyranny, indeed."

Daniel looked at her. "With ships from Taraska we could–"

"Slave ships," she interrupted. "Don't forget that."

"We can't afford to be picky," Bill said. "With their ships we can control the ports, interrupt transit of the Empire's supply boats, stop food getting through to the outlying islands."

"It was you who first drew our attention to the importance of the supply chain, Eleanor," Don said. "You can't deny this is a good way to do it."

"I was talking about starving the Empress out of her palace, not depriving the islands of their food supply. Anyway, wait until you hear the rest: they want the right to plunder any Imperial ships, payment in food for their oarsmen, and the new government to pay a percentage of all the Empire's produce in tax to Taraska. Indefinitely."

It was Don's turn to look troubled, now. "That's a high price," he said.

"Too high," Gerald agreed. "Can we negotiate?"

"If it ends the war quickly, it might be worth it," Daniel said. "We could always change our minds about the taxes, later."

"And invite them to turn their armies on us?" Don asked. "Better not to get involved in that sort of double-dealing."

"Maybe we should think about commandeering a few ships of our own, though," Eleanor said. "Who's heading to Almont next?"

"I think Andreas will be," Don said. "Why?"

"Tell him to find the First Revolutionary Guards – they're probably still concentrating on the northeast gate – and tell Violet we need her."

"Violet?"

"Don't let the pretty name fool you, she's the toughest sailor I know. If anyone can build a navy for us, she can."

"Meanwhile we must press harder on the Empress and her family," Daniel said. "Nothing would inspire the revolutionaries more than a few royal bodies."

Eleanor wanted to say something, but Taraska was more important. If she started arguing too hard against a systematic erasure of the Imperial family, they might decide to reconsider the question of forming that stupid and dangerous alliance. So she kept her mouth shut as the meeting proceeded to draw up a list of targets from the Imperial family.

"What about that child Eleanor hid away?" Daniel said, looking straight at her, just as it had seemed everyone had run out of suggestions.

"I don't think we'll find him again," she said. "I didn't even catch his name."

"Then how were you planning to reunite them?"

Eleanor wished she'd paid more attention to what she'd told Daniel at the time, but now there was nothing for it but to persist with the lie. "That was never part of the deal. I promised I'd keep him alive, that's all."

Daniel looked skeptical, but he didn't say anything more

about it until the council dispersed and he managed to catch her alone.

"They would want their son back," he said. "Did you already tell them where he is hidden?"

"I told them nothing," she said, truthfully. "That was the safest thing."

"And if the Empress sends the Shadows to torture you, you would not be able to tell her how to find the one heir we will not have killed?"

"The Empress doesn't even know there's a child to look for."

She turned on her heel and left him standing alone in the corridor. He didn't believe her, but he didn't have the evidence to call her out in front of the council, so it didn't really matter.

"How was the meeting?" Lauren asked when Eleanor arrived to pick up Isabelle.

"Lucky escape," Eleanor said. "If Taraska's price wasn't so high, a lot of them would've wanted to go for it."

"You can't let them."

"No."

As she carried Isabelle back to her room, Eleanor wondered at that. How could Lauren understand so much better than the others? And why couldn't at least Daniel take her at her word when she said it was a bad idea?

Chapter 25

Eleanor swung the harping knife around, using the long blade to block Lauren's dagger thrust and flicking her wrist around to pin her back against the wall with the second, shorter blade.

"You're almost as good as Ivan with that thing," Lauren said, moving away from the wall and dropping into a low guard ready for another bout of sparring. "I never could get the hang of it myself."

"It took me a while," Eleanor said. "But it's the one weapon that makes me feel confident in hand-to-hand. You know I'd generally prefer to take down my enemy from a distance."

"That's why you prefer a longer blade."

"I think so, yeah."

Eleanor spun the harping knife casually between her hands; Lauren was far enough away that she could afford to be flashy without risking the initiative. The twin blades glinted in the lamplight.

"When are they going to start trusting me?" Lauren asked, watching Eleanor's movements but making none of her own. "It's been three months, and still the only job they'll give me is training the kids."

"Patience," Eleanor said. "There are plenty of good people who've spent years training new recruits. It's not the worst job."

"It's not the best."

"No. Would you prefer to go back out into the districts? I could give you your own guard unit."

"I'd prefer to be useful. To the fullest of my abilities – not as a guard or a glorified schoolteacher."

Eleanor dropped her arms to her sides and sighed. "You were a Shadow," she said. "Their first instinct is to kill you, as was mine. We just need some way to prove your loyalty really is with us."

"Like what?"

"There's a list of Imperial family to deal with, we could pick up one of those. Come back with Imperial blood on your hands and there won't be space for any doubts."

"That could work."

Eleanor started to work through the list, counting names on her fingers as she dismissed them one by one. As Crown Prince, Leon should be the best protected, and she didn't much feel like trying to assassinate him anyway. His brother Rowan was known to be the Empress's favourite, so she would have made sure he was well-guarded, too. Daniel had already worked his way through the Empress's siblings with a series of carefully planned 'accidents'. There were a few cousins, but she wanted something a bit more high-profile to serve her purposes with Lauren.

"Rowan has three sons," she said at last. "Aged eight, eleven, and thirteen. I think any one of those would show you mean business. We can set out in three nights, when the moon is dark, unless there's a good cloudy night before then."

"You don't have to come with me. I'm a grown-up, you know. I'm quite competent."

"This isn't about getting the job done, it's about getting you accepted. That means you need a witness."

"Okay. Do they live at the palace?"

"So far as I know. We have a couple of spies in the household staff who can get the details for us."

"Great, who are they? I'll go to Almont and ask them. You can come out and do your witness thing once I've got a plan."

"Sorry," Eleanor said. "But even most of the council don't know exactly who my spies are, just like they didn't know you were working for me. We can go to Almont together but you'll have to let me do that part alone."

"I understand," Lauren said. If she felt at all put out by Eleanor's reticence, she didn't show it.

As it happened, there was solid cloud cover the following night, and no reason to delay any longer. Eleanor shivered as they rowed towards the mainland; it was a cold night, and it would only get colder as the winter months drew in. She'd told the council of their plans, though she'd phrased it in such a way as to invite no argument. Laban had looked a little surprised – of everyone, he best understood Eleanor's reluctance about assassinating the Empress's every relation – but he'd said nothing to dissuade her. Daniel had been thoroughly overjoyed that she'd apparently come around to his way of thinking, so much so that he'd even kept quiet for once about Lauren's part in the mission.

Lauren paused for a moment, oars resting above the water, to pull her woolen cloak more tightly around her shoulders.

"Cold, isn't it?" Eleanor said. "It'll be a bit less harsh in Almont."

"I should have worn more layers," Lauren said. "It's so warm inside, I hadn't really noticed how close we're getting to winter."

When they reached Woolport they tied up the boat and went to Violet's rooms for the night. The rebel district had loose boundaries here; the town was a trading port above all, and the traders cared for neither the rebellion nor the resistance above their profit. The area wasn't heavily guarded – they were far enough from the heart of the war, here – but Eleanor preferred to keep the Association's location a secret even from those who claimed to be with the revolution. Violet, though, she trusted.

Sally let them in, hung their sea-sprayed cloaks up to dry by the fire, and gave them a pile of blankets.

"I'd join you for a drink, but it's late," she said. "Help yourself to whatever you want, and we'll catch up at breakfast."

"Sounds perfect," Eleanor said. She wanted nothing more than to warm up and rest her aching arms.

"I'd just assumed we'd be riding straight away," Lauren said as they curled up on the floor, close enough to the fire to feel something of its warmth, but far enough to avoid stray sparks.

"Travelling by night looks suspicious," Eleanor said. "And there are spies everywhere. If we can't avoid being seen, we have to look inconspicuous."

In Almont, Eleanor left Lauren in the Old Barrel Yard while she went off to speak to her spies at the palace. She couldn't let herself be seen, so she took a slow route across the rooftops and let herself in through a skylight in the servants' quarters. Allie, her favourite source, should have been back from her evening duties but her tiny bedroom cubicle was empty. Eleanor sat on the bed to wait.

"Eleanor, hi!" Allie's face broke into a smile when she saw her unexpected visitor. "Sorry, have you been here long? Tom's ill so Janine had me doing all sorts of extra errands, I wasn't sure I'd ever get to bed."

"Don't worry, I've got all night. Are we safe to talk here?"

"Yeah, Tom's out like a light, and Amber's on the night shift." As she spoke, Allie indicated the wooden partition walls to either side of her bed. "No-one's going to hear us."

"Great. I need some information from you – on Rowan's children, if you're okay with that."

Allie nodded. "Sure, what do you need to know?"

"Anything you can tell me. For a start, do they live here in the palace?"

"Yeah, in the north wing."

"With guards?"

"Of course. Not too many, though, just occasional corridor patrols. And I think you could pay the C watch to fall asleep on the back gate."

"Oh, really?" Eleanor smiled. "Now that is good to know."

"It is your people, then, who's been causing these so-called accidents?"

"You know I can't tell you things like that."

"Oh, I know, sorry, I shouldn't ask." She didn't look sorry at all. "It's just that I thought it must be you but, well, everyone here's so sure about the accidents. We're not allowed to even talk about the revolution, we have to pretend nothing's happening out there, even now there's so much of the city fallen."

Eleanor nodded and swiftly changed the subject. After she'd got all the information she needed about the boys and their protection, she headed back to the Old Barrel Yard for the night. Except for the guards hovering by the door, the bar was empty when she got in. She knocked at Lauren's door but got no response, so she pushed her way inside. The bed was empty, sheets undisturbed.

She went to the next room and knocked, rousing Ade from his bed and causing Nasha to murmur in sleepy protest.

"Have you seen Lauren?" she asked. "She didn't tell me she was going out."

"She left not long after you," he said. "She didn't say where she was going, though, and you know I'm not daft enough to ask questions of a woman like that."

"Okay, thanks." She went back to her own room in silence, a little troubled. Lauren surely wouldn't be stupid enough to just go out for a walk, when any of the Shadows would recognise her for a traitor. And if they did find her, what then? Would they kill her straight away or torture her for information on the revolution? If they guessed that she'd gone into the Association, they'd realise she had valuable knowledge.

Dawn was beginning to break – and Eleanor had hardly caught a wink of sleep – when she heard a door swing open. She sat up, throwing knife grasped in her left hand while her right hand gripped the hilt of her stiletto. It hadn't been her door, anyway. Hoping the hinges were still well-oiled, she opened her door and looked around. No signs of life.

She padded across to the top of the stairs, bare feet making no sound on the wooden floorboards, and peered down into the dark hallway below. There was a glimmer of light filtering through the crack under Lauren's door.

She walked down and knocked, weapons still ready in case it wasn't Lauren who'd come back.

"Eleanor," Lauren opened the door with her shirt half unfastened, and her hair falling loose around her shoulders. "What's up? I was just getting ready for bed."

"I wanted to check you were okay," Eleanor said.

"Yeah, I'm fine. Why wouldn't I be? I was just scoping out the palace."

"You went out in the city without telling anyone your plans. And anyone could have seen you."

"You worry too much." Lauren continued undressing as she spoke, and climbed into bed. "I've been looking after myself in the big city for years. See you in the morning."

She turned to face the wall. The blatant dismissal grated, but Eleanor could hardly blame her. She'd react just as badly faced with the level of mistrust they'd inflicted on Lauren. She turned and tiptoed back to her own room, trying to avoid disturbing Ade and Nasha again.

She slept more soundly now she knew Lauren was back, and woke late. Not that it mattered; there was little enough they could do today. The guards Allie had talked about, the ones who might be sympathetic if a few dollars passed their way, wouldn't be on shift for another two nights.

Eleanor dressed and went down to the bar to see what Ade could offer by way of breakfast. She found Lauren already hunched over a bowl of millet porridge.

"Sorry I was short with you," she said, blushing as she looked up. "But I get... kind of frustrated sometimes."

Eleanor nodded. "I get it."

"You do?" Lauren smiled, her whole face brightening. "Of course you do. You're very like me."

"So what did you find out?"

Lauren looked confused for a moment, then: "Oh, at the palace! Yeah, it doesn't look too bad, does it? I mean, we can take them on. No problem. It's not like they've put Shadows watching the kids."

"I've got even better news," Eleanor said. "My source says the guards who'll be on the gate the night after tomorrow could be persuaded to turn a blind eye, for a small incentive."

"Do we even need to wait for that? It seemed manageable. If we wait, we just give them time to find out."

"I trust my contact," Eleanor said. "It won't leak."

"Thought you didn't trust anyone?"

"I don't trust anyone with everything, but I trust her with this. It's a gift, we might as well take it."

Lauren looked about to argue, but thought better of it.

They spent the next couple of days hanging around in the tavern, occasionally stepping out into the courtyard for some friendly sparring. Various guests dropped in, once word spread that Eleanor was back in town, and for her part she was glad to be back in a place where no-one challenged her authority. Well, no-one except Lauren, and she did it only with sullen looks when she thought Eleanor wasn't watching.

At last, evening fell on the appointed day. Ade prepared a quick dinner of sausages and potatoes, they refused their usual spiced ale in favour of cold water and steady hands, and they went to get ready. As Eleanor strapped herself into light leather armour and fastened weapons against her skin, she wondered again why she'd talked herself into this. She didn't even agree with Daniel – and, if she was honest, most of the others who also took the same view – that it was the quickest way to end the war. On the other hand, her abstention would change nothing. The children were as good as dead; this way, their deaths would help Lauren if no-one else.

Lauren was waiting for her in the bar, chatting and joking with Ade. "Ready?" she asked as Eleanor came downstairs.

"Ready," Eleanor said.

They made their way to the Marble Quarter over the rooftops, as usual, although Eleanor insisted on taking a route that was even more indirect than usual, following paths she hadn't used since her days at the academy. She didn't want any chance that they'd be intercepted on their way.

The palace stood too far removed from its neighbouring buildings for a rooftop approach to take them all the way. In a broad street behind the royal stables, they dropped to the ground and looked around. As expected, it was quiet. In their camouflage greys they blended easily into the shadows between the colonnades, but if they had to walk through wide avenues in the open then their very disguise would make them conspicuous.

They'd discussed their plans endlessly over the preceding days, so there was no need for words as they crept along, keeping close to the walls for cover. One of the horses reared and neighed in panic behind the stable door; they froze as the stablehand went to comfort the animal, but thankfully he didn't turn to see what had caused the disturbance. Maybe the horses often took fright at nothing. Eleanor would have thought better of the Empire's best mounts, but she was glad of the servant's casual inattention.

They made their way to one of the palace's many back gates. Eleanor had her darts at the ready lest the guards be less co-operative than Allie had predicted, while Lauren drew her dagger, keeping the blade out of sight beneath her cloak. They waited in the shadows until they saw the perimeter patrol guards go by, leaving just the two men with crossbows who flanked the gate.

Eleanor hung back, blowpipe gripped between her teeth, while Lauren stepped forwards to offer them money and sleeping potions.

"We're happy to compensate you for your trouble," she explained. "And you'll feel just fine when you wake up."

"What if I don't trust you?" asked one man, levelling his crossbow bolt towards Lauren's chest. "It could be poison."

"If I wanted to poison you, I wouldn't be asking your permission. Now are we going to do this the easy way or the hard way?"

The two men looked at one another, then one of them reached out his hand. "Deal," he said.

Lauren passed him five dollars, which he pocketed, and a vial filled with a gentle sedative. He threw it back in one mouthful, and sat back against the wall to wait for the effects to kick in.

"And you?" Lauren asked the second guard, who still held his bow uncertainly.

"Fine," he said, as his colleague's head started to droop.

Eleanor breathed a sigh of relief as he, too, drank the potion without any further complaint. This was so much less messy than the alternative. Once they were both unconscious she pulled a flask from her waistband and splashed spirits over their shirts; if the men were discovered, it would just look like they'd had a little too much to drink. They'd be punished, of course, but being drunk on duty was hardly a rare occurrence. Unlike if they'd needed to slit their throats, this shouldn't cause anyone to panic or search for intruders.

Lauren leaned over the first guard and slipped her hand into his pocket.

"What are you doing?" Eleanor asked.

"Getting our ten dollars back," Lauren said. "They'll be strung up by morning, so they won't miss it."

Eleanor didn't know what to say to that.

"What, you didn't think they'd get away with this?" Lauren asked. "They'll make an example of everyone on duty in the north wing tonight."

Allie's instructions had been detailed and precise, leading them through silent corridors towards the suite of rooms where the young princes were housed. They moved steadily and with caution, but as expected, they passed no more guards. Protection was always focused on the outer walls; a threat from within was an idea that had never been taken seriously in an Empire whose power was kept strong by its citizens' own belief in the notion of perfect assignment, and if Allie was right, the palace was still in denial. For decades the rebels had been viewed as nothing more than crazed drop-outs, with only themselves to blame if they'd rejected their assignments, or religious nutters whose views couldn't be taken seriously. Despite the war raging outside their gates, the Imperial family was clearly having a hard time keeping up with the threat. It was only recently that their 'rule by consent' had come under any serious question.

Eleanor caught herself enumerating all the things she'd do differently if she was in charge of palace security. A few traps in the corridors, perhaps, or just armed guards at every doorway. She caught herself, and almost laughed at her own naïveté. Of course they'd rejected such ideas. Within the palace, the Imperial family wanted to be able to come and go as they pleased without worrying about traps. And they certainly didn't want to see guards everywhere, spying on their movements and reminding them of their own mortality.

They reached the door they'd been looking for and Lauren kicked it open, clearly enjoying the chance to extend her muscles. The crossbow bolt came as if from nowhere, and she threw herself to the ground just in time. Eleanor stepped across and flung two battle stars through the door, though she was too startled to aim properly and his cry of frustration told her that she'd wounded rather than killed the shooter. As she flattened herself against the wall outside the door, she cursed herself for being too hasty. She probably hadn't done enough damage to stop him using his bow, meaning he could easily take another shot at her when she went back to finish him off.

Lauren had rolled out of the way and crouched on the other side of the door. Eleanor waved at her to get ready, and once they each had stars in both hands she leaned around the doorframe, aiming more carefully this time.

It was then that she saw their assailant wasn't alone. Far from it, in fact. The little reception room was positively crowded with armed guards. She took down the original bowman and one of the others, and Lauren mirrored her actions – catching one and missing another – but seven still stood.

She caught Lauren's eye and held up her fingers to signal how many they were up against. Only one of those remaining had a crossbow, the others just carried swords, but they were sufficiently outnumbered that it would still be a tough fight. Eleanor took the harping knife from where she'd strapped it across her back, and pulled a stiletto from her boot sheath. By the time they looked around the door again, she was sure, the guards would have ducked for cover. There was no way to take them down without going in themselves.

"Should we go?" Lauren asked. "Come back another day, when they're not expecting us?"

Eleanor shook her head. "Let's finish this."

They stepped into the room together, and Eleanor ran headlong towards the sofa which partially shielded the guard with the crossbow. A couple of others came at her from the side, but she ignored them, even as she felt the first blows. She had to put the bow out of action before she could even think about hand-to-hand.

Lauren came up behind her and engaged one of the swordsmen, buying her enough time to vault over the top of the sofa and stab the short blade of her harping knife through the throat of the bowman. When she turned back Lauren was fighting with both hands. The remaining guards had surrounded her, and she was surviving only by keeping those she was fighting as a living shield between her and the others.

Whenever one of them tried to dodge around and bring his sword down, she forced one of his colleagues to duck in such a way as to deflect the blow. If it hadn't been so serious, Eleanor would have enjoyed the show. Here was a master at work: Lauren danced with her blades.

But there was no time for appreciating artistry. One mis-step would be all it took for the whole thing to come crashing down. Eleanor pulled throwing knives from her belt and watched for a few more heartbeats until she was sure she'd got a feel for Lauren's rhythm. Then she stood, loosed two blades towards the guards on her left, turned, and flung two more to her right. Three of the four blades sank home in the throats of their intended targets; the fourth clattered to the ground.

Two guards turned their swords on her then, leaving Lauren fencing with just one swarthy woman. Eleanor swung the harping knife in a bold defensive pattern, knowing she could hold them off for quite some time. She didn't even need to press the attack. If she could just keep them occupied, Lauren would finish the job.

She fell into an easy rhythm, knocking away attacks from one side then the other, trying at every turn to cause the two of them to get in one another's way. Block, turn, block, twist, block, step, block, duck... and then, from the corner of her eye, she saw Lauren go down.

Eleanor threw herself to the ground, rolling between her opponents' feet, relying on the element of surprise to buy her a few heartbeats. She arrived just in time to knock the woman away from Lauren, smashing her head into the stone floor.

As the others came for her again, she knocked the sword of one through the chest of the other, and sliced his throat open while he struggled to free his blade.

She stopped to draw a couple of deep breaths, then turned to help Lauren to her feet. "Are you okay?"

"Fine. Just bruised." Lauren dusted herself off, and started to retrieve her weapons. "You swore this wouldn't leak."

Eleanor stared at the bodies now surrounding them, hardly believing it herself; she counted ten.

"I was so sure," she said, shaking her head. "But this is why we don't trust anyone, right?"

Even as she said it, though, she couldn't bring herself to believe Allie had turned against them. Allie, who'd frequently been beaten and raped by Rowan himself when she'd lived in the Imperial harem, before he'd grown tired of her and had her dismissed into the palace cleaning staff. If even Allie couldn't be trusted, what hope was there for anyone else?

"Right," Lauren agreed.

Eleanor pushed open the door to the boys' sleeping quarters. "So we'd better get on with this before someone notices this mess," she said.

Thankfully, the noise outside didn't seem to have woken the children. But then a sleeping draught was common in schools, where a single unruly child could otherwise disturb the sleep of a whole dormitory. Perhaps the Imperial family didn't operate entirely differently to normal life.

Eleanor stood guard by the door as Lauren went through to finish the job. Watching out of the corner of her eye, she saw Lauren hesitate before sliding her poisoned blade against the throat of the youngest. She frowned in sympathy. Killing children had never formed part of her life's ambition, either, but she was fast learning to put her sentimentality aside.

A few heartbeats later, and Lauren was back by her side.

"Done?" she asked.

"All three."

They walked home in silence, keeping to the shadows, weapons concealed but no less ready for that. Allie. Eleanor couldn't get over the idea that the girl had betrayed them. She just wouldn't, not unless... but that was even worse. If her rebel sympathies had been discovered, and the information forced from her, then that left an even worse taste in Eleanor's mouth.

The next morning, the Old Barrel Yard was full of uncertain whispers. There was a rumour of deaths at the palace, and someone had pinned up notices announcing a display of public executions at noon. Eleanor and Lauren ate their breakfast in silence, volunteering nothing, and no-one dared approach them to ask if it was coincidence that they'd been in town when it happened.

"I'm going to go to the hangings," Eleanor said. "I need to see who they decide to blame for this."

Lauren looked horrified. "Are you sure that's a good idea? They might see you."

"I'll be one face in a crowd, it'll be fine. But you don't have to come."

"No, I'll come with you."

After a quiet morning, they left the rebel district and joined the flow of people moving towards the Grand Square for the hangings. Public executions were a rarity, usually reserved for serious and high-profile crimes, so anyone without urgent duties would make their way to see what the fuss was about. Eleanor overheard snippets of conversation as they walked: talk of spies and traitors, rebels and assassins.

"They got her, you know," one woman was telling her friends. "The killer. She worked at the palace."

Eleanor's chest tightened a little at that, but she pushed all her guesses from her mind. They'd see soon enough.

The crowds were thick in the Marble Quarter, and merchants had set up little stalls selling food and nicknacks just as they would for a carnival.

"We won't see much," Lauren said. "Are you sure you want to do this?"

"We'd make ourselves far too conspicuous if we turned back," Eleanor said. Everyone in this part of the city, today, was here to show their Imperial pride by watching the Empress dispose of those who'd attacked her. Besides, Eleanor needed to know if they'd managed to pin something on Allie.

They heard a gong, and then a cheer went up from the crowds in the Grand Square. Eleanor started to elbow her way forwards but by the time they managed to push their way into the square the charges had been read, the scapegoats condemned, and the nooses tightened. Nine bodies hung limply from the scaffold, feet dangling in the air. Eleanor had to scramble up onto a nearby wall to see, but there was no mistaking Allie's slender form. As Lauren had predicted, the others looked to be palace guards, presumably those unlucky enough to have worked in the north wing.

It was all she could do to force herself to wait in the square until the crowd dispersed, and she didn't say a word to Lauren as they walked back to the Old Barrel Yard. Allie had been a sweet girl, and a good source; the loss hurt in more ways than one.

Chapter 26

It took a lot of persuasion for the council to agree that bringing Violet to the Stacks would require less effort – and draw less attention – than if they went to see her in Woolport. She was not Association, numerous voices repeated. Eleanor and Don seemed to be the only ones who understood that they could no longer be 'just' the Association; that if they thought they were organizing a revolution then they'd better get on with actually organizing it, and for that they needed to be able to hear reports from their new naval captain without transporting the whole council to the mainland. Eventually they'd decided that Eleanor could fetch her if she agreed to be blindfolded during the trip across.

As she rowed back now Eleanor couldn't help feeling that the precaution was as stupid as it was unnecessary. Violet was an intelligent woman, and she'd see the inside of headquarters soon enough. Only one of the sea stacks was even remotely large enough to conceal such a place, so they were insulting her for no gain. But Violet just laughed when Eleanor tried to apologise.

"Your kind have to be careful," she said. "I understand."

Lauren and Stefan were on guard when Eleanor steered the boat between the rocks which sheltered their harbour.

"You can uncover your eyes now," Eleanor said as the boat knocked against the quay. "I'll need you to see where you're going."

She handed the rope to Lauren and led Violet through the corridors to the chamber where the council were waiting for them. She was about to start introductions when David waved her to silence.

"We have no need of names," he said. "Let's get straight down to business."

Eleanor rolled her eyes at Violet, and said, "Okay, Violet's here to talk about our new navy."

"Such as it is," Violet added. "These things take a while to build up, as I'm sure you know. I wouldn't call it a navy yet."

"How many ships?" Ragal asked.

"Four we can call our own," Violet said. "Three medium-sized fishing craft, and one that was a local supply ship. Traders are much more reluctant to get involved."

"That'll change when we start disrupting their routes," Eleanor said.

"What about smugglers?" David asked. "Or pirates?"

"Smugglers think like traders," Violet said. "But much worse. They'll keep their heads down for as long as they can turn a profit, and don't mind their devotions, either. And you don't get pirates this far into the archipelago."

"Not Magrad pirates, no," Eleanor agreed. "But are there any common criminals looking for plunder?"

Violet shook her head. "The navy keeps that down. Why risk being sunk for piracy when you're safer with landlubber crimes? It's harder to run at sea, and Our Lady might scuttle you even if you evade the Empire's forces. We'll get more ships, though, don't you worry."

"Let's focus on what we've already got," Don said, striding over to the large map they'd hung against one wall. Red lines marked the frontiers of rebel districts and towns which had already fallen to the revolution, while pins with little blue flags marked what they knew of the Imperial armies: a couple of battalions that had been pulled back from the mountain regions and were now camped near Bastion, a strong force still along the coast, and several units marching to converge on Almont.

Don had made some new pins topped with a tiny ship motif. In his optimism before the meeting he'd prepared three dozen, of which he now selected four. "Where are these boats of ours, then?"

"One here in Woolport," Violet said. "One at Pierston, one at Westquay, and one over on Hope Island. Keeping them spread out so we're not spotted before we're ready."

Don inserted pins along the coast at the towns she'd named.

"And you're stripping out the fishing tackle and whatnot to load up with weapons, right?" Eleanor prompted.

"We will be," Violet said. "We only get ships when we win over a captain, and usually at least a couple of crew, though we should be able to capture some once we're ready to show our hand. For now it's best to keep up the fishing – looks less suspicious – but we're starting to make spikes and rams."

"How long until we're ready to fight?" Bill asked.

Violet turned to him. "To do what? We could be making a nuisance of ourselves within a turn of the moon, if we were minded to, but they'd come for us and they'd win soon enough."

"We need to build up more of a force down here," Eleanor said, "while the Empress is still concentrating on keeping pirates out of the north. We need enough to control a decent area before we give our plans away."

"So how long?"

"Six months to find enough ships," Violet said. "Another two to fit them out and give the fishing crews some half-competent defensive skills. That's assuming you'll give us men to do the actual fighting."

Bill whistled. "Eight months."

"Never said it was going to be quick," Violet said with a shrug.

"Recruitment will be easier once we've got something to show off," Eleanor said. "Just like in Almont – we got new volunteers for the rebel guards every time we struck out. Once it's clear we've got a navy, we'll get captains with rebel leanings coming forwards, but we can't afford to waste ships on exhibition raids until we've got enough to defend our own forces."

"Any more questions for Violet?" Don asked. There weren't, and Eleanor escorted her back down to the harbour.

"Stefan can row you back," Eleanor said. "I really need to stay for the rest of the meeting, but we'll catch up soon."

"After the baby comes?" Violet asked, with a glance at her bulging stomach.

"I should have a couple of months yet, before I'm too big to move. I'll come over for a day or two when I can get away."

"Get back to your meeting, then," Violet said, waving her

away as she scrambled into the little boat. "Who knows what they'll be deciding without you?"

Violet re-tied her blindfold without needing to be asked, and Lauren hopped into the boat with her. Eleanor turned and paced back to the council chamber with an uneasy feeling in the pit of her stomach. She'd never said mustering a navy would be easy, but she'd hoped it would progress more quickly.

"–much too slow," she heard Daniel say as she reached the door. She hesitated outside.

"I agree," Gerald said. "We shouldn't be so quick to dismiss outside help."

Now Eleanor pushed the door open, so vigorously that it slammed into the wall behind. The gust of air set their battle map flapping, and one of the pins fell out onto the floor.

"Not this again," she said, sinking back into her chair. "We all agreed it was too expensive, quite aside from anything else."

"And what does all this waiting cost us?" Bill said. "We're using up our reserves. This can't go on for ever."

"We have enough funds," Nathaniel said. "And with access to the rebel supply chain, we're not spending anything right now. We can afford to be patient."

"Better to wait than to bankrupt the Empire with promises to the Taraskan lords," Laban said. "But you're right, we must end this as soon as we can. Ordinary people are starting to suffer."

"Anyone who hasn't joined us yet has chosen to stay a slave of the Empress," Don said.

Laban gave him a withering look. "Do we believe our own propaganda, now? Most people only care that they have food in their bellies and a roof over their heads. What does it matter to them if the Empress is a little overzealous in protecting her personal interests?"

Don shrugged. "She's overstepped a lot of boundaries. If they don't care, they should."

Chapter 27

Eleanor lowered herself into the bath and shuffled to try and get comfortable. As the baby grew inside her it was getting harder and harder to find any good places to sit, but the water gave her some support and the warmth soothed her aching muscles. And if there was only one advantage of being a few short weeks from her due date, it was that someone would invariably offer to carry the buckets of water to fill the tub.

Since Daniel had taken Matt to the mainland looking for mistflowers, it was usually one of the new recruits who would offer, but today Lauren had insisted.

"It's my fault," she'd said. "If I hadn't told you about the mistflowers, Daniel wouldn't have gone off and left you."

Daniel had put on a good show of feeling bad about the trip, offering to stay right up to the moment he left, but she'd always known he would go. As she scraped the cleansing oils from her skin, Eleanor smiled at the memory. The mistflowers bloomed for such a short season in the early spring, and if he missed it he'd have to wait another whole year to finish his experiments. At least he should be back in time for the birth, to hold her hand and feed her poppy extract again.

She pressed both her hands against her belly and waited for the child to kick. He – or she; she wasn't going to make that mistake again – was more active than Bella had been, always turning himself around and pushing against her insides.

Lauren came in with a neat stack of clean clothes, placed them carefully on the sideboard behind Eleanor's head, and bent to pick up the tunic she'd discarded earlier.

"You don't need to do that," Eleanor said. "Seriously, I can clear my own laundry."

"Relax." Lauren continued to collect up Eleanor's trousers, underclothes, and clanking weapons belt. "I know bending down is awkward for you at the moment. Anyway, maybe you can return the favour one day."

Eleanor stared at her. "Is there something you should be telling me?"

"Not yet!" Lauren called out, laughing, as she carried the dirty clothes out of the room.

"You haven't found your dream man in our little Association, yet, then?"

Lauren came back with a towel draped over her arm, closed the door, and moved up beside Eleanor's head. "Not exactly," she said, and as she spoke she dropped the towel and Eleanor saw something glint in her hand.

"Lauren, what–?"

"Be quiet and listen to me," Lauren said, the jovial tone of a moment earlier now gone from her voice. She pressed the flat of her blade against Eleanor's windpipe, leaving no doubt of what the edge could do in a heartbeat. "I don't want to kill you."

"Is that why you've got a knife to my throat?" Eleanor asked, quietly, trying to work out what she could possibly have done to bring this on.

"Fair point." Lauren took one small step to the side, keeping the knife poised in her hand. "But I'd hate to underestimate you so I think I'll keep this out, just in case."

"What's this about? Are you still frustrated that some people don't trust you enough?"

"Oh, I think you'll find you've all trusted me far too much," she said with a bright smile.

Eleanor's stomach flipped as she realised what she was hearing. This wasn't like the time she'd drawn her dagger on Mikhail in a burst of emotion. This was something much more serious.

"I lied about my role in the Shadows," Lauren continued with barely a pause. "I'm one of Ivan's own special agents."

"Okay." Eleanor nodded. "But why tell me this at all? Why haven't you killed me already, if you're working for them?"

"You know Ivan, he's a practical man. He's always been a pragmatist, and he really believes you're the same at heart. Why hold a grudge when there's more advantage to be had by moving on? I'm only to kill you if you turn down our offer."

"That's what he told you, is it?"

"He told me you'd admire his artistry in sending me to betray you, just as he admires the way you talked Nicholas into setting a trap for himself. Of course we saw straight through you, but you know that by now."

"You weren't even with the Shadows then."

"No, but I've heard all about it. Here, do you want this?" She reached beneath her shirt and pulled out a small silver key.

Eleanor recognised it immediately as the one she'd failed to recover. "You know we don't need it any more."

"That's why you can have it. Ivan said this way you'd know the offer really came from him."

"Oh, I believe you speak for him, but that's no reason to trust you. Now run home and tell Ivan that, as much as I admire his style, this war is a long way from being over."

"Sorry, Eleanor, I can't let you say no."

"Let me? I'm giving you chance to walk out of here with your life, which is much more than I should."

Lauren laughed, though she was careful not to relax her guard for even a moment. "You're in the bath, Ellie. You're not even armed."

"Do you want to risk it? I only have to scream, and you'll never get out alive."

"Save yourself. The fact that I'm here surely proves the Association has no secrets left. Come with me before we turn this place inside out."

Eleanor toyed with the pendant at her neck, wrapping the thin chain around her fingers. "I think we have a few secrets left."

"And what about Bella? Are you going to condemn her, too?"

"Where is she?" Until that point Eleanor had felt only the cool anticipation of a fight on the horizon, but fear suddenly gripped her as she realised she'd too often left Isabelle in the care of this traitor. She hadn't seen her daughter since the early morning. "What have you done with her?" she demanded, tension edging her voice.

"She's perfectly safe. I sent her ahead of us to the *Albatross*, we'll see her when we get there."

Eleanor brought her pendant down in one sharp movement, breaking the chain and slamming the point into Lauren's knife arm.

"Sorry," she said as the poison began to work its way into Lauren's muscles. "I would've preferred it if you hadn't made me do that."

Lauren tried to raise her dagger, but her arm was already locked. She tried to lunge, staggered, and fell.

"One last chance," she said, struggling to push herself up to her knees. "Whatever you've just done to me, fetch the antidote. If we don't leave tonight then you'll be surrounded by dawn. They're expecting us, and Bella..."

"Sorry, no antidote."

"How many days do you think you can survive a siege?"

Eleanor ignored her, concentrating instead on heaving herself out of the water. She suddenly had a lot to do.

She dried herself imperfectly, pulled on some clean clothes and ran through the corridors, banging at the doors of lounges and common rooms, calling for the council. By the time she came to the council chamber herself, the room was already half filled with those she'd summoned first. Others followed closely behind her. They muttered to one another, expressions puzzled or curious or simply creased with frowns of irritation at her unexpected interruption of the day.

She slid into an empty chair and pounded her fist on the table to silence the room. Her other fist still gripped the pendant that had saved her life, though the broken chain had slid between her fingers as she ran, dropping to the floor somewhere between Lauren and the council.

"We have a problem," she said once all eyes had turned on her. She fought to keep her voice as flat and emotionless as she could, but she was struggling to catch her breath and her words came out in uncomfortable bursts. "They know we're here. We're surrounded by ships."

The room erupted with so many shouted questions that Eleanor couldn't even pick the words apart, and this time it was Ragal who slammed the table to bring the meeting to order.

"Let her talk," he said. "Everything you know, Eleanor, and quickly."

"Lauren betrayed us to the Shadows."

A couple of mouths opened again, but a quick glance from Ragal kept them silent.

"She said that the navy has us surrounded," Eleanor went on, her breathing beginning to steady. "Though I haven't looked out to confirm it. I don't think they'd be stupid enough to attack the island but they won't let us out, or supplies in. And one of those ships has my daughter."

"We can wait out a siege," Dek said, forcing a cheerful note to his voice that contrasted sharply with the uniformly grave faces of the others. "They'll get bored soon enough."

"With fresh supply lines, they can wait forever," Don said. "We can't."

Ragal turned to Nathaniel. "How long will our stores last?"

"Around six months if you don't mind living off bread and porridge."

"We can still fish," Albert said. "We'll drop lines inside the harbour. The catch won't be quite up to the usual standards, but we'll get something."

"You can help Nathaniel with rationing, then," Ragal said.

Don got to his feet. "If food isn't an immediate concern, we should turn our thoughts to action. I'm going to see exactly what they've got out there."

Eleanor was about to follow as he strode from the room, but Ragal called her back. "Eleanor, stay. Tell us exactly what happened. Where is Lauren now?"

"Her body's in my rooms, I was in the bath when she–"

"How can we question her body?" David interrupted.

"I know, I know. She picked her time carefully," Eleanor said. "I was almost unarmed, so I used the only poison I had to hand."

"Why did she bother to tell you she'd betrayed us, anyway?" Bill asked.

"She wanted me to come with her. Apparently the Shadows still thought they might win me over." Eleanor couldn't help laughing at the absurdity of it, but no-one else looked amused.

"I suppose she thought threatening Bella would be enough to make me play along, but she just made me angry."

They were interrupted by Don's return, with news of the few ships he could see and warnings about the likelihood of others waiting beyond their sightlines.

"We need to send someone to the mainland," he said. "Who's our strongest swimmer?"

"Probably Lukal," Bill said, and no-one could think of a better name to offer.

"With a breathing tube, a man might be lucky enough to sneak between the ships, and once he makes Woolport he can send the word out. We don't want anyone falling into this without warning."

"The others should stay away," Laban said. "At least for now. Tell them to stick to the rebel districts."

"For now," Don agreed. "But they should plan to be nearby, and look for chances to break the siege."

"Someone needs to build a trebuchet," Dek said.

"What makes you think we have enough wood for that?" Nathaniel asked.

"Not a trebuchet, then. Some other way of throwing fireballs at these pesky ships."

"Is that everything for now?" Ragal said. "We can all spend a little time thinking about ways to scuttle their ships, and we'll meet again tomorrow."

"I'll need some help to get Bella back," Eleanor said. "I'm not exactly in top form."

Everyone stared at her for a long, silent moment. It was Don who eventually spoke: "Are you seriously asking us to risk good men to go and rescue a baby?"

"We're always risking good men," Eleanor said. "That's just life."

"You're suggesting suicide, though. Those are navy ships – armed and full of soldiers."

"And we need everyone we've got to defend ourselves," Albert added.

"Lauren mentioned one called the *Albatross*," Eleanor persisted. "So it's not like we have to search every ship."

"We should vote," Ragal said. "If you believe we should move to retrieve the child, raise your right hand."

Eleanor thrust her arm into the air, but no-one joined her. Even Laban kept his hands folded neatly in his lap. It wouldn't have made any difference to the outcome, but she would have liked someone to be on her side.

"Daniel would vote with me," she said quietly. "If he was here."

The meeting broke up and Eleanor walked briskly back to her rooms, ignoring Laban's attempt to catch her eye. She didn't really want him to tell her that he'd been right all along: that now she had a child, she cared too much for her own good. His words rang in her ears quite well enough without needing to hear him repeat them.

Her mouth set in a determined line. So what if she was over-reacting? Bella was in trouble, and no-one else was going to deal with it, so she'd just have to do it herself.

She wrote a short message, wrapped it in a sealskin pouch, and went to ask Lukal to deliver it as soon as he reached the shore. Once he'd gone, she started to gather other young recruits together in a small, out-of-the-way chamber. Tal and Gaven and Simeon and Kit from the year before; Daryl and Billy and Bren who were still wet behind the ears and full of boyish enthusiasm. They were all she could find of those she'd recruited in person.

"Is this about the siege?" Tal asked once they were all seated.

A few of the others looked at him in surprise, but it was Simeon who asked, "What?"

"If you haven't heard the rumours, it'll reach you soon enough," Eleanor said. "The navy have got us surrounded. It's nothing to worry about, yet, we'll just be cooped up for a bit while we work out what to do. But that's only half of why I brought you here."

They watched her expectantly.

"The council doesn't approve this," she said. "So I won't try to make you, but I'm asking for your help. They've taken my daughter."

No-one interrupted her as she explained, to the best of her knowledge, what had happened and where Isabelle was now. She told them about the note she was sending to Violet, and her plan to approach the *Albatross* herself.

"So you see, I just need some backup in case things go wrong," she concluded. The lads nodded. "Thanks. I hope we'll be ready to go before daybreak."

"I wish you'd been right," she said to Gaven as they walked to the dining hall. "If she'd been a boy, she might be safely in Venncastle right now."

Nathaniel and Albert had wasted no time on setting up a system of rations, and dinner that night was a rather subdued affair, though they all knew it would get much worse once the fresh meat and vegetables ran out. Eleanor picked at hers but she wasn't hungry and she ended up passing her plate to Simeon, food almost untouched. She excused herself, whispering to her co-conspirators that they should get some sleep and she'd come for them once she was ready to go.

Back in her rooms, she sat on the floor beside Lauren's body and studied her, as if by staring at the corpse she could understand how she'd managed to lose her judgement so entirely. That Ivan had known her better than she knew herself, well enough to orchestrate such a scheme, was just salt in the wound.

Eventually she forced herself to get into bed and close her eyes. Sleep seemed unlikely, but moving her swollen figure around was exhausting at the best of times and she needed to get whatever rest she could before Violet arrived.

She must have slept, though, because she woke with a jolt when Daryl came to tell her that Violet was waiting in the next room.

"Thanks." She rolled into a sitting position and pulled on her boots. "Could you go and wake the others? Gather them all by the boats, okay?"

He nodded and was gone, leaving her to hobble alone through to where Violet was inspecting Lauren's corpse.

"Interesting times," Violet said, standing to greet her. After swimming from the mainland she was soaked to the skin, but somehow she managed to look composed despite her dripping clothes. "You sent for me, cap?"

"I need your help," Eleanor said. "I have to attack a ship."

"One of those big navy beasts?"

"Something like that," Eleanor agreed. "They've taken Bella onto a ship called the *Albatross*. I need your help to get her back."

"How many men have you got?"

Eleanor smiled ruefully. "Ah, that's where it gets tricky. The council aren't really interested in rescuing a toddler, so I've just got half a dozen kids who've agreed to pitch in. We're not going to win this by the numbers."

"I know that look," Violet said. "You've got a plan. Let's hear it."

"The traitor," Eleanor pointed at Lauren, "thought she could persuade me to go with her. The *Albatross* is expecting two of us to arrive before dawn. Now, you don't look much like her, but you'll be rowing with your back to them."

She picked up Lauren's cloak and draped it around Violet's shoulders. She loosened Violet's tight bun and re-fastened her hair into a low ponytail that matched Lauren's usual style.

"You've the right sort of colouring, the right sort of build, and it'll be dark. I, on the other hand, will be facing them from the back of the boat – and there can't be that many pregnant redheads on this island."

"They'll drop ladders for us," Violet said. "I like it. We'll be on deck before they notice I'm not her."

"In my dream world, they won't notice at all," Eleanor said. "She must have been there this morning to take Bella, but now it's night, and a different crew should be on shift. If we're lucky, they'll assume you are Lauren and show us through to our cabins."

"What about the others?"

"They're our emergency plan," Eleanor said. "If everything goes well, we'll pretend to go to bed and then sneak back to our boat when no-one's looking, quiet as anything. But if we have to fight, we might need a few extra hands."

They made their way to the sheltered harbour where the

Association's boats were moored, safely out of sight of the surrounding forces. The youths Eleanor had called on were sitting on the quayside, waiting. Eleanor considered the options and then settled herself on the stern bench of a little black row-boat.

"Why this one?" Violet asked. "She's not the nicest here."

"I'm trying to think like she would," Eleanor said. "If she took the best, someone might think there was something to notice. This one's inconspicuous."

Violet stepped past Eleanor, seated herself in the middle bench, and slid the oars into the rowlocks. Eleanor turned to loose the mooring line.

"I hope we won't need you," she said to the boys as she pushed the boat away from the quay. "So I hope we'll see you right back here."

Violet pulled on the oars and the boat slid through the water towards the mouth of the harbour and out into the pre-dawn light. She swung the boat left around the island, towards the huge hulk of the *Albatross*, and Eleanor squinted to try and spot the ship's lookouts. It had taken longer than she would have liked for them to get going, but she hoped it was still dark enough to disguise their approach.

As they neared the *Albatross* a young man noticed them. Eleanor waved at him, but he didn't lower his crossbow.

"Turn around and give them some kind of hand signal," she said to Violet. "But turn back quickly so they can't see you're not Lauren."

Violet twisted to look over her shoulder, raised her hand to acknowledge the youth, and was hunched back over her oars within a few heartbeats. "How's it look?" she asked.

"They're not shooting us," Eleanor said. "That's a good sign."

Violet continued rowing until their little boat bounced against the hull of the *Albatross* and the youth threw down a mooring line. Once Violet had secured them he dropped a couple more ropes, and Eleanor saw the winch above their heads.

"He's not going to try and pull us all up, is he?" she asked

Violet, who laughed and shook her head as she tied a complicated self-tightening knot around one of the rowlocks.

"Nah, he'll throw us a ladder once we're ready. Here, you could help – tie this one to the stern bar there."

Eleanor took the line and looped it around the bar. It had been quite some time since she'd needed to know sailing knots, but she thought she probably remembered enough. Then the youth lowered a rope ladder from the deck and she started to pull herself up, cursing as the ladder swung and she knocked her knees against the hull. Eventually she managed to get her hands onto the gunwale, and the youth finally dropped his crossbow to give her a hand with the last section of the climb.

"I think you're expecting us," Eleanor said.

The youth nodded. "Yeah, you're headed to Almont, aren't you?"

"Is the *Albatross* sailing all the way up the coast?" Eleanor asked. She wouldn't mind a lift to the city, but it would be a long time to hold the pretence.

"No, we've a job to do here," he said, motioning back towards the Stacks. "We've just to get you both back to the mainland."

"We have a carriage arranged from Woolport," Violet said, in a voice that sounded nothing like her own. Eleanor started; she hadn't even heard her come up the ladder.

"Great," Eleanor said. "Then we just need to get Bella. Where is she?"

The youth started to wind the winch, slowly lifting the little boat. Water poured from the hull at first, slowing to a steady drip as it rose towards their level.

"Lauren can show you to your cabin," he said. "And you can both rest a while. It's the morning watch who'll see you safe to Woolport."

"Yes, come on," Violet said, striding across to where a covered trapdoor led down below decks. "Follow me."

Eleanor followed, and it was only when they'd both descended the steep metal ladder that she said, "But you don't really know where we're going."

"I know all these ships are built the same," Violet said, back to her own voice again though she spoke in an uncharacteristic whisper. "This here's all the officer sleeping quarters – how long can it take to find a baby?"

They walked across the ship, from one end of the corridor to the other, but there was no familiar gurgling or crying from behind any of the cabin doors.

"What now?" Eleanor asked. "Is there anywhere else?"

"It must be one of these. The kid said we had a cabin, and it's all open bunks to the stern." She glanced both ways again, and then rapped her knuckles against the nearest door.

Eleanor started to ask what in all the Empire she thought she was doing, but she closed her mouth as soon as the door opened.

"Excuse me," Violet said to the bleary-eyed woman who answered. "I'm ever so sorry, I seem to have lost my way. I never can tell the back from the front of one of these boats. I was here earlier with a baby, they showed me to a spare cabin but–"

"Must be that one." The sailor pointed across the way, yawned, and closed the door. Violet turned to Eleanor with a smug grin, and pushed her way into the cabin.

It was immediately obvious why Isabelle hadn't been crying. She was in a deep, motionless sleep, strapped into a bunk to keep her from falling as the ship pitched and yawed.

"Sedated," Eleanor said, putting her hand to the child's cheek. Her skin was cold and clammy. "Lauren was probably going to shock her awake, but I don't have the right potion. We'll just have to carry her as she is. If anyone asks, you thought it'd be safer to keep her sleeping until we reach land."

"Are we leaving now?"

"No." Eleanor loosed the straps holding Isabelle down, and crawled onto the bunk beside the unnaturally still body. "We'll do as the lad suggested and get some rest. If they're going to take us to the mainland, we might be able to do this without giving ourselves away."

"But sleep with one hand on your knife," Violet said. "For when they realise I'm not her."

"I always do."

354

Violet climbed up onto the cabin's second bunk, and they laid for a while in silence. Eleanor pulled a blanket over Isabelle and hugged her tight, but she couldn't warm the child. She drifted into an uneasy sleep, waking with a start every time a board creaked on the deck above her head, until eventually a knock came at the door.

Eleanor rolled into a sitting position and sheltered Isabelle behind her, while Violet dropped from the top bunk with an immediacy that suggested she hadn't slept a wink.

"You ready?" a male voice called from beyond the door. "I'm to row you to shore."

"Almost," Eleanor called back.

"Well, come up on deck, I'll be getting the boat ready."

They listened as his footsteps receded.

"*Are* we ready, cap?" Violet asked.

Eleanor scooped Bella into her arms and turned to the door. "I think so."

"Okay. Time to pretend to be a landlubber again."

Back on deck, they found an ageing, weather-beaten sailor hauling a boat across the boards to the winch.

"Need a bigger craft than that little wreck you came in, if we're to get you comfortably to shore," he explained when he saw them watching. "You must be Eleanor, and Lauren, is it?"

"That's right."

He stared at Violet. "You've seen the sea yourself," he said.

Eleanor saw Violet's muscles tense, and hoped the reaction wouldn't be so apparent to the sailor's untrained eye. She willed Violet to bluff it out.

"We trained everywhere," Violet said, putting on her best Lauren voice again. "In my line of work, you can't afford to have limits."

Eleanor had to bite her lip to stop herself from grinning as the sailor nodded and turned back to the winch.

Once the boat was safely lowered, and a rope ladder snaked down after it, the sailor called across to a young woman – looking barely old enough to have left school – who was to help him row them to shore.

"We can do our share," Eleanor offered, but he was having

none of it, and the four of them took it in turn to clamber down into the boat.

Eleanor settled herself uncomfortably in the bow with Isabelle resting between her knees, Violet sat cross-legged at the stern, and the two sailors shared the middle bench, each with a single heavy oar. They loosed the winch lines and the girl used the end of her oar to push the boat away from the *Albatross*.

"You don't look how I imagined you," the girl said to Violet as they moved out from beneath the ship's shadow. "Mikey said you was hot, but I don't see it."

Violet shrugged. "Maybe you and Mikey have different taste in women."

"He said you was hot even with the scars," the girl continued without pause. "But you don't have scars. And you look older than he said."

"What are you saying?" the older sailor asked.

The girl waved at Violet. "Are you sure this is the right woman?"

Eleanor caught Violet's eye as she got to her feet, leaving Isabelle propped against the side. She balanced herself along the line of the keel and crept forward inch by inch, glad she'd practised keeping her balance so that even with her swollen belly she could move without rocking the boat. She pulled the garrotte wire from her belt and looped it over the head of the old sailor just as Violet launched herself forward and thrust her knife into the chest of the girl beside him. Eleanor pulled and tightened the wire, holding it just long enough to be sure he was dead.

"We won't risk turning," she said, pushing the bodies out of the way so she could move onto the middle bench. "We'd have to go within reach of their crossbows to get back to the island, so we'll keep on towards Woolport and just hope no-one saw that."

She reached out to where her oar was now floating beside the boat. Violet sat beside her, took up her own oar, and slid it into the rowlock. It took them a few awkward moments to get into a regular rhythm, but soon the boat was gliding towards the shore again.

"Well, we knew it couldn't last," Violet said. "I'm not that much like Lauren."

"I almost believed it'd last until Woolport," Eleanor said.

"It almost did."

They rowed in silence for a while, listening to the waves lap against the boat and the regular splash of the oars. In the distance, there were faint sounds of the town waking up: market traders calling out to advertise their wares, carts trundling to and from the docks, and shipwrights hurrying to effect repairs.

"I'll take you back to mine," Violet said. "You can stay until this nonsense dies down."

"I'm not sure it's going to," Eleanor said. "But I'll stay until the baby comes, at least. I'm no use to anyone until then."

"I'm not sure about that." Violet glanced down at the bodies by their feet.

"Is there somewhere we can moor up out of sight?" Eleanor asked. "Dead bodies tend to attract attention, even when there's a war going on."

"Nothing convenient." Violet stopped rowing for a moment, leaned forwards, and pulled a thick tarpaulin from beneath the stern bench. She arranged it over the bodies. "How's that? We should be able to get home before anyone pokes around in here."

Eleanor nodded her approval, and they covered the remaining distance at a steady pace. Violet steered them into a space between a small fishing trawler and a trader's ketch, and went ashore with a rope. Eleanor turned and lifted Isabelle from the bow, and was about to step out of the boat when she saw the six soldiers marching towards them. They were in regular army uniforms and marched in two columns of three. The townsfolk milling around the harbour moved swiftly out of their way without needing to be told.

"Eleanor," said the one with a star on his jacket, nodding in her direction. "Lauren. We've a carriage waiting for you."

Violet was bent over the mooring post and Eleanor tried to signal that she should stay as she was, with her back to the soldiers. Violet adjusted the rope with her right hand, and pulled her dagger from its sheath with her left.

"Are you all escorting us to Almont?" Eleanor asked. "That's a lot of manpower that could be out squashing pockets of revolution."

"Special favour for a friend," the soldier said, glancing towards the back of Violet's head. "Lauren always gets what she wants."

"I'm sure she does." Eleanor shifted Isabelle's weight onto her left hip, and extended her right hand. "Can you help me up?"

He reached out to take her hand and she gripped his wrist, ducked suddenly, and pulled him down into the boat where she could drop Isabelle safely out of harm's way before knifing him between the ribs.

One down, five to go.

As Eleanor jumped out onto the quay, daggers in both hands, Violet turned and slashed at the nearest soldier. From the corner of her eye, Eleanor could see people turning deliberately back to their business. Woolport didn't see many skirmishes, even now – and regardless of which side won, no-one wanted to be noticed watching.

The soldiers were young and poorly trained, at least by Association standards, but they had the advantage of numbers and Eleanor found herself facing three of them almost as soon as she set foot on solid ground. She turned side-on to keep the bump out of the way of her arm as she blocked blow after blow from their identical short swords, while with her right she fumbled at her belt for throwing stars. The only way to get the distance she needed was to step back onto the boat, balancing between the accumulated bodies. She took a deep breath, felt the boat rocking beneath her and, once she knew its rhythm, timed her throws so each one would slice the neck of an approaching soldier. Not one of them knew how to block such an attack, and they tumbled where they stood.

She turned to where Violet, down on one knee, was struggling to fend off the two remaining soldiers. Eleanor thrust her dagger into the side of the nearest man as his sword came down. He crumpled and fell, but his blow still connected with

Violet's shoulder and she fell backwards with an involuntary cry of pain. Eleanor turned and swiftly dispatched the final soldier with a slicing cut beneath his jaw, then bent to help Violet to her feet.

Violet groaned as she tested her weight on one shredded leg, and leaned unsteadily against the nearest wall. "Where's Bella?" she asked.

"In the boat. Can you hold yourself up while I fetch her?"

Violet nodded. Eleanor left her for a moment and went back to the boat, where Isabelle was slumped on the tarpaulin. There was blood smeared across the tiny forehead, but when Eleanor wiped at it with her sleeve it came away without revealing a wound. She was still breathing slowly, and didn't move when Eleanor picked her up.

Violet leaned on Eleanor's shoulder and limped, cursing under her breath, as they made their way past dozens of people who tried to avoid looking at them. Woolport was, above all, a trading town, and the traders would stay out of the war for as long as they could escape it. If someone came to ask about the missing unit of soldiers, no-one wanted to have seen anything.

Violet and Sally's attic room was above a silk trader's workshop. Eleanor had met the man a couple of times before: he was sympathetic to the rebels, but a couple of spare rooms was the extent of his contribution to their cause. She struggled to avoid getting blood on anything as she squeezed between the dye baths and the rolls of raw cloth.

"What happened?" Sally appeared at the bottom of the stairs, staring at them. "By the flaming lady, Violet, what happened to you?"

Violet managed a weak smile. "Made the mistake of coming ashore," she said.

"Do you have woundwort?" Eleanor asked. "And we'll need clean water, and bandages."

Sally nodded, her face pale as she led them up the steep stairs into the attic.

Eleanor helped Violet into bed and laid Isabelle down beside her. She stripped Violet's blood-stained clothes away, and Sally returned with a bowl of warm water and a cloth to clean the wounds. The cut to Violet's shoulder was deep, and it felt like a chip had come out of the bone. Eleanor fought to stem the flow of blood with compresses and bandages, but every layer was soaked red almost as soon as she applied it.

Sally sat in silence and watched as Eleanor worked, occasionally passing a clean cloth or more bandages without needing to be asked. Violet herself let out an occasional curse, but was otherwise still. Aside from a few minor scratches, the other main damage was to her leg, where one of the soldiers looked to have caught her repeatedly with shallow, ragged slashes that had torn through the flesh.

It was after she'd patched up Violet's leg, and was about to turn her attention to waking Isabelle, that Eleanor felt an unexpected contraction in her belly, and wetness dribbling down the inside of her leg.

"Not now," she mumbled, then gasped as a second contraction hit her. "Not now, it's too soon."

"Baby?" Sally asked.

"It's too soon," Eleanor repeated. "Should be a month away, at least."

But she didn't have to wait a month. Aided only by the tiny quantity of poppy extract that Sally happened to have in her medicine pouch, she was holding her new baby boy before the sun even reached its zenith. Isabelle came round while she was nursing him for the first time, and bawled until Sally carried her across to Eleanor's side.

Eleanor looked down at where her new son was nestled in the crook of her arm. The tiny size of him terrified her; he was maybe half the weight Isabelle had been at her birth, and looked ridiculously fragile. Isabelle prodded him with one curious finger.

"Bella, this is your new brother Martin," Eleanor said, moving the girl's hand aside. "You have to be nice to him."

Chapter 28

It was three weeks before Daniel and Matt returned from the mountains with a sack full of delicate mistflower stems. A couple of others had already responded to Lukal's messages by coming to Woolport, and they had formed a sort of council in exile. Naval ships still hovered in the waters beyond the harbour, and they'd failed to communicate any further with the island headquarters: the first time Lukal had tried to swim back, he'd been seen and had returned with an arrow in his shoulder. After that they'd been more cautious.

Daniel found Eleanor at Violet's bedside, Isabelle playing at her feet and Martin asleep in her lap. She jumped up when she saw him and pulled him into as a tight an embrace as she could manage with Martin still in her arms.

"I'm so glad you're back," she said. "You have to help Violet, I'm afraid we're losing her."

Daniel looked down at the bed. "What happened?"

"Just a few cuts, I thought, but this one's deep and it's gone bad." She peeled the bandages away from Violet's shoulder to reveal the wound. The surrounding flesh was swollen and red, and thick yellow pus had leaked into the dressing. Violet moaned a little, but didn't open her eyes.

"Violet?" Daniel patted her cheeks, and lifted her eyelids one by one to look into her eyes. "Violet, can you hear me?"

"She's been delirious for a few days," Eleanor said.

"She has a fever," Daniel said, as if he thought she might not have noticed. "Tell me everything you have done."

"I washed it as soon as we got here, bandaged it up with woundwort, and gave her poppy milk for the pain. Then the baby came, but Sally's been changing the poultice every day. It looked like it was going to heal nicely, at first."

"Go and ask Sally for the strongest spirits she has," he said. "I will wash it again and cut out the rotten parts. Then all we can do is wait."

Since Violet had been incapacitated, Sally had taken over her role in the revolution's infant navy, co-ordinating the volunteer sailors and commandeered ships. They didn't yet have anywhere near the force they would need to break the siege, but Sally had thrown herself into the work with a level of dedication known only to those who are trying desperately to keep their minds away from some other train of thought. She returned every night, to burn prayer offerings and sleep on the floor beside Violet's sickbed, but during the day she would be out negotiating with half-drunk sailors in the taverns around the harbour or – as Eleanor found her today – shut away in her tiny office poring over charts of the archipelago.

"Daniel's taking a look at Violet's shoulder," Eleanor said. "He wants the strongest bottle of spirits you've got."

Sally picked up a small, dark bottle from beside a half-empty glass. "You won't get much stronger than this," she said, holding it out across the desk. "This stuff is the only thing keeping me sane through all this."

"Thanks."

"Will she..." Sally started, but thought better of the question. "Just tell him to look after her for me, okay?"

"He'll do everything he can."

Eleanor took the bottle back to Daniel. He poured a slug of liquid onto the wound, scraped at the skin with his tiny herbalist's knife, and then doused the area with spirits again. Violet moaned and her eyelids flickered, but she still didn't respond to her name. Eleanor watched as Daniel spread a thick layer of honey across her shoulder, sprinkled bright yellow powder on top, and bound the whole thing with fresh bandages.

"Will she be okay?" she asked, voicing the question Sally had been too afraid to ask.

"There are no guarantees," Daniel said.

"But you'll keep trying?"

"I have done what I can. But now we have a war to win – I cannot afford to spend all my time tending one woman."

"She was helping me to rescue Bella," Eleanor said. "We owe her for this."

"I heard about this." Daniel didn't look at her as he packed his things back into his apothecary case. "I wish you would learn to think before taking such risks."

"Risks? I had to rescue our daughter – how can you possibly doubt that was worth the risk?"

"You knew Lauren was in the Shadows. Had you not brought her to the heart of the Association, this would not have arisen. As it is, you have traded one of the best sailors we had – for a toddler."

Eleanor stared at him. "Are you saying I should have left Bella with them?"

"I am saying you have made a lot of mistakes."

She wanted to argue – wanted, really, to shout and scream and rail against him – but there was nothing she could think of to say. There was too much truth in his words. If she hadn't been so totally taken in by Lauren's act, Bella never would have needed rescuing in the first place.

"That doesn't change anything," she said at last. "None of that was Violet's fault. She just helped me to get Bella home."

"And I have tried to help her." Daniel said. "Now come away, she needs rest."

He took Isabelle's hand in his and led her from the room, leaving Eleanor to carry Martin after him. Matt and Lukal were sitting in the small lounge, making toast on the fire.

"Council tonight," Lukal said, handing a slice of toast to Eleanor and skewering a fresh piece of bread on his fork. "We can see if Matt and Daniel have any more thoughts on breaking this siege."

"You do not need to come," Daniel said to Eleanor.

She eyed him suspiciously. "Why don't you want me there?"

"I know you are tired," he said. "You should stay here with the children."

"Either you've completely lost faith in my decisions," she said, "or you're planning something I won't like. Which is it?"

He shook his head.

"I know you better than you think," she said. "And if you don't tell me, I'll definitely have to come along to find out."

"We need to reexamine the question of outside help," he

said at last.

It took her a moment to catch his meaning. "Taraska. You want us to sell our souls for a little extra manpower, is that it?"

"A lot of extra ships," he said.

"Slave ships," Eleanor said, but she could tell she'd lost him. "You're mad if you think I'll let you discuss this without me."

"Eleanor." He rested a gentle hand on her arm. "You will be outvoted whether or not you are there. Your presence will change nothing."

She glared at him and shook off his arm. "I'm coming with you. I have to make it clear just how strongly I oppose this idea."

"Everyone knows how you feel," he said. "We know you were hurt. But you are taking it personally – you cannot expect kindness from an enemy."

"They're inhuman. You weren't there – you can't begin to understand."

"Then how can you expect to persuade the council?"

He almost looked sorry for her, which made her feel nothing but angry. If her own husband thought she was being unreasonable, what hope was there that the others would understand? But she couldn't just let this one go.

"I'm coming down," she said. "And that's final."

"You will only tire yourself."

It was true that she wanted nothing more than to curl up and sleep, but this was more important. It was almost more important than the whole of the revolution. What good was winning if it came at the expense of everything they thought they were fighting for?

"I'm coming," she repeated.

They finished their toast in silence, and made their way to the drying room, a vast space downstairs at the back of the workshop where they'd taken to having these not-quite-council meetings. The old hierarchies had been thoroughly disrupted by the siege. Doubtless the official council was still meeting across the water, making plans of rationing and defence and, possibly, occasional attempts to get someone to the mainland – though no such attempt had succeeded, not since Tal had swum across to see what had happened when Eleanor didn't return. But the decisions here in Woolport were being made by those who had turned up, meaning that a lot of votes went to youngsters like Matt and Lukal who'd never come close to a real council seat.

When Daniel suggested they approach Taraska and request their help to break the siege, Eleanor put forwards all her usual arguments, and then – when the others seemed far from persuaded – she tried to tell them that they had no right to make decisions on behalf of the whole Association.

"You should have thought of that when you made the one decision that got us into this mess," Daniel said.

"And the others are in no position to negotiate anything," Tal added. "So we've got no choice but to do it for them, have we?"

Eleanor knew then that she'd lost. She felt tears welling up, and blinked them back. She couldn't afford to cry. But she thought of Isabelle and Martin, and the world they were going to grow up in, and she could barely manage to suppress her sobs.

There was nothing else of importance to discuss. Daniel put himself forwards as the best person to approach the representatives of Taraska, and everyone except Eleanor voted in favour of his proposals. He would go to them and ask their assistance to break the siege around the island, and in exchange they would get all the payments and taxes that they'd demanded.

After such an emotive meeting sleep was hardly an option, but Eleanor went to bed anyway. Daniel had gone back to studying his mistflower harvest, and for once she was glad that he was preoccupied. She wrapped her arms around her children and hugged them tightly to her, glad that they didn't understand what was going on – and gladder still that they couldn't read the thoughts going through her mind.

Laban had warned her, and it had happened just like he'd said: she could imagine no other pain even approaching the magnitude of what she'd felt at the very idea that she might lose

Bella. It had blinded her to anything else. There was no question, if she forced herself to think about it rationally, that her love for them was clouding her professional judgement. They'd all agreed long ago that the revolution didn't rescue people: the end was worth more than any individual lives. And yet she'd gone running to Violet and talked her friend into helping her do the one thing that, logically, they shouldn't have done.

Isabelle and Martin were sleeping soundly, so Eleanor tucked the blanket around them and tiptoed through to the little study where Sally was still examining her charts by lamplight.

"I'm sorry," she said, pushing the door closed behind her. "I realised I haven't said that yet."

"Sorry?" Sally looked genuinely puzzled at that.

"I asked Violet to help me when I shouldn't have. It's my fault she's sick."

"Only the gods can decide when our time's up," Sally said. "I hope they'll give her back to me, but if they don't, it won't be your doing."

Eleanor nodded. Sally had been one of the least devoted of the rebels right up to the point where Violet had been injured, but now she prayed every night.

"Anyway, it worked," Sally said. "You got her back."

"But the price was too high," Eleanor said. "I can't let that happen again."

"You'd better keep those kids safe, then."

"That's what I'm thinking. It was a mistake to try and keep them with me, wasn't it? My life just isn't safe."

Sally poured an inch of dark spirits into a chipped beaker and passed it across the table. "Here."

"Thanks."

"There are good people who'd take care of them if you ask, here or in Almont. What about Rosie?"

"I don't want them to be revolutionaries." Eleanor took a long swig of the drink. "I want them to be safe."

"Do you think we're going to lose?"

"I think we're not stupid enough to go and decimate the Imperial schools if we win – whereas they'll kill any rebel child who crosses their path."

"And you'd really give them up to keep them safe?"

Eleanor nodded, tears streaming down her cheeks. "I think I have to."

"Is there anything I can do to help?"

"No." Eleanor wiped her eyes and downed the rest of the spirits. "I think I've had quite enough help. Just... don't tell anyone where I've gone. Daniel won't approve."

Sally offered to top up her glass, but she shook her head.

"I need to move tonight," she said. "I'd better stay sober."

Next she summoned Tal to meet her down in their makeshift council room. She'd expected him to ask why she'd sent for him, but he just sat, waiting.

"Have you worked out why you're here yet?" she asked when it became clear he wasn't going to break the silence.

"I assumed you'd tell me, eventually."

"I don't mean here in this room. I mean here, fighting this war, rather than back there with your schoolmates trying to defend the Empire from our insurgency."

He thought about it for a moment. "You gave me an offer I couldn't refuse."

"Indeed."

"So what?"

"It's time I told you how I did it."

"Why?"

"It's almost that time of year again, and I'm not going to be able to do it myself this time. I was hoping I could persuade you to take my place, especially when it comes to Venncastle."

"Well, I'm sure I could..."

"Oh, anyone could go," she said, cutting him off, annoyed at his casual tone. "But you have to be prepared to do the real work. And that means you need to know how I did it."

"Don't you think I can recruit from my own school?"

"Simple methods work for most of the kids, but if you turn up and suggest this directly to Venncastle boys, they'll just say no. Yours isn't like other schools."

"No."

"So you'll have to be a bit more subtle."

She wished, not for the first time, that she was having this conversation with Gaven. But Gaven was trapped on the island, and Tal was the next best thing. It certainly beat the idea of sending Lukal to Venncastle.

"And now you're going to tell me what you did?"

"Something like that."

"What makes you think I won't tell the school about your techniques?"

"You're welcome to – they already know. I'm not doing anything very different to Venncastle's own imprinting."

"Their what?"

"The way your school generates such legendary loyalty. And they've probably guessed that's what I'm doing. Some time when you have a spare moment, you might want to consider why they've never told you their own secrets. But first, tell me what you think I did to win you over."

"You..." He hesitated. "You arranged for us to ambush you. You made us fall into our own ambush. I still don't quite know how you did that."

"I can tell you if you like, some time, but it's not very important. I couldn't force an ambush more than once."

"But that is what you did. You manoeuvred us into a position where we had to fight for our lives."

"Well, we're at war now, there'll be plenty of natural opportunities to bind the recruits together. That comes later. The first thing you have to do is find a way to make them turn up, when you haven't got an ambush to tempt them out of their beds."

He nodded, just waiting for her to go on.

"You'll start with two or three names. Anyone that comes to your attention is going to be good, but you have to pick out the one you think is slightly less good than the others. The one who'd be flattered if you tell him you think he's the best."

"How will I know?"

"Read the records, and use your instincts. Venncastle students are famously overconfident, but you usually have a fairly good feel for how you fit into the order of things, don't you? Like you've always known Gaven was slightly better than you."

He blushed, and blustered, but she waited out his temper and he managed to contain it without saying anything he might come to regret.

"So when you've got one boy in your sights, take the usual approach – visit in the middle of the night, memorise his records first, make sure you know his weaknesses as well as his strengths. Be prepared to fight if he doesn't want to listen, but in time, he'll listen. When the time is right, make it clear you're only approaching him."

"But you just said to pick out the weakest."

"Exactly. The others will be so affronted when they find out that they'll have to make their own attempt to get your attention."

He nodded. "They'll come to me."

"Then you ignore them, and they'll become even more determined. You've got them all then – the one through flattery, the others through the insult."

"I see."

As she went to collect her things together, Eleanor realised there was one advantage to dealing with Tal. It hadn't even crossed his mind to wonder why something like that would suddenly have become urgent. And she was glad he hadn't asked, because the fewer people knew she was leaving, the fewer could try to stop her.

It was hard work riding with two children, and harder still that she had to keep them hidden under folds of a spare cloak. She was careful to stop only in towns with strong rebel leanings, or sizeable rebel districts where they could stay, but to do so she had to take a somewhat circuitous route north.

It would have been more direct to go to Venncastle first, and up to Mersioc later, but at Venncastle someone might notice Isabelle. Whereas this way, if she could get to Mersioc without being spotted, she knew she could afford to travel openly back to Venncastle. Martin still looked like a tiny newborn.

And so it happened that one night the most natural staging post happened to be in Almont, and she decided to take the opportunity to visit whatever was left of First Corps at the northeast gate. She came into the city from the south, and worked her way up to the edge of the rebel district without trouble. Once she'd exchanged pass phrases with a couple of guards, she could finally let the children out of hiding to see the city. Bella gaped up at the huge city wall, as Eleanor led the horse into the shade and tied him by troughs of hay and water. Then she made her way across to the gate itself and knocked at the little door.

Dash stepped out in front of her, his huge frame almost blocking the doorway.

"Password?" he asked.

"What? Which password?"

"You need to give me the password before you can come through."

"But Dash, you know me."

"I'm sorry, you need to give me the password."

"I'm here, aren't I? And you know me. This is virtually my second home."

"We can't let just anyone through, you know. You taught us that. You've got to have the password for the gate."

"I don't have the latest one. You can test me on any of the old ones, I can even give you a list of active codewords, but I've been out of town for a while."

"Sorry." He centred himself in the doorway; there was no way she could squeeze past without a fight. "You're the one who told us we had to be careful."

"Yes, that was me. Precisely. I'm still me, I'm still on your side."

"Sweetie, what's up?" A thin arm wound around Dash's waist, and a moment later Nicole's head popped out from beneath his arm. "Eleanor, hey! Welcome back."

"She doesn't have the password," Dash said. "I was explaining that she can't come in."

"And I appreciate your thoroughness," Eleanor said. "But let's stop this now, shall we? I need a drink, and the kids need some sleep."

"I'll tell you the password," Nicole said. "Then he'll have to let you in."

"I don't think that's how it's supposed to work," Dash said, but he let her past to whisper in Eleanor's ear, and when Eleanor gave the right password he moved out of her way. Upstairs, Jace was on duty with a young man Eleanor didn't recognise.

"So how's it going?" Nicole poured ale for both of them and plonked the tankards hard onto the table, splashing her drink across her fingers. Dash kissed her on the forehead and went back to his post. "What's been happening out in the big wide world?"

"Not much," Eleanor said. She settled Isabelle and Martin on blankets in one corner, and came to sit with Nicole. "I'm on my way north. But I see you've got news. You and Dash?"

"Yeah we... we hooked up. We're still living here, obviously, keeping your gate for you. It's nice. He's a nice guy."

"Don't let it get in the way," Eleanor said, though she felt like every kind of hypocrite as she spoke. "It's important not to care too much, in times like these."

"Oh, I get it," Nicole said, taking another swig of her beer. "Dangerous times. And this is a dangerous job. We know."

"As long as you understand that the revolution comes first."

"Yeah, of course, this is bigger than us all. This stuff matters."

"Well, I'm really happy for you. I think it's great that my little guard unit gave you two the chance to get to know each other."

"Yeah, I never would have thought it. Not with his attitude, all team-leader, bigger-than-you crap. But he's nice when you get to know him. Real nice."

"I could have told you that," Eleanor said, laughing. "Leadership isn't a character flaw, you know."

Nicole shrugged. "I don't much like being told what to do."

"No... me neither."

They'd almost finished their drinks when Rosemary came down from the sleeping loft.

"I thought I heard a familiar voice," she said, crossing to

give Eleanor a hug. Then she spotted the children in the corner. "Oh, and this must be Bella, isn't she growing up fast? And the baby...?"

"Martin, my little one."

Bella had started crawling across the floorboards at the sound of her name. Eleanor stepped across and lifted her to her feet.

"You're a big girl, Bella, you can walk now. No need to crawl around on your knees."

"You're not working, then?" Rosemary said. "Not with the children."

"No, I'm..." Eleanor hesitated, trying to think of how to explain without alienating everyone. "I'm taking them to see my mother. It's not safe for them to live in the Association with me."

"Do you want me to look after them for a bit?"

"Sally suggested the same thing," Eleanor said. "But I really want to get them further away from the war. I don't want them growing up in the middle of this."

"Have you seen much of Sally?"

"And Violet?" Nicole chimed in. "We miss them, when can we have them back?"

Eleanor finished her drink and poured herself another before answering. "Violet's the reason I'm here, really. She got hurt helping me to rescue Bella."

"Oh no. Is she okay?"

"We think she'll recover, but one of her wounds went bad. She's very sick at the moment. Anyway, I can't let that happen again, so I have to get the children out of danger."

Chapter 29

If she leaned hard against the bars of the cell and angled her head just right, she could see the guard at his post along the corridor. He was young, and had seemed a little kinder than the others when he'd brought her evening meal.

"Hey!" she shouted, and he looked up. "Do you know a man called Raf?"

It was a long shot, but she was desperate. The boundaries of the rebel districts were shifting, shrinking under Imperial pressure, and Eleanor had found herself on the wrong side of an imaginary line after dark the previous night as she'd tried to leave the city. She could have taken down a couple or even four of them with no trouble, but she'd been unlucky enough to run into half a unit of city guards who'd been determined to sweep her and her illegal children straight into Almont's gaol. Faced with that number she'd thought it better to go without a fight rather than draw attention to herself, but she was starting to question the wisdom of that decision.

"He's probably quite high up in the Shadow Corps by now," she went on when the guard didn't respond.

"I know one who goes by that name," the man said, eyeing her suspiciously.

"From Venncastle school?"

"What's it to you?"

"Oh, it's nothing," she shrugged, going to sit down again with the children at the back of the cell. "I just wondered how he was getting on."

The guard marched across and glowered at her through the bars. "Tell me what you want with the deputy."

"Your deputy commander?" she asked, keeping her voice soft. "Well, what's an elite recruit like you doing guarding the dungeons, then?"

He didn't answer, so she tried again, dropping her voice to a conspiratorial whisper. "Listen, I wonder... I can't help feeling it might help your career if you went and told Raf that you have his old girlfriend captive."

"You're not his girlfriend," the guard said, but she heard a hint of doubt in his voice and knew she had something to work with.

"Oh, I haven't seen him in a while," she said agreeably. "It's been a couple of years. But we parted on very good terms."

"Why should I believe that? You're married." He indicated her bangle. She could hardly deny her status when Daniel's name hung from her wrist.

"As I said – it's been a couple of years. Things happen. But I still think he'd like to see me."

"I don't believe you."

"If you want to check we're talking about the same man, his identity number is V-N-five-nine-F-six-two-E-Y-G."

If this guard really was in the Shadows then he shouldn't have any problem remembering an identity code for long enough to check.

"Do you think it would be worse for you," she asked sweetly, brushing a few stray hairs from her face and fluttering her eyelashes, "to keep the deputy commander's sweetheart locked up, or to waste a few moments of his time if it turns out I'm lying? At least in that case the blame would clearly lie with me."

"What if you're planning to hurt him?"

She forced a gentle laugh. "You think I'm dangerous? And the children?"

The guard leaned heavily on the bars. "Who are you?"

"Tell him you have his first girlfriend in your cells. He'll know."

The guard squinted at her for a moment longer, then turned on his heel and left without another word. She hoped he'd made the right decision.

A short while later Raf strode into the cells, the guard rushing two steps behind him. He was dressed in a smart uniform of deep blue linen, the Imperial insignia on his chest, with four small silver stars arrayed above the crest. He snatched the heavy keyring from the guard then barked: "Leave us!" The guard obeyed instantly and Raf turned back to the captives, his voice a shade more gentle. "Ellie? What are you doing here?"

"I was taking my children to school," Eleanor said, coming up to the bars. "And I got caught."

Raf turned his attention to the two children. Isabelle was cowering in a corner, her arms wrapped protectively around Martin; both were quiet.

"Why aren't they already at school?" he asked.

"We made a mistake. I'm taking them now... well, I was. Please, can you help us get out of here?"

"Ellie, Ellie!" He reached a hand through the bars to ruffle her hair. "A girl like you really should be able to get out of a shoddy place like this without my help."

"Not with two little ones." She glanced back at the children, giving Isabelle a reassuring smile when their eyes met although she didn't feel reassured inside. "Will you help us?"

He hesitated. "They're... Daniel's children?"

"Raf, please." She could hear the pain in his question, but this was hardly the time to go over everything that had happened in the years since they'd last seen each other. "They're my children."

He took a step back, suddenly serious. "How do you think my wife would've felt if she'd been there when Senn came to tell me he'd got my 'girlfriend' in his cells? And with two children."

"I'm sorry," Eleanor said quickly. "It was the only thing I could think of to make sure you came. I didn't mean..."

"I don't want to upset her."

"No, of course not." She looked at the floor, wishing the ground would swallow her. Somehow, she hadn't even imagined he might be married. The odds of him helping her felt a lot slimmer in light of that knowledge.

"She's the head of the Empress's personal staff," Raf continued. "She's far too useful to me."

"You..." Eleanor faltered, somehow struggling to make sense of the words. "She's useful?"

"Yes, very."

"Don't you love her?"

He laughed then, and his laughter echoed back from the walls of the cell. "Of course not. We have nothing in common. But she holds a good position and she keeps her ear to the ground."

"Oh."

They regarded each other in silence for a long moment, and Eleanor felt she was separated from him by more than just the iron bars which stood between them. He'd changed in their years apart; hardened.

"I'm useful to her, too," he added as though that made sense of it all.

"So will you let us go?"

"Ellie, you're a fugitive and a criminal..."

"I know that," she snapped. "I'm not asking for your moral judgement – I'm just asking you to let me out of this cage."

"You'd do well to remember who you're talking to," he said, taking a small step backwards.

She gripped the bars of her cell door firmly, leaned forwards, and glared at him. "I'm not the one who's in danger of forgetting who my friends are."

He drew himself up tall, unconsciously adjusting his uniform. "I am deputy commander of the Imperial Shadow Corps."

"Yes, and you used to be my friend." She met his gaze fiercely, daring him to argue back. Shouting mindlessly was by far the easiest thing to do.

"You're right," he conceded after a momentary pause. "Okay, come on, let's talk somewhere more comfortable."

He unlocked the door, steered Eleanor into the corridor, and locked the cell again behind her.

"I know you won't try anything while we have your kids in there."

Tears welled up in Eleanor's eyes as she looked up at him. "When did you get so cold?"

He avoided her gaze. "It's a cold world, Ellie. I'm sorry, it isn't personal."

"Don't you trust me any more?"

"It's not about trust," he said, going to put his arm around her shoulders. She shrugged him off irritably. "Officially, you're the enemy. And I know just how good you are."

He led her along the corridor, signalled to the waiting guard that he should resume his post, and beckoned her to follow him up a broad flight of stairs.

"Where are we going?" she asked.

"Just up to my private quarters," he said. "Where we won't be overheard."

"What about your wife?"

"Oh," he waved his hand dismissively. "She'll be working well past sunset. Besides, she wouldn't dare to disturb me if I hadn't summoned her."

"Well, I'm glad I didn't marry you!" The words snapped out of Eleanor's mouth before she had chance to think, and she instantly regretted them.

Raf stopped in his tracks, halfway up the stairs, and turned on her. "What?"

"If that's how you think about her, I'm glad we never... I mean, I'm glad... Not that we ever..." She stopped, wondering why she'd said anything, realising she'd accidentally begun a conversation she really didn't want to finish. True, she'd often wondered what might have happened if he'd stayed with the Association, but they'd never talked about their relationship in terms of marriage and this didn't seem like a particularly good time to start.

He came down two steps towards her and took hold of both her hands. "If I'd been lucky enough to marry you, that would've been very different. But I was never going to find another girl like you, so I did the next best thing and found someone useful. I don't have to like her."

They walked up the rest of the stairs in silence, and though she was still annoyed at him she didn't withdraw her hand from his this time.

Raf's rooms were on the third floor, as large and imposing a suite as befitted a high-ranking official of the Empire. "So this is what you get for selling out," Eleanor muttered, only half joking, as he waved her into the room.

He pointed her in the direction of the window-seat, then

poured them each a glass of spring nectar before seating himself beside her.

She sank back against him as she sipped from the glass. The familiar taste combined with the warm closeness of his body revived too many old memories in her, and she caught herself longing for the simplicity of their days at the academy. She pulled sharply away from him, annoyed that she'd allowed her emotions to be manipulated so easily. She knew she mustn't stop thinking of Isabelle and Martin – locked alone in the cells, the children were relying on her to get them out. She couldn't afford to be sidetracked by memories.

"Why can't you just let us go?" she asked.

"This isn't like the old days. The men here are selfish, they've got no loyalty."

"Who are you to talk about loyalty?"

"Don't fight me, Ellie." His voice cracked a little as he spoke, and he hugged her closer. She didn't resist. "I need you to understand. Senn came to fetch me because he thought I might make it worth his while, but if he spots me doing anything out of line he'll report it without thinking. I can't be seen to help you."

"Then what can you do in secret?"

"I'll think about it."

She opened her mouth to press him further, but he put his hand gently across her lips.

"Shhh. I'll do what I can, I promise, but I need time to think it through."

"Okay." It was hard to be patient knowing her children were locked in a cold stone dungeon, but it wouldn't help her cause to hurry him. She swallowed the rest of the nectar in one long gulp, relishing the way it burned at her throat and hoping the alcohol would help to numb her mind.

He topped up her glass and pulled her round to face him. "I know it's hard," he said. "But you've been through much worse. You'll work it out."

"I will," she agreed. "But the children..."

He nodded his understanding. "How old are they?"

"I've had Isabelle for a year and one season. Martin's not

even two months yet."

"And remind me again why you're taking them across the Empire, in the current climate?"

"I'm just taking them to school." She finished her second glass of nectar much too quickly, and he poured her another top-up. "But most places wouldn't take a toddler, so I have to go back and try my old school." She wasn't sure what kept her from mentioning that it was her own mother she'd be visiting; somehow, it didn't seem prudent.

"One thing I could do is to take your son to the nearest school here in Almont. He'd be safe there, away from the war. Or..." He stopped, a thoughtful smile spreading to his lips. "Actually, I'm sure I could make an argument that a child of yours and Daniel's is suitable Venncastle material."

"Would you?" She could hardly believe her luck. "That's where I was going to take him."

"It would only be reasonable. I don't know why anyone thought to lock up a baby in the first place, when clearly what we should be doing is making sure he's removed from his criminal mother and placed under proper care." He grinned at her. "Yes, I'm sure I can make a case for that. And it's one less thing for you to worry about."

She wanted to throw her arms around him in thanks, but something made her hesitate. "How do I know I can trust you?"

"You've always been able to trust me."

She raised a questioning eyebrow. "You've a funny way of showing it."

"Ellie, you have no idea how many times I've saved you."

"What?"

"I've done everything in my power to persuade them that you're not worth looking for, ever since the rift. Everyone else who stayed with the Association is being hunted day and night – you're the only one who's slipped off the end of the list, and if you hadn't, you wouldn't have stayed alive long enough to ask to see me tonight. But trying to run across the Empire with illegal children is asking for trouble."

"Sorry," she said. "Though if we're talking about stupid things we've done to save one another's lives, you might think about that time you woke up in the street, when you were pretending to be a palace guard."

"Someone hit me with a sedative before I even... that was you?"

"I took my revolutionaries out for a little guard-hunting. I didn't expect to find you wandering around in disguise."

"Well, I suppose that makes us even."

They fell into silence. Eleanor watched the fountain sparkling in the evening sunlight and wondered whether the old Association buildings were still in use for anything, but she knew better than to ask. Raf continued to fill her glass as quickly as she could empty it and before long she was feeling drunk and sleepy. She curled herself against his chest, drifting in and out of consciousness as he held her and wishing, not for the first time, that life could be simpler. He stroked her hair softly as she slid into a deeper sleep.

When she next awoke it was almost dark outside, and Raf was running his fingers along the contours of her face.

"About what you said earlier..." he began when he noticed her eyes flicker open.

"Forget I said anything."

"But..."

"Forget it," she insisted, pulling herself up into a sitting position, suddenly fully awake and sober. She didn't want to expose herself to those feelings again.

"Ellie, if you'd ever even hinted that we could be together, I would've stayed, no question."

"You had to make your own decision," she said, wondering why he had to open up these old wounds again. It was too late; talking over it now could only cause them both more pain.

"But if you'd ever told me... If you'd ever..." He paused, trying to compose himself. "My decision would've been different."

"I kissed you. What more did you need?" She didn't bother trying to keep the incredulity from her voice.

"I thought that was goodbye."

"It didn't have to be." Tears rolled down her cheeks. "Daniel understood – enough that he's never really forgiven me."

"Why did you tell him?"

"I didn't. He saw us."

"Ohhh."

"It was enough to split us up for almost a year. When I came back here for the key... if you'd been here..." She shook her head, blinking. "I really wanted to see you again."

She thought she saw a tear glistening in the corner of Raf's eye, though she knew he was unlikely to let himself cry. "Then stay with me now," he said, squeezing her hand.

"It's too late." She wished that it wasn't true, but she knew she was right. "The Empress would never pardon me for my crimes, not even to keep her best Shadow happy, and the Association wouldn't trust you if you tried to come back. Besides, I have the children to think of now."

He ran two fingers along the scar which cut across her cheek, from her nose right down to her jawbone, reminding her of the way he'd gently tended the wound when it was fresh. However much he seemed to have hardened against the world, she couldn't forget everything they'd shared. He pressed his lips against hers and she returned the kiss with desperate intensity, trying to make up in those few heartbeats for everything they hadn't had chance to share over the preceding years.

"At least stay with me tonight," he said as he pulled away.

Before she could respond, he picked her up and carried her easily into the next room where a sumptuous four-poster bed stood proudly in the centre of the floor. Rich green curtains draped to the floor, and matching silk sheets covered the bed.

"But you're married," she protested as he set her down on the divan.

"So are you."

She fingered the gold bracelet which was still fastened round her wrist. "I don't think I will be, by the time I get home," she said, suddenly feeling a great sense of loss. Daniel would never forgive her for taking the children away, and certainly not if he found out that Martin was off to Venncastle. "Besides, Daniel isn't here – but your wife might want to share your bed."

Raf shook his head, and began to loosen the laces of her shirt. "Janine has her own rooms. She'd never expect to sleep here without an invitation – and I don't often invite her. She knows well enough where she stands."

"That's... sad."

"I don't know how you can be so righteous about it when you married Daniel. You never even liked him."

"It seemed like the right thing to do."

"Right?"

"We were having children for the revolution. Once we'd decided to be a little rebel family, there wasn't much sense in staying resolutely unmarried. Besides, we'd already done it once."

He pulled the cord through the last set of eyelets and dropped it to the floor, then slid his hands beneath the loose folds of fabric. "Done what?"

"Been married. On that Faliska mission, didn't I tell you?"

"Somehow you managed to forget that part of the story."

"I tried to put it out of my mind." She frowned, wondering whether she would have thought twice about agreeing to marry Daniel if it hadn't been the second time.

"Shall I get one of the servants to run you a bath before bed?" Raf offered.

"Won't they find that a little strange?" She thought back to what he'd said about the lack of loyalty: she didn't want him to get into trouble.

"Oh, I won't mention you, obviously. I often bathe at night."

"Okay, then. The hot water might help my shoulder."

He took hold of her right shoulder and started to knead the muscles around the site of her old injury, making her wince although she knew it would help. "Did you wrench it again?"

"Yeah, trying not to get captured."

"Wait here, and I'll fetch you once the water's ready."

She finished undressing while he was gone, and folded her clothes into a neat stack on the sideboard. After a moment's hesitation, she unclipped her name bangle and rested it on top of the pile; it felt strangely liberating. The wedding-band had felt like a shackle lately. She was still deep in thought when Raf returned for her, and she was certain a man of his observational skills would notice what she'd done.

She followed him back to the sitting room where the servants had placed a large iron bath by the window and filled it with steaming, scented water. He held her hand as she clambered into the tub, then stripped off and lowered himself into the water to face her. He'd made sure a fresh bottle of spring nectar was easily within reach, and handed her glass to her as soon as they were both settled. She accepted gratefully; she'd sobered up after her nap but she wasn't sure she wanted to be fully in control of herself tonight. Besides, there were few enough times these days when she felt safe enough to relax her guard.

They stayed in the bath long enough to fill and empty their glasses three times, then Raf rang for the servants to clear away the tub while he led Eleanor back to the bedroom. Somewhere at the back of her mind she knew she should insist on going back to her children for the night, but they were going to have to learn to live without her soon enough. She could afford to stay a little longer.

Raf pulled back the blankets for her, snuffed out the room's torches and then pulled the curtains closed around the bed before coming to join her between the sheets.

Eleanor woke early as usual, but she squeezed her eyes closed against the world and snuggled up to Raf instead. She didn't want to think about her real life; the illusion was much nicer despite her blinding headache. She could almost believe she belonged here. He put his arm around her and pulled her close to his chest, and she drifted back to sleep in his arms, wishing she could put off the day ahead. Then she remembered the children, and how she'd meant to go back to them last night, and suddenly she was wide awake and with guilt wrenching her stomach.

"I should get up," Raf said, tweaking the curtain just enough to flood their faces with light. "But I really don't want to."

"Me neither. I want to stay in bed forever. Shhh," she added, hugging him tightly and pressing her fingers to his lips to stop him speaking. "Don't tell me we can't, I know that."

He ran his fingers through her hair, tilted her face up towards his, and kissed her lightly on the forehead. "They'll be wondering where I am."

"Who's in charge these days?"

"Above me? Just Ivan."

"Well, he'd understand, wouldn't he?"

Raf frowned. "Ivan hasn't been quite the same since he lost Lauren."

"Mmm?" Eleanor asked, nestling her face against his neck to avoid his gaze.

"He really thought you'd come with her but even if you didn't, I don't think it crossed his mind that she might not make it home."

"It's an occupational hazard."

"But we had you surrounded. We didn't think we could lose."

"Arrogant as ever," Eleanor said. "But I was going to let her go, until she threatened Bella."

"You killed her?" She felt his body stiffen. "You? Personally? If you ever do see Ivan again, I really don't think you should tell him that."

"Why's he taking it so personally?"

"Why?" He stared at her for a long moment. "Oh, shit, she didn't tell you? She was his wife."

Eleanor shook her head. "She didn't say."

"No, I suppose she wouldn't."

"I'm sorry. I had no idea."

He hugged her tightly, speaking into her hair. "You did what you had to do. You couldn't have known."

She pulled away and started to get dressed. The spell was broken, the magic of pretending no-one else existed replaced with the harsh realities of war. She hadn't known but if she had, she couldn't help wondering, would it really have made any difference? She had little enough time for sentimentality towards people who weren't trying to kill her.

Raf stepped up behind her as she laced her shirt. He

smoothed her hair, then swept it up and pinned it into a bun at the back of her head.

"Can you get your daughter out of the castle?" he asked.

She reached up to feel the strength of the pins he'd used on her hair. "Yes," she said. They'd be just about good enough for those locks.

"Concentrate on that part. I'll think of a plan for the rest."

Raf took the guard's keys from him and led Eleanor back down to the cells.

"Mamma!" Isabelle cried, throwing herself against the bars of the cell as soon as they came around the corner and into sight. "Mamma! Mamma! No no no!"

"What's wrong?" Eleanor asked, reaching between the bars to touch her daughter's hand.

Raf unlocked the door, and Isabelle ran out and wrapped herself around her mother's legs, sobbing and repeating "Mamma, mamma!" until Eleanor shushed her.

"What is it?" Eleanor asked again.

"Marty," Isabelle said, pointing back into the cell where Martin clearly wasn't.

Eleanor glanced round at Raf and he winked at her. She turned back to Isabelle, wondering how put it in words that the girl might understand.

"It's okay," she began. "Martin's going to school, like other children. Come back inside and I'll explain." She prised her daughter away from her knees and lead her towards the cell.

"No," Isabelle said, shrinking back and shaking her head. "No no no. Nasty."

"I'll protect you, baby. It's not for long." Eleanor picked Isabelle up and lifted her back through the cell door, at which point she began to scream. Eleanor just rolled her eyes at Raf, and indicated that he could lock them in again.

"I can get away in six days," he said as he turned the key. "But you should go as quickly as you can. Wait for me in the rebel quarter – I'm sure you can find someone to take you in."

"I'll stay at the Old Barrel Yard, they know me there."

"I'll meet you at midday on the bridge where the silk road crosses the river, that should be far enough from the palace for safety."

"Hmm. You shouldn't need a pass phrase, but you'd best not wear your uniform if you're coming that close to rebel districts."

"I know. I may be an Imperial chattel, Ellie, but I'm not stupid."

"No, you're not."

"Six days, midday, at the silk road bridge."

"We'll be there."

Eleanor settled on the floor with Isabelle beside her, and a moment later the guard had resumed his post, sitting in his little office on the other side of the bars. She fiddled with the pins in her hair and wondered how soon she'd have chance to use them. She thought that she'd prefer to make her escape without needing to kill any of the guards, if she could help it, and then she laughed at her own soft-heartedness. She was worrying far too much about protecting Isabelle from the sights of war. The girl had already seen worse than the quick dispatch of one or two Imperial mercenaries.

Her opportunity came two days later when one of the guards left his shift early, leaving his post deserted. She pulled the pins from her hair and reached around the lock, working as quickly as she could.

"Mamma?" Isabelle asked, tugging at her shirt. "Mamma?"

"Shh, baby. Mamma's busy."

"Want..."

Eleanor turned to face her. "Right now, you want to be quiet. We're leaving, okay? You just have to give me a moment."

Isabelle hung on to her mother's leg while she worked, affecting Eleanor's concentration a little and causing her to stab her finger with the sharp end of her pins more than once. But somehow she still managed to swing the door open before the replacement guard arrived.

"Eleanor!"

The voice came from another of the cells; she turned and saw Eric with his face pressed between two of the bars of his cell.

"Eleanor! It is you!"

"I don't have time to get you out," she said, indicating Isabelle with a wave of her hand. "We're in a bit of a rush. But here, take these, I'm done with them."

She handed the hair pins through the bars. He thanked her and slid them out of sight under his clothes just as the new guard came around the corner.

Eleanor grabbed Isabelle, ducked into the guard room, and pushed the girl to the floor and out of sight. The guard stopped short when he saw the empty cell, and Eleanor launched herself out of her hiding place before he had chance to work out what was happening.

They'd confiscated all her weapons, so she took advantage of his momentary surprise to snatch a dagger from his belt and plunge it straight between his shoulder blades. It was a boring, functional blade but it was sharp enough to do the job. Eleanor wiped it clean on his one leg of his trousers and tucked it into her belt.

She turned to fetch Isabelle and saw the girl peering out of the doorway, a stunned expression on her young features.

"Don't ever do that again," Eleanor said. "If I put you out of harm's way you have to stay there, understand?"

Isabelle nodded.

"Come on then, let's get out of here before we're found out. Good luck, Eric."

She took Isabelle's hand and they walked together along the corridor, Eleanor constantly alert for any sound that might indicate they were about to have company.

"Where?"

"Shhhhhhh." Eleanor put her finger to Isabelle's lips. "Let's play the game where you try to keep silent, okay?"

The streets were eerily quiet; evidently the people of Almont had finally given up their dogged insistence that everything was normal. Even outside of the rebel districts people were staying in their houses now, keeping out of the way in case something happened. The curfew wasn't official, but it was practical.

Eleanor walked through the checkpoints without needing to

respond to even one challenge. Usually two or three of her guards would have emerged from the houses, crossbows levelled, issuing one half of a pass phrase whose response would determine whether or not the visitor would live. But not tonight. Tonight they stayed in their houses and let her pass. She was a well-known figure in her own right, she knew, and usually she still had to answer. But nothing demonstrated loyalty to the revolution more than being accompanied by a small child.

She sighed. They'd have to have serious words about this. It wouldn't do for the Empire to be able to infiltrate any rebel stronghold with no tactic more sophisticated than borrowing a child from one of their own schools.

"Home?" Isabelle said, squeezing Eleanor's hand more tightly. "Home?"

"Almost." The tavern was just around the next corner, and only when they were safely out of the range of any possible spies could they risk talking about the next stage of their journey.

Ade welcomed Eleanor with some surprise. Her usual room was occupied, but although he offered to free it up for her, she settled for the best of those that were already empty. The grubby window looked out over the yard to the back. She settled Isabelle on the bed while she took a few basic precautions to secure the room against unwanted visitors.

"This is a tavern run by some friends of mine," Eleanor told Isabelle as she worked. "We're going to stay here for a couple of days."

"Why?"

"We're waiting for someone."

"Home?"

"Not quite yet, sweetheart." She couldn't quite bring herself to explain that Isabelle would soon need to learn a new meaning of that word. "We've got another trip to make first."

"Where?" Isabelle bounced on the edge of the bed, caught between excitement and fear. "Mamma? Where? Marty?"

"We're going to visit my old school."

Chapter 30

Isabelle was disturbed by the sound of the door behind her clicking closed; she hadn't heard it open. She turned away from the stack of seventh-year reports to investigate the intrusion, and stared in open astonishment at the young woman standing by the door.

"Eleanor?"

Eleanor nodded but said nothing, waiting as Isabelle's reactions played across her face. She'd aged dramatically over the last few years, her auburn hair had greyed and her face was creased with wrinkles that had been mere laughter lines when Eleanor had left school. It didn't take long for her to compose herself again – long years of experience in the school had given her practice at dealing with surprises in many forms.

"I'd ask how you got in here, but I probably don't need to."

"I always did take after my father," Eleanor said. "However much you may have wished I wouldn't."

Isabelle took a deep breath. "So. You know all that."

"I know his version."

"I doubt he'd lie to you."

"No."

"You've followed your father's path completely, then? I had my suspicions when you refused your assignment, of course, but... well, that didn't seem like a good time to talk about it."

Eleanor picked up a chair and moved to sit alongside her mother. "Can we be honest with one another now?"

"I'd like that."

"Why did you never tell me?"

"If you thought about it, you wouldn't need to ask that."

"You kept me in your school. Wasn't that breaking a dozen laws already?"

"I wasn't the headmistress when I had you, just a young art teacher. I only needed a couple of friends to cover for me."

"Even so. You could have trusted me."

"I wanted to – every day I wanted to – but I couldn't."
Isabelle's eyes were moist with tears. "I was already breaking all the rules by keeping you in my sight. And if the school had done its job properly and persuaded you that your first loyalty was to the Empire, then you shouldn't have wanted to know. Far better you grew up like everyone else. No child wants to be marked out as different, even if it's just in her head."

"I was always different."

Isabelle stared at her hands for a long moment's silence. Eleanor watched her, waiting for this new relationship to start to make sense. She could see an echo of her own decision in her mother's actions – but she'd make sure the younger Isabelle would always know her heritage.

"Can you forgive me?" Isabelle asked at last.

"I can try," Eleanor said.

"But that's not why you came here."

"I have a daughter too. She's called Isabelle, after you. I wanted her to meet you."

"Surely you didn't come all this way just for that. Not the way things are out there."

"She's been living with us, but the revolutionary life isn't right for a child."

"Ah." Isabelle nodded her understanding. "So now you want to give her up?"

"Of course I don't want to." Eleanor dabbed with her sleeve at the corners of her eyes. "It's breaking my heart just thinking about it."

"But you will."

"I know it's better than watching her be unhappy and in danger all her life. The schools should be safe from all this nonsense, shouldn't they?"

"We can only hope so."

"I didn't know where else to come. Will you take her?"

"I'd love to, of course, but how old is she?"

"A year and a quarter, more or less."

"With no assessment records? It's going to look very suspicious."

"Does the school keep copies of all the girls' assessments?"

"Of the tests, yes."

"You need to get me copies of a complete set for a girl Isabelle's age. I'll make you a new set for your records, and I'll see to it that a copy is inserted into the appropriate files at the College. Then we just need to force a change of assessor for Mersioc, and no-one will be any the wiser."

"Except for my staff, and her new classmates."

"The girls won't remember in a year or two. I don't remember anything from that age."

"Maybe, but the staff will. You're asking me to make a lot of people complicit in your crime, Eleanor."

"You probably made a few of them complicit in yours. The point is, she's family. Your own granddaughter. You can't condemn her for my mistakes."

"No, you're right. I can't." Isabelle nodded. "Bring her, then, as soon as you're able. We'll work something out with the records."

"I can bring her today," Eleanor said. "We're camping out in the forest."

Isabelle glanced out of the window, and smiled. "You always did like that forest."

"You have no idea. So, you'll get me some papers to copy? Probably best to do this as quickly as we can."

"I'll go to the records office now," Isabelle said. "Meet me back here once you've fetched your daughter."

Eleanor took a more direct route out of the school, ignoring the curious glances of the few girls who were playing on the lawns, and disappeared into the forest.

"And?" Raf asked when she dropped down into the cave. "Did she agree?"

Eleanor nodded. "Yes. Bella, are you ready?"

"What ready?"

"To go to school."

Isabelle chewed her lip, then shook her head. "No mamma. No no no."

"Bella, sweetie, we have to do this."

"Why?"

"You'll have fun," Raf said, dropping down to his knees to

face Isabelle at her own level. "I loved my time at school. You'll have chance to learn more and more about whatever you're interested in, and you get to try all sorts of different things."

"No," Isabelle repeated.

"It's better than being stuck with whatever your parents happen to be good at, isn't it?"

Isabelle wrapped both arms tightly around Eleanor's legs and squeezed her eyes closed.

"You won't be on your own, if that's what you're afraid of," Eleanor said. "There's a whole school full of other girls to keep you company."

"Daddy?" Isabelle asked, looking round. "Marty?"

"Bella, we've had this discussion." Eleanor smoothed her daughter's hair. "Daddy's working right now. We'll come and see you as soon as things are a bit more settled, but now I need to take you to the school."

"No."

"Come with me now, and if you really don't like it we can come back, okay?"

She took Isabelle's hand and led her to the mouth of the cave.

"Do you want a hand?" Raf asked.

"I think we'll be all right. Bella, sweetie, get on my back and hold on tightly, okay?"

"Okay."

Eleanor knelt down so that Isabelle could climb up. "I really mean it about holding on. Put your arms round my neck and hold really tight. Don't let go for anything."

"Okay."

With the child's weight heavy against her back, Eleanor stepped across to her usual foothold at the side of the cave and began to climb the rock face. She tried to climb quickly despite the extra weight, knowing she'd never feel entirely comfortable with trusting Isabelle's safety to the child's own grip.

She knelt at the top of the cliff to let Isabelle down to the ground, but the girl kept her arms wrapped tightly around her neck.

"Fine, stay up there if you like."

Eleanor got to her feet again and started to walk down the most gentle route she knew between the trees. As they neared the edge of the forest, though, she stopped again and lifted Isabelle to the ground. They walked hand in hand towards the school, attracting suspicious glances from groups of girls who pretended they hadn't been looking the moment Eleanor turned towards them. Eleanor led the way straight back to the headmistress's office, where Isabelle was waiting for them.

"Isabelle, meet Isabelle," Eleanor said. "Bella, this is your new headmistress."

The younger Isabelle buried her face in her mother's legs and refused to speak while the elder one watched, looking faintly amused.

"Isabelle," the headmistress said softly, touching the child on her shoulder. "Would you like to come and see your new bedroom?"

The girl shook her head, face still hidden.

"Well, would you like me to fetch your new classmates?"

"No."

"She's not usually like this," Eleanor said. "But we're not having a good day, are we, Bella?"

She prised the girl away from her legs and picked her up. Sitting on her mother's hip, Isabelle leaned her head against Eleanor's shoulder and sucked on the collar of her tunic.

"You're behaving like a baby," Eleanor said. "And I know you can be a big girl when you want to be."

"No."

"Suit yourself, then." Eleanor turned back to the headmistress. "Did you find me those forms?"

Isabelle handed her a small sheaf of papers and she read them quickly, recognising the style of the pages from the files Lucille had loaned to her in the past, although she'd never paid much attention to the early questions. She was pretty sure she could represent Isabelle's development fairly, and they could administer the most recent tests for real.

"I'm going to need to put you down, sweetheart." She lifted the reluctant Isabelle to the floor. "Sorry, but mamma needs to do this for you."

The elder Isabelle found a couple of wooden toys for her young namesake, and the child sat on the floor to play while the adults considered her paperwork. Eleanor took a blank sheet of paper and started to construct the record, starting with things she was sure of like the age Isabelle had been when she'd taken her first steps and spoken her first words. For other, subtler milestones she had to guess: she hadn't been paying much attention to when the child first sat up on her own, or responded to her name, or put a strange object into her mouth.

"This must be really hard," she said. "You have to watch out for a lot of things."

"That's almost all we do for the first couple of years," Isabelle said. "It's easy enough to note something down when it happens."

"But with a whole group of babies..."

"There's always something to write down, yes. But we're specialists, just like you are."

"Of course." Eleanor turned back to the papers. "How am I supposed to know which of these tests she would have passed in the first year battery?"

"The traditional way is to enroll her before that age and let us do the tests," Isabelle said dryly. "But since you missed that boat, I suppose you'll have to guess. Which ones are you looking at?"

"They look like fairly elementary reasoning."

"Almost nothing is elementary to a toddler."

"Working out which box a toy is in – that's pretty simple."

"How often do you get impatient with her when she looks in the wrong place for something? That's a clue."

"And this one, testing whether she eats a cake – that's just bizarre."

"It's an important test, it measures a child's understanding of delayed gratification. But at one year old, she'd definitely fail."

"Definitely?"

"Most girls don't pass until they're five or six, sometimes even older."

394

"Then why test so early?"

"You have to have something to identify the kids who are years ahead of their peers. There won't be many, but it's important to find them."

"Bella's very smart, but she's a bit clumsy," Eleanor said as she considered the questions.

"She strikes me as a fairly normal toddler," Isabelle said. "Which is precisely what you want at this stage. An exceptional record would stand out too much, with what you're trying to do."

"You're right, of course."

"So don't try too hard to make it right. Worry more about making it normal – if she starts to excel as she gets older, that's great, and it can be handled then."

Eleanor made a few more notes, then looked up. "Do you promise me you won't interfere?"

"Why would I do that?"

"Laban told me it was you who steered me away from the subjects I enjoyed. I couldn't bear to see that happen to Bella."

Isabelle flushed. "I tried to keep you safe, that's all. I hoped you'd find something you enjoyed that didn't involve risking your life every day. But I realise that was wrong for you."

"It was never your job to shelter me."

"No."

"So will you promise me you won't try anything like that with Bella? Even if, some day in the future, she seems to take after me?"

"I promise."

"I don't think she will. I don't think she's like me – that's part of the problem. She's too clumsy to live out in the rebel districts."

"Eleanor, she's one year old. At that age anyone can be forgiven a little clumsiness."

"Forgiven, yes, but it's impractical." She glanced towards the window. "Out there, when there's a war going on. Wars aren't designed for children."

"Don't worry, we'll look after her."

"I'd like to show her round before I go," Eleanor said. "I'll bring her back here."

She took Isabelle's hand and led her down the stairs and through a couple of quiet corridors to her old dormitory. She knocked at the door, but wasn't surprised when no-one answered. It was the middle of the day; the girls were in classes, or playing outside. She pushed the door open and lifted Isabelle over the threshold.

"This used to be my room," she said. "I slept in that bed, just there."

"Mine?" Isabelle asked.

"No, sweetheart, there's another girl living here now. But I can show you where you'll be sleeping, if you like."

"Okay."

The headmistress had given Eleanor directions to an unfamiliar corridor, but she found the room without difficulty. A large number seven hung in the middle of the door. Again she knocked, and again the room was empty; this one was a nursery room, with cots for ten girls and a bed for the teacher who'd stay with them overnight.

After a brief tour of the buildings, taking in the dining hall and a couple of classrooms, Eleanor took her daughter back to Isabelle's office.

"I made a copy of Bella's file," Isabelle said, handing the papers across. "If you really can get these into the right branch of the College, that would help."

"Dashfort, isn't it?"

"That's right."

"I'll do it tomorrow. They'll never know the difference."

Isabelle bent down to take her young namesake's hand. "Bella, are you ready to come and meet your new friends?"

"No," she said, but the fight was gone from her voice, and she even smiled when Isabelle handed her a doll.

Eleanor kissed her daughter's cheek, and stood to let herself out. "I'll come and visit you as soon as it's safe," she said. "But right now, it's not safe for you to be seen with me."

Raf knew better than to try and talk when she got back to the cave; it was all she could do to keep herself from breaking down in tears. He wrapped his arms around her and stroked her hair in silence, and only after the sun had set did he suggest they might want to start their journey. She nodded, and helped him to pack, and tried not to think about how soon they would also have to part ways. He had a job to get back to, and she had paperwork to file in the archives of the Assessor's College at Dashfort.

They hiked well into the night, keeping a safe distance inside the forest. It was slower to walk through the undergrowth, but they were out of sight of the road here. Besides, neither of them wanted to hurry. Eventually they stopped, roasted sausages over a small fire, and pitched their tent for the night.

Eleanor had only stepped out of the tent to relieve herself when she heard her name whispered from between the trees. She spun round, knives in both hands, but it was only Daniel.

"What are you doing here?" she asked, keeping her voice to a whisper.

"I came to help you," he said.

"You're too late if you were hoping to make me change my mind."

He shook his head. "We can talk later, it is not safe here. Strike your camp and come with me."

"How did you even find me?"

"Laban thought you would be here. He said... well, it seems we have much to talk about, but this is not the time."

"No, it's really not."

"Ellie?" Raf called to her from inside the tent. "Who's there?"

"It's nothing," she called back. "I won't be long."

"Who are you with?" Daniel asked.

She shook her head. "It's nothing to do with you. I've taken the children out of harm's way, that's all."

"Only one person calls you Ellie. Why are you with him?"

She didn't answer.

"I came to help you, but instead I find you with him." He glared at her, and for a moment she thought he might hit her. "You betrayed me."

"If Raf hadn't helped me I'd still be locked in an Imperial dungeon somewhere," she said. "With both our children."

"That is no excuse for running around with the enemy. And him. I told you you could never be friends with him."

She met his gaze steadily. "You never did have the power to tell me who my friends were," she said. "I've done what I needed to do, for Isabelle and Martin."

He grabbed her arm and, before she knew what was happening, yanked the name bangle from her wrist. He threw her backwards; caught by surprise, she lost her balance and fell heavily to the ground.

"Why did I ever try to be with you?" he said, flinging the two halves of her own bangle back at her. The metal stung where it whipped her flesh. "You never really wanted to be a proper wife."

Eleanor picked herself up slowly, and clipped her name bangle back into place on her left wrist. Single again. She felt more relieved than anything.

"I did care for you," she said, realising as she spoke that the past tense was more than appropriate. It had been many months since she'd felt anything but frustration and disappointment. "But you've never owned me. Perhaps if you'd realised that, things could have been different."

"While you act like this, it could never have worked." He spat crossly at her feet. "I hope you do not think you will be coming back after this. No-one will welcome you when I tell them you have been sleeping with the enemy."

"How dare you–" she began, but looking at him she knew exactly what he would dare. She felt sick to her stomach. Where would she go if she couldn't return to the Association?

"You have betrayed us," he said. "You have betrayed me and you have betrayed our children into Imperial slavery. There is nothing you can do to put this right."

He turned and strode away, and she went back to the tent, still in shock.

"What was that about?" Raf asked as she slid in beside him and rested her cheek on his chest.

"Didn't you hear? Daniel. He says I can't go back home."

"That isn't his decision."

"He'll tell them about you, he'll tell them that I sold our children into Imperial slavery, and he'll make stuff up if he has to. And he's going to get back before I do. So he's right. I can't go home."

"Then what will you do?"

"I don't know. Do you have any ideas?"

"I wish I could help you." He hugged her closer. "I wish I could bring you home with me, but you know that I can't."

"I know."

"You'll have to flee the Empire. What else can you do?"

She looked up at him and he met her gaze, sadness in his eyes.

"What do you want me to say? There's a war on, and you've managed to make enemies of both sides. How else can you expect to survive?"

"Yes." She nodded. "You're right, of course. I just have to survive until it's over."

"Where will you go?"

"So you can lead your men to hunt me down?" she asked, unable to keep the bitterness from her voice.

He reached out and placed one hand firmly on her shoulder. "Ellie, it's still me. I want to come and get you once all this is over."

"Probably the mountains," she said, hoping against hope that she was right to trust him. "No-one would bother to look for me there."

She fished around in the bottom of her bag and pulled out the emerald pendant he'd bought for her in Taraska. It was still missing one gem; she'd never asked Harold to fix it in the end, and since then she'd always worn the poison-tipped copy.

"Keep this for me," she said as she pressed it into his hand. "If you ever need to send me a message, I'll know it's really you."

They couldn't exchange bangles, not while she was a fugitive and he was wedded to some Imperial wench, but symbolically this was the closest she could think of. If he was ever able to fetch her back to the Empire – if there was even an

Empire left to return to – she hoped he'd free himself to marry her. But she didn't dare ask for that much. Not now.

He nodded his understanding and slipped the trinket into his pocket. "Thank you."

"I never thanked you for getting Harold to make me that copy."

"I hope it was useful."

She thought of Lauren's crumpled body. "You don't want to know," she said. "Not while we're on different sides of a war."

"Then I'll take that as a yes." She wasn't looking at his face, but she could hear the smile in his voice, and he ran his hand along her back.

"You'll give me time to get out of the way, won't you, before you set your men searching for me?"

"I can't do anything till I get back to Almont. You have time to disappear."

She wrapped her arms around his waist and hugged him as tightly as her injured shoulder allowed. "Send for me once it's safe," she said, tears stinging her eyes.